The Wishing Tree

JAMES BUXTON

The Wishing Tree

ORION

The right of James Buxton to be identified as the author of
this work has been asserted by him in accordance with the
Copyright, Designs and Patents Act 1988.

First published in 1996 by
Orion
An imprint of Orion Books Ltd
Orion House, 5 Upper St Martin's Lane,
London WC2H 9EA

A CIP catalogue record for this book
is available from the British Library

ISBN 1 85798 479 X (cased)
ISBN 1 85798 478 1 (trade paperback)

Typeset at The Spartan Press Ltd
Lymington, Hants

Printed in Great Britain by
Clays Ltd, St Ives plc

I would like to thank my agent, Sara Fisher, for her encouragement; my editor, Caroline Oakley, for her inspiring advice; and my wife, Liane Jones, for just about everything else.

Prologue

1

In those days the forest was much bigger.

Apart from the main bulk that squatted like a great green roaring monster four or five miles to the west, there were its offshoots: wood connecting copse connecting spinney connecting wood, as if the forest had tentacles or roots, depending on which way you looked at it, trailing from its ancient body.

But I'm going to take you to a copse of hazel and birch, and a couple of hundred yards away, standing in the middle of a ploughed field, a rather thin, rather cold child. Today, if the copse is still standing, you would never connect it to a forest, but then, only thirty years ago or so, it was recognisably a part of something bigger.

So, a copse of birch and hazel, bare wood softening at last with the first gauzy shoots of green, but very dark under the low afternoon sun. The copse dipped into a fold in the ground, straggled on to form a narrow wedge between two poor fields, was squeezed into a single strand of willow and beech as it edged nervously alongside a drainage canal, then gradually took on substance as it joined Woodmane Hill – almost anything qualified as a hill around there – with its heavy growth of hornbeam, elm, and oak.

That was where the voices came from, the child was sure, although she wasn't sure who they belonged to. Could fairies call to you from woods? The child looked, and looked, but the voices only came when she turned away from the trees. Sometimes she thought they had to be in her head, but they were too real for that.

The wind was cold on the child's knees and blew through clothes that were too small. After 8 April the heavy prickly winter clothes were packed away and the thin, worn summer ones laid out, but 8 April was long past, and summer would not come for a long time yet: one month, two? The wind came in from the east, from the Ural Mountains of Russia according to the child's father. He also said that the house stood on the first hill between here and there. The child had no idea where the Ural Mountains of Russia were, but knew they sounded cold. The child also knew that the cold would last for another two months at least.

She shivered and pranced like a pony, lifting her knees, one two, one two, then wincing as a scab split. She put a hand out and felt nothing, but then you didn't feel blood, not at first, not until it cooled and began to crust. The child rubbed finger and thumb together, and felt the stickiness as the blood set. She lifted the skirt that flapped around her knees and tucked it into her knickers, as taught, in case the wind blew it against the wet red streak and stained it.

That would never do.

Across the bumpy field, the house stood foursquare to the world. It was built of dull red brick and the lower courses were stained green from damp. The window frames were painted brown every two years. The child's father had laid a strip of concrete all around it, and extended this into a long thin tongue outside the kitchen for the washing line. The child watched him do it over a week two years ago, first digging out a shallow trench, then laying the hardcore, then pounding the hardcore down, then the careful alignment of the wooden shutters (endless, grunting work with a spirit level, culminating in the announcement over dinner that the fanny who'd built the house had put it on a slant), then mixing the yellow, gritty sludge, then the pouring and finally the wet dabbling with a board. He had surrounded the house in a day and the child had imagined, standing in the field, that the house had been lassoed by a collar of concrete and might be snatched away for ever.

The child looked down. Today her shoes had not got too dirty – this wind had sucked the moisture from the ground underfoot. Also Mother hadn't run outside, waving and flapping her arms and shouting: 'Run around, run around, you dirty little spider,' waving and flapping until the child did start to run and the shoes got dirty and she had to answer for it in the basement.

She was meant to stay in sight of the sitting-room window. It was in there that her mother sat and darned every day from half-past four, and the child had to stand outside. The cold had blotched her hands and legs with purple. The wind was vicious on her exposed thighs. She turned and hopped by flexing her toes, not wanting to break the scabs, not in this cold.

Then the feeling came: a cold burning on the neck, and a sense, growing with sudden, steady strength, of being watched.

The child turned. The spinney blurred black against the grey sky. She gasped. A row of figures, small and grey, stood in the shadow of the trees, flickering like smoke, almost disappearing in the evening gloom. She heard the voice again, thin and rough, a dry whisper of dead leaves across a concrete floor: something saying nothing, nothing saying something.

That night the child lay on a rubber sheet, and tried not to move. Cold again. Her night shirt was stained with blood. No one ever seemed to change it; it just grew darker and stiffer.

She thought of the bar in the cellar that rested on two wooden trestles, and again wondered, tried to imagine through the pain, what had happened today that had led to the beating, what had happened today but not yesterday. Had breakfast been eaten too fast or too slow? Had Mother not liked the way she smiled or looked? Had she not washed her hands well enough for lunch? Had she not made her bed, swept the room, washed the floor, beaten the carpets – how had the tasks performed today differed from yesterday?

The answer was as big a mystery as the future, the vacuum between one blow and the what-would-happen-next. Another blow, or not? The child never knew. Until it happened, or didn't happen.

There was a moon tonight. No blankets because of the blood. The moon moved across the window from left to right, and by the time it was sliced to nothing by the right-hand frame, the child was asleep.

She dreamed of a tree in the wood a long, long way away. She was told by an old woman who might have been her grandmother, or her grandmother's grandmother, how to get there, and she was shown what to do. The dream was as grey as smoke and as fine as cobwebs, and faded and faded . . .

She awoke and shivered, turned and fell asleep again, reluctantly because this time she knew what was coming.

She was lying on her back and growing, flesh spreading out from the skeleton, pooling around and then pouring over her fingernails, growing with solid, vegetable strength. She was the earth under the forest and there was a roaring vastness in her head that made her feel sick. A flash of black, a terrible, vertiginous awareness that slid through a slash in her brain of things she didn't want to know about, growing and dying and rotting and birthing. Her body was caves and mountains and swamps and rivers and pools, but harnessed by an awful awareness of the slow motor of growth and decay. A thick tail grew from her spine and rooted her to one place so that even as she shrank, as her edges shrivelled and decayed, it held her still and forced her to gather all the rotting sweetness in. It made her live off that.

She awoke to the sight of the streetlights through the curtain, waited till they clicked off in the dawn and then got up.

2

Marcus woke up suddenly. He could see the shape through the thin curtain, a shadow cast by the streetlight. It was hunched, as if ready to pounce, squatting down on its heels. At the moment it was looking at the street; any second now it would turn and waddle clumsily down the window sill, trying to peer in through the gap in the curtains. Exasperated and not quite understanding, rather than angry.

It thumped on the window and whispered his name. The words erupted through the dark and the quiet. He lay quite still, aware that he was acting strangely, and wondering why he didn't scream, wondering how he was able to dismiss the fear that was crawling down his back. It was like being cold: no different from that. A feeling that was uncomfortable but bearable if you put your mind to it. He would like to see the thing if it could not see him.

He had a vague feeling of déjà vu; he knew it was about to walk down the window sill towards him. That was something worth waiting for and he wasn't scared, which meant it had come before and nothing had happened. The more he thought about it, the more certain he was.

The thing stood and scratched its hip. It was child-sized and child-shaped. Slight. He could tell that even though the silhouette was distorted by the fold in the curtain. There was a weird contrast between its shape and its awkwardness. Things that thin, shaped like that, should be graceful, he thought, like fairies.

He thought of fairies. In some books with old-fashioned illustrations, fairies were girls with long hair, dressed in gauzy wisps. Sometimes you could see their breasts. He looked at the

5

thing outside the window with sudden sharpness. Was it wearing clothes? Were those wings? Suddenly he was reminded of a picture of a sick African child he had seen on TV. It had been naked, thin, long-legged, reduced by illness rather than starvation. The reporter had said it was wasting away, but it didn't want to die.

The thing arched its back and should have done something dramatic, but instead it squatted down again, slowly, as if it didn't quite trust its knees . . .

we want . . . you want . . . you help . . . we want you . . . what you want . . .

Just words, but words divorced from breath fell oddly on the ears and the mind. Want you? Help you? What you want? The list of things he wanted – new this, new that, a trillion, zillion pounds, a neverending supply of wishes – a list he generally carried around with him, adding to, subtracting from, fine tuning, dreaming about, had evaporated like ether.

help you . . . want you . . . your mother . . . quick . . .

Suddenly it was as if a blindfold had been pulled off his head. He was awake in bright sunshine without ever having re-membered waking up. The dream – if that was what it had been – was gone. Except it didn't feel like a dream. Dreams were things that happened in the long drift of sleep. This had happened in a special room inside his head, except it had been outside his head as well.

The bedroom door opened. 'Oh, darling, you're awake.' His mother looking crumpled and yawny; the T-shirt she had been wearing in bed embarrassingly short, he thought. He yawned. Odd, the longer he stayed in bed, the more tired he got. 'Wake up, sweetheart, wake up. Come on, you know you have to. Look at the time. Be quick before I turf you out.'

Mother.

help you . . . your mother . . .

His mother, his mother . . .

quick . . .

Chapter 1

'Who was your friend?' Caroline asked.

As Marcus turned to look up at her she saw his wet skin glisten and slide over his ribs. There were slight shadows under his eyes. His cheeks were pink from the heat of the bath.

'What?' He twisted his face in the disbelieving way that was a new and irritating habit he had picked up at school.

'Your friend. You were talking to someone through the fence. Someone on the other side.'

He shook his head and pushed at the water with the heel of his palm.

'I wasn't talking to a friend.'

'Who then?' she persisted, mild curiosity curdling into suspicion.

'Just a kid,' Marcus said. 'Jesus, anyone would think . . .'

He said it so loftily that Caroline smiled. Marcus was nine, and had all the confidence in the world!

'And what were you talking about?'

'Oh, he just wanted to play with me in the woods.'

'And didn't you want to play?'

He turned back towards her. 'I shouldn't go into the woods just like that,' he said. 'You wouldn't like it.'

'Well . . .' Caroline said. The thought that she might be restraining Marcus pulled her up short. She was about to say that, well, perhaps he was old enough now to go off on his own more, when she realised that Marcus had orchestrated the conversation to go this way. She looked down at him, then said: 'Next time, why not ask your friends in?'

'They're not my friends,' he answered. 'I told you.'

Caroline twisted a Rug Rat's head back on and absent-mindedly wiped a dribble of bubble bath from its neck. The bathroom looked as if a small tornado had hit it. Wet towels lay strewn across the floor, one wet sock stretched over a tap. Why? How? The other one was lying on the loo seat, trousers and shirt were soaking nicely in a puddle on the tiled floor. Some comic she had never seen or heard of (she liked to vet them) disintegrating in the sink, purple Body Shop butterfly soap softening in the plug hole, high tide mark three-quarters of the way up the side of the bath.

My baths were six inches deep and the bathroom was always freezing, Caroline thought, remembering grey, rough enamel that put your teeth on edge and greasy soap in lukewarm water. She remembered the momentary pleasure of the lather on her skin, then the discomfort when the water cooled on her body and there wasn't enough in the bottom of the bath to get properly covered – and anyway you weren't meant to dunk yourself in case you got your hair wet, and wet hair meant, obscurely, a cold on the chest. Things had changed; left to himself, Marcus ran baths you could drown a small horse in.

She took a rag from where it hung under the wash basin, knelt by the bath and began to wipe the worst of the grime off, surprised at the grittiness of it and what looked like bits of leaf clogging the plug. Had he been in the woods? She stopped humming then. Big deal, she said to herself. She felt un-expectedly happy, but then expectation did that to you some-times.

'Marcus,' she called, 'how come every time you have a bath, more water ends up on the floor than in the tub?'

There was a scurry and a thump from the bedroom. Mistake, Caroline thought.

'What?' Marcus stood in the doorway looking pink and fresh. His pale skin was still flushed and his damp hair stood up in a lopsided cockscomb. 'Sorry.'

He started kicking one of the towels through the puddles to sop up the water.

'Oi, you. I asked you a question. I didn't mean to give a naughty piece of baggage an excuse to get out of bed.'

'Just helping,' he said. 'Like Dad said I should.'

That's clever, Caroline thought, he knows how to shut me up. Mildly surprised by this further small revelation, she watched him skate across the floor on the towel, one hand holding up his pyjama bottoms which were a bit too big, the other waving in the air for balance.

She reproved herself: Don't blame the child, blame the parents. And when she thought of her ex-husband Tom smugly telling his son to help his ex-wife, found she had no problem in blaming Tom for almost everything.

'What were you humming then?' he asked.

'When?'

'When you were cleaning the bath.'

Caroline rewound, paused, hummed a few bars and couldn't remember the title until she reached it.

'It's a song called "Wishing Well" by a group called Free. One of Daddy's favourites.'

'Huh,' Marcus said. 'Tell me about it.'

He was sitting up in bed, looking tired but alert. 'Why are you going to bed so early?'

Caroline looked at him closely. He was acting out a part. Some other question lay behind the words.

'Why do you want to know?'

'Isn't something happening for you?'

She smiled. 'You are getting altogether too – oh, I don't know. Yes. I've got that job interview tomorrow.'

Marcus appeared to think. 'And you want it?'

'Yes. Yes, of course.'

'Why?'

Something had got into him tonight. There seemed to be a bright light behind his face. He was buzzing with energy.

'Well, there's the money. That's going to come in useful.'

'But why in particular?'

'Are you all right, darling?'

He nodded, looking intent. Perhaps he just needs reassurance, Caroline thought.

'It's a bit hard to explain but, to be honest, things are beginning to wear out. I mean, all the things we had when Daddy was still here lasted well but now they seem to be going all at the same time. The house could do with a lick of paint, the car's getting on, the cooker's old. All those things. They're fine, it's just – well – '

How could you explain?

9

'I get it. And you don't want to ask Daddy?'

'That's it.'

'Tell me about the job?'

'Oh, pretty dull, I expect. I'll be working in the office, doing typing – if I get it, that is, and it's quite a long shot.'

'If you want something, does that mean you get it? I mean, the more you want it?'

'The more you want it, the harder you have to work for it,' she said.

'And if you work really hard, do you get what you want?'

Caroline sensed a trap. 'Not necessarily.'

'So what's the point?'

'If you work hard at something you make your own luck. The harder you try, the more likely it is you'll succeed,' she said.

Which in her experience was a lie. In her experience there were good things and bad things in life and you crashed into them more or less at random. The trick was to know when to grab hold and when not to.

'And suppose you wish?' Marcus asked.

Caroline stiffened. 'Wishing's lazy,' she said.

Marcus was looking unconvinced so she changed the subject.

'If I get the job, you know I'll have less time for you? But I'll make sure I can leave early to be here when you get back from school.'

'Oh, no. Simon Pears always lets himself in and he drinks a whole big bottle of Coke if he wants to.'

'Which is exactly why I'm going to be here.' She paused. 'Is that what you wanted to find out?'

'Yes.'

'But I will be cooking less.'

'Yes.'

'And I'll be more bad-tempered.'

'Yes.'

'And when I come back I'll hit the bottle and start to smoke and become unmanageable about the house.'

'Like a dog?'

'Worse. Like a mad camel.'

He was laughing now. 'Camels don't smoke.'

'They do after a hard day's typing. You all right now?'

'I just wanted to know.'

'And now you're satisfied?'

'Yup.'

'Keep your fingers crossed then.'

'I'll do better than that,' Marcus said. And kissed her unexpectedly on the cheek.

He lay down and closed his eyes. End of conversation. She pursed her lips, raised her eyebrows and kissed him. As she turned in the doorway she saw his eyes were open and he was looking at the computer.

She was smiling again as she walked out of the room. I might have known, she thought. Marcus had always instinctively understood the concept of enlightened self-interest. The thought of a new computer made her new job a more exciting proposition altogether.

Chapter 2

She did not like to say that money had been tight the previous Christmas. The fact that you did not want to spend £150 on a computer games console was not exactly a valid indicator of poverty, although here, in the wealthy, far-flung outskirts of London, some people thought you were engaged in a limbo dance under the breadline if your second off-road recreational vehicle didn't have a car phone.

But without money being exactly tight, she still had to play the either-or game. Either Marcus gets a computer or he gets new trainers and a jacket; either we stay in England for our holidays or no new clutch for the Nissan. And now that a vital unguessable invaluable something else had gone on the car that had to be replaced immediately, *and* the clutch was still slipping and juddering, it meant that the pretentious trainers she had bought in order to compensate for the absence of Sega or Nintendo, and the continuing, awful humiliation of a steam-powered Amiga, were looking like a frightful extravagance. A really frightful extravagance. An extravagance he was going to grow out of in a few months' time, and what value then the ridiculous go-fast stripes and pressure grid soles or whatever that were going to make him capable of a three-minute mile and twenty-metre long jump?

But, what the hell. There were no big problems. Warm clothes, a freezer full of pizzas, a big car that more or less worked, a mother who mopped and a weekend father who smiled – these things were the basis of security. And it was not as if Marcus was without toys; it was simply that he could not always have exactly what he felt he needed.

Which was fine. Fine, sharp and clear. Because desire sharpened the senses, she thought. Even wanting this job felt good. She took a deep breath, checked her face in the mirror above the fireplace, checked again. The slight sagginess had gone, along with the line between her eyes. There was something different about her. Something prepared. Battle bright. She was ready for change. Whether she got the job or not, it was important to have found that out.

She looked out across the garden from the sitting room: a big garden to go with a big house. Through sliding glass doors the grass of the lawn was yellow in the lights of the living room, black where the light did not fall. The swing – a blue plastic seat, yellow nylon ropes, bright red metal frame – swayed an inch or two either way in the breeze; beyond it she noticed a strip of black shadow down the side of the gate that was cut into the slatted wooden fence. Marcus must have left it open again.

When she and Tom moved in ten years before, house and garden had seemed like the shape of their future: new, well thought-out and sensible. There were four bedrooms and space to convert the attic, a large sitting room, a kitchen big enough to eat in, plus a small ground-floor room with bookshelves which the construction company salesman had referred to as the library.

And it backed on to the forest. While she was carrying Marcus and they were just getting ready to move out of their tiny flat in Bow, Caroline peopled her daydreams with the big family she thought she wanted. Three, maybe four children (hell, she felt so good why not five or six?), running pell-mell through house and garden. Lazy, sundrenched, green-shaded afternoons, with Tom reading in a deckchair, battered Panama on his head; she playing with the latest baby on an old tartan blanket on the lawn; the gate that led to the forest crashing open and the two eldest running in, faces flushed and bloomed with sweat, toy bows and arrows in hand, scavenged feathers in hair, fresh and muddy from an imaginary raid on imaginary enemies.

It had not quite worked out like that. The house had emptied, not filled. A tide she had not known about had ebbed and carried her dreams away. Marcus was an only child: her oldest and her youngest. The forest had stayed the other side of the fence. It was wild; their house was home.

Caroline sniffed the air. Barbecue somewhere. She listened. Opera from next-door on the right; TV laughter from next-door on the left. She walked across the lawn barefoot, the dew cold on her feet, the wet grass stinging her ankles. The gate had sunk on its hinges which meant it scraped along the ground and was hard to bolt. She pulled it open and peered through the gap. Between the fence and the forest was a narrow trodden grass path. It was lined with high grass, cow parsley and the odd patch of blackberries. She heard a rustle. Something had slipped into the forest, something bigger than a rabbit and the wrong shape for a deer.

'Hello? Is anyone – '

She started. Was that a whisper?

She took a step backwards and stood slightly away from the gateway, the gate in her hands, ready to slam it.

'Is someone there? Hello?'

She thought she heard a voice say: 'Marcus.'

'If that's the little boy from two doors down, you should be in bed,' she said.

Immediately in front of her the wood exploded. A crow blasted from a tree and flapped into the air above; the undergrowth crackled and parted. A muntjak deer darted into the path ten feet away. Caroline's heart was pumping and her mouth was dry. Crows didn't fly at night; muntjak deer never showed themselves. Something must have flushed them out.

She looked to left and right. She saw the roofs and dormer windows of the other houses in the Close and heard a swishing noise which turned out to be Maurice Temple, a neighbour. He was smashing at the heavy froth of wildflowers that grew on the forest side of the path with a walking stick and, as Caroline watched, he stopped, crouched and peered through the gap he had made. He straightened up when he saw her, overbalancing slightly. He looked caught out.

'Lost something?' Caroline called. He advanced down the path. He had a deep tan from gardening, she saw. His forearms were thin, hairless and tensed. He wiped the sweat from his forehead with the back of a hand, leaving little beads of moisture on his bald pate.

'Did you hear something? I thought I heard something.' He sounded uncharacteristically harassed.

'Me too.'

'Really? I mean – ' He seemed more confused than the

14

occasion demanded and Caroline wanted to find a way to back off. She believed that other people's embarrassment was their own concern.

'Something flushed out a crow and then a deer. I heard rustling but perhaps the deer was just going crazy, frightened the crow, then frightened itself? Anyway I'd best be – '

'A fox? Surely not.'

'Well, I thought it might have been a child.'

'A child?'

'I caught Marcus talking to one earlier. I mean, I think I did.'

'You can't be too careful.'

Temple's voice became oddly insinuating. It sounded as if he were trying to soothe her.

'I saw him talking to you the other day, for that matter,' she said. 'In the Close.' She immediately regretted it but Temple gave a short, harsh laugh.

'What a pompous old bore I've become,' he said. 'Pompous old bore.'

'I didn't mean – '

'I know, I know. Of course you didn't. But I am. "You can't be too careful." Who am I to talk? I like Marcus. He's a nice boy. You must be proud. Yes. He was asking me about the forest. Its history, legends, that kind of thing. Showed a surprising interest for a child of his age, I thought.'

Caroline felt as if she had been turned and herded away for a reason she could not fathom. She had not even known where she was in the first place.

She said: 'I'd rather you didn't – ' but Temple stopped her with a quick nervous movement.

'You didn't see a child out here, did you?' he asked.

Whatever emotion he was feeling was stronger than the façade he had erected. She suddenly saw a small, middle-aged man, diminished somehow by yearning, eyes searching her face. The change was sudden and a little bit shocking. What was it about Maurice Temple? That was it – he was a watcher. It could be a habit, she knew, or an affectation. But watchers were also people who cared too much about other people's reactions, who needed to know what other people were thinking because they had something to hide. She knew that because Tom had

15

called her a watcher once, and ever since then she had been at pains to disguise it.

'No,' she said. 'No.'

'Ah, well. That's that.' And he walked past her with a curt bow, swinging his stick from side to side, staring straight ahead.

Caroline stepped back into the garden and pushed the gate shut. She had to lift it up and batter the bolts into their sleeves with the side of her palm. She caught the side of her hand on a jag of metal and as she sucked it was unable to tell rust from blood.

She forced herself to kneel and look in the rabbit hutch, listening all the while. Nothing. Nothing climbing over the fence. The crow frightened the deer; the deer panicked. But what had frightened the crow? Anyway, the two movements had been simultaneous. Had Maurice Temple been looking for a child?

There was fresh grass and dandelion leaves for Snowball the rabbit in the hutch. The animal waddled towards her. She poked a finger through the mesh and tried to scratch him between the ears. He did a half-hop backwards then advanced, leading with his nose.

''Night Snowball the rabbit,' Caroline said. 'Hope that fence is fox-proof.'

She heard the rustling again and walked backwards to the house. 'Rubbish,' she said to herself as she slid the french windows shut. 'Phooey. Nothing's the matter. I'm just jumpy tonight. Nerves . . .'

A good soak in the bath, twenty minutes with Ruth Rendell, then sleep.

Chapter 3

Caroline stood in the car park and shook, feeling sick with humiliation and hating herself.

The office manager, an unruffled, cool blonde, had said that the interview should never have been arranged: the man who had told Caroline about the job had been misinformed, the manager she had called had had no right to arrange an interview, and Caroline herself had been naive not to check before she had come in. Why? Because the job had been promised to someone else already. She would take some details and put them on file, but really – raising an eyebrow as she scanned Caroline's blank-ish CV – she could not be very encouraging.

That was bad enough but then Caroline made her mistake. Instead of losing her temper or just walking out, she had said in a trembly voice that she really believed that she was owed more than an apology and could she at least go through with the test? The officer manager had yielded. Caroline failed the test disastrously and was interviewed by a departmental manager who stared at each segment of her body from her chin to her knees, leant back in his chair and said: 'Right then, tell us what you can offer Smith's Car Parts apart from your lovely smile?'

The air she sucked in tasted of car fumes. She felt cheap and shapeless, like market-stall clothes. Her body prickled with sweat. She looked up at the sky, surprised at how overcast the weather suddenly was, and how the heat was building up, and then as her eyes swept down, she saw something under the trees that overhung the car park. Her heart did something awful in her throat. It was a dead child.

She blinked and looked again; air, sounds and sensation funnelling into a cone that led from her eyes to the shadows. She

17

had to be wrong. A child asleep, even injured, but surely not dead.

It was lying just off the tarmac, under the trees and close to where the big executive saloons basked in the shade. Signs were hung on a steel mesh fence: 'Sales Manager', 'Managing Director'. She took a step towards the body. There! The child had moved, just a flicker of the hand. She stopped moving; so did the child. But it had twitched. Or was that just the play of shadows? She took another step. Every movement seemed to make the child move, in the same way the world trembles and swoops through a camcorder's viewfinder. Every step she took brought her closer, but even though she screwed up her eyes to try and sharpen the focus she could not make out the child's face. It seemed to be a blank. Now she was going to have to walk around a Transit van. It blocked her view for a second or two and when she looked again the child was gone. She put her hands through the mesh and clung there, staring into the forest.

On the other side of the fence was the stuff that always gathers on the border between road and country: paper; empty packets; a black refuse sack; some clothes – a shirt maybe or a pair of old trousers, thin grass growing over and through them.

She began to doubt what she had seen. She peered through the fence, screwing up her eyes as if she could penetrate the gloom. There was little undergrowth – only leaves from last winter. It couldn't have moved out of sight in the time it took her to get round the Transit. Something rustled in the foliage above her and she glanced up. There was a dark shape in among the leaves. A child? *The* child? Was this some kind of prank? The trees were all beeches – thick smooth trunks with no handholds for a good ten feet, and near impossible to climb.

'Hello,' she said. 'Hello?'

'Hello,' said a voice behind her.

She yelped and turned. The man who had interviewed her, Mr Carstairs, was standing by a car that looked too big for him, his keys pointing in her direction.

'Talking to the trees?' he asked, looking smoothly insolent. He shot his cuff and glanced at his watch.

'I thought I saw something in the wood,' Caroline said.

'Oho?'

'No, no. A child. I thought he . . . it . . . looked hurt.'

Her fingers were dirty where she had hooked them through the mesh. Carstairs stepped towards the fence, keeping his eyes on Caroline's. When she looked away he kept on looking.

He stood beside her and shouted: 'Fuck off, you little fuckers! Should be in school anyway!'

His words soused Caroline in panic. 'Oh my God, what's the time?' She looked at her watch. Christ, what with everything she'd be late for Marcus.

'Need a lift, Miss Waters?'

'Mrs. No, I've got a car. I'm late.'

Carstairs shrugged and jerked his key at his car. The locks clunked open. He swept out of the car park as Caroline was still trying to get her engine to start.

She pulled out into the constipated, mid-afternoon traffic. Her lane stopped moving. She revved and tried to pull into the fast lane. A man in a black Mondeo braked an inch away from her front wing and yelled: 'Fucking bitch!' at her until the cars behind him started to sound their horns. He roared off, then his lane ground to a halt as Caroline's began to move again. She was so shaken that she did not want to move up next to him. She turned left down a side road and watched him slide into the space she had vacated.

She found herself in a street lined with pebble-dashed semi-detached cottages with mock Tudor gabling. She knew where she was. Marcus's friend Toby lived two streets away. She should be able to cut through. But she had to stop and squeeze into driveways so that other cars could get past. She got lost in the gently meandering roads, took a right instead of a left, and suddenly found herself driving between green fields and hedgerows in the wrong direction. All the time the clock was ticking away on the dashboard. She met a milk float out way past its bedtime, and a muck-caked muck-spreader being towed by a no-neck orc on a clapped-out old tractor that had just escaped from a Museum of the Countryside.

A balloon of panic began to swell inside her head. She had to stop the car, open the window and take huge breaths of air. She felt the sweat on her forehead, on her upper lip, on the nape of her neck, above her breasts, in the small of her back. She imagined the air filtering through her, aerating her. She felt it move through the membranes of her lungs, react with her blood, flow into her head, carry the bad thoughts away. Away. Away. No dead children in the woods. Marcus would be fine. What was there to worry about? Marcus would be fine. There was nothing to worry about.

She slid to a gravelly halt outside the school fifteen minutes late but pleased with herself for making up time by finding a real shortcut. There were still kids milling by the playground gates and she counted the ticking sounds of the cooling engine to show herself she really wasn't worried. She rolled her face against the breeze. Nice day actually. Clouds and sky and things.

She stepped out of the car, her legs still shaky but okay, and looked at the playground gate. Marcus was not there. Of course he wasn't. He had waited there for a while, then wandered off to kill time. He was in the playground; he was waiting in the school; he was talking to teacher . . . There were already far fewer boys by the gate, and they were all three or four years older than Marcus. That made her feel bad again. She started to walk faster.

Now she could see the playground. No Marcus. She looked up and down the road for his small frame, even ran a few paces in either direction. No Marcus. She searched her memory, thinking perhaps that she had seen him on the way, but been too preoccupied to recognise him. No. The panic balloon began to inflate again.

Breathe slowly. Slowly. Breathe it out. That's it.

A teacher caught her eye. Caroline walked towards her.

'I'm looking for my son. I can't seem to see him.'

'I'm sorry, Mrs . . .?'

'Waters. He's Marcus Waters. I'm late. I know I'm late.'

The teacher looked understandingly at her. 'Everyone's late occasionally, Mrs Waters.' She put a hand out and touched Caroline's forearm. 'Now, you've checked the road and the front. Have you checked round the side?'

'No.'

'Well, you do that. Wait a minute – tell me what form Marcus is in and I'll pop inside to see if his class teacher is still there.'

'Dunlop. Miss Dunlop's class.'

'I'll find Margaret Dunlop. Please don't worry.'

The teacher walked quickly inside. The playground ran down the side of the building to one side; to the other were milk crates and dustbins in an enclosure. Caroline checked behind and inside the enclosure. She turned away from the school, managed to keep the panic contained, and looked at the field opposite.

The street made a border between village and country. In front of it lay agricultural land. A tractor was harrowing a bare field. The tines seemed to float through the dry soil, breaking it, spinning it off on either side while behind and above seagulls wheeled. Caroline stayed still but the world rocked. One way, then the other, then back again.

She turned, closed her eyes, breathed deep.

'Mrs Waters?' It was the teacher again. 'I'm afraid Margaret had to leave as soon as lessons were over. Nick Pullin was looking out for her class. Now he knows your son, and tells me that Marcus said he was starting home by himself, that you'd arranged it. You were going to meet the other side of the golf course, near Granton Farm.'

'What?'

'He asked Marcus if he was sure, you know, just to check, and Marcus swore that was the arrangement.'

The teacher's voice showed concern but not guilt.

'But that means he'll be walking through the forest for some of the way! You let him – '

Dead children.

'Mrs Waters, I'm sure Marcus is a sensible boy. People do let their children find their own way home at Marcus's age, you know.'

'But I don't!' Caroline shouted. 'I don't! And the forest!'

The teacher closed her eyes in a way that Caroline found insulting. 'The forest isn't full of wild animals, you know, and parents do let their children manage on their own, and Marcus did say – '

'I don't care what – '

The teacher looked at her watch. 'Listen, if you take the road by the side of the golf course, follow it round and turn sharp left by Granton Farm, you'll meet your boy coming out of the wood, exactly where he said you should. Now he knows that's

21

the plan, so your best bet would be to follow it. Hmmm?'

Caroline realised that what the teacher had said made sense. Without another word she got into her car.

She drove fast between low fields. Seagulls filled the emptiness to either side.

Marcus was sitting on a low barrier across a forestry tractor track, chatting to a girl.

Caroline had a fleeting impression of a young, plump figure, thick blonde hair cut short and a pretty round face. Marcus slid off the barrier as soon as he saw the car and ran towards it, grinning and dragging his little rucksack through the leaf mould.

The girl watched, waved as he turned and waved, gave him a big smile and strode into the woods. She had a modern, business-like riding hat under one arm and a carrier bag in her other hand.

He dragged open the passenger door.

'Mummy, Mummy, I made a – '

He stopped as Caroline grabbed his wrist and pulled him down. She had thought that she might slap him on the back of the hand but when she saw his face, all lit up with excitement, she forgot and pulled him towards her in a sort of bear hug.

Then she took him by his shoulders and looked him in the eye.

'Marcus, you must never, ever do that again. Do you hear?'

'But – '

'No. No buts. You lied to the teacher, didn't you?'

'I just said – '

'Marcus.'

He settled back in the seat, folded his arms and pushed his lips forward in a pout.

'Marcus!'

'All right. Yes.' He stuck out his feet. They did not quite reach the floor of the Nissan so he jammed them against the glove box.

He turned his head and looked hard out of the side window, his eyes glazing over with tears.

Caroline was surprised. Something was wrong. Like last night, he was not acting in the way she expected. He was almost sulking now, as if she had let him down somehow. Caroline knew she could not stand another argument. She started the car and prepared to turn it.

'Who was that you were talking to?' she asked, lightening her voice.

'Where?'

Caroline glanced into the rear-view mirror. It stole some of the light from the forest. The ranks of trunks, grey-green and smooth, faded into darkness. She looked over her shoulder. Much lighter. She caught a glimpse of bright blonde hair slipping between the trees.

'On the gate there.'

'Oh, just a girl.'

An idea struck Caroline. 'Was that who you were talking to yesterday?'

'What?'

'The person on the other side of the fence?'

'No!' He sounded outraged.

'Did you arrange to meet the girl?'

'No! I just met her. She was on the way to the stables. Said she'd walk me out. To be honest, I got a bit lost.'

'You got – '

'I'm sorry.'

The way he said it, it came out 'sorr-eee', implying she was nagging him.

'Look, Marcus, all I want is for you to be safe. What made you take off like that? Have you been talking to people?'

The forest dropped away on the left; the houses started.

'Marcus.'

'Yes?'

'All I want is for you to be safe.'

'Your job.'

'What?'

'I wanted to help you with your job.'

Caroline inhaled sharply. What did he mean? Then worry suddenly sluiced off her and she was warmed by sudden relief.

'And you thought if you met me on the other side of the wood it might be quicker, if I was coming from work?'

There was a pause. Marcus sniffed and looked down, his nose out of the window. He had to tilt his head to see, the seat was so

23

low for him. Caroline loved him. She could not help it. She
began to grin.

'Marcus Waters,' she said.

A pause.

'What?'

'Thank you. That was a nice thought.'

Another pause.

'Sorry.' It was so faint it sounded like a mouse burp.

'Didn't hear that.'

'Didn't say anything,' he said, trying not to smile.

Chapter 4

Tina called at about quarter to seven. Marcus had arranged various monsters, musclemen and dinosaurs on the carpet and was zapping them with the remote control. Caroline took the call in the hall. There was a phone in the sitting room but conversations with Tina were uninhibited.

Tina and Caroline had been at college together. After they left, Tina had gone round the world and come back with an Australian accent – not that she had stayed long there, just that every second person she had met on the road had been Australian. She had worked as a temp in Glasgow, run a massage parlour in Bristol, been a music industry publicist in London, and given that up to teach sailing in Turkey. These days she was running a small residential health centre outside Hertford. It was always full and made a bomb and she was on a profit-sharing scheme. Things tended to go well for Tina. She screamed with laughter as Caroline described her interview.

'You must have looked ridiculous! Fancy thinking a word processor was like a typewriter. You get your arse up here and I'll let you loose on one of our computers for an afternoon.'

When Caroline began to describe the interview with Carstairs, Tina said: 'He fancies you.'

'Lay off, Tina.' Knowing it was true.

'I'm serious, I know all the signs.'

'You may know the signs, but I was there. I can tell you, he looked at me as if I was dirt.'

'Men like dirt, babe. You've been in purdah too long. With your figure and face, men don't act like that unless they've got a twitch, and as soon as that happens they have to try and assert their little manly selves.'

'All right.'

'There's something else, isn't there, chuck? Come on.'

'One of those days. You won't believe this but I've been seeing things. In the car park, by the office, there was this child lying on the ground. I mean, it was in the forest. When I got closer it went.'

'You mean, ran away?'

'I suppose. I'm sure it was hurt . . . the way it was lying.'

'You told anyone?'

'I tried. Just now. I called the police station but the lines were busy. I'll try again. I – '

Caroline's attention was caught by an image on the TV screen. Trees. A track in the woods. A reporter in a light-weight suit looking serious. Something on the local news. It looked like the forest; more than that, it looked familiar.

'You what? Caroline?'

The television was right at the other end of the house – across the hall and through a glass connecting door.

Marcus must have switched over to the news from *Babylon 5*. Caroline had a thing about the news. There was so much shit in the world she did not want to know about, and did not want Marcus to know either.

Another image. A girl's face spilled over the edges of the screen.

Caroline walked into the sitting room, handset sandwiched between ear and shoulder, extension lead snaking behind her, Tina saying: 'Cooo-eee, is anyone there?' in one ear, TV in the other.

'. . . in Epping Forest. The thirteen-year-old girl, an only child, was on her way to a riding lesson . . .'

The face was familiar, and the hair. Not the child in the car park but . . .

'. . . raised the alarm. But it was too late. Dana Watkins's body was found at five o'clock by a . . .'

'Marcus!'

'Hey, what's going on?' from Tina.

'MARCUS!'

'. . . assaulted, dragged some distance and bludgeoned to death . . .'

'Mummy!' His voice was a desperate wail.

'What's up there?'

A new face on the TV, a middle-aged policeman. '. . .

begging the public to come forward as soon as possible. That is why we've issued the picture so fast . . .'

'That was her,' Marcus said in little more than a whisper.

Caroline dropped the phone, fumbled for the remote that Marcus was waving around like a magic wand, pressed for the off-switch, grabbed him. 'I know, darling.'

'She's dead! They said! She was killed!'

'Oh, darling.'

'I saw her. She helped me. She was nice.'

Golden hair, a glint of sunlight in the forest, walking into darkness.

Marcus was stiff and quiet and cold in her arms.

What do you do? You say 'hush' but they're not saying anything; you say 'it'll be all right' but you don't really mean it; so you wait quietly, holding them, not saying anything. Children do not understand why adults feel that they have to put words to everything. They usually prefer to be held on a lap, against a breast, in silence.

Still Caroline was unprepared for the way the news took Marcus. After the shock he said nothing; hardly cried, just shook, as if he were more scared than sad.

The telephone handset stopped beeping and started to wail. She untangled Marcus and got up. After sitting bolt upright in the chair for a second, he followed her across the room with his fingers hooked into the hem of her sweater.

As soon as she put the phone on the hook it began to ring.

'Caroline, is that you?'

'Yes?'

'It's Marina here.'

Caroline's mind skidded. 'Marina?'

'Tom's on his way over.'

'What? What's wrong?'

'Well, he thought that something might be wrong with you.'

'What? Why?'

'Tina rang. She said she was chatting to you and you dropped the phone as if something was wrong. She thought she heard you shout something, and then Marcus began to scream – ' Marina's voice was breaking up. She sounded tearful.

'Oh, that.' Caroline acted more casual than she felt, thinking that she could not stand the thought of Marina snuffling over Marcus at the other end of the telephone. It was difficult to be cruel to Marina, even for Caroline. She was so fluffy, so pretty, so soft and pneumatic, so strangely asexual and negligible that cruelty was superfluous. Tina had once pointed out that people who loved animals liked Marina; Tina had a theory that she slept in a basket.

'He saw something disturbing on the news, that was all. He's much better now,' Caroline said soothingly.

'Oh. Good.'

Caroline smiled down at Marcus. He was looking better but she wanted him looking much better before Tom arrived. She mouthed 'Snowball the rabbit' at him and made nibbling motions with her mouth. Marcus nodded and trotted off.

'He's just feeding the rabbit right now,' Caroline said.

'Oh, good,' Marina said, her voice honeyed with genuine relief. 'And how is he?'

'What? Marcus?'

'No, silly. Snowball the rabbit.'

Caroline was about to say something sharp but realised that Marina was never sarcastic. They talked rabbits until Tom's new Citroën drew up outside the house.

Tom looked thin and fit. He was wearing jeans and an expensive soft leather jacket, all pleats and flaps. He strode purposefully to the door. Caroline opened it before he had a chance to ring.

'Caroline.' As always his eyes slid past her and started darting around the house. She never knew what he was looking for: boyfriends, pentagrams, Marcus? It was never just Marcus.

'What's up? Something's wrong. Can I help?'

He demanded involvement.

'Tina got totally the wrong end of the stick. Marcus was upset by something he saw on telly. I came over to turn it off and she rang off before I had the chance to explain. He's outside now with the rabbit. I've been on the phone to Marina. I told her all about it.'

'What, Marcus?'

'No, the rabbit,' Caroline said sweetly. 'She wanted to know about Snowball.'

Tom shook his head in irritation. 'Well, can I come in? Can I see him at any rate?'

Caroline stepped aside. 'Everything's fine.'

They stood in the picture window, three feet apart. At the bottom of the garden Marcus had the rabbit in his arms and was stroking its head.

'What was it?' Tom asked. 'I'm sorry about the panic, but the way Tina sounded I thought you'd been attacked or something.'

She decided to own up. Better that than him finding out from Marcus. 'A girl was murdered in the forest this afternoon. I – I was late picking him up from school. Marcus snuck off. I suppose he was hoping to get home on his own. Anyway he took a short cut through Burrows Corner – you know, at the back of the golf course and the riding school? – and he met a – he met *the* girl who was murdered. Apparently she was nice to him. Walked him through the wood. I saw her briefly just before she turned back.'

Caroline found that she was talking more and more slowly. She suddenly saw the reality of it all. She had seen the girl walk to her death. The girl who had helped Marcus. If she had not helped Marcus, he might be – If she had gone straight to the stables, she might not be –

'Caroline? Will you be able to cope?'

'What?'

Tom was looking concerned. 'Because if it would help – '

'Tom, it's fine.'

Marcus poured Snowball the rabbit into the cage and locked it, crouching down on his heels. He put his palm against the wire mesh.

If anything happens to Marcus . . . Caroline thought.

The child turned, saw Tom and ran across the lawn to the window.

'How come you were late?' Tom said to Caroline, as Marcus began scrabbling to push the window open.

'Round the side, and wipe your feet!' she shouted through the glass.

Tom waggled his fingers at his son. 'I asked – oh, forget it. Have you spoken to the police?' He cocked an eyebrow at her.

'No. Haven't had time. It's just – I didn't want Marcus to – '

She could see Tom thinking. She guessed he found it

satisfying to insist she talk to the police (owning up), but at the same time did not want to expose Marcus to any more grief (caring dad).

Marcus rushed into the sitting room, leaving a trail of dampish grass on the carpet.

'Shoes!' shouted Caroline. Marcus retreated and sat on the kitchen floor where he tugged his shoes off without untying them. His old Reeboks, Caroline noticed. She was sure he had been wearing Nikes when he went off to school that morning. If he'd lost them . . .

'We just saw someone who was killed,' Marcus said. 'I was the last to see them.' His voice was laced with excitement.

'I'll call the police,' Caroline said.

Tom wanted to stay for the interview, 'to keep an eye on things'. Caroline thought company would be nice but balked at the idea of Tom's. He always wanted to help, but while *he* was sure he did it for the best of motives, Caroline knew he was trying to work off a lingering sense of guilt. He had left her for Marina; the very least he could do was trust her to get on with her life now, thank you very much.

The police were round in five minutes. Tom was barely out of the door. Caroline watched them drive up in a standard-issue Metro and imagined the curtains twitching up and down the Close. She looked in some of the windows. Two people were staring hard at her house: Hugh Frobisher, a retired bank manager with a drink problem who lived opposite, and a woman two doors down from him whom Caroline did not know. Hugh Frobisher turned away quickly when he saw Caroline looking back at him; for the first time she realised that net curtains were useful to hide behind too.

A policeman and woman got out and looked around, pulling their tunics down. The policeman was a large man who rolled when he walked like an old-fashioned sailor. The woman had the brisk, purposeful gait of someone going places.

This time Caroline waited for them to ring before opening the door.

'Thank you for coming forward, Mrs Waters,' the policeman said.

'I just hope we've been of some help.'

The WPC smiled encouragingly at Marcus who had been bug-eyed and monosyllabic throughout the interview. Caroline had done most of the explaining – about her lateness, about Marcus wanting to help.

'You're a very brave little boy,' she said.

'He's very tired,' Caroline said. 'We're both still – '

The policeman looked at her. He had shrewd eyes; high, fleshy cheekbones gave them an odd slant. At one stage, Caroline noticed, his eyes had rested on the ring which she still wore, then looked around the sitting room. It was as if he were comparing what was there with what might have been.

'I know,' he said. 'Shock doesn't quite cover it, does it? Isn't a big enough word.'

Caroline had in fact been about to say 'shocked' but had thought it sounded too lame.

She nodded appreciatively. 'It's just the feeling of helplessness. I mean, uselessness. I mean, why are we here if . . . when a girl walks off like that . . . I mean, how come we don't have some idea? How come we can't help? I saw her; I saw her hair. She might have been killed a minute after that. Oh my God!'

'What is it?'

'It's just – it's probably not important. It's just I saw a child earlier today in the wood. Or thought I did.'

The man and the woman exchanged glances.

'You see, I thought it looked hurt, but it was the other side of a fence and when I got to the fence it had gone, and I couldn't get through because it was a high fence and anyway I was late for Marcus. I called the police station but you were engaged.'

The policeman nodded. The WPC took out a notebook. Caroline told them where the car park was, and where the child had been. 'It's probably nothing,' she said. 'I mean, I even doubted it myself.'

'Well, we'll look into it.' The policeman blinked deliberately. 'If Marcus remembers anything, anything at all, the way you've just done, please call me immediately. Memory does funny things; it doesn't work to order, does it?' His eyes flicked from Caroline to her son. 'Are you with me, Marcus? Can you use a phone?'

Marcus's eyes lit up. 'Yes, but I'm not allowed to all that much.'

'Nonsense, darling. I just don't want you calling those dreadful joke-line things.'

The policeman dipped a hand into his top pocket and pulled out a couple of cards. He handed one to Marcus and one to Caroline. 'That's my number,' he said.

'And you've got to remember that you're in no way to blame,' the WPC said. 'And you're helping now. You've helped us a lot.'

The policeman was sitting in the armchair next to the wall. He was fiddling with the fabric, Caroline saw. Big hands covered in sandy hair. While the WPC was talking, one of the big hands appeared to climb over the arm of the chair and disappear into the gap by the wall. It re-emerged holding a large model aeroplane.

It had been an expensive present from Tom and Marina, one of many. This one had a rasping petrol motor that took an age to start, and wire controls so that you could fly it like a stunt kite. Marcus sort of adored it but it was far too advanced a toy for his age – far too advanced for Tom for that matter. All the damn' thing ever did was nosedive.

'Its speciality is crash landing,' Caroline said.

The policeman was holding it out, squinting down the length of it. Marcus watched with a glimmer of interest. The policeman shot him a glance.

'Crashes, eh? Hold it for me, will you?'

Marcus slid off the chair and walked across the carpet.

'That's right, under the belly and round the wings is where it's strongest. That's it. This is a beauty, you know that?'

Marcus nodded.

'They fly them on Sundays in the forest. Once he'd seen them . . .' Caroline said.

'I know,' the WPC interrupted. 'Don't tell me. Once they see something they like . . .'

'Right, now, if you give Nancy the wires to hold – ' Marcus handed them to the WPC ' – and you hang on to the fuselage, and then Nancy waggles the wires a bit and I do this – '

While he had been talking he had gripped the tail with one

hand and slipped a couple of fingers into the body of the plane where the wings joined it.

Like a conjuror he was talking to Caroline and Marcus simultaneously without really seeing them.

'Hey, presto!'

There was an audible click. Two flaps on the tail started to move up and down.

'Wow!' said Marcus.

The policeman smiled in embarrassment. 'Ailerons jammed.'

'Of course,' said Caroline. 'Come round any time. There's a tap dripping upstairs.' Her voice sounded sharp. To cover it she said: 'Marcus, say thank you.'

The WPC stood up to go.

'Can you fly it?' Marcus said.

Caroline held him by the shoulders and mussed his hair. 'Now the airywhatsits are fixed, perhaps Daddy can fly it.'

'Oh, where is Mr Waters?' asked the WPC.

'We're divorced,' Caroline said simply. For some reason she looked at the policeman. Something about officials brought out a strong urge to confess.

'Anyway,' the WPC said, walking towards the door, 'my name is Nancy Freeman and this is Sergeant Willis. Do call us if anything else comes to mind. You've been very helpful. Sorry to keep you up so late. You do understand how important it was for us to see you?'

'I understand. Do you think you'll catch him?' Caroline asked.

Willis looked at her directly. 'We'll certainly try.'

Chapter 5

Sergeant Willis had Nancy Freeman drop him off at the car park which served Smith's and a couple of other offices on the small industrial estate. The car park had been carved out of the forest. Trees pressing up against the high mesh fence, so that in places leaves bulged through the links like fur through chicken wire.

He stood where Caroline had stood and looked at the forest. He could not distinguish a thing in the twilight, only the trunks of the trees. He pressed his face to the fence, seeing only litter. He took out a map and compared the location of the car park with the murder scene. Supposing the killer had attacked twice and the second body had not been found yet? A big supposition. There had been no reports of missing children and it seemed rather slim justification to pull people off the fingertip search.

He walked round the side of the car park and into the forest, sweeping the ground with a small torch. He saw the same rubbish, the same old pile of clothes as Caroline, and decided her eyes had tricked her. He shone his beam at the trunk of the nearest tree, then up into the branches. The light gleamed on something high up on the trunk. Beads of moisture clung to the bark. He reached up and touched it. Sniffed his fingers. Definitely not sap. Animal, not vegetable. He walked deeper into the woods, surprised at the quality of the light. It was dim, but clear. You thought you could see more than you could, like that child . . .

He swung his head round to stare. There *had* been a child but it was gone now. It had moved like something wild. He tried to see it in his peripheral vision – the corners of the eyes pick up more light than the centre – and sensed movement rather than saw it. There! It was running away from him. Without thinking, he gave chase. The child was about the same build as the Waters boy. And yet, what would any child be doing in the woods at this time of night?

He could just see the figure flitting from tree to tree ahead of him. It was moving quickly and smoothly but Willis thought he was gaining. And then, very suddenly, he stopped wanting to gain. The child was not running – it was flying! That was the only explanation. It was moving like a big, heavy insect, in bursts, swaying slightly from side to side. The realisation came in two stages. A sort of slow freeze that made running hurt, followed by the body blow of terror. That lasted a second. Then reason caught up with him. It was impossible.

He had stopped running and was standing opposite a small clump of hazel. His body was making a lot of noise in his ears: forty-year-old noises. Shadows leaked menace. A clump of hazel took on a dark significance. Above him the breeze began to ruffle the leaves. Above him . . . He looked at the heavy tree trunks all around. He began to walk, slowly at first, then more quickly in silly chicken steps, like a child trying to get to the loo before it bursts. He began to trot. Ahead of him the forest began to glow. There were noises, voices now, ahead of him, behind him, around him. He burst through a veil of foliage into a clearing that blazed as bright as day with a flat, dead light, and an invisible voice said in front of him, beyond the glare of the lights: 'Fuck me, look what the cat's brought in. Trying to pick up some overtime, Sarge?'

Willis blinked, then shaded his eyes from the vicious glare of the mobile arc lights to try and see beyond them. He heard the tinny growl of a mobile generator, now, and people talking.

'What do you make of it?' It was DC Benson, one of Nancy Freeman's young admirers. He was always polite to Willis, not seeing him as a threat.

Willis turned. He was standing in a glade that was roughly circular and grassed over. At one end stood a great, dying oak tree. Two lights were pointing at it, making it look very black. Its branches, barely carrying any leaves, were hung with scraps of cloth.

Willis had seen something like it before and racked his brain to think where. His body still hurt from running. Benson came and stood by him.

'Interesting, isn't it? Some kind of folk thing. Genuine rural myth. Sort of thing you'd expect to find in a remote French valley, not in the middle of Essex.' He glanced at Willis. 'You make a wish on the tree, tie your rag to it, and – hey, presto. Some people write the wish down. That cleft in the middle's plugged with soggy paper. You read about it from time to time, you know. I mean, if you went back to Fraser and *The Golden Bough* . . .' Willis cut him off with a gesture.

Against the backdrop of forest, the tree looked as if it were shedding black shreds of skin. He now saw that there was a ladder propped up against the trunk.

'Evidence?' he asked.

'Murder took place twenty yards away. Fingertip search over fifty-yard radius from scene of. This is within fifty yards.'

'But surely – ' Willis looked up at the tree. 'How old are those things tied to it?'

'Some of them are falling to bits. Old. Feeling superstitious, Sarge?'

'Seen any kids?' he asked.

'Heard plenty of them. Bit of fun, isn't it? Mucking around in the bushes. Didn't catch any though. That's all murder means these days – although again, sociologically speaking, I suppose we're providing them with an alternative focus.'

'What?'

'It allows them to share in the experience of death without getting too involved. There's no harm in that. You wait, tomorrow the place'll be covered with cut flowers. Floral tributes. Floral tributes in the middle of a fucking forest! Ironic, really.'

'Highly,' said Willis.

Chapter 6

Marcus was in bed and Caroline had just stretched out her legs on the sofa when there was a knock at the door. She groaned. She wanted time to think. Something about Marcus, something about some of the answers he'd given the policewoman, worried her. It was nothing she could put her finger on at the time, but now she thought his answers had come out too quickly. Had been too pat. Even when he hesitated, it looked as if he were acting a part.

She tried to identify her caller by the blurred silhouette behind the glass door. Too narrow for either Tom or the policeman. The policewoman? Wrong shape altogether. She put the chain on and opened the door, and tried to look through the gap as if she were not cowering.

A small man, thin with receding hair. Maurice Temple.

'Ah,' Caroline said. 'Yes.' She closed the door to release the chain, then regretted it when he said: 'May I come in?'

She was reluctant and made sure he knew it, but he refused to give way. After a pause she stood back and let him in, hating herself for doing so. He smelt of grass and pipe smoke. She pointed him to the sitting room.

'It's really nothing,' he said. 'I saw the police here this afternoon and heard about the murder in the forest. I really just wanted to check that everything was all right?'

He sounded sincere but he was watching her again. 'I'm sorry if it seems nosy. After we met last time and you seemed so upset . . .'

'Marcus saw the poor girl just before she was murdered,' Caroline said. Her voice sounded level and harsh in her own ears. And it was he who had been upset.

'Oh dear. Oh my. How awful. I mean, the girl and all. That is awful. But to see her . . .'

37

'He's fine. I mean, he's shocked but fine.'

'That's . . . good.' Now he seemed to be at a loss.

'There's something I wanted to ask you,' she said. 'The last time I saw you – on the path. We had a conversation about children in the forest.' She picked her words carefully. 'I thought I saw one the other day.'

'Yes?'

'It was the same day that the girl was killed. I was in the car park by the Oaklee industrial estate and thought I saw a child lying on the ground. I went over to see if I could help but it was gone.' She shook her head. 'It's been confusing me.'

Temple looked concerned. 'Perhaps – ' he began.

'It's confusing me, but I'm not confused,' Caroline said. 'I thought I saw it. I suppose I'm wondering if you've seen anything like it?'

Temple looked at her closely. 'And have you ever seen anything like it before?'

'No,' Caroline said quickly.

'A premonition perhaps?'

'Do you believe in that sort of thing?'

'Perhaps "believe" is too strong a word.' He shrugged. 'Perhaps we could just say that I've knocked about the world long enough not to discount anything. What did the child look like?'

Something made Caroline say: 'You sound as if you've lost one. It was thin-looking. Brown-skinned, I thought.'

'Well,' Temple said, 'all I can suggest is that you report it to the police.'

'Yes. I did that.'

He looked at a coffee stain on her carpet. 'I see,' he said. As if she had imparted some fact for which he was grateful.

He looked up and she was surprised to see how wet his eyes were. 'I'm very glad,' he said, 'that all is well.'

'Thank you,' said Caroline.

'Very glad.' He stood up suddenly and blundered towards the front door. He was on the verge of tears, she realised.

Caroline woke up and glanced at the alarm clock as the glowing figures flashed from 1:59 to 2:00.

The bedroom was stifling. She kicked the bedclothes off and

went and stood by the window where there was a sluggish flow of cooler air. She heard tiny clear night-time sounds, and behind them all the fizzing roar of the M25 where it passed under Bell Common.

Marcus stirred. Perhaps he couldn't sleep either. The house creaked as she walked to his room. He was up, she saw with a shock, staring out of the window at the forest.

He jumped as she stopped in his doorway. The window framed different kinds of darkness: the wood's heavy silhouette; the night sky, rusted by the glare of motorway lights. Marcus's face looked blue, his lips and eyes black.

'What is it, darling?'

'I woke up.'

'What's the matter, precious?'

'I wish – ' he said, then stopped suddenly as if he'd remembered something. 'I don't like the trees. They're too tall. I feel ill. Can I have a Dispirin?'

'You don't need one, darling. Yesterday was a horrid day. What you need is sleep to make a new day.'

That's what her mother had said: You make a new day when you sleep.

'Go to bed. I'll sit with you.'

She sat on the edge of the bed. Marcus climbed in.

'Is there a monster in the wood?' he asked.

'What – oh, darling, of course not.'

'The man on the news said that only a monster could have done it.'

'He just meant a very bad man. But there's nothing to worry about now. You're safe with me, my darling.'

Marcus nodded and closed his eyes. One minute he was awake, staring at the ceiling; the next his eyelids had fluttered and he was asleep. Caroline stayed there a while longer then went to her bed.

The back window on the landing faced the forest. She had stood there many times in the darkness, looking at the trees. She knew that by staring at the dark she could keep at bay the nightmares that gathered under the hissing leaves and the hard web of branches. Now it seemed the nightmares were pressing for release and the massing darkness outside was stirring a shadow in her head, another darkness she thought she had

39

buried, something she had come back to the forest to confront and defeat.

It had died, she knew that, but now perhaps it was coming back to life. It was not the nightmare that frightened her so much as the fact that it could come back. She closed her eyes and squeezed and squeezed them, tighter and tighter until her eyeballs ached, as if the pressure might wring the fear from her mind.

Chapter 7

The North Forest Police Authority knew about death and knew about bodies. At times the forest seemed like a clearing ground for crime. Old scores might not be settled in it but a great deal of the fall-out ended up there, though now the habit seemed to be dying as gangland, like so much else, changed. There was a period during the 1980s when the supply dried up altogether, but property was booming then and suddenly there were a lot of very deep holes being excavated all over London: the foundations for a new generation of high rises.

Still, when a body was found, certain procedures swung into motion and people knew what to do. There were routines, fallback positions, questions to be asked, answers to be listened to, near-standardised press releases, ways of fudging if you wanted to fudge and pushing things along if you wanted to do that, even jokes to take the sting out of what you were doing.

All that was fine if you were dealing with the skeletonised corpse of a white Caucasian male aged anything between eighteen and fifty. But the case of Dana Watkins was different. Everyone, it seemed, came across some fact or detail about the case, some little barb, that sliced its way under their tough hides and stuck there.

Some of these were relevant to the case.

Fact: she had been seen fifteen minutes before she died – an accurately timed sighting by a woman who was meeting her young son on the way back from school.

Fact: she was found barely fifteen minutes after estimated time of death. Her body was still warm.

Fact: neither the blood on her face, breasts and thighs, nor the so-far unidentified white-ish liquid pooled in the cleft of her buttocks, had had time to dry.

Fact: the body carried bite-marks up the right side, then

41

across both breasts. They had been made after she had died.

Fact: fifteen minutes before she died she had been a virgin.

Fact: she was blonde, and it seemed that gentlemen – coppers or psychos – prefer them.

Fact: she was on her way to the riding stables to help teach Downs Syndrome children to ride.

Fact: she was an only child.

Cause of death was suffocation, as opposed to strangulation. This was considered odd.

Sergeant Willis worried a nail with his teeth. It tore clean across the top, baring a strip of undernail, then continued down the side, ripping away a thin strip of quick. He swore and flapped his fingers, sucked the blood. The case just kept on worrying away at him, leaving him feeling just as raw. He was supposed to be writing up his notes from the Waters interview but couldn't keep his mind on the job.

Dana had died in a plump sachet of red time. She was seen just before her death; she was seen just after. Whoever had killed her had taken an enormous risk. And as far as Sergeant Willis could see, if she had not bothered to help the little boy find his way back on to the path, in all probability she would still be alive: heart beating, hair shining – all that banal stuff you had to get through. But that was a profitless way to think: empty philosophy, thought without consequence, because the consequence had already been decided. Sure, Dana would not have died if she had not talked to the Waters boy, but then it was possible that she would be alive if she had not eaten Kellogg's Frosties and Marmite soldiers for breakfast. Or if that butterfly hadn't flapped its wings somewhere in the Andes. He had to hold to the idea that it was by no means Caroline or Marcus Waters's fault. It was just one of those things, and with any luck when they worked it out they would see it like that too.

The mother and child, Caroline and Marcus Waters . . . Nice people; the sort of people a policeman would be proud and honoured to protect. The sort of people you might like to meet and the sort of people you wanted to accept because, well, sometimes you just got sick of suspecting people. But . . . something was nagging him.

He glanced down at the notes he had taken during the interview. At some point, and it would have to be soon, they would have to make a sworn statement. When he looked at the notes and when he played back the interview in his mind, he knew that what they had told him wasn't all of it.

He stretched his legs under the desk, barking his shins on the modesty panel. He clicked his fingers and scratched his Nicorette patch to try and jiggle a bit more of the drug into his bloodstream. He looked across the incident room where Nancy Freeman was prodding at a typewriter the size of a Victorian doll's house and about as good at producing readable copy.

The room was crowded. A line of computer consoles hooked up to telephones ran along one end of the room and everything else had been squashed into the remaining space. Draftees to help with the searches and compile the preliminary database were mooching around in the tiny gaps between the desks – officers from the country, officers from the city, mixing it on the border. There were three half-finished cups of coffee on the edge of Willis's desk, two with fag ends floating in them. He leaned sideways in his chair to peer around a pair of serge-swaddled buttocks and waved until Nancy Freeman looked up. She clattered to the end of a line, dabbed Tippex on a couple of places, stood back with one eye half-closed then pushed her way across the room to join him.

'Well, I'm here,' she said. The man by Willis's desk looked at her, looked at Willis and jokily said: 'Oi, oi!'

Willis looked down. Nancy Freeman pushed the man away with her fingertips pressed on to his chest and an expression that was not forgiving. She grabbed a chair and sat down.

'So what did you think of the woman and the boy yesterday evening?' Willis asked abruptly.

Nancy Freeman frowned. 'Caroline Waters? I thought she was – er – brittle. Her voice was anyway. Perhaps "brittle" isn't quite it. She looked like someone used to living on their nerves, but so used to it she knows how to cover it up.'

'Could have been shock?' Willis suggested.

'Really, sir? I thought you said that was an inadequate term.'

Willis rubbed his eyes. 'Did I? Probably just showing the human side of the force, Constable. Actually I agree with you.'

Nancy Freeman thought for a second. 'It could have been shock, sir. It's hardly likely that they *weren't* shocked. I just thought there was something – watchful? defiant? protective? –

something like that. I mean, the way she related to the boy when he told his story.'

Willis scratched the underside of his chin. He found a place his razor had missed and stroked it.

'Protective? Not surprising really. Boy meets girl. Girl gets killed. You'd expect the boy to be a bit upset and the mother to get a bit protective.' He exhaled noisily. 'Watchful. Defiant. Protective. Ye-es. Defiant and protective. That's okay. She doesn't want us messing around with his brain. But watchful. At the time I thought she might have been watching the boy – I mean, watching him closely, like she wanted to learn something from him.'

'Didn't get that,' Nancy Freeman said.

Willis rubbed his eyes. 'Kids! I hate anything to do with them.'

'You mended his aeroplane.'

Willis spread his fingers. 'Surgeon's hands, Constable. They must mend, they must cure.'

'Bollocks! You just wanted to bring a smile to his wan little face.'

'Bollocks! I fancied his mum.'

There was a pause. Willis jiggled his feet. 'Something else is bothering me. How long would it take a kid to walk from the school in Burrows Way, down the lane, into the wood, get lost, meet Dana Watkins, get back on to the path and be sitting on the barrier by the time his mum comes by? That's not a rhetorical question, by the way. I haven't got a clue. Oh, and incidentally, it's a bloody crackpot scheme having him walk through the woods to that place. Once you've taken all the turns into account it'd be further away from her office than the school. And she says it was all to speed things up.'

'That's a point. And all she had was an interview; it's not as if she's got the job. And suppose it's raining anyway. What does the kiddie do then? Walk through the forest in the rain? Suppose it's raining really hard? Suppose it was winter and getting dark? He'd be petrified. I would be, I know. You're right, it doesn't quite add up.'

'Bastard bloody kids. It always happens,' Willis said. 'I know it's nothing, I know that there's a perfectly simple explanation, but it's nagging me. Oh, there's another thing. What about him

44

losing his way? Do you know that path?'

Nancy Freeman shook her head.

'It's five feet wide and gravelled. I just checked with lover boy Benson. It's not the sort of path you lose.'

'Could have wandered off, lost his sense of direction . . .'

'Children!' Willis said. Nancy cocked an eyebrow at him.

'You're not saying he's lying?'

'I bloody well am.'

'Come on, Sarge. A kid does something wrong that he doesn't want to own up to. While he's doing that, he's not going to admit to seeing anything else. If a kid nicking sweets saw an armed robbery, it'd deny it just because it didn't want to get found out about the sweets.'

'Okay, okay. So we have to find out if he was doing something wrong so that we can find out whether he saw anything. And anyway, it won't stand up in court.'

'No leads so far?'

'There's that bloody weird tree, but it's more a distraction than a lead.'

'Pop over to the Waterses?' Nancy Freeman asked. 'Quick chat with Mum then have a look at the path and the route he took. It's all just-in-case stuff, I suppose, but you never know.'

'No, you bloody don't, do you? Okay. Here's the plan. I want you to wait in the car because I want it to seem that I'm only going to be in a short while – just dropping in to clear something up. Nothing heavy. And there's my constable waiting impatiently in the car to prove it. You can wait impatiently, Constable Freeman?'

'I can wait any way you want, Sarge.'

'Don't tempt our fat-arsed friend,' Willis said. 'He wants to ask you out.'

Nancy Freeman squinted at the man she had pushed out of the way. He raised an eyebrow at her.

'He's been doing that all day.'

Willis narrowed his eyes. 'Is he pleased to see you or is that a walkie-talkie in his pocket?' he said in a bad W.C. Fields voice.

As they headed for the car park Nancy pointed out that it was a quote from Mae West, not W.C. Fields.

They hit rush-hour traffic. Willis grew bored, looked at houses,

45

looked at cars, clicked his knuckles until Nancy asked him to stop, thought about cigarettes, Mars Bars, clogged arteries, his sister who lived in Cleethorpes, mud, earth, dead teenagers. There was summer dust on the windscreen; a dead summer leaf under a wiper. He fiddled with the heater controls.

'See that VW Polo, Constable? Do you think it's got a murderer inside?'

'Seriously, Sarge?'

'Yes.'

'No.'

'Statistically, I wonder how many cars I would have to get you to look at before you said yes.'

'Might depend on the car. Now if you'd said Vauxhall Astra . . .'

'The constable jokes.'

'I thought *you* were joking.'

'I was speculating. There's a difference. What happens in a man's brain when he's walking through a forest, or sitting at home reading, to make him suddenly change from being a bloke walking through the forest or reading a magazine, into a murderer?'

She said nothing. Willis said: 'Do you mind talking like this?' Some people did, but Nancy was merely frowning thoughtfully, a little furrow deepening between her eyebrows.

'It's like everything changes but everything's the same,' she said. 'It's like when the streetlights flicker off in the dawn. The moment when everything turns.'

The traffic thinned, gaps opened between cars. They turned into Kingsmeade Close. As Willis was squeezing out of the little car, he said: 'Another thing. Why do waves always break on to a beach and not off it?'

Nancy just mouthed 'Silly wanker' at his back.

Willis slithered out of the Metro and straightened up. He caught a scent on the air and sniffed appreciatively. There was jasmine growing somewhere nearby. That was one advantage of not smoking. Taste and smell seemed sharper somehow. He sniffed again, spotted the plant about two doors down from the Waters' house and wondered if anyone would notice if he snaffled a cutting.

He looked around. No one visible, but his eye was caught by a sticker in the window of the front room of the house: Neighbourhood Watch. Philosophically speaking, the scheme made no sense at all, because its ultimate success – the entire country watching itself – would result in its failure. Because if your neighbour was a villain, and he was watching you . . .

He turned to the Waters' house, noted the coach lights, calculated from the number plates that the Nissan was six years old, glanced around, saw that none of the other cars in the Close was more than two years old, and without ever really thinking about it walked up the narrow brick path to the front door with the idea forming in his head that Caroline Waters had been divorced between four and six years, had kept the marital home and family car, was worse off than most of her neighbours (without exactly being poor), and had not noticed that the door frame needed a lick of paint.

He lifted his hand to the doorbell –

The scream was hard, harsh and desperate. It ruptured the afternoon quiet and stopped him dead.

Willis looked around for Nancy but she had driven on round the corner, looking for a place to turn, and was out of sight. There was no time to waste. The scream had come from outside and behind the house.

The front door was closed; the fence abutted the right-hand side of the property, but to the left there was a narrow path between the fence on the other side and the house, blocked off by a high gate. Two hard kicks with the soles of his size twelve shoes, one on the middle, one at the bottom, and latch and bolt tore loose. He shoulder charged the gate open, pounded down a narrow concrete alley and stopped in the back garden.

A frozen tableau.

At the end of the garden, a gate similar to the one he had broken down stood open. The boy was standing framed in it, the aeroplane under his arm. Behind and above him the trees massed. He had turned in mid-stride and was looking up at the house.

Willis followed the boy's eyes. Caroline Waters was staring out of the window at her son, her face twisted in shock. The boy looked rather calm, Willis thought, considering his mother had

47

just thrown a complete fit. But then perhaps she had them all the time.

Caroline Waters looked down at him.

Willis said: 'I heard screams. I'm sorry, I thought . . .'

She said: 'No, I'm sorry. I saw Marcus about to go into the forest from the window. Marcus, you're a *very* bad boy. What can I do with you?'

Marcus said to Willis: 'I was only going to find some dandelions for Snowball.'

Willis said to Marcus: 'With an aeroplane under your arm?'

The boy gave him an it's-a-fair-cop-guv smile, and put the aeroplane carefully down on the grass.

'I'm coming down,' Caroline said.

'I wanted to ask you something. Will what you did stop it crashing?' Marcus asked from the other side of the garden.

Willis walked towards him, peered left and right at the green path and closed the gate. 'Nothing's going to stop it crashing,' he said, 'but at least now it's got a fair chance. I mean, model aeroplanes always crash eventually but at least now you should have a bit of fun with it before you smash it up.'

'Could I work it or would it have to be with a grown-up?'

'Well, you probably should – '

He broke off as the mother walked across the grass. She had just showered and her hair was brushed straight back over her forehead. For a second he saw another person there, someone looking at him with an adolescent's detachment. Then her face shifted into a big, almost flashy smile.

'What?' the boy asked.

'Have an adult with you,' Willis snapped. For a second, before her face changed, she had reminded him of someone and he found himself wondering if he'd ever booked her. Wishful thinking. Willis was surprised by a particular golden surge in his solar plexus. Her wet hair darkened the T-shirt at the back of the neck.

'Is he bothering you?' she asked.

'Not in the slightest. I'm being put on the spot but I can manage, I think.' Christ, she was gorgeous.

'If I kept away from wires, cars and houses and trees, I'd be all right?' the boy pressed.

Willis felt stumped.

48

'A grown-up would have to check, darling.'

'I don't care about that,' Marcus said.

He ran off, holding the aeroplane, roaring in the back of his throat as the plane turned, swooped, dived.

'He's still upset,' Caroline said. 'Can you be quick?' She glanced up at the trees. 'We'll go inside to talk,' she said.

Nancy had pulled up in front of the house and was looking bored.

'Your colleague. Would she like to come in?'

'No, no. I just wanted a quick chat, that's why I left her outside.'

Caroline walked down the room and stood by the sliding glass doors. Willis stood to one side.

'You said you had some questions for me?'

Willis studied her. She was in profile. 'It's about the arrangement you made to pick Marcus up after school. I wondered if you had anything to add or perhaps that you'd forgotten? To be perfectly frank, it's a terrible arrangement.'

To his surprise she smiled. She did not look at him, just said: 'I can't tell you what a relief it is to hear a smartarse comment from someone other than a nine-year-old boy. Yes, you're quite right. I was late picking him up and by the time I got to the school he'd taken off. He told the teacher that he had arranged to meet me on the other side of the wood, but there was no such arrangement. You see, I felt ashamed at being late. When I spoke to you the first time, I'd narrowly avoided a lecture on parental responsibility from my ex-husband so I picked up on Marcus's story. It was naughty of him, but he was trying to help.'

'Help you do what?'

'It was to do with a job. Didn't I say? All rather academic now. I screwed up the interview. Anyway, Marcus left a message with a teacher about where he was going to meet me. The teacher told me so I knew where to go.'

'So he knew you'd be going to the school?'

'Of course.'

'So he wouldn't be helping you. He'd just be making you drive, what, twice as far?'

For a moment she looked confused. 'Yes, that hadn't

occurred to me.' Her face brightened. 'And if it didn't occur to me, it probably didn't occur to Marcus. Oh, you must know what children are like. You're not suggesting, you don't think that he – '

'What?'

'Saw . . . no, I'm not thinking straight. He couldn't have seen anything. I saw the girl after he got lost and she was fine then.'

'That's right,' Willis said. 'You said you did.'

'I *said* I did? But I did!' The outrage looked genuine.

'Sorry, force of habit. I honestly am not implying anything. All I meant was – if he was doing something he shouldn't, he'll probably lie about everything. What I want to do is tell him that we think he's hiding something. It doesn't matter what that is, but it's terribly important he doesn't hide anything else. All right?'

'All right.'

She tapped on the french window. Marcus looked up and she beckoned him in.

'Now, Marcus,' Willis began when he'd joined them, 'we want to retrace your steps because we want to find out exactly where you met Dana Watkins – the girl. It'll help us a lot if you can remember.' A shadow moved across the boy's face. Willis pushed quickly on. 'Now you said you got lost, yes?'

He nodded.

'That means you probably left the path.'

Another nod.

'Can you tell me where?'

'Well, it wasn't very far in. When I looked back I couldn't see where I had come into the wood but I wasn't far in.'

'Less than halfway?'

He nodded.

'On the left or the right? Did you go off the path to the left or the right?'

The boy waved his arms and wrote with one of them in the air. He thought for a second. 'Right,' he said brightly. He crossed and uncrossed his legs and smiled.

'Are you sure?' Willis asked.

The boy did the mime with his hands again. 'Quite sure,' he said.

Willis looked sideways at the mother who was looking puzzled and worried. That's the lie, he thought.

He smiled. 'Now, Marcus,' this was the hard part, 'we know that you didn't have an arrangement with your mum to meet her the other side of the wood. We know that she was late and you went off on your own. We know that the only reason you did it was that you wanted to do something. Okay. But I've got a problem. I need to know everything that everybody in the wood was doing when you were there. Even if you were doing something secret that you don't want to tell us about, did you see anyone before you saw the girl?'

Marcus looked at his mother. He had opened his mouth to protest. Now he closed it.

'A man or a woman, maybe?' Willis prodded.

'I was only trying to – '

Then there came a sudden series of events as if they had been stacking up, waiting for a pause. A car door slammed, the telephone began to trill and the front doorbell rang, one of those silly sounds that went 'ding-dong'.

Willis swore under his breath. The boy rushed past him just as his mother reached the phone and opened the front door to Nancy who was looking very excited. Caroline, with the phone in one hand, nodded to her and jerked her head at Willis.

'We might have a result, Sarge,' Nancy said. Marcus had followed her into the room and stood behind her. 'Suspect a couple of miles away. Sex offender name of Tailor out on parole in Harris Drive. They're taking him in. We're wanted for back-up, pronto.'

The boy moved between them. His head swivelled from Willis to the WPC to gauge the importance of what was being said.

Behind him Willis heard Caroline Waters say: 'But that's – I thought – No, of course – Yes – Tomorrow then.'

He hesitated.

'It's an emergency, Sarge.'

He shrugged and nodded at Caroline as he walked out.

The boy followed them. As Willis was folding himself into the passenger seat, he called: 'Your side gate. It's open. Broken. Tell your mother to wedge it shut with something. Can you do that?'

51

The boy nodded.

From the back of the hall Caroline Waters looked at him with an expression that was frankly bewildered. She gave a half-wave as the car pulled away. She was looking at the telephone as if it was the Holy Grail.

She said 'yes' a few more times then, 'Thank you very much. Thank you VERY much. I'll be there.'

Marcus looked at her, frozen with expectation.

'It's happened, Marcus. I got the job! Your clever mummy got the job. Oh, darling!'

She knelt to hug him but Marcus did not come towards her immediately. For a second he looked bewildered, an expression that was overwhelmed by something else that seemed to be welling up inside him. Caroline spoke his name, and his eyes suddenly fixed on hers.

'Clever Mummy got the job,' he repeated. 'I knew you would.'

'Which was more than I did. Marcus, this is going to be a whole new beginning.'

'Good.' He wriggled out of her arms.

'Where are you going?'

'To tell Mr Temple.' He sounded surprised that she had had to ask.

'But – '

'It's all right,' he said. 'Back in a minute.' He paused by the door. 'He asked me to tell him.' Another pause. 'Perhaps he fancies you.' Then he was gone, looking gleeful.

Chapter 8

The house was a large, square detached villa at the end of a terraced street. It was built of grey local brick; the window frames and front door painted green. Three windows were broken and patched up with cardboard. The others shone like gems.

A small crowd of nine or ten people had gathered in the short space of time since the first police cars had arrived. Nancy and Willis were waved through. Looking up through the window of the Metro, Willis tried to read the faces. They were curious, even light-hearted, but then hangings at Newgate used to turn into massive street parties.

'So what are we doing?' Willis asked. 'Rounding up the usual suspects?'

Nancy parked at the end of the road. 'He lives with his mother,' she said as they got out and leaned against the Metro's wing. 'Currently out on parole from Wenlock Green Prison. You know, the one with the famous rehab' unit. Responded well to therapy, counselling, that kind of thing. Never missed a session. Model prisoner.'

Willis grunted. He was not really listening. When he had told Caroline Waters that he was going to try to trap her son in a lie, she hadn't protested. He was trying to work out whether that was strange or whether he was just being oversensitive.

But Nancy was talking again.

'He could have got into the forest that way,' she said. There was a narrow alley at the back of the house overhung with branches. 'How was the interview with the boy?'

He shrugged. He didn't want to talk until he was clearer in his own mind. Better to concentrate on the matter in hand.

'What did this one do to deserve our attention?'

'Rape. Teenage girl.'

'Ah.'

'That's all I heard,' Nancy said. 'But there are similarities.' The car radio squawked before Willis could ask for details.

'Here we go,' she said.

A tall man was being bundled down the steps of the house, an anorak over his head. A tall, bony woman with tightly curled old-fashioned hair looked on from the doorway of the house.

'Must be the mother,' Nancy said.

'And that's trouble.'

A man and two women had broken through the cordon and were running down the pavement towards the house. The man was screaming, 'Bastard, bastard!' The women were just screaming.

Willis moved up to intercept. He body-checked the man; the two women collided with him. Glancing over his shoulder, he saw Nancy press down on Tailor's head as she helped guide him into the car. He looked down at the man who was whooping for breath on the pavement.

'You can get up now,' he said.

'I'll get you for this,' the man said. 'I'll sue.'

'Do you want me to arrest you for assaulting a police officer?' Willis asked.

'Fuck you,' the man said and picked himself up. He looked over his shoulder and yelled as the car drove past, 'Bastard! Fucking shit bastard! You deserve to die.'

One of the women shouted: 'Hang him!'

The other: 'Keep away from our homes!'

The small crowd tried to move in on the car. There were a couple of bangs as someone hit its roof, then it was off.

In a flash of clarity, Willis looked up at the big grey house and thought: that was a family home too. For some reason it reminded him of the Waters home. He searched for the reason, then got it. Two people in a big house. Mothers looking out for sons. Sons doing things in the forest. Maybe.

Coincidence?

Maybe.

Nancy was looking at the hand that had touched Tailor as if she wanted to amputate it.

Chapter 9

Tailor was being sweated but not talking. Willis was doodling on a piece of paper. Dana Watkins. Tailor. Marcus Waters. He had even drawn a little sketch map of the area.

On impulse he drew in the car park where Caroline Waters had seen, had *thought* she'd seen, an injured child. He drew a vector line to show the route he'd taken, chasing, or *thinking* he was chasing, a child that floated. The memory made him feel queasy.

He thought about the suspect in the cells. Tailor. His solicitor was talking harassment; he was talking but not saying what they wanted to hear. Yes, he had been in the forest. No, he hadn't seen Dana Watkins. No, he had no hand in her death. He often walked in the forest. He found it restful.

And that was that and all there was likely to be. Grey, the interrogating officer, had not had a breakthrough, and, in Willis's opinion, had no chance of achieving one. Tailor had an ominously simple story and was sticking to it, and everyone knew that simple stories were the hardest to break down by frontal assault.

Willis felt frustrated. He had not been allowed to see Tailor's file because Grey was sitting on it. Because Grey had been shouting at Tailor for eight hours with no results and he still hadn't ordered his team to try alternative courses of action: extensive interviews, a wider search; anything to place Tailor somewhere other than where he claimed.

Dana Watkins. Marcus Waters. Tailor.

Tailor was 43 years old. Since his release from Wenlock Green four months ago, having served five years of an eight-year rape sentence, he had lived with his mother. Ten years prior to his long sentence, he had served two years for an assault on a minor.

But those factors did not explain why Grey was going for him so hard, why it had become a sort of mark of honour to break him down. The reason was that Tailor was not just scum. He was élite scum. Scum-de-la-scum. He was the evil bastard, the evil guilty bastard, who played the system and got away. It had happened once before, the reasoning went, and they couldn't let it happen again.

The last time they had been sure that Tailor was guilty of rape and murder. In fact, they had been so sure that they had planted evidence in the Ford Transit he used for deliveries from the factory where he worked. The evidence could have led to a mistrial and Tailor walking free. As it was, the judge had placed particular emphasis on other forensic evidence during his summing up, evidence (hair, coat fibres) that placed a young, asthmatic teenage girl in Tailor's van and was proof of a struggle with him (skin under her fingernails; scratches on his neck).

Three factors weighed in Tailor's favour. One, the rope the police planted under the front seat of his van to match the marks around the girl's wrists. Two, the lack of evidence that she had died in his van. Three, the asthma attack that the defence claimed killed her.

Anyway, her body was found in woodland three days after she had disappeared, covered in human bite marks, and Tailor was identified as the man seen picking her up in Chingford. He admitted propositioning her, admitted rough sex, but claimed that when he chucked her out of the van, she had been fine. (His words.) The fatal asthma attack must have come along later.

The prosecution accepted that Tailor might not have set out with the intention of killing her, but claimed she had died of terror in the course of a savage sexual attack. In the end, the jury went for a compromise, and convicted him of rape, not murder. Some said that if they had gone for manslaughter, the jury would have found for the prosecution all the way.

Willis half listened to Nancy talking across the room to a colleague: 'I thought I'd be excited,' she was saying, 'but I started thinking about what he had done, I mean to that asthmatic girl, and suddenly I felt like shit. And when I touched him, it's like the first time you see an autopsy. You're all right on one level but while you're saying, "this is fine, it's just meat," you're fainting. I've seen rapists before. I suppose he's the first psycho. I don't know. Grey says the bite marks are identical. The whole thing just seemed ludicrous: to be bundling him into a car, to be protecting him. I wanted to kill him. Not for Dana Watkins, not until there's evidence, but for the other one. I've never felt like that before. He just looked so unbothered, and I was thinking: It could have been me. I was young when he did the first one. He would have used me like a handkerchief to come into and chuck away. That was the first time the reality really sank in.'

The men around her looked uncomfortable. Nancy looked across at Willis. Her eyes were bright. Something was flying behind them. 'No anecdotes, Sarge? No wise cracks?'

He winked at her. 'You understand computers, don't you, Constable?'

'Yes.' She blushed.

'Help me.'

He walked across the room to one of the new toys: a computer loaded with identikit software.

'Was I talking too much?'

'It's called displacement.'

'Shit,' Nancy said.

'Displace on this. I'm sure I had to sign a chit saying you were worth training on it.'

They built up the face from a series of menus. Shape of head, face, jaw, mouth, hair type, eye colour.

Unfamiliar with the technology, Willis had Nancy print off a couple of blank faces – just the outline of hair and jaw and cheek so he could doodle features on them. He left one blank and stared at it, thinking that the empty, featureless face was how so many investigations began. Slowly, feature by feature, you built it up into something recognisable, something with significance. You had to really. Beyond the job, beyond the desire to catch the bad guy, beyond the fight between order and chaos, good and evil and all that, there was a simple compulsion to fill in the unknown because the unknown was frightening. After they got the basic shape Nancy kept on wiping it clean until they got the nose, then the mouth. Half an hour later Willis was satisfied. Quite a good likeness if you just glanced at it. He took the print-out, and a blank one for reference.

'What's it all about, Sarge?'

'Just a hunch. I want to check if Tailor saw the Waters kid.'

'You don't think he'll admit it?'

Willis shrugged.

'How are you going to get past Grey?'

Willis shrugged.

'Can I help?'

Willis shook his head.

He walked down to the interview room, the print-outs rolled up and warm in his hand. A constable was standing outside the door. Willis peered through the small square of wired glass. Inspector Grey was shouting at Tailor; Tailor's solicitor was shouting at Grey. Tailor was not doing anything except sit very still and look at the wall behind Grey's head. He had a curiously big face, dominated by the eyes. His skin was whitewash white like the wall. A skin disease had played a part in his transfer to a prison with a liberal regime. He couldn't go out into sunlight without protective covering or sunblock.

'How long since Grey had a piss?' Willis asked.

'He's not been out for two hours.'

There were three polystyrene cups on the table, all in front of Grey. As Willis looked, he pushed back his chair, pointed at Tailor and walked from the room. Willis stepped back, Grey walked down the corridor without seeing him and Willis slipped through the door into the interview room where Tailor and his solicitor were just rearranging themselves into more relaxed positions. They stopped as they saw him.

'Oh no you don't,' said the solicitor. 'We're owed a break.'

'I've come in to offer you some tea.'

'White with.' Tailor had a pleasant, light voice. Willis glanced at him and smiled.

'Coming up. Oh, by the way, have you ever seen this boy?'

The solicitor half rose from his chair and said, 'Watch it!'

Willis unrolled the print-out and held it flat on the table. He kept his eyes on Tailor. Tailor glanced down, blanched, then opened his mouth. For two seconds he was silent; Willis clearly heard the second hand of the big wall clock tick twice. Then Tailor began to scream. It was a high-pitched, helpless scream.

A child's round-eyed, paralysed scream. The solicitor snatched at the print-out and stared at it, looked up at Willis in bewilderment, who returned his look, matching his amazement. Willis had accidentally laid out the blank print-out with only the outline of the face.

Tailor began to drum his heels on the floor. His lower lip was puckered to make a sort of spout and it began to overflow with spittle.

'Who is that?' The solicitor waved the picture. Willis heard the door open. He knew the situation was slipping away from him and all he wanted to do was find the switch to turn off the noise. He smelled urine and heard the splash of it hitting the floor. Tailor started to shake, first his hands, then his head.

'Get a doctor,' the solicitor said in a tight voice. 'What have you done?'

Willis shook his head in horror, not at his own action, simply because he was looking at someone who seemed to be breaking up in front of him. Fear had risen off the flat surface of the identikit picture and was tearing Tailor apart.

'It's a fit,' said Willis. 'It must be.'

Tailor spasmed. His feet shot out and rocketed the chair backwards. It tipped. His head clunked against the wall. He slid down and stopped moving.

'I'll get an ambulance,' Willis said.

He walked to his flat – the top floor of a Victorian conversion in a quiet street between the High Street and the tube.

He opened the south-facing dormer window. By virtue of an unexpected wrinkle in the ground, this window looked out over the rooftops to the green mass of the forest beyond. By leaning out of the window and craning his neck left and right he could see a messy patchwork of fields – tawny fields of dusty wheat, squares of rape in Benetton yellow, the green of set-aside or pasture.

Willis changed out of his uniform and put on a worn towelling bathrobe. He wanted a bath; he wanted to wallow in warm, soapy water with a beer at his elbow and a book on the soap rack. Ross Macdonald, maybe. Or he'd just bought another Carl Hiaasen.

He looked across the fields to the forest where Dana Watkins

59

had died and *something else* had happened. While people were drinking tea, scratching their arses, watching telly, a man had held Dana by the throat, raped her, killed her by holding a plastic bag over her head (it was assumed) and, after she was dead, bitten her on her side and breasts. And the man they thought had done it had been scared into near insensibility by an empty face. *Something else had happened.*

Willis's shower produced a miserable stream of water. He dribbled it over his body, worked up a lather, then spent ten minutes trying to rinse it off.

He got dressed in an old pair of corduroys, an M&S sports shirt and old desert boots. He pulled a Centenary Trust map of the forest from the bookshelf and, feeling surprisingly buoyed up by anticipation, left the flat.

He drove to Marcus's school, West Forest Boys', and parked. From the school gates the way home was more or less self-explanatory. The school buildings backed on to allotments which in turn ran as far as the woods. A quarter of a mile away a spur of forest jutted out, causing much grief on the eighth hole of an adjacent golf course. Then there was a patch of scrubby open common, then the last stretch of real forest before the houses began.

He leaned on the school gates and shook out the map. A broad path led from the end of the road halfway through the wood, but Willis saw that in order to get to Kingsmeade Close you would have to branch off it, take a smaller path, and in the end cut through the undergrowth to the back gate of the house. Wait a minute though, he thought, the boy got picked up before he had to take the turning. He would still have been on the main path. Willis folded the map and walked towards the forest.

There was hardly a breeze but the forest was sighing: a slow, constant arrhythmic susurration that sounded both thin and deep. Layer after layer of whispers, hissing, rustling high above where the boughs of the trees spread out in frozen green explosions of bough and branch and twig and leaf. The wood closed above him but there was no sense of claustrophobia. The trees, hornbeam and beech, with smooth grey trunks slightly greened by lichen, were evenly spaced on the russet carpet of dead leaves. Above he could still catch glimpses of the early-evening sky – surprisingly light compared to the sombre gloom of the woods.

Willis was alone. He adjusted his speed to that of a boy. Was he dawdling, dragging his satchel or rucksack or whatever they had these days behind him, stopping to peer at leaves, mushrooms, beetles? Or was he hurrying on, intent on getting back to something he had marked on a nature ramble and was determined to find: a dropped toy, a watch, a piece of jewellery lost by lovers on the forest floor? Did that sound like childish behaviour? God only knew, but it was a theory, a premise to work from.

He stopped. A sudden flash of movement to his left. When he looked he could see nothing. The slow draining of light from the sky, the thick canopy of leaves, the ranks of tree trunks, thickening and massing into a grey wall, made him feel that he was standing in clear grey mist. He blinked. Opened his eyes. There! How could he have missed it? A deer, not fifteen yards away, looking at him in exactly the way he was looking at it. It had danced into focus like a fish under water; now in a flicker (he must have blinked) it was gone.

Had the boy seen a deer? You're brought up on Saturday-morning TV, climate-controlled cars, instant access to almost any form of entertainment, comfort, or even discomfort, and then suddenly, you're all alone in the forest and you see something beautiful, *and you can't control it.* It's from another sphere of life. So you stand, spellbound. A flicker and it's gone. What do you do if you're a kid? You follow. The ground's clear and level with little undergrowth.

But where? Willis thought. Then he stopped and whacked his knuckles into his palm. He was going about this the wrong way. They knew the boy had strayed from the path, but the girl – she had no reason to do anything except make her way to the riding stables by the most direct route.

He took out the map again. She lived in a village north of the forest. He knew it: all the old houses had been bought up, tarted up, sold on. On the outskirts of the village was the council estate which was the only sort of home that the locals – or those who had once thought of themselves as local – could afford. They were being squeezed into the margins, those people, just as this forest, which had once covered England from the Channel to the borders, had been slowly pared down to a slice of green moated by wide grey roads.

Concentrate! A girl was killed. You're tracing her path. Come on, think. The bus would stop at the High Street, then again outside the hotel. Then there was another stop in the middle of the forest. She'd get off there, by the old Roman fort in fact, then probably follow a small footpath across the wood, leaving it just – *there* – and cutting straight through the forest to the stables.

He retraced the route with his finger, imagined the boy leaving the path, and came up with a rough area where the two of them might have met.

Elementary, my dear Watson. Another hundred yards or so and I branch off. Left or right? Well, the boy said right and I'm sure he was lying, so left it is.

The character of the wood changed. The great beech and hornbeams continued to the right of the path, but to the left the ground began to break up. There were spreading clumps of bramble here and brakes of hazel. Silver birches slanted in crazy obliques across the orderly verticals of the bigger trees. The ground was wet underfoot. Willis walked a few yards on, saw it grow increasingly boggy, walked back and turned off the track.

Thorns snagged his shoes. The ground sloped gently down on either side; as he walked the little puddles consolidated into a thin stream. The wood seemed to get colder; he caught an odd smell of dustbins; a bramble caught his shin; cobwebs tickled his face. He turned. The path had disappeared. The ground he was on was dropping slightly and the clumps of hazel – once regularly coppiced for their wood but now growing wild – formed an effective barrier.

Easy to get lost. He found what he thought was a path but it petered out. He saw another and hopped across a little patch of bog, walked a few yards down it, then swore. There was a deep patch of mud in front of him and what looked like mire on either side. He turned left, hopping from clump to clump of grass, feeling the water begin to seep into his shoes, lost his footing, sploshed into deep mud, staggered forward, almost overbalancing, held himself upright and swung himself through a veil of leaves.

And stopped dead.

He was back in the clearing. Tied to a tree near him were scraps of the blue tape that the police used to demarcate scenes of crimes. The ground underfoot was firm where he was standing and covered in closely cropped grass but the grass was strewn with the wreckage of mangled flowers and florist's paper.

Benson had been right: people had brought cut flowers to the scene but someone had been there since and had ripped them to shreds. He picked up a card: *To a dear innocent.* There was a brown smear along the top of the card that smelled like shit. Willis dropped it. The press would have a field day here, he thought. Who would do a thing like this? they would ask. Who would do such a thing?

He walked further into the glade. The tree was dying: you didn't have to be a surgeon to see that. There was a pool of water in the soft fork of the trunk; the branches were almost bare. Only at the tips did a few thin twigs carry new leaves. A few scraps of fabric trailed from the branches. The bark was green with lichen and moss.

At waist-level the trunk was heavily scarred. Wood had swollen and grown around a slit. He ran a finger over the cut, knelt and peered at it. He felt dizzy. The air was resisting him, almost as if he was trying to move through a thin layer of latex. Around the clearing the air crinkled, as if suddenly crazed by a dark, deep heat, except Willis felt nothing. He blinked. The sky went back to normal.

He turned. He was sure something small scurried out of sight behind a veil of leaves. It seemed to be grey, hunch-backed, but moved with the darting, clumsy certainty of a pig.

He stretched out his hand again; this time disturbed by the sudden spurt of a screaming jay across the clearing and the eruption of a flock of crows, rising thickly like a puff of black smoke from the trees in front of him. Benson had said that when they were doing the search of the glade they had been disturbed by kids. Willis had never heard of anything like it. He wheeled round, half-expecting to see eyes in the forest wall. He saw only leaves.

63

Come on, Willis. He took out his penknife and dug into the wood. The blade hit something hard. He hacked away around it until he had exposed a thin crescent of metal. He ran his finger over it. The edge was milled. It was a coin. Someone had sliced into the living tree, and banged the coin into the cut. He hacked away but even with the coin two-thirds exposed he could not work it loose. The tree did not want to give it up.

All those other marks in the tree, all those other coins . . . He looked up at the branches. Had the boy been here? Seen this special tree? To prove anything he would need evidence, and the evidence would be sitting in little plastic bags back at the station being studiously ignored by everyone who was certain that as soon as Tailor came out of hospital, he'd be nicked again. Willis thought he would be too, but wished the enquiry were continuing with a bit more energy. Wished there were more evidence full stop.

When he saw the eyes staring at him his heart almost stopped. They were five feet away from him and partly hidden in the middle of a thicket of hazel. He stood very still, staring at the eyes while the eyes stared at him.

'It's all right,' he said. 'Don't be afraid.'

The eyes did not even blink or waver. If anything their gaze intensified. Then their expression changed. They were child's eyes, Willis thought, a girl's, and they were not expecting him. The forest was no place for a young girl. He craned his neck forward, trying to get a glimpse of the body. He gave a little cry; he thought he had seen it, a body so torn and beaten it looked as if it were wearing its skin inside out. Red, yellow, white, wet. Slick to touch. No. He had just imagined it. In the absence of a body, his imagination had provided one.

Willis took a step towards the thicket. There was a sudden swirl and something hit him in the face, burning and blinding him. He sank to his knees, rubbing heavy warm mud from his eyes, convinced something large had passed over his head. When he looked up, there was nothing in the bush and the branches of the trees overhead were beginning to dance as a light breeeze stirred them. An odd certainty had planted itself in his mind. The child had not been expecting him. It had been expecting someone else. Was that Marcus Waters's secret?

Chapter 10

'So there you go, sweetheart. Maybe clouds do have silver linings.' Caroline and Tina were lying on sun loungers in Caroline's back garden. Even the late-afternoon sun was hot. 'Just when you least expect it something comes out of the blue like this.'

'I can't get my head around it. I mean, me. Working. I'm going to have to get clothes – I'm going to have to get back in the whole swim of it.' She looked at Tina's trim body. Even when she was lying down she looked as if she were perching, ready for anything. Caroline groaned. 'And you don't help. You make me feel like a jelly that hasn't set.'

'I'd die for your figure, Caroline.'

'You wouldn't die for my head.'

'You celebrated?'

'You could call it that. After Marcus had told his new friend about my job, I managed to get him feeling festive with a bottle of Coke and ice cream. So we toasted each other and when he went to bed I finished off the Coke with some poisonous whisky, staggered up and spent half the night trying to stop the room spinning. Celebrating isn't quite the word I'd choose, unless it's changed since the last time I did it.'

'Which was when?'

'Maybe when Tom got his first contract.'

'Where's Marcus now?'

'Oh, I don't know. In the house somewhere. We had a bit of a spat this morning. He's getting so hard to read.'

'And you're feeling hard done by because he's not cockahoop about Mum being out to work all day long?'

Something in Tina's voice made Caroline open her eyes and squint at her.

65

'That sounded rather knowing. Oh God, I'm being a cow. It's –'

'Caroline baby, listen to Auntie Tina. You are by far the bravest, most courageous person I've ever met. Anyone else with your past, with everything that happened, would be shattered. Completely shattered. I've always thought it. You don't give yourself enough slack, though. I've noticed it before. When Marcus gets a little bit shirty you start to blame yourself –'

'I'm so worried – it's this girl. I hate to think of him being – seeing. He's been different ever since.'

'Come on, it must be doing you in as well?'

'I suppose so.'

'I'll go and find Marcus and we'll have a talk, me and him. Woman to man.'

'He'd like that.'

Tina stood up. She tied a wrap around her waist. 'You stay here. I'll go and do my stuff.'

Caroline let the sun push her down and then further down. Her headache lifted slightly. She heard the gentle sighing of leaves; even on the stillest day, the forest was never silent. That was a fact. Another fact was that it had taken Tina to point out the simplest of truths to her. Of course Marcus was a bit apprehensive about her getting a job. All his life she had been at home. Now she wouldn't be. She'd have to find ways to reassure him.

'Caroline!' Tina's voice sounded urgent. It came from behind and above. She twisted round.

'Marcus isn't in his room. Or yours. I can't find him anywhere.'

They spent the next five minutes searching the house, the next ten walking up and down the Close. For some reason Caroline tried to look unconcerned and the strain of that, coupled with the anxiety, made her feel lightheaded. Every corner she looked round, she thought she'd see him. Every time she didn't she felt tighter, lighter. One more shock and she'd explode. She and Tina knocked on doors. Where people were in, and an awful lot of them weren't, they shook their heads and said of course they would keep a lookout, and you couldn't be too careful what with maniacs on the loose. Concern always seemed to be mixed with relief. The mouths said: He'll be all right, I'm sure. But the eyes said: If the monster's got hers, it won't want mine. Caroline imagined Marcus in the forest, every step taking him away from her and nearer danger. She glanced at her watch, appalled at how time was racing. Every second seemed sickeningly significant. Then she remembered the card the big policeman had given her. Call me any time, he had said. Any time. She ran back to the house and dialled the number. The phone rang, each ring another two seconds, each gap a second. At last it was picked up by someone who wasn't her sergeant. Caroline gabbled her message. He was slow, unbelievably slow. She felt his attention slip, slip then grip. 'If you want to report a missing child – ' he said.

'Just tell Sergeant Willis,' she shouted. 'Now!' She slammed the phone down and ran back outside.

She met Tina at Maurice Temple's house, at the end of the cul-de-sac. Caroline could hardly raise her finger to the bell.

Temple opened the door. He looked delighted to see her.

Caroline felt her voice tremble: 'It's Marcus. Is he – ?'

Temple said: 'But of course. You look upset. It's not, oh my! If I'd known . . .' She heard his voice follow her down the hall, then pick up as he explained to Tina, 'I had no idea. I assumed you knew where he was. We've been having a fine time. Walking . . . yes, walking.'

Caroline pushed open a door. There was Marcus, sitting at the breakfast bar, eating ice cream. He looked exhausted and relieved to see her.

'Marcus, I was worried sick!'

He shook his head. 'Mum, I've been out plenty of times before on my own.'

'But not when there's a maniac loose!'

'It's all right, I was with Mr Temple the whole time. We were . . .'

'Walking in the woods,' Temple interjected from the doorway.

Chapter 11

Willis had not really been able to refuse when Grey told him to watch Tailor's house. Tailor had been released from hospital with a bump on the back of his head, the official line being that he had collapsed from exhaustion. Neither he nor his solicitor had mentioned the blank identikit picture, and this made Willis curious. Grey simply did not know about it, but blamed Willis for being there when Tailor had fallen off his chair. That was why Willis was on surveillance duty.

Tailor's street was a long, tree-lined cul-de-sac which led off High Street and ended in woodland. At the back of the Tailor house was a path that led to the forest and that was being covered by a lucky constable on overtime.

Willis had four newspapers – the *Mirror*, the *Sun*, the *Telegraph* and the *Guardian* – a thermos of coffee and a stack of cassettes to ease the boredom. He had two packets of Polos, three packets of Orbit and a set of worry beads to stop him biting his nails. He was listening to 'The Girl From Ipanema' and going 'ahhh' when A Girl From Essex ran down the steps of one of the Victorian semis, glanced at Willis curiously, and walked self-consciously up next-door's garden path, puppy fat rolling round her midriff. A young man with a rockabilly quiff was buffing pitted chromework on a Ford Zephyr.

Kids. The vandalism, the destruction of the flowers, had been the sort of thing a child might do; there had been children at the scene of the murder, before and after it, if you counted in Caroline Waters's sighting and DC Benson's report. There were also the eyes Willis had seen in the bush. Whoever it was had thrown mud at him and escaped; he assumed they had also destroyed the flowers. A disturbed child loose in the forest? Disturbed children? He tried to open his mind to other possibilities but shrank from them. You get scared once and everything seems frightening. Be rational. Concentrate on the job in hand.

Willis closed his eyes deliberately and let the sun touch his face with heat. He opened his eyes for a split second then analysed the snapshot behind the warm red screen of his eyelids.

The rockabilly rebel was running a comb through his hair in the mirror; a cat had jumped on to a wall and was staring with slitted eyes at a butterfly; a boy was running his palms over the wheels of a skateboard. Nothing. He opened his eyes and put his mind back in neutral, and found it drifting back to the evening after Tailor had had his fit . . .

Movement . . . He rubbed his eyes but had missed it. A curtain twitching? A face appearing for a second in the window, caught by the single strobe flash of daylight on his retina?

God, the Tailor house was depressing. Drawn curtains; the air of pinched shabbiness. It was as if all the hatred in the community was bombarding it with malign radiance, a feeling that now seemed to infect the whole police station as well. It had only happened once before in Willis's experience: that wave of dull, resentful hatred sweeping over an entire group of professional police officers. Curiously enough it was at the very moment when all professionalism had broken down – when young men talked in huddles in the locker room, by the vending machines, in the corridors – that the police were closest to the man in the street, or at least the men in Tailor's street. Hanging was too good for him was the general consensus, as was just about every form of torture ever invented or imagined by the good citizens of this solid suburb.

Willis shifted in his seat. Sweat was beginning to pool in the small of his back and round his balls; Toyota car seats did not breathe.

The sun moved across the sky; the shadows moved across the car. And Willis waited, and thought. It occurred to him that he was more frightened of the elusive children in the forest than the killer in the house in front of him.

69

Chapter 12

Movement.

He had been looking straight at one of the upstairs windows when the face had appeared like a big white penny. It had been looking at him, he was sure. He would have been surprised if it hadn't.

So, the watcher was watched. He wondered if PC Henry, who was keeping an eye on the alleyway at the back, had also been spotted.

He looked up at the sky. A few clouds, very high, very small, were slipping across the frame of the windscreen. He was off at six – half an hour to go. Please God, let nothing happen. Let me still have time to see the Waterses then go to the pub.

The door of the Tailors' house opened. Tailor, swathed in a baggy blouson jacket, baseball cap pulled down over his forehead and wearing incongruous wraparound dark glasses, stood a moment on the doorstep then trotted quickly down the steps and got into a brown Allegro parked in the concrete-covered front garden. The engine coughed, blue smoke blew out of the tailpipe and began to float down the road. Willis slid down in his seat and radioed Henry.

'Tailor's out and in his car. I'll follow.'

The constable acknowledged. Willis started his engine, and waited for the Allegro to back out of the Tailors' drive and travel fifty yards down the road. Then he moved the car round the corner and followed at what he imagined was a discreet distance. The Allegro turned left then right, then left again on to the High Street, sluggish with Saturday shoppers. Willis kept four or five cars between them. He could see Tailor's back, head hunched over the wheel, and occasionally caught a glimpse of his profile, or what little of his profile he could see between the upturned collar of the jacket and the heavy sunglasses.

Tailor had a skin complaint that made him susceptible to sunlight but perhaps that was the way sex offenders always dressed. There was always a risk that they would be recognised. Was every parent an enemy? Would this be like the final scene in *Marathon Man*, with the Nazi walking down the street in the diamond district, suddenly realising that everyone around him was a Jew? What was it like to be responsible for a death? Had it frightened him or excited him? If he had killed Dana Watkins, did he kill because he wanted to, or because he felt that circumstances demanded it?

They were out of the High Street and heading for Thornwood Common. Willis experienced an odd nausea accompanied by a crawling in his stomach and groin. Thornwood Common was where Dana came from. Surely he wouldn't be passing her house.

No. The Allegro turned right and headed for the motorway. They were in farmland now. Hedgerows on either side of the road, tractor mud on the road, a hand-painted sign, 'Danger: Farm Vehicles'. The Allegro maintained a steady forty-five miles an hour. A barn loomed on the left. The car slowed down for a corner and for a moment was out of sight.

Willis heard the squeal of tyres, a dull crunch, and was on to the crash almost before he had time to react.

The Allegro's bonnet was wedged underneath the high sides of a trailer, the metal rumpled like a stiff sheet. The impact had slewed the trailer across the road. A farmer was standing beside the car, peering through the passenger window.

'The driver just took off,' he said. 'Bugger just ran.'

There was an open gate in the hedgerow. Willis ran to the gap. Tailor was halfway across the field, arms flailing, running with strangely short strides.

Willis found himself running after Tailor without making a conscious decision to do so. He was overweight, unfit, and his shoes slid on the grass. Even so he found he was gaining on Tailor who was making heavy going of it.

He heard the farmer shouting, 'Watch my fucking grass,' and increased his pace. He could hear Tailor panting and gasping shrilly for breath. He drew level, grabbed his shoulder, suddenly aware that Tailor was a good six inches shorter than he remembered, also that the muscles were slack, the shoulder very thin.

Tailor collapsed. The sunglasses slid off his face. Willis was staring down at Mrs Tailor, who in turn was looking up at him defiantly.

He swore and hit her hard on the shoulder when she tried to sit up, then stood back, revolted equally by her behaviour and his own.

'Where is he?' he shouted.

She said: 'Bastard, you bastard!' and tried to spit up at him but her saliva was thick from running. It flew from her mouth in a long stream, then slid across her chin and neck.

'Where is he?' This time he was almost screaming.

'You'll not get my little boy again. He just went out for a walk! He just went out for a walk. That's all he did! He just went out. No one understands. No one!'

She was lying on her back, drumming her heels into the ground. Her eyes were closed and her mouth was opening and shutting as she gasped for breath. She was like a baby, screaming so much that she had forgotten to breathe. As she sucked in air, it rattled down her throat.

It was imperative that Willis contact Henry back at the Tailors' house. He reached into his inside pocket for his radio. It was gone.

He felt in all his other pockets. It must have dropped out some time during the chase across the field. He left the woman lying on the grass and walked back, watching the ground. They had left a clear trail across the field but the grass was long enough to hide a small radio easily, and it could have flown off to either side. He walked the hundred yards back to the gate without finding it, and turned to go back.

Mrs Tailor was standing in the middle of the field, watching him. Behind her, crows were slowly circling a great elm tree, turning in the air like a ragged crown.

Time had slowed. Willis felt as if his brain was stuck in freeze frame. He needed to act and think fast. What the hell was Tailor up to that he needed his mother to be his decoy? Where was he going? What was he doing?

He began to walk back along the trail. Then stopped. Suppose he missed the radio again? He looked at Mrs Tailor who was unpeeling layers of clothing. Not so much a disguise, more an advertisement.

There would be a telephone in the farmhouse.

He climbed the gate. The tractor and trailer had gone. The battered Allegro was ticking and dripping, pushed at an angle off the road. How long had he been in the field? How much time had he lost? He ran into the farm yard. On his left a tractor shed with a big Ferguson and a rusty seed drill in it. In front a large, enclosed breeze-block building. The yard stank of cow shit. A gutter ran with brown liquid from the building to a drain in the middle of the yard. Willis could hear the movements of cows in the shed. Time weighed slow and heavy, while he was broken and dripping. Useless.

The farmhouse made up the other side of the yard. He walked carefully over sun-baked cow dung and straw and wondered what it smelled like when it was wet. He rapped his knuckles on the glass of the back door. In an outbuilding there was a sudden explosion of barks and scratches. The door creaked and rattled in its frame.

He knocked again, then tried the door but it was locked. He waited. The dog was going mad and the house was empty. He had no choice but to go back to his car.

The Toyota grumbled and squealed round the bends of the narrow roads. He tried to remember how long he had been following Mrs Tailor.

A diversion. Think. They knew the house was under surveillance. Mrs Tailor left, drawing Willis from his post. He had radioed Henry who would probably have stood down immediately.

Tailor would then have slipped out. Why?

First possibility: he was doing a runner. Willis turned that one over in his head. If he was running, the chances were that he was guilty.

What else could he be doing? Anything. He could have been overcome by an attack of claustrophobia, he could be picking flowers. Now there was one fruitless line of thought. Put yourself in his place. If I'm guilty, I might be doing a runner,

73

or . . . going back to the scene of the crime because I know there's something incriminating there. Something the plod have missed. No. If I'm guilty, the tests would show it and I've agreed to tests. So, back to the beginning again. I'm guilty and I'm running.

Willis was on the point of stopping to call the station when a third possibility entered his head. Tailor was innocent but was being drawn back to the forest, just as Willis had been. There was a mystery. It had touched Willis. Why should it not have touched Tailor? A blank face had terrified him, and his refusal to mention it later just compounded things. Damn it! This was getting complicated. Instinct told Willis that Tailor was back in the forest. It also told him that if he wanted to find out what Tailor was doing, he would be better off on his own.

Willis reckoned he must have been taken out for at least half an hour. Barring accidents, which Tailor and his mother could have not anticipated, he should have been out of action for half the day. She could have driven to Cambridge and back.

What would he have done? Allowed five minutes, maybe ten, to make sure the coast was clear before leaving. The house backed on to the wood. He would have gone out the back way. There was a path leading south to where Dana's body had been found.

Willis tried to relate the route that he thought Tailor would take to his own position. There was a chance . . . if he bypassed the High Street, entered the forest by one of the side roads, he might intercept Tailor en route – if he was right about the path that Tailor was going to take.

Christ! It had so nearly worked. He imagined himself following the car down country lanes, always keeping a few hundred yards behind. Then somewhere the car would turn round and drive back. He would have followed it back to the house, seen Tailor get out and been none the wiser.

He hit the steering wheel in frustration and felt it shudder. Still, he thought, if I can find him, if I can follow him, if I can catch him . . .

The road entered the wood. There was the parking area, half-full of cars. That was good. The forest was still crowded. That would afford some protection for possible victims. Willis

74

forced himself to breathe deeply and relax, then got out of the car and orientated himself.

The light was green; noises were faint and muffled, apart from the clear sharp tapping of a woodpecker. Willis looked around him. Even on a warm Saturday evening, with the dry ground freckled with light, people kept to the paths.

There were always parts of the wood that were empty.

It all depended on where Tailor was heading. He would be approaching more or less from the north; Willis from the south. The killing ground lay in between them. Nothing for it but to get a move on.

The path swept round in an arc. An elderly couple in matching grey tracksuits and striped trainers fast-walked towards him; behind them were two women on horseback, high rubber boots flecked with mud, hard hats and hard faces.

Willis left the map folded in his pocket. It was too late to plan or calculate. He would have to act more or less on instinct. May the force be with me. On his left the forest opened up before it was taken over by a dense screen of birch and hazel. Willis left the path and pushed through. As far as he could estimate, Dana had been found about half a mile to his left. He veered slightly in that direction.

The forest was appreciably darker here; the ground sticky clay underfoot. The ground began to slope down and Willis was standing on the rim of a shallow valley with a stream-bed winding through it. He paused and scanned the valley for movement. Every time he moved his head a tree moved as the perspective lines shifted, so he kept his head, kept his eyes still, and willed the scene to pour into his consciousness. For the second time that day he was looking for Tailor and for the second time he saw movement, a tiny flicker through the trees on the periphery of his vision, a flicker that died to stillness when he looked straight at it, and began again shyly when he looked away.

He slipped as quietly as he could from behind the rough trunk of an old oak, feeling the primitive thrill, the adrenalin rush of the hunter, and began to move.

Tailor was working his way across the valley floor. He was heading away from the area where Dana had been killed. Dark glasses hung on a cord on his chest and his cap had been pushed back over his high forehead. He had an ugly walk – cocky and ungainly. Each foot was thrown forward in a strange jerking movement as if it were loose and heavy on the end of the leg, but at the same time the head was held high and the shoulders pulled back so he seemed to breast the air as he passed. A rolled-up newspaper stuck out of his pocket.

Tailor was on his way home. Willis followed, keeping above him and thirty yards behind, moving quickly from tree to tree, slowing when Tailor slowed. Every now and again his right hand crept upwards to his pocket and tapped the newspaper in a nervous, unconscious movement.

During a pickpocket awareness course that Willis had once been on, they showed film footage of people passing in front of a poster on the London underground that warned people of the dangers of pickpockets. Of the men who noticed it, six out of ten patted either their front trouser pocket, their back trouser pocket, or the breast pocket of their jacket. As a study in unconscious body language it was funny, but not as funny as the way the pickpockets peeled off and began to trail their victims, having been alerted by their gesture as to where the wallet was.

The newspaper. Why would he be worried about that? He had dropped something. He was looking for something. With a quick flare of insight Willis thought of the life the Tailors would lead: they would go out as little as possible; milk and newspapers would be delivered. Newspapers that were delivered usually had a name pencilled on them, and an address. Suppose Tailor had come out on that day with a paper, dropped it or even just thrown it away in a bin? Yes. That had to be it. It was the clearest way imaginable of connecting him to the forest: not only a name but a date as well, and the delivery time would narrow the field of possibilities. It would be enough to re-arrest him.

He was not aware of anyone following either him or Tailor; the first he knew that anything was wrong was when Tailor stopped, thrust his head forward, and seemed to be straining to see something ahead of him.

Willis looked down the valley. He saw a flash of movement, golden as it passed through sunlight. A child running?

Tailor had stopped dead. Willis was reminded of nothing so

76

much as a big cat. He was still, but you sensed the tension building and the potential for sudden movement.

He took a step, then another. Willis matched him, trying to see what he had seen. A child. He had thought it was a child. A child in danger?

He risked moving forward, dropping slightly below the edge of the valley so only his head would be visible if Tailor looked up.

Tailor was moving forward now in bursts of three or four steps, doing what Willis was doing himself.

Stalking.

Willis dropped down the other side of the rise, ran about twenty yards then came up by a brake of hazel. He lost Tailor for a second then saw him, further back than he had thought, and followed his line of sight. The shock sent his heart up into his throat where it still insisted on trying to beat. He was looking at a child.

It was dancing in a small patch of sunlight. A wisp of a thing; made of light and shreds of cobweb, except that just had to be an illusion, an effect of light dappling a slim body, seen from far away. Except –

No. He squinted. It was so damn' hard with the shadows and tree trunks and constant shifts of light through leaves. He thought he'd seen wings. He also thought it was floating. The body was thin and upright, the hair long and golden. It ran with head tipped back, arms and legs carried like a dancer's. It was as light as a flame but at the same time oddly clumsy. I've been here before, thought Willis. And so, for my money, has Tailor.

The fairy was naked. He saw that when its body flared into a shaft of light. No. He only said that because he couldn't see any clothes. The skin was grey and patchy. It was getting to him. He wanted to – what?

There was a sudden red shift in his head. Blinded for a second, he saw himself rearing over the still, thin body, his erect penis, blood-swollen, ploughing and plunging through papery flesh. He heard himself grunting like a pig.

He staggered back. That had come from nowhere: a ghostly prickle of infantile curiosity and – wham! Grotesque amplification and mad distortion.

He stood still for a moment, trying to even out his breathing and will his swollen flesh to subside. He closed his eyes. His mind had been invaded. He felt defiled and debased; feelings that were made worse by the knowledge that the pictures that had flooded him had not been implanted, they had been uncovered.

And what were the implications of that? His brain felt flash-fried and refused to work logically. He allowed thoughts to flow and grow that he had purposely kept stopped up. He had followed a child that flew; he had seen eyes in the bushes – eyes that seemed detached from any body. Now a naked child dancing. Fairies. Sprites. Wood elves. His mind taken over. At least that might explain how they had kept hidden. You wouldn't admit to seeing a fairy if your first reaction was to think of raping it . . .

Somewhere, some way away, he heard a pigeon croon and was brought back to reality.

Willis looked around and saw Tailor moving again. He had broken into a run now just like the fairy thing. It ran like a happy child, jumping, leading with a pointed toe, slowing, swooping, arms stretched out and fingers extended. Tailor ran low and fast and smooth, like a cat after a bird, or a dog in heat.

Willis shouted and started to crash down the hill, waving his arms. But he misjudged the pitch of the slope, his shoes had no grip and he found himself out of control. He threw himself sideways, slipped over, and his hip crashed on to an exposed tree root. He rolled down the slope in a small avalanche of leaves and twigs, then splashed heavily into the stream.

He lay in the water, stunned and half-winded, vaguely aware that the sound of Tailor's movements had faded to nothing. He sat up, spat blood from a cut somewhere in his mouth and pulled himself to his feet, using a rotten birch as support. His left eye ached; his hip was badly bruised. He took a step, felt his leg try to give way, forced himself to take another and another, and got the blood flowing. He stepped up the pace, punting himself along on his good leg, leaving his bad one to trail behind.

He shouted: 'Tailor!' but his voice was deadened by the smooth trunks of the trees. He stumbled forwards, feeling

78

hopelessness and impotence descend on him like a physical weight.

'Tailor!'

He held his breath and tried to listen but all he heard was the empty soughing of the leaves high above his head. He slid against a tree and rubbed his cheek against it until it hurt. And then he thought he heard laughter. The sound mingled with the sounds of the woods: the creaking of living wood, the steady rippling of the stream. His breath sounded coarse in his head. Old man's blood was pounding in his ears. The laughter was a note of innocence that played inside him like an echo of youth. He gathered himself and staggered on, moving in the direction that Tailor had taken, the direction of the laughter. The wood thickened. Branches whipped his face. Spider's webs clung to his face. The air grew heavy. He was bathed in sweat. Water had begun to seep into his shoes. The ground was turning boggy. He knew this place. In front of him was a wall of hazel. And he pushed through it for the third time with a feeling of sick anticipation.

Tailor was standing in the middle of the clearing at the foot of the old, half-dead tree. He was standing in a mire because his feet and ankles were sunk into the ground. He was stuck, Willis thought, but more than that: transfixed. He was moving, but not in any way that suggested he was trying to get free. It was as if he had forgotten the fact that he was stuck, so fascinated was he by what was going on around him. He was peering, first one way, then the other, following movement around the clearing. When whatever he saw (or thought he saw) got behind him, he twisted quickly round the other way and followed it round again.

Which is fine, Willis thought, except I can't see anything.

Tailor stretched out a hand, leaned forward too far and fell. His body shuddered. He sank in a good foot further. He pushed himself upright with his arms and then seemed to grow aware of his situation. He pushed down with his hands. They sank into the mud, and in his efforts to get them free he slipped in further still. He was up to his groin now. Willis stepped into the glade. And stopped because he saw what was on the tree.

At first it had no face: a complete, shocking blank. Then it

79

was patterned like the floor of the forest, a hideous organisation of leaf and mould, twig and earth. Natural things. Good things. A shiver passed through it and suddenly he was looking at a thin creature wearing Dana Watkins's face. He was familiar enough with it from the scene-of-crime photos but even those images of blue skin and red swollen tongue and bulging red eyes did not compare to this. Those, when you got over the shock, excited only compassion. This excited revulsion. That was death; this was a macabre parody of life. The face was round but stiff, plump but hard. The eyes were chinks in a mask, black and blank as a bird's. The mouth was red and wide. The creature looked at Tailor, then smiled in a movement that sent flurries panicking up its cheeks and into its leafy hair. It ran a blunt hand over its body. A tongue, as sudden as an animal, appeared between its lips. It split, bloomed into a brown flower and wrapped itself around its face. Tailor screamed. He worked a hand free from the mud and tried to cover his face with it.

Everything happened very fast. The entire quality of the air changed. It became darker and clearer. Willis thought he saw wisps of smoke moving around the edge of the glade but when he looked again they were grey figures; sharp, angular and flat. His hair bristled. Shivers convulsed him. He could not have moved even if he had wanted to and somehow he knew that movement was useless because in that second the forest was infinite and stretched for ever and this was a small glade of horrifying clarity in mysteries too big and too grey and too old to comprehend.

Tailor saw him and opened his mouth. He shouted, 'Look!' The ground beneath him convulsed. He was thrown into the air, arms and legs akimbo, spreadeagled in a big cross of celebration and held there as shapes flew from the clearing's edge, clustered on him, and stuck to him in a heavy lumpish swarm. He screamed as he fell through the earth that was as liquid as water and disappeared as quickly as a pebble falling into mud. There was a beat, a heartbeat, or was it the sky stretched like a drumskin above them, then Tailor reappeared – erupting from the mud in pieces.

His trunk had been sheared of its limbs; his face still looked surprised; dark blood pumped in streamers from the ragged blurs of darkness on his hips and shoulders, and Willis thought

80

he could see the smooth white of the sockets before they were covered by the falling blood, by the shreds of flesh, by the stinking grey mud that had erupted around him.

The main bit of Tailor fell, hitting the ground with the heavy thump of a sack of coal. His arms and legs, which had been flung higher still, pattered down around him.

Willis, one foot in the air, mouth as wide as a railway tunnel, thought: The poor bastard's probably still alive but thank God I'm asleep. He glanced at his watch like a real pro, then felt blackness swim up in front of his eyes like a third eyelid.

Chapter 13

Caroline began to shiver by the cereals, got really shaky as she passed the deli counter and was forced to stop pushing her trolley and try and relax opposite the fresh meats. The cold white glare and blasts of refrigerated air oppressed her; her sense of smell seemed particularly sharp and she was tasting the cloudy fug of cold fat on her tongue.

People strolled past on either side. No one looked remotely interested in her. The shivering stopped. What did people say? Someone's stepped on my shadow . . . something like that. She turned. No shadows in a supermarket. Even though the place was half-empty she felt unaccountably crowded.

In the middle of the display was a row of white polystyrene trays under a big yellow sign which read: 'Low in fat, high in protein. Try natural, country-reared rabbit. Special offer – please take recipe for Essex Coney Stew'.

Caroline stared. The flesh was a fresh, delicate pink, firm and channelled into purposeful twists and bunches of muscle. Under the tight glaze of the shrink-wrap it glowed with a miraculously smooth lustre. She stared at it, thinking of Snowball, and suddenly the meat changed from being potential stew to rabbit, ex-rabbit, dead rabbit, rabbit corpse, rabbits with their feet chopped off, their heads chopped off, and the skins ripped over the little bloody stump of their necks. And equally suddenly, with a woman behind her promising to buy her son a Snickers bar if he was good, Caroline started to cry because in some awful way the rabbits reminded her of Marcus.

She had wanted to gate him, of course, after the initial explosion of rage and relief. Temple had begged her not to take it out on the boy – he should have thought of clearing it with her, but as it was he had seen Marcus going off and thought it wise to accompany him. Caroline was almost completely

82

oblivious to his entreaties, concentrating with fierce intensity
on Marcus, crying and shouting, hating the sound of her own
voice, hugging him, shaking him, and making him swear not to
go into the forest on his own, not ever, because Mummy loved
him and was very angry, and was very angry because she loved
him. Marcus had been very still, she remembered, eyes closed
some of the time.

Obscurely she remembered a beach holiday, two years or a
lifetime ago, in North Wales, near St David's, where the sea
had been grey and freezing for the entire two weeks. On the
last day she had seen Marcus walk out into the sullen, slatey
waves and brace himself against their heave and sting; not to
enjoy it, simply to undergo it. His expression in the sea,
tense and braced, had been his expression in Temple's
kitchen.

The rage passed and she walked him from the house. On the
way out she glanced into the sitting room. Temple was looking
out of the window at his garden. On the mantelpiece were three
pictures of a girl. As a baby, as a child, as a young teenager.
Then Temple shifted and she hustled Marcus out, not wanting
him to see her in case he started apologising again.

Tom's car was standing outside her door, glistening as if it
had been sucked clean; there was the look of smug reproof on
his face to deal with, Marcus's over-loving reaction to seeing his
dad, her exhaustion. They had driven off, Tina had driven off,
and she had crashed and slept like a dead thing.

And now it was rabbits, and rabbits were somehow translat-
ing themselves into a message: Marcus was in danger.

Suddenly Caroline knew she had to call Marcus and could not
delay. The feeling grew like the need to be sick. She ditched the
trolley and ran to the check-outs, pushing past the queue, down
the narrow channel by the till and then to the phone by the
door. She fed the machine some coins and punched Tom's
number.

'Oh, Caroline,' Marina said. 'It is you. Just as the phone
was ringing I said to myself, "Now that will be Caroline." I suppose – '

'How's Marcus?' she interrupted, feeling the fear wash in the
back of her throat.

'Well, he's much better,' Marina said in a sing-song voice. 'It was very sudden. We're waiting for the doctor now, no crisis or anything, a bit of a mess but fortunately it was mostly cornflakes, bless him, and the kitchen tiles wipe down very easily. I blame myself, Caroline. It's these bloomin' chilled meals, though I'm always most careful – '

'What are you talking about?'

'What am I talking about? Oh, I'd have thought you'd have heard. It's when they cook them or chill them, or when you cook them and there's bacto – bacteri – oh, you know, germs in the chicken's armpits – '

'What are you saying about Marcus?' Caroline shouted.

'That he's better.'

'But what was wrong with him?' she whimpered.

'I thought you knew?'

'I just telephoned. How the hell could I know?'

'You do have an answering machine,' Marina said poutily. 'Ah, there's the door. Tom, that's probably the doctor! I'd better get it. You can come over any time, you know.'

'Don't hang up, let me speak to Tom – '

But Marina had hung up.

There were three messages on the machine. Marcus had been having a mid-morning cornflake snack when he had suddenly been sick. His forehead was hot to touch and they had put him to bed. Tom sounded efficient but worried. The next two messages were blanks – Tom trying again.

Caroline splashed water on her face, did something quick and clever with make-up so that she looked better without looking made up, ran her fingers through her hair in the hall mirror and drove quickly but safely over to Tom's. She felt curiously well. Worried sick but well. She had thought that there was something wrong with Marcus and she had been right.

'Look, I'm sure it's nothing to worry about,' Tom said as he opened the door. 'Dr Macdonald said it's almost certainly something he ate, and now he's got it up he'll be fine.'

Caroline pushed past him and trotted briskly up the stairs to Marcus's room. It was a pretty, low-ceilinged room at the end of the house where the sloping roof came down almost to ground-floor level. Scalextric was laid on the floor, the track threading its way through a junkyard of props, crash barriers, wires, and toy soldiers for running over. There were books on the shelves; pictures of cars on the wall. Caroline had never been up here before. She felt startled, as if she had just discovered that Marcus led a secret life.

He was lying in bed, staring at the ceiling. His hair was flat on his forehead as if he'd pasted it down with water. His eyes darted towards Caroline.

She sat on the edge of the bed, hand reaching out automatically to smooth the hair and feel the temperature.

'Hello, darling.' In that special voice.

'I was sick,' Marcus said. He started to smile, stopped as the muscles round his mouth began to pull downwards. 'It came up like a geyser.'

'Old faithful.'

'All over Marina.'

'Oh, darling.'

'It just came. I didn't feel sick. I was just feeling,' he frowned and tiny furrows appeared on his forehead, 'thundery. Hot and sort of full. Then – '

He made a vomiting noise. Suddenly he looked scared, and sagged over the edge of the bed. He began to pant with his mouth open and saliva fell in skeins into Marina's washing-up bowl. Caroline felt the muscles in his back go into spasm. She thought of the rabbits and shivered. Marcus's back was wet with sweat through the dinosaur pyjamas.

He sat up, eyes watering. 'I don't really feel ill though. Just hot and dirty inside.'

'Thundery,' Caroline said.

He nodded. She bent over to kiss his forehead, then recoiled. He had exhaled and his breath smelled of dead meat and . . . leaf mould. Gone now. Just a sweaty sick boy. Her lips tasted salt off his skin. She wanted to lower him into warm water, bathe him then pat him dry with a huge towel in a clean sunny room. She wanted him to be a baby again.

'I'm taking you home for the night, young man.'

Marcus closed his eyes and nodded.

Caroline found Tom and Marina in the kitchen, not looking as miserable and guilty as they should. The room smelled of lemon disinfectant; the quarry-tiled floor was still damp in places.

'How was he before?' Caroline asked.

'Fine. Look, if the doctor said –' Tom said.

'Food poisoning?' Caroline asked sarcastically. 'He did tests?'

'Well, if you –'

'He says he feels thundery.'

'What does that mean?' Tom asked.

'I've no idea,' Caroline said.

'Are you all right?' Marina raised her eyebrows. 'I mean, you sounded so – worried on the phone. Let me make you a nice cup of something hot.'

'Yes. I'm sorry I snapped. Oh, nothing to drink for me,' Caroline said, but Marina had flicked the switch on the kettle anyway. 'I've got this awful feeling that something's wrong.'

'Wrong?' Tom asked sharply. 'What do you mean? With us? With Marcus?'

'I can't shake it,' said Caroline. 'With Marcus. Ever since the murder.'

Tom shook his head solicitously. 'I wonder whether this isn't delayed shock on his part, you know. The mind and body are linked, after all.'

'And Caroline's linked,' Marina said unexpectedly. Caroline looked at her sharply, unable to explain the sudden rush of fear, the feeling that the finger had just pointed at her. 'Something was wrong and you knew, Caroline. It's amazing. A mother's love.'

She relaxed. Marina's hands strayed to her stomach and folded over it, and Tom looked suddenly so proud and protective and Marina so withdrawn and thoughtful that Caroline knew that she must be pregnant. And you don't have to be telepathic to know that, she thought. There was a pause while she waited to see if they were going to tell her, but they did not so she broke the silence by saying: 'Would it – I mean, I would like to take Marcus home.' She was not sure whether or not there would be any resistance. But Marina only looked mature and concerned and said: 'Of course. Of course you do.'

And Tom shook himself out of his reverie and said: 'Yes. Yes. You'll be all right?'

'I hope so,' Caroline said. 'Oh, by the way, was he doing anything – this morning, I mean?'

'No. Why?'

'Just wondered. Nothing.'

'No. If you've got something to say – '

'I just wondered what he was doing before he was sick?'

'Right,' said Tom. 'Sorry. What was it on the telly, love?'

'Some nonsense – Arabian nonsense – Arabian Nights. A cartoon, that's right – about a little boy who went back to the Arabian Nights.'

The kettle roared.

'He was given three wishes by a fish.'

'Right?' said Tom. 'No more arguments then, Caroline?'

Caroline lost her bearings for a second. Marina looked embarrassed.

'What?'

'Well, what he said was that you'd lost it with him a few times recently.'

'Perhaps things have been getting on top of me just lately,' said Caroline, wanting the conversation to end. 'Can't be too careful. I'll just go and get his things together.'

'Oh, no. Marina and I will do that.'

Caroline went outside to turn the car.

'Keep a close eye on him, won't you?' said Tom through the open window as she pulled away.

Chapter 14

She did not want to leave Marcus and go shopping but equally felt she needed to do something. She was used to filling her weekends. So, while he lay on the sofa and watched cricket on the television, Caroline went into the garage to sort out supper and the next day's meals from the freezer.

He had been sick and she had known. Or was the danger she had sensed something deeper? Something coming from her? No. Her fears were just that. Hers. Not his. There couldn't be a link, could there? Was her mind so stuffed with bad things that they were escaping again? Was that possible?

She tried to consider the question rationally but it was impossible. There was too much static.

She deliberately recalled the exercises she had been shown and the small things she had found out for herself. Your mind is a house. There are no rooms that need to stay dark. Go through the house and switch on lights, draw back curtains, throw open windows. Welcome reason and light, light and reason.

Caroline closed her eyes. Her mind was a house. She turned on the lights and threw back the curtains. Outside the house, all she could see was trees.

Enough. When she had been told to confront her fears, she had taken it literally. Moving to the edge of the forest had been one way of doing it, of proving that there was nothing to fear. The fear of the children was supposed to go away with the fear of the forest. She had worked out that it was a manifestation of her own wretched experience so she'd tried to conquer that in the best way she could – by marrying a man who wanted a big family. She had grown Marcus inside her, given birth to him, and there she had stuck. Still, even having one child seemed victory enough.

She took herself in hand. Now what you've got to do is go into the sitting room and look at him. And you are not looking at him to see if he's all right, you are looking at him because you *know* that he is all right, and you want to prove to yourself how stupid you have been.

She stood up and rubbed her hands which were cold from the freezer. While going through the food she found a couple of Chicken Kievs that were over a year old; the whole thing would need clearing out, but for that she would need a sweater against the cold. Good, so she would walk past the sitting room on the way to the stairs and look in on Marcus then.

He was lying on his side and looked asleep. His eyes were closed and he had kicked the blanket off the sofa. Out of the garage the house was warm – as the day went on, the heat seemed to be piling up under a pale, thick sky. No wonder he felt thundery, Caroline thought.

She opened all the windows on the first floor, picked an old sweater out of the cupboard in the spare room and went downstairs. Marcus was still on the sofa. Poor thing. Food poisoning was a bitch, especially from those germs that lived in chickens' armpits.

In the garage she opened the great sarcophagus lid of the freezer and watched the mist swirl in the fluorescent light. Then she bent over it and got to work.

When you did something like that thoroughly, it was hard work. First to pick through everything, checking the dates. Then to try and guess which of the use-by dates were honest and which were exaggerations, then to put everything back in the way you had been planning, and discovering halfway through that there was a jolly good reason why things were done the way they were and not any other way, and then to create a little area for all those foods that you had forgotten and needed to be reminded of, then to stretch and ease your back and rub your hands warm – it took a lot of time.

In the end there were half a dozen frozen pizzas that needed chucking, a bag of prawns that she did not trust, some trays of frozen meat, indeterminate, and a few cubic feet of frozen gooseberries she had picked herself from a soft fruit farm in prehistoric times. She put them in a bunny bag and tied the ears tight.

While she was securing it, she had been aware that she was

hearing a rush of water in the pipes. The mains riser ran behind the freezer. She immediately thought of Marcus; immediately assumed he was being sick again.

She ran into the sitting room – the sofa was empty, the blanket lying in a crumpled heap on the floor. Downstairs loo. Empty. The clock on the video told her that she had had her head in the freezer for almost two hours.

She trotted up the stairs calling: 'Marcus, Marcus.' Now she could hear the taps in the bathroom. She turned the handle and pushed the door, expecting to walk right in. It was locked. She actually knocked her forehead on the wood.

'Marcus? Marcus?'

She could hear nothing over the sound of the water, even when she pressed her ear against the door.

She knocked, first with her knuckles, then with her fist, knelt and tried to peer through the keyhole.

'Marcus! Open this door! Marcus! Will you open this door!'

The sound lessened as first one tap, then the other, was turned off.

'Marcus!' Bangbangbang.

'Yes?'

'Marcus, why is this door locked?'

'I'm having a bath.'

'I know, darling, but you don't usually – '

She heard herself – whining, cloying, overprotective, maddening, claustrophobic – checked and began again.

'Sorry, darling, I was just worried, thought you might be sick. I wanted to make sure you were all right.'

'Feeling much better.' He did not sound much better. His voice was wobbly. There was an odd rubbing sound which she could not identify.

'All right, darling, don't be too long.'

She called Tina, thinking it would be nice to have her over soon, but Tina was in a meeting. Then she remembered the old pizzas and bag of prawns that were defrosting on the garage floor and that made her think of the dustbin and that made her think of the side gate which the big policeman had kicked in.

In the garage she picked up a screwdriver, a hammer and some four-inch nails, then went outside.

The sky was darkening. She could feel moisture on her cheek; her T-shirt stuck to her.

She tested the latch which was quite firm, but she tightened the screws just to make sure, and locked it by banging a nail into the post just above the catch so that the lever would not lift. She liked doing things like that. It was satisfying, and logical. No one had ever taught her how to use a screwdriver, let alone secure a gate, but she had done it.

The bolts at the top and bottom would be harder to fix because the creosoted wood was splintered around the fixing screws. When she tried screwing them in she found that one at the top and one at the bottom gripped the wood, but the rest had ripped through the grain and the threads would not bite. She decided to nail the gate shut as a temporary measure, and so banged a couple of four-inch ovals through the side of the gate at an angle and into the post. She gave the whole structure a good pull. It was firm, and she knew that eventually, when she got round to it, she could fix it properly by unscrewing the bolts from where they were hanging and moving them down a couple of inches to where the wood was sound.

She stepped back, knocking the dustbin with her knee. The locking lid slid a couple of inches off centre.

Because of the foxes, she was always very careful to lock the lid by pressing down and turning it. She always did that. Had the foxes learnt how to open sealed dustbins, like the blue tits had learnt how to drink the cream off the milk bottles?

She lifted the lid.

The dustbin was full, and she didn't remember filling it. On the top, crushed and lumpy, was a bunny bag. She thought of the food from the freezer. No. She hadn't put it in yet, and anyway, the bunny bag looked odd. There was dark liquid smeared on its inside; you could see through the thin plastic. The same liquid, hardening to dark specks, was smeared on the ties. The ties themselves had not been knotted properly, just folded round each other. She always tied them in a granny knot.

Very, very slowly she opened the bag.

Marcus's pyjama top lay bundled up in the bag, sticky with some dark red liquid.

Vomit? He had been vomiting blood?

Blood?

She pulled the garment out of the bag and held it up. The front was dense and heavy with blood, a large, clumsy, irregular stain over the belly, finger smears radiating from it in rough rays. Blood dripped on to the concrete path at her feet, and a minute at least pooled between each drop.

She held the garment at arm's length, eyes sweeping round the alley as if there might be a clue in the brick and concrete. At the bottom of the garden, framed by the wall on one side and next-door's fence on the other, was Snowball the rabbit's hutch. The door was open.

She looked more closely at the stain on the pyjama top. Stuck to the blood was a fragment of fur. Rabbit fur. Stained red though it might once have been white.

She dropped the pyjama top and looked further into the bag.

A pair of rabbit ears poked up from under a pile of potato peelings. A rabbit head but no rabbit neck.

She held up Snowball's head. It was so light, so small. One of his eyes was out. She emptied the contents of the bin on to the concrete path. Bits of Snowball, leg bits, body bits, ripped open, blue guts, white guts, green guts, guts –

'Oh God,' she said. And ran straight up to the bathroom.

The room was empty; the bath grinned at her. It was clean. Marcus never left a clean bathroom. Absent-mindedly she ran a finger over the tiles above the sink. They were wet. All around the sink was too, wet as in wiped down.

The bath too – he'd even cleaned the high tide mark. At the end, in a droplet of water under the mixer tap, she thought she saw a thin pink wash.

She opened the dirty clothes basket, and shook the towel out. It was sopping and still twisted from attempts to wring it dry. But it was covered with faint pink stains.

She dropped the towel. Her hands were trembling.

Marcus was standing in front of the television set, waving the remote control as if he were conducting. She could hear the jags of sound as the channels changed. He had dressed himself in jeans and a plain sweat shirt. His face was very pale and the rings under his eyes were very prominent.

Her lips pursed to make an M.

Marcus looked at her.

'That's all you ever say: Marcus, Marcus, Marcus!' he shouted at her shrilly.

She bore straight down on him, grabbed him by the shoulder, pulled up his shirt.

His belly and back were smooth and white, shadowed by bone and muscle, faintly marbled with green and blue veins.

She took his hands. He twisted and wriggled them, and kept his fists closed. She pushed him down on to the sofa. He squirmed and pulled and wriggled like a cat, seemingly careless of whether he put his shoulder out, screaming: 'You're hurting! You're HURTING!' Caroline forced her thumb into the tight-clenched tunnel of his fingers, worked it in, then forced the fingers open.

His hand was scratched and there was a dark crescent under a couple of his nails.

'What, Marcus? What?'

It was all she could think of saying. What have you done, what have you found, what happened –

Marcus exploded into shrill tears, twisted away from her and tried to bury himself in the corner of the sofa. She touched his back, although she did not want to. It was as tight as bowed metal. He was burrowing into the fabric, rocking from side to side, howling.

'What is it, darling? What happened?'

She said it over and over again, like a mantra. She did and did not want to know. If there was some rational explanation – But could there be?

'What is it, darling? What happened?'

She felt as if she were on the brink of a momentous discovery, and the thought terrified her.

'What happened? What did you do?'

Marcus opened huge, teary eyes at her. Shocked. Dear God, I didn't mean that, she thought.

'What is it, darling? What happened?'

Marcus turned away from her, his face twisted into a strained mask. Tears had reddened his cheeks; snot lay in a transparent curtain over his mouth.

'I found him!' he howled.

'You found who?'

'I didn't do it!'

'I know. I know that. I'm sorry. Tell me what happened?'

'Snowball the *rabbit*,' he stammered, his jaw trembling, his eyes wide in an expression between terror and wonder.

'Found Snowball the rabbit, darling? Where? Found him where?' She had a hand on his belly. His heart was thumping, but the racking spasms were slowing.

'On the *grass*.' Still emphasising the last word, as if it were obvious and she was failing him by not knowing.

'Tell me, darling.'

His body was almost back to normal. She felt the tension leave his stomach.

'I was on the sofa watching the cricket. I thought I heard a noise. I looked out of the window and Snowball was lying on the grass – I mean, all over the grass,' he added.

'Snowball had been – '

'He was all cut up in little pieces. I'll show you,' he seemed to plead.

He took her hand and led her out. There was a gorgeous dewy dampness in the air. The trees beyond the fence were still.

'There,' he said, pointing to a patch of lawn where the grass was blackened and flattened as if oil had been poured on to it.

'And there. I couldn't clean that bit up properly.'

White strands and what looked like sick clung to the grass stems.

'But, Marcus, why? Why did you come out here? Why didn't you tell me?'

'I don't know! Snowball's dead!'

'What were you frightened of?'

'I don't know.'

'What did this to Snowball? Is it anyone you know?'

'No.'

'Why didn't you tell Mummy?'

'Let go, you're hurting me!'

'Who are you frightened of?'

'I'm frightened of YOU!'

She dropped him as if he were hot to the touch. On his arms the white stripes where she had been gripping him turned quickly to red. Marcus rubbed them. His face was filmed with tears and snot.

Caroline felt tears start to her eyes. She held her arms out for him and he walked towards her. As she held him close she felt like a traitor.

She let him watch while she hosed the lawn down using a hard jet. Sod the drought.

She fed him spaghetti hoops on synthetic bread and a Munchbunch yoghurt. He ate sloppily, with his mouth open; the food, twisted by his tongue, went up and down and round and round.

Caroline was half-revolted, half-dismayed by feeling revolted. She knew he was not aware of what he was doing. You chewed automatically. It was a reflex. You could be thinking of something totally different but the food would still be churning in the mouth. On and on. On and on. Like thoughts in the back of the mind. Thoughts you were not quite aware of, but nonetheless just went on churning. *What did you do?* She had really meant it.

She closed her eyes and clenched her jaw. Be still, she pleaded. Be still.

She sat with him on the sofa and watched *You've Been Framed*. He stared meekly as a succession of fat men in shorts and white socks were hit in the testicles with golf balls, pogo sticks, children, wives, and fence posts; as a succession of fat ladies crashed into swimming pools, off rostra, bicycles, camping chairs and hammocks; as a succession of children fell into flower pots and lavatory bowls, over patio steps and kerbstones, off school stages and more school stages and more school stages.

None of them hid bits of bunny in bunny bags. That was a disaster that no amount of public display could dilute.

Marcus was submissive and tired. He went to bed meekly when Caroline noticed that the rings under his eyes were like ink stains. It was still light outside. He closed his eyes in the false night of his bedroom and fell asleep in about two minutes. She washed up, poured herself half a tumbler of hock from the wine box in the fridge, topped it up with soda water and called Tina.

'Oh, hi,' Tina said. 'Listen. What would you do if one of your clients who happened to be a senior backbench politician asked you to tie him up with your stockings, shove your panties in his mouth and whip him with a rubber fan belt from his Roller?'

'He did what?' Caroline asked.

'I'll take that as a rhetorical question. It was during his two-day assessment – we give them progress checks and they like to hear it from the boss. He's sitting there in his hideous pyjamas which are too short – he's got shiny shins incidentally – and he just puts it to me. Says he has been led to understand that we cater for special needs. You know what I thought? I thought I'd do it, then tell him I had thrush.'

'Tina!'

'Sorry.'

'What did you do?'

'Signed him up for combined fast and double enema treatment. *Mens sana in corpore sano.* He won't last twelve hours and for the rest of his life he'll go into a cold sweat whenever he sees a nozzle.'

There was a pause. Caroline knew she should have been laughing.

'Still Marcus?' Tina asked.

'No. It's nothing,' she said wanly. If Tina could cope with being taken for a prostitute, surely she could cope with being a mother.

'Come on.'

'No, I really don't want to – I mean, it sounds like you've got a lot on your plate at the moment.'

'Sweetheart, when you talk like that I want to punch you in the throat. Now what's bothering you? How's Marcus?'

'Oh God.'

'No comment?'

'Either Marcus has done something terrible or I'm terrible for thinking it.'

'Something else? Or are you worried he's going to divorce you?'

'Right now I think he might have a case.'

'Uh oh. Feeling good about yourself, aren't you?'

'I just feel I'm going a bit crazy. It's being with Marcus all day – I feel as if I'm losing my bearings.'

96

'Ye-es. Now tell me what you mean?'

'Snowball – you know, Marcus's rabbit – was killed this afternoon.'

'What? Who? I mean how?'

'Unfortunately "who" was what I thought, and for a minute I suspected Marcus.'

'You thought Marcus killed his rabbit? Caroline . . .'

'I know, it sounds awful, but first he won't tell me why he was in the forest, or how he happened to meet Temple. Then he was at Tom and Marina's and he was sick. Not just sick but sick in Marina's lap – and she's bloody pregnant!'

Caroline described what else had happened that afternoon, finding Snowball's body and how Marcus had attempted to cover things up by cleaning the bathroom.

'I don't know if I'm worried about what I'm thinking or why I'm thinking it. When I saw the bathroom had been cleaned, what I thought was that Marcus had killed the rabbit. What I thought was – I mean, suppose he was so disturbed that he went outside and killed the fucking thing?'

'Oh, come on. Because his stepmummy's preggers?'

'I mean it. He's acting oddly. Running off into the woods. The police have been asking more questions because they think he was lying. I even thought – no, I didn't think but I allowed it to occur to me that he was involved in, you know, the girl dying in the wood. I know it sounds awful and I hate myself but the thought just came to me and I couldn't stop it and now the rabbit and I just thought – it all just – '

'Hush,' Tina said. 'Hush. Listen to me, Caroline. Listen to me. Marcus is a wonderful sensitive boy. Very sensitive. And what he's gone through in the last few days – well, it's enough to upset anyone and make them act out of character. The kid's going through a lot.'

'Do you think Tom and Marina told him she was pregnant? Tom would have said.'

'Oh, come on, Caroline. Use your brain. You guessed she was pregnant and they didn't tell you, did they? It was just body language. Children live off body language but it's that much more confusing for them because they don't know what's going on. Look, sweetheart, he didn't kill the fucking rabbit. A fox killed the rabbit. Marcus is feeling involved with that poor girl's death, and when a kid's involved in something bad they can get to feel guilty. They don't understand where their responsibility begins or ends.

'So this is what I think. Marcus is feeling ill. He was the last person to see a girl who was murdered. Something's up with Dad and his fluffy pet wife which Marcus doesn't understand, his mum's probably acting weird, he thinks he's the cause, he sees his rabbit strewn all over the grass, and something short circuits in his brain. Perhaps he just touches the fucking thing, gets blood on him, panics, and it all leads on from that. What do you think? Sounds good to me.'

Caroline exhaled.

'It would sound good to me but I can't find a place where the fox could have got in, and I've never heard of one dismembering a creature like that.'

'If not a fox then a dysfunctional dog. Caroline, *anything* is more likely than its being Marcus. You're just giving yourself things to worry about.'

'I suppose I'm feeling a bit uptight about everything, what with work starting on Monday. This has been such a crazy weekend I forgot. They called me last week. The one who got the job originally has dropped out. I was next in line.'

'That's great – I hope.'

'Well, I suppose so. If I can learn to use their machines.'

Tina hooted with laughter, then said: 'Shit, my bleep's gone off. Perhaps the MP's finally cracked. Look, I'll see you both soon. 'Bye.'

Caroline, who had been meaning to ask her over for Sunday, put the phone down. She closed her eyes and sat on the floor with her back against the wall. A fox. A dysfunctional dog. Anyone but Marcus. Marcus was not a dysfunctional child.

But she was still bothered. Tina was good at defining her problem but sticking a label on it did not mean that the problem went away.

Come on. It is not a problem. It is not a thing. It was a fox. A dog. Think that and don't think anything else.

Tomorrow they would take things very easy and if he was not well on Monday, she would just have to take the day off work.

Which would get her off to a wonderful start but you had to have priorities. What could she do the next day, something foolproof to make him feel good?

Chapter 15

Caroline woke up with a start. Something odd and dark had just lurched into life in her brain.

She had fallen asleep on the sofa with her third tumbler of wine by her side on the floor, an Aga saga comfort novel ('wholesome people dealing with their problems in lovely settings') splayed on her chest and too many lights on for the room to seem cosy.

She sat up. Her neck ached. Two-forty-five in the morning. Getting on for the dead hour of three o'clock which is the true grey edge between night and day, when more people die in their sleep than at any other time.

She checked the front door. The frosted glass was orange from the street lamps in the Close. She twitched back the curtain to check the lock on the sliding doors. The glass was shining jet; the garden invisible.

Something moved?

Are my thumbs pricking?

Upstairs she dashed warm water over her face and rubbed a toothbrush over her gums. In the bedroom she drew the curtains, undressed, and lay on the bed. The air was still and heavy. She pulled all the blankets off and lay under a single sheet. It was cool for a while, then got too hot. She kicked it off. Three-thirty.

Air. I want air.

She drew the curtain and pushed open the window.

The sky was flat and dull and the air was strange. The garden was grey; the trees were black.

There was not the slightest breath of wind and the garden swing was moving. Not just moving, swinging, jerking at the top of each arc, swinging back, higher, higher. She could hear the tiny squeaks of the metal frame – the wind rush on the ropes.

It was moving and there was no one on it. Higher, jerk, higher. Filled with an impossible momentum, it carried her terror with it, higher and higher, a tightening of the body, a strain that pulled her mouth open into a silent scream, stretched the sinews of her neck into wire coat hanger rigidity.

Suddenly the seat sprang, fell back loosely against the ropes, dangling and twisting. Caroline knew what had happened, or at least she knew when swings did that: when a child jumps off in mid-swing.

The forest gate opened, then whacked shut. The trees were still. Someone had been in the garden. Someone who wasn't there.

Sweat seemed to dry on her in a thin rime of ice. She moved her hands quickly over her belly, her breasts, to remind herself that she was real. Flesh was real. She stepped back from the window. Floor under her feet. She pressed herself. Rough hair; soft belly and breasts; nipples roughened in alarm; ripples of gristle behind the skin of the neck. Chin, nose, eyesockets.

Real.

She moved towards the window and the garden unrolled from beneath the window sill.

The swing was moving gently and the forest gate was shut. She put a dressing gown on, sat on the edge of the bed and stared at the gate until it was light. Little children, she thought. Little children who wanted to play. With Marcus. Her nightmare.

Then she went out into the freshness and the dew and the clear dawn light and slid the bolts across. The sky was blue and feathered with delicate shades of yellow and pink but all she could think of was Snowball's guts.

Eventually she slept.

Chapter 16

WPC Nancy Freeman was sitting at her desk, trying to coax some white stuff to transfer from a matted Tippex brush on to a piece of typed paper. Mike Rawson and Bobby Collins were over by the window talking Youth League soccer in low, serious voices, but apart from that it was as quiet as a church in the big, low-ceilinged room, and almost as empty.

For days it had been like Gatwick Airport on a summer bank holiday. Two dozen officers on the phone taking calls from the public. Another dozen collating their notes. Half a dozen on computers. The same number sifting the scene-of-crime evidence. God only knew how many doing house-to-house. Now they'd gone. The case notes would be bundled up into fat, papery pillows and shelved somewhere, along with the computer disks and little lock-top evidence bags with their chewing gum wrappers, used condoms, unusual-looking bits of wood, scraps of fabric – all the scene-of-crime evidence that might or might not have meant something.

The strip lights hummed. A desk fan creaked, swinging its head like a bored animal. A fair number of officers were doing overtime at an open-air pop festival out in Suffolk. A quiet day. No one committed crimes on a Sunday.

Willis snapped a bin bag off the roll in the stores cupboard and started pulling the drawers of his desk out. There was hardly anything to take. He'd have to leave his notes and he was not in the habit of turning his desk into an alternative home base, with photos of children and wives and souvenirs, not that he'd got any. The only things he found were things he had forgotten – a recipe for fishcakes his sister had sent him; a headscarf that a girlfriend had left in his car; a single glove that was probably half a Christmas present. Two messages from

102

Caroline Waters: one to tell him that Marcus had disappeared, the other to say that he hadn't.

He glanced at the recipe. His sister ran a bed and breakfast in Maplethorpe on the Lincolnshire coast. She had been pressing Willis to stay with the family for years, literally years. If staying in the neat terraced house got too much – or if it miraculously filled with guests, although with the recession etc, etc, chance would be a fine thing – he could always camp out in the shally on the beach and just take his meals with the family. Willis had stuck at the word 'shally' until he had said it out loud. Chalet. Beach hut. East-coast vernacular. A week by the sea in Lincolnshire sounded just what the doctor ordered. What on earth was the coast like in Lincolnshire? Did it have cliffs? Did it have harbours? It had Skegness, and Skegness had Butlin's, but there had to be more to it than that.

Nancy was staring at him quizzically from her desk. He raised his eyebrows at her. She raised a hand and smiled out of one side of her mouth – the side the rest of the room could not see.

Willis thought of the report that Chief Inspector Grey and Superintendent Thackeray were reading now.

Better keep away from me, WPC Freeman, he thought. Keep your illusions intact. Keep the faith. Keep believing that any offence imaginable can be dealt with by arrest. Keep believing that the world can be described in the soothing rhythms of officialese which people laugh about ('I was proceeding through the housing estate in an eastwardly direction when I became aware of a dark-coloured liquid on the pavement that I took to be of the nature of blood') but which do the job because, like all acts of translation, they require you to think, to put a distance between yourself and the facts.

So that the little bastard who chewed the nipples off an eighty-five-year-old pensioner and then squirted ammonia into his face was a 'juvenile GBH suspect in possession of a bottle made of some plastic substance containing a strong-smelling chemical'.

So that the loving mother who ironed her darling baby's back off because she heard a voice telling her to had been 'apprehended in the act of applying a heated household appliance to the dorsal region of the eight-month-old's torso'.

So that the rapist who superglued his naked victims to the wall was . . .

He thought of his own report. He thought he'd made quite a good job of it.

'Sarge.'

He had his head deep in the middle drawer, wondering how many pens to nick. Nancy was standing just behind him.

'Careful. I'm contagious.' He tried to keep his voice light.

'What are you doing?'

'Clearing my desk.'

'Why?'

Willis gave a wolfish grin that showed a great many of his teeth and sharpened his face unexpectedly.

'I'm anticipating my imminent suspension.'

He looked around. Mike Rawson and Bobby Collins had stopped discussing the finer points of training and the Bobby Charlton Skills School and were looking hard at him and Nancy.

'You really think – '

'I really do.'

Nancy looked upset. 'I don't understand what you've done.'

Willis waved a hand to stop her. 'Don't worry on my behalf. I mean it.'

Two pink spots appeared on Nancy's cheeks. She said doggedly: 'It's just that if you did – er – if you were unable to stop what happened for whatever reason, Sarge, you know the lads are behind you. He'd gone down, he'd got out, and he just did it all over again. The important thing – what's *really* important – is that he won't do it again.'

She paused, flushed but looking pleased that she had spoken, pleased and expectant, as if she thought he was going to thank her. When it was clear that he was not going to place his head in her lap and cry sweet tears of gratitude and joy, she deliberately deadened her face.

'You're telling me,' Willis said.

'Telling you what?'

'That he won't do it again.'

'I'm not saying I approve. I'm not saying we should kill everyone we think's done a crime. Or even anyone – '

'Well, that's a relief.'

Nancy blushed again but pushed on. 'But now that it's done . . . well, what's done is done and it might be for the best.'

'If you think actions can be disassociated from motives, you're in the wrong profession, Constable.'

'Every cloud has a silver lining, Sarge.'

'In this case, the cloud and the lining are one and the same thing, aren't they? Tailor's death.'

'No. You've got it wrong, Sergeant. Tailor's death – that's wicked. The fact that he won't murder any more young girls – that's good. So – '

'So if I could have stopped it, but turned a blind eye or arrived five minutes after my vigilante pals tortured and dismembered him, that's all right – that's a good result, is it?'

Nancy exhaled with her mouth open and looked stubborn. 'The lads just wanted me to tell you, anyway.'

'Say hello to the lads from me then, will you?'

'What were you going to say, Sarge? Earlier, when I interrupted you?'

Willis said simply: 'If you ever get to read my report, I'd like you to believe it. And if you get the chance, do a thorough comparison of Dana Watkins's mutilations with Tailor's first victim. Maybe you'll find out why Grey was so jealous of the file.'

She nodded curtly, turned on her heel and strode back to her desk, flat shoes squeaking.

Thackeray's secretary put her head around the door and said in a bright, soothing voice: 'They're ready to see you now, Sergeant.'

Her head looked detached. She wiggled it and smiled until Willis stood up, then held the door open for him, leaning sideways into the room and semaphoring joy to the world with her neatly plucked and pencilled eyebrows.

'This report won't do,' Inspector Grey said.

'Isn't it clear, sir?'

'It's pathetic, Willis. It isn't even a decent lie.'

Grey was a local man, resentful of outsiders. There was a rumour that he had made a serious mistake early on in his career. He checked as the Superintendent held up an elegant hand. Thackeray liked to think of himself as a bit of a grandee.

He wore expensive three-piece pinstripe suits, and when he stretched, which he did with well-rehearsed grace, he showed a pair of bright red felt braces in the gap between waistcoat bottom and trouser top.

This was a typical set-up – the Inspector looking blunt and rather sweaty, boring away like a good 'un, going over the same point, once, twice, three times, looking more stupid than he really was, while Thackeray leaned back in his chair, looked at the ceiling, steepled his fingers, ran fingers through well-cut, floppy hair, eventually coming out from his side of the desk to perch on its edge and look more dynamic and steely and competent than *he* really was.

He half-closed his hands and looked at his long, pale, polished finger nails. 'My advice, Sergeant Willis, is to tell the truth. I'm sure we'll all feel a great deal better.'

'What I saw is in my report,' he said. 'I don't quite see what the problem is?'

Thackeray had a good reading voice. He picked up the form in front of him and read aloud: '"At this point the subject stopped. From my elevated vantage point I could see him examining the young person while at the same time attempting to remain hidden from said young person.

'"I estimated the young person to be aged between ten and twelve. He/she was semi-naked and performing some rhythmic movements of a repetitive nature." Sounds a little bit porny but let it pass,' he said, turned a page and picked out the odd sentence. '"Knowing the subject's record I abandoned my surveillance role blah blah blah . . . In the course of my attempts to warn said young person I tripped over a tree root and was precipitated downward blah blah blah . . . struck a tree . . . attempting to move I discovered that I had sustained injury to said hip . . . the young person proceeded in an easterly direction . . . was unable to maintain visual contact with subject . . . re-established visual contact . . . in a clearing . . . legs had sunk into the ground above the ankles . . . time was approximately 11.40 or 11.42 . . ."

'Here we are: this is where it gets good.

'"The suspect appeared to be sinking rapidly. I was following the movement of persons or objects in the clearing but I was unable to see them despite having a clear field of vision.

Between my arrival on the edge of the clearing and my attempts to enter the clearing, I estimate time elapsed to have been between half a minute to one minute. In that time Tailor had sunk to his waist into the ground." Ground, Willis? Don't you mean the bog?'

'I'd been there the day before, sir. The ground had been firm enough then.'

Thackeray and Grey exchanged a look that Willis was meant to see.

'"I realised that precipitate action was required of me." Willis, this is positively baroque. "Intending to enter the clearing with the intention of aiding the subject, I stepped into the clearing and immediately began to see things differently." Now this is the bit I *hate*. "The day seemed to grow both darker and brighter. I saw smoke on the edge of the clearing that coalesced into flat figures. Simultaneously the rate of Tailor's descent accelerated quite considerably and he disappeared under the ground with sufficient rapidity to force me to the conclusion that he had been pulled down from underneath. He disappeared for the space of perhaps five seconds. He was then ejected from the same spot, dismembered. His trunk was propelled into the air to a height, I estimate, of approximately twenty feet, followed by his limbs. I collapsed and lost consciousness due to extreme fear.

'"When I recovered consciousness I was some distance from the clearing where the above-mentioned events took place. I reported to the station at the earliest opportunity that I had been following Tailor and that I believed he was dead. However, owing to certain peculiarities, I could not be sure."'

Tailor had been found by a local family giving the Dobermann an outing, Willis had been told subsequently by a deadpan Nancy Freeman. The dog had run off with the left arm and the father had tried to pocket Tailor's bloody sunglasses as a souvenir. They had been lying on the ground some distance from the head and were still shading the eyes from the sun.

Tailor's trunk was impaled on a reasonably straight tree branch that had been stuck into the ground. Twigs had been rammed into his eye sockets. His remaining arm and legs had been stacked like firewood under the dead tree.

'What do you mean by extreme fear, Sergeant?' Thackeray

asked, sounding and looking like a Harley Street psychiatrist. 'Help us there.'

Willis looked around the office. It was neat and clean and square with vertical blinds angled against the sun. Fear was like pain – you remembered having it, but the mind lacked the facility to recreate it so that it seemed, in retrospect, less awful than it had been.

'I can't really describe it, sir. I have been frightened before, but in the past it was accompanied by an adrenalin reaction. This time it was different. It made me helpless.'

'Smoke, Willis? Frightened by smoke?'

'It was all in the way it moved, sir.'

'This young person, Willis. The one you saw earlier. Strike you as familiar in any way?'

'I didn't notice, sir.' He hoped they didn't notice him sweating suddenly.

'But you noticed everyfuckingthing else, man! You noticed the precise order that Tailor emerged from the ground.'

'I was concerned for his or her safety.'

'Ye gods! Concerned for his or her safety while a group of psychopathic vigilantes are hiding nearby? This person led him to them, I know that. It's clear from this. Oh, yes. So where the fuck are they?'

'Who, sir?'

No one had ever heard Thackeray lose his composure before.

'Who? The people who tore Tailor limb from limb. Literally tore.' He rubbed his shoulder tenderly. 'I've asked around. It would take a lot of very strong people quite a long time. In the olden days when we used to do this kind of thing in public, it was done by four horses, and even then they used to cut the tendons in the hips and shoulders. So, what we are looking for, Willis, is descriptions of them: how long it all took, where they dispersed to, and what the fuck you were doing in the meanwhile. That's what we want in the report, Willis.'

A ray of sunlight crept across the desk top. Willis said: 'I've written down what I saw, sir.'

'Better not to have written down anything, wouldn't you say?'

'We'll dump it,' Grey said. 'We'll shred it. We can't have this shit used at an inquest, let alone a trial. And he's not going anywhere near a witness stand.'

'It's what I saw, sir.'

Thackeray spoke again. 'I'm not going to shout, Willis, I'm just going to put it to you straight. We've got you over a barrel. So far as any enquiry goes, you were engaged in unauthorised surveillance on a murder suspect whom you followed into a forest. All this – ' he gestured at the typewritten sheets on his desk ' – we don't know what game you're playing. Frankly I don't give a shit, but unless you give us some answers you've fucking had it.'

'Who did you tell, Willis?' the Inspector said. 'Come on. Give us something.' He gestured with both hands.

Suddenly Willis felt bored. He had run all this through his head in advance – what they would say to him, and how – and it was no fun going through it a second time. All he wanted to do was get out, beat a strategic retreat, regroup. In real life that meant having a break and trying to make sense of what he had seen.

'What I saw I put in my report. I can't say more than that.'

Thackeray leaned back and left the field to the Inspector. 'You're suspended. You're finished. I'll fucking break you for this, you bastard!'

Willis said: 'I've cleared my desk.'

'We had a result. We had a fucking result and you . . . And you – '

'And what did I do, sir?' Willis asked, turning, looking, thinking that if there was a switch he could flick that could transport him somewhere else, anywhere else, even if it meant leaving and losing everything in his life, if there was a switch like that he would flick it right now and disappear into a parallel universe.

'You blew it, chum,' the Inspector said, inadequately but viciously. 'You blew it for me and you blew it for you and you blew it for a whole fucking team of coppers.'

Willis nodded to the room and left.

The High Street was like a race track on Sundays, what with the shops being closed, next to no buses and only a scattering of pedestrians to work the crossings. On Sundays Essex Man liked to drive Essex Woman as fast as Essex Car would take them into

Essex Heaven – a big country pub with three brands of lager, four fruit machines, chilli con carne and Thai chicken dips for dinner, and outside tables so you could keep an eye on your motor and kill anyone who touched it.

Willis felt dazed and disjointed. His mind kept on taking funny turnings along unexpected avenues. He got the first stirring of an erection as he thought about what Essex Man and Essex Woman might be doing in the woods.

Senility strikes, he thought, and wondered whether he should book one of those natty little soft-top Mazdas for jumping a pelican crossing on red, for heaven's sake.

The light started to flash amber. The car behind hooted him. He stayed stationary well into the green because he felt like winding someone up, and then, when he pulled away, the engine stalled.

Senility strikes again, or perhaps I'm regressing, he thought. They'll love it when I block the road to turn right.

A bluebottle was bumping fatly against the glass of his windscreen. He wound his window down and ushered it out but it seemed to be held by an invisible strand of elastic. Every time he pushed it towards the open window it bounced back and panicked against the glass. More horns sounded in a ragged scale. He leaned back in the seat.

'Get out, fly,' he said. It whirred around his head and left. That's all it takes, he thought, and started to laugh.

He heard a car door slam. A heavy pair of thighs in jeans appeared in the square of the window. A fist thumped on the roof. A face appeared at his side. Gelled hair. Flinty little eyes. Fat sunburnt cheeks.

'Move your fucking car, Shirley Temple.'

Willis grabbed the man's shirt front, pulled the head in through the window, banged the throat down against the edge of the door, and held it there for a count of five using his right arm while his left hovered around, wondering whether to do something terrible to the man's eyes. Then he let go suddenly. The head sprang up, smacked against the roof. The man fell backwards into the road, making a noise like a ratchet spanner.

'I just felt like doing that,' Willis said out loud. 'And now I feel like getting drunk.'

He drove off, cut dangerously across the oncoming stream of

110

traffic and parked at an angle in front of his house.

One of his downstairs neighbours was clipping the low privet hedge in a small front garden.

'It's all in my report,' Willis said to him. He felt pretty drunk already.

He filled an ice bucket, because he felt like maintaining a pretence of gentility, found a bottle of soda water, a tall glass and a three-quarters-full bottle of Famous Grouse. Whisky and hot Sunday afternoons did not seem one hundred per cent compatible but if he mixed them long and put in plenty of ice and called them Highballs as the Americans used to, perhaps it would work.

He was wearing a straw hat he had bought in southern Spain, a loud shirt he had bought in the West Indies, a pair of shorts he had bought in British Home Stores, and a pair of Ray Bans that had fallen from a felon's breast pocket in the course of an arrest. He looked a fright and did not care.

At the back of the house was a tiny garden, big enough for a lawn the size of a hearth rug, with a flower bed around it. Willis had lopped off every branch of every overgrown tree that overshadowed his patch, and planted an assortment of shrubs and perennials that would more or less look after themselves. In the spring snowdrops, tulips, peeping toms and crocuses poked up through the lawn, and the flowering cherry littered the lawn with its fragile papery blossoms. Summer through into autumn a honeysuckle, grown from a cutting from a scented hedgerow in Shropshire, filled the evenings with its heavy scent, which mingled nicely with a bank of lavender which the previous owners had left. There was an old English dog rose on a trellis by the back door which was pretty but always picking up diseases.

Willis opened up his deckchair, poured himself a drink and forced himself to sink back into the canvas. His immediate surroundings – the garden, the wall, the back of the house – receded. He was sitting alone in the middle of thoughts that danced in his head like bluebottles. There was something out there; something in the forest.

He thought about Tailor, the murdered murderer, killed underneath the tree. He thought of children who floated, vigilante groups you didn't see, and a big, beautiful blonde woman with shadows behind her eyes who lived near the forest but was scared stiff of it. Well, he'd joined the club. And now he had nothing to do with his time except think about it.

Chapter 17

'Marcus, will you hurry *up*?' Caroline shouted from the kitchen. The sky outside was high and blue, the air was warming but still carried the damp freshness of night. She wanted to be able to enjoy it for a second but Marcus would not come down.

'Marcus!' The walls and floors in their house were thin enough for sound to carry across two rooms and up the stairs.

She waited for the thumps that should have started echoing through the house as he put on his shoes and came running downstairs.

Silence. She put the milk carton down on the table too hard. Milk geysered up through the spout and a splash landed on her shirt. She swore. Milk stained. She ran to the sink and dabbed at it with a soapy J-cloth, then walked quickly and angrily to the hall.

'Marcus! MARCUS!'

She trotted up the stairs, pausing halfway, just catching a snatch of looping electronic music.

'MARCUS!'

She threw open the bedroom door. He was standing by the bed holding his school books, face already twisting into indignation.

'Ow!' he said. 'You almost hit me.'

'Marcus, I told you. No games before breakfast. It's hard enough to get you off to school as it is, but I've got to be on time. I wish I'd never bought you that dratted thing.' The dratted thing was a Nintendo that had pushed her Access card to the limit. It was hooked up to an old TV that had been lying dormant in one of the spare rooms. Marcus had been agitating for that one to go down into the sitting room and the good one to go into his bedrom. He said the resolution was better.

'Now how do you turn it off?' she said.

Marcus didn't say anything. Caroline turned the TV off.

'You probably damage it that way,' he said, and pushed past her to get out of the room. Caroline paused in the doorway, looking at the machine, not understanding why Marcus liked it so much. A memory – lying on a bed, watching TV in a student flat in Birmingham – bad video footage of punk rockers throwing themselves against each other in a club. Then the commentator, all paunch, make-up and seventies hair asking the viewers: 'Where's the fun in that?'

Half the point in fun was other people not understanding it.

'There was a message from Miss Dunlop on the machine last night,' Caroline said. Marcus splashed milk on to cornflakes.

'Do I have to eat this?' he asked.

'Yes. Any idea what it's about?'

'Why don't you ask her yourself? The phone's in the hall.'

Caroline nearly slapped his wrist. 'I wanted to ask you first.'

Marcus opened his mouth wide enough to be disgusting. 'Better eat your cereal,' he said. 'Your boyfriend's arrived.'

The extra money from the job meant that Caroline was able to afford the school bus which picked Marcus up from the bottom of the Close. That was fine; she no longer had to drive him to school, but she was less sure about the other half of the arrangement which had come about after three days at work. She had been delivering the mail to Mr Carstairs when he'd asked her suddenly to fetch her CV from the file. He had looked at it and announced that, as he drove past her house every day, he'd pick her up and help do something about the greenhouse effect. He was a keen environmentalist, he said, somehow imbuing the word with innuendo. Caroline accepted the offer, telling herself that she could change the arrangement whenever she wanted and use Marcus as an excuse. It worked out fractionally cheaper to accept the lift there and take the bus back, once you took into account the state of her car and the fact that she didn't have enough seniority to use the staff car park.

She raised an arm to him through the window. While Marcus dawdled to the door she threw the cereal bowls into the sink and ran cold water over them. By the time she got to the car and Carstairs had turned it, Marcus was at the end of the Close, waiting on the corner for the bus. He did not look up as they drove past.

Caroline worked in accounts for Maggie. Maggie had been working at Smith's for two years. She had a round face, grey hair that was cut in a rough fringe and flew away at the sides in a ragged helmet, and a shiny mole on her cheek. She wore corduroy trousers with elasticated waists and generic trainers, and made Caroline feel like a frilly bitch.

'Well,' she had said bluntly, the first morning that Carstairs had driven her into work, 'is this foreplay or the morning after?'

Caroline had gone red and stammered that it was neither.

'Just don't expect anyone to believe it, that's all.'

Maggie's manner was brusque without being frosty, whereas the attitude of the other women in the office was positively glacial. There was a girl with a vaguely punk hairstyle, and two more copy typists who worked at the other end of the office. They stopped talking when Caroline came near to give the impression that they were talking exclusively about her, and if she walked past them and then turned she found them all staring at her. Tina told her that it was the politics of the disenfranchised: a pathetic attempt to validate their lowly status and dead-end jobs. Caroline wasn't so sure. She felt real hatred.

She was entering figures on to a spreadsheet when she remembered the message that Marcus's class teacher had left. She swore under her breath. Maggie looked up.

'Sorry,' said Caroline. 'Just got to call my son's school. I feel like I'm waiting outside the head teacher's study.'

'How old is he?'

'Nine going on thirteen,' Caroline said. 'Premature adolescence.'

Maggie laughed. 'Mine were always getting it in the neck. Doing all right now, though. People always say that thing about them going through phases. Well, they never stop.'

'Great,' Caroline said.

'You're missing the point. If they never stop, it means that you never stop. Ask your parents.'

'They died when I was a child,' Caroline said. 'But I take your point.'

'Whoops,' Maggie said loudly. 'We've been caught talking by the head girl.'

Barbara Neilson, the office manager, ignored Maggie and told Caroline that she was wanted by Mr Carstairs for dictation in ten minutes. One of the other girls, walking past, said: 'Dick, more like.' Ten minutes later, as she walked past the small typing pool at the other end of the office, she heard someone say 'Bitch', just loud enough for her to hear. She turned. Three faces met her challengingly. She blinked, swallowed, lowered her head and turned away. They wanted a confrontation; they wanted her to retaliate. Why?

Caroline was kept busy until lunch. She caught up with Maggie as she slouched out at one o'clock, leaving the three weird sisters to their own devices at the other end of the room.

'Can I join you?' Caroline asked.

Maggie looked rather pointedly at her empty hands. She had a Tupperware box in one hand and a can of Fanta in the other.

'I don't want your lunch,' Caroline said. 'I – just want to talk.'

Maggie shrugged. 'Suit yourself,' she said. 'I only go up to the roof to get some fresh air.' She led the way down the corridor, pushed open a fire door, wedged it open with a fire extinguisher and walked up a flight of concrete steps. There was a breeze blowing from the east. The town spread out below, a messy grid of roofs and roads. Caroline looked above the roof tops to the great ground-hugging green-backed monster of the forest.

She began speaking abruptly.

'Those three at the other end of the office are trying to pick a fight with me. It's getting worse. One of them called me a bitch this morning. I'm not going to give them the satisfaction of spitting back, but I'm not going to back down either. Will you help me?'

Maggie looked startled. 'Why ever should I?'

'Because it's unfair?' Caroline said. 'I just need to know what's going on.'

Maggie looked as if she was about to say something, then held back.

'Look, I think there's more to the way the others are

116

behaving than just Carstairs giving me a lift to work, isn't there?'

Maggie shrugged. 'Well, they assume he was just looking for a chance to bring in his fancy woman, I suppose. It's a bit awkward . . .'

'It's not my fault that the other woman turned the job down. Surely they can see that?'

Maggie looked taken aback. 'Yes, but steady on. She's a friend of Simone's.'

'Well then. Simone must know why she turned the job down? It's got nothing to do with me.'

'Well, I've got you wrong. I was beginning to like you. Everyone knows why she turned the job down. Simone probably thinks they should have held it open.'

Caroline said: 'Everybody knows? *I* don't know. I don't know why she turned the job down. Look, I admit it was stupid of me to accept lifts from Carstairs but I've been a bit out of the swim and I thought it was a way to save money. Tell me what's going on?'

There was a pause. Maggie seemed to be examining Caroline's face. 'So you really don't know?'

'No,' she said.

Maggie looked wary. 'Jesus wept in a bucket!'

'I don't know what you're talking about. I don't know anything. Please believe me.'

'You're saying they didn't tell you when you got the job?'

'Tell me what? Barbara Neilson called me at home and said the job was mine if I wanted it.'

'God, she is *such* a cow,' Maggie said vehemently. She sat down on the low parapet that edged the flat roof. 'She's got to fill the position so she just – Oh, it makes me so angry!'

'What?' Caroline tried not to yell but she felt her voice rise. 'Tell me.'

Maggie shook her head and looked at Caroline. She spoke in a low voice. 'The woman who was offered the job in the first place is called Mary Watkins.'

Caroline shrugged. 'Who's she?'

'Mary Watkins is Dana Watkins's mother. She *was* Dana Watkins's mother, I should say. Dana Watkins was the poor little – '

It was as if the air snapped at her. The parapet swerved; the roof tilted; the forest jumped, a place that bled shadows, a place where girls died. She found herself on one knee, with something screaming in her brain.

'Steady on, pet,' Maggie said.

She put an arm round Caroline's waist and made her sit on the parapet. She kept an arm behind her back, pushing her forwards and her head down.

'Sorry,' Caroline muttered thickly. 'I didn't know.'

'Sorry I broke it to you like that. It was stupid. What a shock. What a horrid shock for you.'

She was looking at Caroline closely, with a sort of detached interest.

'So Mary Watkins was offered the job and turned it down . . .' Caroline's voice trailed off.

'Well, it was assumed, what with everything else, that she wouldn't want to take it on so soon after – you know. I mean, how anyone could be expected – Simone thought that they should have waited but – '

'Of course they should have waited!' Caroline said. 'Of course they should. I feel like a – Oh, I don't know. But it seems like I'm just taking advantage of this awful tragedy. I can't do it. I'm going to hand in my notice.'

'Oh, I wouldn't do that,' Maggie said. 'Look, if you don't do the job, someone else will. And if you're worried about the harpies at the other end of the office, I'll deal with them. They're frightened of me because I don't wax my legs. But you just hang on and things'll get better. You see if they don't.'

She unpeeled the plastic lid to her lunchbox. 'Now then, after a shock you have to eat to get your blood sugar up. Come on. It's nothing to do with you. Just one of those things. Have a sandwich and stop shaking. It's all right,' she added.

Caroline bit into wholemeal bread, lettuce, tomato, Marmite. She hated Marmite. It reminded her of her childhood and her mouth was so dry that the food impacted to a solid paste and she could hardly swallow.

It's nothing to do with you. It's just one of those things. And at least something has been cleared up.

Except something else was nagging her, something beyond the horror of Dana Watkins's death. Sitting on the roof, staring across to the forest where the murder had taken place beneath those selfsame trees, she saw Dana Watkins's golden hair blazing in the shadows, saw little grey children, and saw her son's taut, angry face. She tried to cast the web of her mind over the whole area that stretched from inside her head to the farthest point of the horizon, but the web would not stretch and things would not gather.

Chapter 18

There were flatlands behind him and flat sands ahead. A mirage hovered above the horizon – he could not tell what it was but it looked like a cross between an oil rig and an oil slick. Two windsurfers were slapping over the little brown waves that lifted weak heads and fell exhausted on to the sand, one after the other after the other in quick, anxious succession. The sea panted asthmatically here.

'You don't get crime on a beach,' Brian, his brother-in-law, said. Willis looked at the families dotted sparsely over the beach, separated by densely corrugated steppes of khaki sand. 'No crime here.' Brian pursed his lips and smacked them. 'And good fresh air.'

His dark hair was cropped short and his widow's peak seemed to peck at the air as he talked. He was small and wiry; his wife broad and tall. They obviously complemented each other but Willis still could not see how their marriage worked. Some detective, he thought.

'That's because you'd have to walk half a mile to mug anyone,' he answered, his voice sounding distant in his own ears, as it had ever since his suspension.

Brian nodded as if to acknowledge his point. Cordy, his child and Willis's six-year-old niece, was squatting over a pile of sand, whacking it with a plastic spade. Every now and again she would dip her hand into the hole the sand came from and splash water on the pile.

'I wonder what she's thinking,' Willis said.

'Ah, kids. We like to leave their heads free,' Brian said. 'Let them develop on their own, you know?'

He had been a psychotherapist in Suffolk but had had a nervous breakdown the year Connie fell pregnant. Now he helped out in the B&B and did plumbing jobs around Maplethorpe.

Willis caught the implication that simply by framing the question, he was in some way *not* leaving Cordy's head free. He was always snapping at Brian, and Connie was always telling him that he was too uptight and Brian just had a way of talking . . .

'Mind you,' Brian continued, 'if you think this is empty you should see up the coast at Saltfleet. That's north of here incidentally. Miles of golden sand and not a soul to be seen. Seals maybe basking on the sandbanks; birds, you know. But basically you're on your own. That's empty.'

'Sounds nice,' said Willis pointedly. He had gone out that morning hoping for a stroll along the front, a newspaper, a cup of coffee with a whisky in one of the pubs, or maybe just to sit on a bench and watch the world – or what little of the world took its summer holidays in Maplethorpe – go by. 'Oh, we'll come and keep you company, won't we, Cordy?' Brian had said as Willis had tried to tiptoe out of the front door. Twenty minutes later, once Cordelia had put on her swimsuit, found her spade, gone to the loo, lost her spade, then found it again, they were off.

Cordy found something in the sand and trotted over to her father.

'Look, Daddy. It's a watch.'

'Yes, darling. A plastic toy watch.'

'It's still going,' Cordy said. 'I can tell the time. It's midnight at the ball. I want a picnic.'

'At midnight?' Willis said. 'You'll have to go to the land of the midnight sun.'

Cordy squinted up at him and smiled. 'Stuff and nonsense. Stuff and nonsense. Snuff and ponsense. Is that like the Land of Green Ginger?'

'Better,' said Willis. 'Because the sun goes round in circles and everyone eats bilberries and whale blubber pizza. And the watches don't have numbers. The hands just go round and round in opposite directions.'

'It's one o'clock, two o'clock, three o'clock, four o'clock rock,' Cordy said. 'Seaside rock. On my watch. What's the land of the midnight sun, really?'

Willis opened his mouth. Brian frowned him into silence, then said to Cordy: 'The land of the midnight sun is a long way north of here in the Arctic Circle. Now, during the summer

121

seasons the sun circles the horizon without ever going below it so it never gets dark, and even though it's midnight, you can still see the sun.'

'Sounds stupid.' Cordy looked at him sceptically, dropped the watch in front of them and ran back to her hole. 'We like to be realistic, Don,' Brian said. 'That's the way we like to bring her up.'

'I think deep down he's rather frightened of her,' Connie said after lunch.

They were in the large, tidy kitchen at the back of the house. Metal teapots on system shelving and the eight-ring cooker gave it a semi-industrial air. A big window above the double sink looked out over the small back garden that was entirely hidden by sheets flapping on lines. The sheets glared in the sunshine and made the room a cube of light.

Willis wished he felt better.

He had meant gently to point out in a lighthearted, humorous fashion how Brian had contradicted himself, first claiming that he wanted to let Cordy 'develop on her own', then doing the opposite, but he had found that he was losing his temper as he told his sister.

'Frightened of her?' Willis said. 'Come on, Connie. All he ever does is correct her. But at the same time he's trying to make out that he's Mister Liberal.'

'Exactly. He wants to be liberal but he's frightened of it. Kids can be scary little things. More tea?' She wiggled a metal teapot at him. Willis held out his mug.

'I know some are bloody awful, but Cordy? Surely you don't have problems with her?'

'It's obvious you've never spent much time with kids. You've never seen Cordy lose her temper. I mean a proper strop, a tantrum. It's like . . . like a storm passes through her – I mean a real hurricane.'

'Cordy?'

'Yes, Donald. Even Cordy. And she's no different from other kids. But sometimes, when she's in a mood and we've said no to something she wants, and she loses it, you just look at her and realise that she's out of control. I mean, literally out of control. Sometimes she's screaming so loud you think she's going to tear a vocal cord or something, and you wonder how you created something that is – well, beyond you.' Connie's hand pressed her belly, as if to reinforce her point. 'Brian, for all his talk, needs order. Desperately. Sometimes I think he does slap her down a bit too much – you know, grounds her – but every parent who's being honest will admit they've been scared by their own child – even if it's just once.'

A man poked his head round the kitchen door.

'Just off, Mrs Ackroyd.'

'There's your packed lunch,' Connie said, pointing to a carrier bag on the sideboard. 'Good weather for it.'

The man bobbed and nodded at Willis before taking the bag.

'Twitchers,' Connie said. 'We're getting recommendations now. It's important. This'll be the first break-even year since the recession.'

Cordy ran in and leaned against her mother, smiling at Willis. Then she went into the garden and began running through the sheets, wrapping herself in them like winding sheets, battering them with her hand.

Willis watched her with narrowed eyes.

'You can talk to me, you know,' Connie said. 'I know you're not on holiday. I know something's happened at work. Have you been given special leave or something?'

'I've been suspended,' he said.

'Oh, Donald! Was it something you did?'

'In a manner of speaking, yes.'

'Well? Oh, Don, it's awful. I don't know what to say.'

'Neither do I.'

His sister's face went from stricken to sympathetic.

'It meant everything to you. I mean, it was everything to you, the police.'

'I don't know any more. As long as I thought I could cope, yes, it was.' He took a deep breath. He had wanted to get away from it all, but perhaps it was better that he talked. 'I was the last person to see a man alive. I mean, I saw him a few minutes before he was killed. They're not happy with my account of it.'

'What – ?'

'I followed this man,' Willis said. 'I was following this man, and I followed him into the wood and he was killed.'

The words came slowly, rising in his throat like bubbles in

thick mud. 'He was sucked underground, then spat out in pieces.'

'And you saw this?' Connie had the knack of being calm.

'I saw him go under and come back in bits. Then I passed out. But no one believes me. I hadn't realised before that we live by consensus. It doesn't matter if you see something, or believe something. If no one else has, or if no one believes you, it might as well not have happened and you're better off keeping your mouth closed. The bitch of it is, that what happened was only what everyone else wants. Everyone seems to think that excuses it.'

'How so?'

'The man who died was a child murderer . . . perhaps. Probably. Maybe.'

Connie folded her arms and said comfortingly, 'Well, if you think that's what happened, you'll have to prove it, I suppose. How will you go about that?'

'I suppose I'll have to find the – ' Willis stopped in midsentence. In staccato phrases that felt as if they had formed in someone else's mouth, he told his sister about Tailor – his history, how he had died. He told her about the child he had followed, how first of all she had had a blank face, then the face of Dana Watkins, and how both faces seemed to be made up of the forest itself.

Connie's face twisted.

'So the guy who you saw had killed a child himself. And you think a child – '

'Lured.'

'Lured is rather a loaded word.'

'I can't think of another one. The child lured Tailor on.'

'So that's why you're looking at Cordy out of the corner of your eyes the whole time.'

'I'm sorry. Connie, I'm actually scared at the thought of it. Can children be evil?'

He had not really thought it before and was surprised that he had said the word evil. Was that because he had been scared? Remembered fear caught him by surprise. The mug in his hand began to shake.

'Not until they are fully formed, no,' Connie said. 'If they're not properly developed, they can't reach any absolute state.

Either absolute state. Good or evil.'

'Even regardless of what that particular child did?'

'Yes. It still holds. You can only be evil if you're fully conscious. Children aren't that.'

Willis was looking at his sister with surprise. 'You've thought a lot about this.'

Connie shrugged. 'You do when you're bringing a child up. What I don't understand is why you're so involved. Forgive me for saying it, but you've always survived in the past by cutting loose. Unless there's a woman.'

'Who's got a child . . .' Willis gave a wry grimace as his voice trailed off. Brian walked in.

'Having a chinwag? Am I included, or is this private business?' Willis shot Connie a despairing glance. 'The guests in the front room have blocked the loo again. What are they putting down it?' he continued.

'What's the mother like?' Connie asked across him.

'Attractive. Nervy. Single.'

'Oho,' said Brian. 'Got that far, have we? Does she have a name?'

'Yes.'

'Come on then, come on. Tell all.'

'Brian . . .' Connie said reproachfully. Willis felt like using him to unblock the loo.

'Caroline Waters,' he said.

'Aha.'

'Brian, don't wind Donald up.'

Cordy appeared in the doorway. 'Donald looks as if he's going to sick something up,' she said.

No child could be evil, adults were scared of children. Something his sister had said kept on replaying in his mind: 'Sometimes, when she's in a mood and we've said no to something she wants . . .'

Could a child flip over into the other world, the evil world, the monster world, just for being denied something? And if it did, what might happen when it was denied its life?

Willis was back in Epping two days later without ever having sampled the delights of the beach shally – some vandals had vandalised it – but taking away memories of high skies and low horizons, deckchairs and fish and chips. The memories were already fading to the pastel gaudiness of a fifties picture postcard. He could have been away forty years ago.

His flat smelled closed and stale. He opened a window and sorted his post. Bank statement, Access bill, police newsletter – aha, something handwritten.

He shuffled it to the top. The address was in Nancy Freeman's rounded handwriting. He tore it open.

Willis,
Just to let you know that none of us misses you at all.
I read your report and came up with a couple of interesting somethings which may/may not have some bearing on the above. Call the station and leave a message for me from PC Fields. I'll buy you a drink.
Freeman

Chapter 19

The Dewdrop Inn was a quiet pub in a quiet, tree-lined back street. It had tiny windows blocked by geraniums, and a long table outside on a wide pavement. A group of New Age travellers, tanned dark brown and dressed in loose, cut-off T-shirts and home-made trousers, were sitting at the table outside. A baby slept in a cardboard box; a man was looking moodily into his glass of beer. One woman was trying to teach a toddler with hennaed hair how to juggle; another, looking tense and ill, was leaning her elbows on the table. There were scratches on her face.

Willis waited by the empty bar, tapping a coin on its surface. The walls were heavily painted tongue and groove panelling, hung with old photographs of forest workers: charcoal burners, chair bodgers, swine herds. There were near-indecipherable lithographs of little children and foxed prints of the High Street. The barman emerged from a back room, recognised Willis, nodded in the direction of the travellers and shrugged apologetically.

'Don't mind me,' Willis said. 'I'm on holiday.'

'They were in the forest,' the barman said. 'Got chased out. Looked well done in.'

'Oh, yes. Who by?'

'Kids, from what they were saying. What's the world coming to, eh? Still, I expect I'd have done the same. We gave the gippoes hell whenever we saw 'em – if they didn't give us hell first, that is. So what'll it be?'

What the man said had given Willis an idea. He was thinking of the forest, and how things happened in it. He'd talk to anyone.

He turned as the door swung open and Nancy walked in. Behind her he saw a police Metro draw away from the kerb. He pushed past her. The outside table was empty. Empty crisp packets, a pool of beer that looked like Greenland. The travellers must have taken off as soon as they saw the police car, and it was a long straight road.

'Were you pushing me out of the way or are you just pleased to see me?' Nancy asked.

'Did you see those travellers?'

'What travellers?'

'They were sitting there a minute ago. Outside at the table.'

Nancy shrugged. Willis remembered that he had been short with her the last time he had seen her. Now he was snapping at her again.

'Let me get you a drink.'

She ordered a gin and tonic and sat down inside, next to the window, placing a carrier bag on the floor next to her and lighting a Silk Cut.

'Sorry about that.' Willis put the drinks down. 'The barman told me that they'd been living in the forest but'd been chased out by kids. I just thought . . . well, you know.'

'What?'

'They might have seen or heard something. They might be able to give us a location.' He blushed. 'You read my report.'

'Yes.'

'Great.'

'I didn't pass it around. I'm friendly with Grey's PA. Let's just say I happened to run my eye over it.'

'So now you know I'm mad.' He dreaded what she would have to say but at the same time curiosity and excitement were making his heart beat faster. He drank some beer. His mouth had suddenly gone dry.

'May I be frank?' Nancy said.

She rearranged her lighter and cigarettes on the table. Willis made a face.

'You're taking all this too personally. You wrote down what you think you saw – '

'I wrote down what I *saw*.'

'You wrote down what you *think* you saw. It's all any of us can do. Now you're getting your knickers in a twist because some of us think you've drawn the wrong conclusions. And if you think this is bad, wait till the inquest.'

Willis groaned.

'But,' she said, 'I have something for you.'

She took a pull of her drink, then reached down and slid a sheaf of Polaroid photographs out of the carrier bag.

'Evidence from the Watkins case,' she said. 'I was boxing some things up in records and came across them. Look at this one first.'

Willis peered at the picture: the dead oak with things hanging on the branches like some ghastly parody of a Christmas tree.

'The first time I saw this all these things had been bagged up.' On the left-hand side of the tree a pair of shoes had been tied to a low branch by their laces.

Nancy pushed across another Polaroid. Same tree but a close-up.

'Training shoes,' Willis said. 'What's the scale? They look small to me.'

The trainers looked new and there was some sort of gadget on the distended tongue that meant they were expensive – the sort you could pump up. They hung at different angles, pointing in opposite directions.

'Why would anyone leave their shoes on a tree?' Willis asked.

'My thoughts exactly,' Nancy agreed.

'To play soccer?'

'Ground's bumpy, grass too long, according to the report.'

'Right. That doesn't work. How about to save them from getting dirty?' Willis suggested.

'But why tie them to a tree? Why not tie them round your neck? Those are expensive shoes. Kids don't go leaving them around. I mean, why take enough care of them to tie them to a tree, but forget about them later? Same again?' She pushed Willis down as he rose. 'My shout.'

While she was gone, he helped himself to a Silk Cut and looked more closely at the shoes.

'There's something written on the tongue,' he said as Nancy put the drink down in front of him.

'Exhibit C,' she said, and gave him the last photograph. It was a close-up of the tongue, folded back. Willis had been right about the shoes being small: they belonged to a child. The writing on the inside of the tongue, written in a bold adult hand, proved it.

MARCUS WATERS 3B.

It was a shock and he felt it in his stomach as if a vacuum bomb had gone off in there, sucking inwards, not blowing out. The boy *had* been there.

'No one made anything of it,' Nancy Freeman said.

'Should have shown up on the computer. The surname, I mean. Should have been cross-referenced.'

'That would have depended on how quickly your report on the visit to the Waterses was punched in. Anyway, chances are that by the time anyone got round to it, Tailor was dead. No one runs cross-reference programmes on a case that's been closed. Results are rare enough.'

'They're calling this a result?'

'They're calling *that* a result. The Dana Watkins case is closed; the body's been released for burial. Tailor's murder is an ongoing investigation. But so far as people know, evidence relating to the one doesn't necessarily relate to the other.'

'That's crazy. Who's got it?'

'Marshall.'

'Oh, they're really taking it seriously,' Willis said sarcastically. 'Are they trying to bury it?'

'Yes. In a word.'

'Does Marshall know about the shoes? I mean, has he connected it with the fact that Marcus was one of the last people to see the girl alive?'

'What do you think?'

Willis made a face. 'One of your loverboys – Benson – told me something. He said trees like this were all tied in to ancient myths. He called it a wishing tree, like a wishing well. Jesus! It's been there all along. He said that all that crap hanging from it was like tribute: you hung something on the tree and made a wish.'

'So?'

'The trainers. Marcus was not only there, he was making a wish.'

'You don't believe all that crap, do you? No, you just want an excuse to go round there again.'

'I'm suspended.'

'They needn't know that, need they?'

'I don't know.'

130

'Jesus Christ, Sarge. For all we know you're under suspicion of murdering Tailor. Now I don't know what the fuck you saw, but I do know it won't hold up in a court of law. If you want a chance to get back on the force with anything like a reputation, you will have to take the initiative. This is a lead of sorts. Now I've gone out on a limb for you on this. What are you going to do about it?'

'I don't bloody well know.'

'Come on. Think!'

'Go and see Mrs Waters? But where will it get me?'

'I don't bloody know either but at least it might start the ball rolling. At the very least ask her if she told anyone else about Tailor.'

Willis looked at her in some surprise.

'It was a big mistake,' Nancy continued. 'I should never have blurted it out like that in front of Mrs Waters and the boy.'

'She was on the phone. She probably wasn't listening.'

'I think she heard. Anyway, you didn't say anything in your report. I owe you.'

'I love it when people say that to me. Thanks.'

'I haven't finished yet.'

'You've been a busy bee.'

'I have to admit I'm getting quite interested. Remember you said I should try and compare the two bodies: Dana Watkins's and Tailor's first?'

'Yes. It was a hunch.'

'Well I did. I mean, I did a complete analysis and comparison of the injuries. They're identical.'

Something peculiar in her emphasis made Willis ask, 'How exactly?'

'Exactly exactly. If you did a tracing of the first and laid it over Dana's, the bite marks, the bruises would map on perfectly. It's not just a copy; it's like a carbon copy.' She looked at him closely.

'Grey knows something.'

'Grey just wanted Tailor,' Nancy said firmly. 'If it came out how precisely the pattern was repeated, you'd start asking all sorts of questions.'

And Nancy didn't, Willis noted. She liked the research; she didn't like the questions. He kept his face blank.

131

'And there's another thing. There was no semen in Dana.'

'Then she wasn't raped.'

'I didn't say that. All I said was that there was no semen in Dana. It's being called unidentified liquid, although the injuries were consistent with rape.'

'But secretions, that kind of thing.'

Nancy pursed her lips and shook her head emphatically. 'The lab's come up with a big zero.'

'And we never found the means of suffocation.' Willis screwed his eyes tight shut. 'Asthma,' he said. 'That's like suffocating, isn't it?'

'You're thinking about the first one . . . Stephanie Temple.'

'If you say so. This whole thing. It's beyond me.'

'And Grey too, I'd say.' Nancy looked at her watch and rose to go. 'Maybe it's nothing but your file was filed.'

'You mean not ritually burned?'

'My friend said Grey made a big play of saying he was going to shred it, then stuffed it in his briefcase and went out. When he came back it was gone from his case. She checked. Doesn't make sense.'

'Neither does anything else. Yet.'

There was nobody at the Waters' house. Willis rang the bell, stood listening, stepped back, gazed up at a jet scratching the sky, looked at his watch, and rang again. Behind him he heard the muffled sounds of locks being unlocked and chains being unhitched. The front door of a house opposite opened. An elderly man with a wispy crown of dirty yellow hair stared deliberately at him, then wrote down his car number on a clipboard. After that Willis felt he had to ring again and wait another couple of minutes before driving off.

It was good, he had to admit it, this business of neighbour looking after neighbour. So why did it all seem so gloomy? Because it was necessary in the first place? Because by tricks that maybe a social historian or an economist could explain, no one was around at three o'clock in the afternoon in this middle-class ghetto apart from an old man with a lot of time on his hands?

Now the old man had gone back to his enormous armchair in the big picture window. Behind him on the television a clump

132

of race horses galloped silently in space, held motionless by the moving camera. Willis wished he could have asked him something useful but there was nothing to ask. He drove off towards the forest. Without actually coming to a decision, he knew he was heading for the clearing again.

It was the same place and the same weird feeling descended on him: sounds were both muffled and sharp, the air claustrophobically still.

Willis peered through the branches. The whole place would have been swept clean by the scene-of-crime squad and nothing had happened to them.

He skirted the clearing until he reached the point where he had stood and seen Tailor.

Looking for something? A clue that half a dozen colleagues, trained to look for and find clues, had failed to notice? He had stood here, peered through this clump of hazel. Tailor had stood there. What had happened to him?

A sudden movement on a branch by his head made him start. A grey squirrel was advancing towards him stealthily, its tail stiffened to a brush, its yellow teeth bared. Willis stepped away. Squirrels were tree rats. This one looked like a mad tree rat. He had no desire to upset a mother squirrel whose territory he had encroached upon.

'Sorry, tree rat,' he said.

Suddenly the squirrel rushed him. It came chattering along the branch, then began to scream. Willis stepped back suddenly, a flare of alarm igniting in his breast. The damn' thing was at eye-level! He threw his hands in front of his face. The squirrel swerved, leapt and disappeared up a tree, frightened by his sudden movement.

The quiet and the still heat closed around him again, like water round a pebble. Shock waves rippled gently through him. He stiffened himself and stepped into the open.

The ground shivered underfoot. Pressing down with one foot would push the other up. It was like walking on a li-lo filled with porridge.

He took one step, and then another. He looked around at the broken wall of forest. Criss-cross patterns of light and shade, trembling leaves, shapes that formed on the edge of his vision.

His eyes raked round. Movement strobed behind the veil of leaves. He was very frightened.

Something splashed on to his shoulder. He flinched and squinted down at it. Bloody birds, he thought. Except this was not a dropping. It was mud.

He flicked it off his shoulder. Very wet mud. He looked up at the blue sky, empty apart from an old prop 'plane, painted bright red, moving slowly across the sky, so high you could not hear its engine. He looked around at the wall of trees. Throwing mud? His heart began to beat faster.

He looked around. There was nothing in the trees. Then he looked up.

The 'plane was banking now. Something was wrong. Something in its movement; its silence. The engine must have cut out. Perhaps it was a stunt 'plane. They would dive, then kick the engine back in. But what was a 'plane doing stunts for above a forest? It was lethal.

As it banked it seemed to slip down the sky – he could measure the drop against the line of trees. Strange-looking 'plane – not only the fact that it was red, but its shape seemed funny, more like a kid's idea of a 'plane than a real one. It was filthy too, covered in – mud? He was slammed by the multiple impact of impressions: a long train of thought hitting a wall.

It was silent as a ghost. Its size was all wrong. It made Willis feel like a stuffed giant. His eyes kept failing to focus. It was diving. It was heading for him. He moved to one side; the 'plane readjusted its course. It was coming for him but still so distant, barely bigger than a kid's aeroplane –

He ducked. The toy aeroplane slashed the air past his face, wheeled and hissed upwards. He looked after it. It had gone. He turned and turned, fear snatching at his belly, clogging his throat. Something was controlling the 'plane. Its propeller had not been turning.

The forest wheeled. Nothing. Something wanted to hurt him. It could aim the 'plane at him without a motor. If it had just been a toy 'plane out of control, it would have crashed. But it was gone. Gone.

Then something made him look up again. The aeroplane was heading straight down on a pile-driver course with the crown of his head. He threw himself sideways and this time the toy brushed past his face and whacked into the ground.

Mud splattered and a single ripple formed the thick, ragged-lipped O of a mouth. It spread in a thick brown grin, then puckered. Before Willis had time to react, half the 'plane was buried and it was sinking fast, the earth heaving and smacking around it. He gripped it by the fuselage, felt the fragile body give, then changed grip, holding it by the wings where they met the fuselage.

Flurries of mud engulfed his knuckles. He pulled and the 'plane jerked upwards, slowly. The mud felt thick and elastic; pliant, almost fleshy. It was like catching a big fish; you never quite knew what was going to break the surface. Flat tyres of earth writhed.

There was something down there –

It reared up suddenly from the mud, long and grey in the bright sunlight. An arm, a hand, grey, thin, slick, turned under his gaze. Lying in the earth was a child.

Its face was extraordinary – leathery, grey but smooth, as if plumped up and ripened by the goodness of earth. Its body was a place where things moved and in that split second Willis saw that it was more like jelly than leather. It began to writhe. The face was like the surface of a bubble. The figure lifted from the mud. Liquid fell from it in curtains and showed a body as slick as a newborn baby's, but plump and voluptuous. The skin had the lustre of wet grapes. Somewhere behind him Willis heard a whirring and as he ran felt something huge try to settle on his neck. His hair was fanned by its wing beats.

Willis ran stumbling from the clearing, holding the plane, careering through the wood, careless of branches that whipped his face and scratched his scalp, trying not to look over his shoulder, feeling terror ball behind him in a great bouncing lump. He crashed through undergrowth on to a path. A woman walking a toddler instinctively threw her arms around it and backed away, trying to scoop the baby along with one arm and drag a candy-striped buggy with the other. Willis stood and quivered. He was rank and sticky with sweat, poisoned by what he had seen. He knew he must look like a maniac – a huge, red-faced man crashing through the forest waving a dirty toy aeroplane – so he backed away from the woman, muttered,

'Sorry,' and walked down the path to his car.

He sat in the car with all the windows open, head down, and waited for the trembling to stop and his heartbeat to slow back to normal. Every minute or so he stretched out his hand and gripped the steering wheel to try and control the trembling. Every time he looked at the aeroplane lying upside down on the passenger seat, dribbling dirty water on to the synthetic weave cover, he began to tremble again.

The trembling finally stopped. The clock on the dashboard said a quarter past four. Now he had to try the Waterses' house again. This time he had two reasons – the trainers and the toy aeroplane. The one lying next to him on the seat was the one he had mended. It belonged to Marcus Waters.

He recognised the Nissan parked outside the house and rang the bell confidently. The paint around the door was peeling badly now and would look shabby next year. He pulled a flake off with his finger and pressed a nail into the wood. It was still sound. He held the 'plane in one hand and was glad that the man opposite was not at his observation post. The 'plane dripped mud on to the boot scraper and it splashed on to a cellophane-wrapped Freeman's catalogue that was obviously too big to fit through the letter box. The door opened hesitantly. The boy stood there.

When he saw the 'plane his face went white.

'Who is it, darling?'

The boy looked up at Willis pleadingly He opened his mouth. Closed it. Shook his head.

'Marcus? Marcus? Who is – Oh.'

She stood in the doorway, rubbing her hands down the thighs of a pair of faded jeans.

She looked at Willis, then at the 'plane in his hand, dripping mud on to her porch, then back at Willis's face. Marcus closed his eyes. Willis was sure the boy was going to faint. He thought fast. He gave a smile that threatened to crack his face, not because it was a particularly broad smile, but because his face felt so stiff.

'Returning one stray model aeroplane, eh?'

He winked down at the boy who was still looking sick, but as the mother could not see his face, Willis thought she might buy

136

the charade. 'That's it,' he said. 'Bet you thought that was the last you'd seen of that?' He tried to chuckle. It sounded like a rusty hinge.

'Marcus, I didn't even know you had lost it.'

He grabbed the 'plane and ran past his mother towards the back of the house.

'Marcus?'

'Well,' Willis said. 'That was a stroke of luck.'

'I'm afraid I don't understand.' Caroline Waters shook her head and smiled as if to say it was just one of many things she did not understand. 'It's Sergeant – '

'Willis.'

'Sergeant Willis, of course. And you mended it the other day as well.'

'That's how I recognised it. I was just walking through the forest and saw it. Something rang a bell and I dug it out. I wasn't sure it was your boy's – Marcus, isn't it? – but it obviously is.'

'He's delighted,' Caroline said.

Not from where I was standing, Willis thought. 'I couldn't just wash my hands, could I?'

'Of course,' Caroline said, wondering how for a man who was standing on a door mat, he looked like a man already inside. He obviously wanted something more and she was torn between avoiding it and wanting to hear – the same sort of impulse that finds you pulling at a scab just to see the blood underneath.

'I was putting the kettle on. Cup of tea?' she said.

'I'd rather have something cold.'

'Dandelion and burdock?'

'You're kidding. I haven't had that in years.'

'The supermarket's just started stocking it. I know the feeling. It was the one treat – ' She broke off and frowned. 'Anyway, come through.'

Willis followed her through into the kitchen, washed his hands, then without thinking dashed cold water over his face. He stood up, eyes screwed tight, and felt a drying-up cloth thrust into his hands.

He spoke, punctuating his words with dabs of the cloth.

'I found it – about a twenty-minute walk from here – in a clearing.'

'Yes?'

'Have you been there with him?'

'Well, no. To be honest I don't go into the woods very much.'

'Any idea how it might have got there?'

'Well, he did say he lost it. Perhaps some other kids found it and took it away. I'm sure Marcus – '

'Tell me, has he lost anything else recently? An article of clothing? A pair of shoes maybe?'

'Why do you say that?'

'A pair of trainers?' Willis persisted.

That got her, but she did not look worried – only confused.

'I have to know why you're asking me all these questions.' Her eyes strayed beyond him to the garden. The boy was looking at his 'plane then looking at the forest.

Willis decided to take the plunge. 'Your son's size four Nike trainers are at present boxed up as scene-of-crime evidence in a basement in your local police station. They were found hanging from a tree in a clearing in the forest. We suspect they had been put there a day before Dana Watkins was killed at the very earliest. It may have been the same day even. That links your son with a spot very close to where she was killed, you know. It's quite a spot. Near where Dana was killed, where I found the aeroplane – and, I'm afraid, the exact spot Dana's murderer was killed. There's a glade in the forest there, and a tree. Now I know this sounds ridiculous but people use this tree to make wishes. I mean, they wish on this particular tree and I think that's what your son's been up to.'

He cut off her protests with a raised hand. 'I'm through with trying to place your son here or there at any particular time but I know that something is going on in that forest, and I know that Marcus is caught up in it, and I know that his possessions have been turning up on the wishing tree. So what I want to find out is what he's been asking for and how it connects with Dana Watkins's and Tailor's deaths.'

'What are you saying?'

'I'd love to know – '

'You're talking about my son!'

'Mrs Waters, I assure you – '

'You're implying he – '

'Might be in some danger,' Willis interjected.

138

She still looked suspicious. 'Danger?'

'Aren't you worried?'

'Well, yes.'

'Did you think I meant something else? Did you think I was implying something else?'

'Yes! No! STOP IT!'

'I wasn't.'

'SHUT UP! QUIET! LEAVE ME ALONE! WHY DON'T YOU LEAVE ME ALONE?'

Willis remembered how close she had been to snapping the time he had seen her before. She put a foot out towards him when she shouted, clenched her fists and tensed her arms. Muscles at the base of her neck splayed out. Her head might have been balanced on spikes.

'Mrs Waters, please tell me what it is you're worried about?'

She shook her head but seemed to relax a little. She was still breathing hard, face flushed, nostrils flared.

'Are you all right?' He wanted suddenly to touch her face.

She nodded. Outside on the lawn Marcus was hosing down the aeroplane but it was completely ruined – even she could see that. The fabric had come away from the body in places. One wing was torn off and held on only by the wires that ran inside it to the flaps. Hopelessly broken.

All Caroline wanted was time to think. She glanced at her watch. Tom would be here any minute; his imminent arrival pressed a lid down on her thoughts and steamed them into disintegration. Danger. Danger. Was that what she had really been thinking? She turned on Willis suddenly.

'Look, just be honest with me. What do you know? Are you saying that you think Marcus could have had anything to do with these – ' She couldn't get the last word out.

Out in the garden the boy had lost all interest in the aeroplane now and was riding round the lawn on his mountain bike. Clockwise, she was glad to see. His lips worked as he made shushing noises. She opened the window, and fresh air, cool and benevolent, poured into the kitchen.

Willis looked embarrassed and was obviously reluctant to pressure her. He said: 'Look, I was clumsy when I came in. The fact of the matter is that I don't know how to proceed – ' He caught her raised eyebrow. 'Sorry, police jargon. The truth of the matter is, I'm stuck. No, worse than that. I'm screwed. And suspended.'

'Suspended?' she said. 'What for? I mean, that's what happens to policemen who are suspected of doing something wrong.'

'That's right.'

'So what did you do?'

'I was suspended because I saw something inexplicable – in the forest – and instead of keeping quiet or inventing a story about it, I tried to report it as accurately as I could.'

'Which was how?'

'You know that Tailor, the man who killed Dana Watkins, was himself murdered?'

'I couldn't very well miss it. There were celebration barbecues all down the Close.'

'I saw it happen.'

'You *saw* it?'

'I saw it and I couldn't stop it happening.'

'What do you mean?'

'It was so ghastly I fainted.' He looked so stricken that Caroline had to stifle a smile. 'Anyway, when I reported back, no one believed me. Basically they told me to change my report or they would suspend me. Underneath, I think they were saying: We're glad the bastard's dead, but for God's sake, go away and come up with a better story.'

'What *was* your story?' she asked, genuinely curious. Her question made Willis flinch.

'I – can't say. Suffice to say, you wouldn't believe me either. But I followed him to his death' (that sounded ridiculously melodramatic) 'and it was about the same time that you left two messages for me, you remember, because Marcus had disappeared?'

'He hadn't disappeared. He'd just gone into the forest. That's right – that was the time he forgot his 'plane, I suppose. He met up with a neighbour. He'll confirm . . .'

The words died on her lips and the world seemed to have folded itself around her, muffling sound and sensation.

'You're not implying he killed Tailor?' She heard a laugh

140

from far away and was vaguely offended, then realised that she was making the noise.

'I'm nowhere near implying anything,' Willis said. 'I just think he's involved. Listen, I've been running away from this thing from the moment it started. The first day I came round I went to the car park where you said you had seen a child lying on the ground. I followed a child all the way to the wishing tree and it floated. I mean it flew. I haven't told anyone that and I haven't been able to build it into a story that makes sense yet. But that's what the two of us have got to do. Throw away our preconceptions and work out what is going on, not what we think sounds plausible. Now two items of Marcus's have turned up at this tree, preceding two murders. That's reality. That's evidence. That is what I would be investigating if I weren't suspended. You with me? Now I've got to know if Marcus was putting things there himself, and if he did, did he know what he was doing?'

'You need more than that,' Caroline said. 'I mean, you need more than children flying.' She loaded her voice with sarcasm.

Willis said flatly: 'All right. We can now place Marcus near the scene of both murders. That's more than a coincidence, that's a connection. I want to know what it is.'

There was the sound of a car drawing up outside. Caroline considered Willis. 'That's my husband. I don't want him involved in any of this.'

'Tell me you'll talk to me later?' he urged.

'No. I can't.'

'You have to.'

'I have to protect my son,' she said.

'What about the rest of us?' He spoke without thinking.

'You feel threatened by a little boy?' Caroline led him to the front door. He walked past a man he identified as her ex-husband, one of those good-looking stubbly types used to advertise cars with family values. When he reached the pavement he turned and looked back. On the ground floor another of those frozen tableaux – the man looking at Caroline; she throwing back her head and laughing gaily; keeping quite a distance between them, Willis noted. The man turned away. Caroline's face seemed to collapse. She was putting on a front the whole fucking time, Willis thought. But what? Why?

Then something made him look upstairs. The boy was staring at him from a window. His face was pale behind the glass and his eyes were dark. His expression, unequivocally, was one of hatred.

Chapter 20

Back in his flat Willis opened all the windows wide and waited for evening to turn into night. He remembered standing outside the front door in Kingsmeade Close and wondering whether the wooden door frame was sound. Why should he care? Because – he cared. Perhaps he had nothing else to care about. He missed his job.

He called his sister to thank her for his stay, but he sounded so distracted she asked him what was wrong.

Willis thought of the model 'plane, the grey hand. 'I'm not sure if I can say.'

'Be careful. I've lived through one breakdown. It's no laughing matter and you never quite get back to normal.'

'What do you mean?'

'Cured can mean a great many different things. Doctors call cancer patients cured when they go into remission. It doesn't alter the fact that the cancer can come back. Brian's cured, but he knows what he's been through. A bit of him broke, and even if it's mended, he's terrified of its breaking again. That fear leads to its own pressures.'

'I'm not going to have a breakdown,' Willis said, wondering if, in fact, he *was* having a breakdown and that explained everything.

Willis lay on his bed and thought about Caroline in a general sense, but somehow the thoughts turned to her jeans and the way that the material had hugged her hips and become worn to pale patches of silky nothingness. In places. He found himself growing aroused and thought of masturbating but felt that it would somehow compromise him. He threw his legs over the side of the bed. Be careful.

He went to the open window and looked up at the yellow

night sky. Two hundred years ago, a tree would have been growing right here, he thought. I'm standing in the branches of a ghost tree. He looked towards the forest. Something inexplicable had happened there. He and Caroline Waters, and the boy of course, were linked by that but hadn't reached a common understanding.

And he had to be careful. Willis smacked his fist into his palm. Who was he to talk about denial? He was the one who was ignoring things under his nose. While he had been complaining that no one understood him, he had completely forgotten what Mrs Tailor had said to him. He had pinned her down and she had looked up at him and screamed: 'No one understands! He just went out for a walk.'

At the time he had assumed that she was making the old, the most awful excuse: No one understands my little boy. But suppose she had meant something bigger than that? Suppose she had meant: There's something going on here that I don't understand? It seemed unlikely that she would talk but it was worth a try.

Above him the lights of an airliner bored into the sky as it dropped towards Stansted Airport. He'd never really seen the point of putting headlamps on aeroplanes – what was there to see up there? Model aeroplanes that try to kill people, he thought, controlled by grey arms that reach out of the earth. The airliner's lights were there to make holes in the darkness, and that was enough.

Chapter 21

Caroline was looking up and saw the same aeroplane. Things were growing clearer in her head.

She was running something over in her mind, a conversation she had had with Marcus on the night before she had gone for the job interview. And she was thinking very hard about the training shoes the policeman had mentioned.

Marcus had hung them on the tree the day he had left school early and walked into the forest.

She had assumed that he had gone into the woods to take a short cut home to lessen the journey time, but in fact he had never said that. He had said that he had wanted to help her. And the night before the interview he had talked a lot about wanting things, had asked her if she really wanted the job. She'd said yes. He had taken the shoes, had hung them on the tree and yes, she had got the job. How? Because a little girl had been killed and her mother had been too shocked to take up her new job. So that it had gone to Caroline instead? The enormity of it made Caroline feel as swollen and numb as a blister of Novocaine.

And the policeman almost knew. She was shaken by a storm of self-pity. Why did everything always happen to her? To be a survivor of abuse, the sort of abuse she had suffered, made her special. She knew that. To help herself to survive, she had told herself stories about fairies. She could still remember the shock when she saw them for the first time, the little grey children who lived in the woods. They had talked to her; she had talked back. They had said they would help her; eventually she had accepted their help. And then?

When she had told the doctors about the fairies, the little grey children, they told her that they had never been outside her head. They were real to her, but not to anyone else. The wishes they could grant, well, anyone in her position would want to escape, so she had made up this story about the fairies and their ability to grant wishes to make herself feel better. But she had to understand that none of it was real. It was just going on inside her.

But now she felt very confused. It was as if the fairies had escaped. They were no longer the shreds and tatters of her damaged psyche. They were real! They were true! And worse than that, Marcus knew about them. Her Marcus!

She hugged her knees, rocked and moaned. Why her? Why did these things always happen to her? And what to do? How could she save Marcus? One thing was clear: he must never know what he had done, and if he suspected, she must somehow convince him that he was wrong.

Chapter 22

Marcus, they both told her, had been wonderful. He had played, he had slept, he had eaten, he had helped. Tom said he sensed a change, a really important deep-down change. Marcus, he said, was growing up. Caroline watched her son say goodbye to his father and stepmother and saw only the jerky movements of a marionette, the taut smile of a child actor. When he got into the car he slumped back into the seat and his face emptied, drained of energy.

'Have a good time?' she asked.

'I'm tired.'

'Ready for bed, then?'

'Maybe.'

His face looked old and twisted. She touched him and he shrugged her hand away.

'What's wrong, darling?'

'Why do you care?'

'That's unfair!'

'Fuck off.'

She slammed on the brakes, turned and raised her hand.

'That's right,' he said. 'Hit me.'

'Marcus!' It was a howl of agony and frustration. 'What is it?'

'Perhaps you should tell me.'

'What?'

'You're the one with the problem.'

'Yes, I do have a problem and I'll tell you what it is. I have a policeman coming round to question me about you! A policeman who says that you've lied to him and lied to me. That's what upsets me, Marcus. *You've lied.*'

Her voice rose and fell like a club. Marcus had been holding back the tears. Now suddenly they came on in a long, gobbling wave.

'I'm sorry.' He finally managed to get the words out. Caroline tried to twist him towards her but he resisted. She rested a hand on his shoulder, thinking perhaps it would be better for him to feel some distance from her.

'Can you tell me what happened? From the start? From the day you didn't wait for me and walked home from school?'

'I did it for you. I was doing it for you.'

Caroline fought with a sudden heart-jolting surge of guilt. Just concentrate on getting to the truth . . .

'All right. You did it for me. What did you do?'

'We decided – '

'We? Who's *we*?'

'No one. *I* decided to help you. So I went to the tree and I wished that you got your job. I did. And you did. That's when it all went wrong. Mummy . . . Mummy . . .'

Caroline felt as if she were freezing. Her blood was slowing and thickening to red treacle.

She turned to him. She tried to keep her voice light. 'Marcus,' she said, 'you know that's nonsense.'

'But I did. I had to leave something. I left – '

'Listen to me! You may have wished, and you may have left something there. That doesn't mean to say it had anything to do with my getting the job.'

'But it's true! It's true!'

'Haven't you heard what I'm saying, Marcus? If you wish for it to stop raining and it stops, it doesn't mean that you really had anything to do with it.'

'But it worked – '

She turned him by the shoulders and bellowed into his face: 'It didn't! It didn't! It didn't!'

Marcus did not answer. She blinked and shook her head. He wriggled away from her and pressed himself against the car door. When she lifted her hand he closed his eyes and screwed up his face.

'Come here, darling.' There was no response. 'Come here,' she said, a bit more sternly. After a tiny pause Marcus leant towards her. Caroline took him and pressed him to her. His hair smelled of sweat. He was hot. His heart was rattling against hers. She willed it to slow down. After a very long while it did.

By the time they pulled into Kingsmeade Close, Marcus was

asleep. Caroline pulled him out of the car and just managed to carry him into the house and up the stairs. She laid him on the bed, wrestled him out of his clothes, got some pyjamas on him and turned off the light.

She was woken by the sound of his crying. She had fallen asleep in a chair in the corner of his room, lulled by the sound of his breathing. He had thrown the duvet off and was rolling from side to side in a way that reminded her uncomfortably of documentary footage of disturbed Romanian orphans. Her bare foot landed on something cold, wet and flat. She flinched and jerked her foot away. She felt something stick, then fall.

His window was open a crack. The air was cold and musty. She knelt by the bed and reached a hand out, synchronising its movements to the swaying of his head. His forehead was cold. At her touch his head stopped moving, his eyes flew open, and he looked at her.

'They've gone,' he said.

There was a sound like tiny waves moving on shingle. Caroline thought she saw darkness retreat over the carpet like water draining away. She blinked. It gathered in the corners and disappeared. The room was lighter now. Marcus closed his eyes and slept. She pulled the duvet over him and kissed his forehead. The skin was warmer now.

On the landing she turned and pushed the door open so she could see what she had trodden on.

She saw a flat, wet leaf.

She watched him closely over the next few days: in the evenings when she was with him. She left explicit instructions with the school to make sure that he got on to the bus in the evenings, and off it in the mornings. She contemplated giving up her job, but didn't, partly to save her sanity. She could see herself pacing up and down outside the school all too clearly, watching, waiting for him to try and escape into the woods.

And Marcus watched her: in the evenings after his bath when they used to talk and sometimes do things together. She sensed that he was looking for an opening and was prepared to wait and wait and wait until one came along.

Chapter 23

It was a normal day when it happened; a normal day apart from Caroline's growing sense that a slow strong pressure was trying to squeeze her from her skin like a pea from a pod; a normal day apart from a phone call from Marcus's teacher the night before asking her to call or come in, to discuss a rather worrying matter regarding her son; a normal day apart from the rain that drove in from the east under vast rolling clouds, rattling on the office windows like grapeshot and running down in a thick, opaque layer. In the end rain was the factor that pulled the rope that closed the sack, but first Caroline had to call the school.

It was like this, Miss Dunlop said. Basically, Caroline was told, there had been some playground teasing in which she had to admit Tommy Robson played a leading role, he being large and low in self-esteem, and the gang which Tommy led had decided to pick on young Marcus. Why? Well, it was hard to get to the bottom of it but it seemed that he had been talking about magical powers that he had together with certain friends who lived in the woods. Tommy Robson and his friends had been told of this, and had cornered Marcus. The whole affair had been over in seconds. He had retaliated and then, apparently, told Tommy Robson he would get him.

Now while she was sure that he wouldn't – er – get him, she wanted Caroline to be clear on two points. One, that the incident was in no way typical – the playground bullying, that was. That didn't excuse it by any means, goodness, no, but she was concerned about one or two other points that she would rather discuss in a face-to-face situation. Perhaps Caroline could come in and they could discuss it. And Caroline agreed. And so the day passed and the streets turned to rivers and the car park to a swimming pool and it all seemed rather appropriate.

*
150

Caroline was watching the clock and the traffic crawl up the High Street, water spraying in grey wings on to the pavements, when Maggie came up beside her.

'Got your wellies?' she asked.

'No, but at least it's Friday,' Caroline answered. 'I don't mind getting wet on Friday. Best be off.'

She turned off the computer and picked up her shopping.

'Good weekend,' Maggie said, looked through the window and snorted.

Caroline picked up her coat and was passing Carstairs's office when he called her through the door.

'Can you do something for me?' he asked.

Caroline said: 'I'm just on my way out. I need to catch a bus.' She had dressed in a hurry that morning and a button had popped off her blouse. As she talked, her fingers moved to pinch the fabric shut. Carstairs noted the gesture with a tiny widening of his eyes and glanced up at the clock on the wall. 'You work until three-thirty?' It was twenty-eight minutes past. 'This will only take a couple of minutes and it's got to go off today.' He shot his cuffs and folded his hands behind his head. 'Look, I've got a meeting down the road at four-fifteen. If you type this letter, I'll drop you off and you'll still beat the bus. How about it? You can do it on my computer.'

Caroline shrugged. It sounded perfectly reasonable but it had the smell of a set-up. Carstairs had a bad reputation, but in all honesty she had not noticed any excessively lewd behaviour from him either in the office or while taking the lift he gave her every morning. In fact, if anything, he was more insinuating in the office, and that made Caroline think that he had a confidence problem rather than anything else. From the odd comment he had passed during the morning run, which was normally a silent duel between his after-shave and the perfume she had started wearing in self-defence, she had built up a picture of a shy, rather lonely man who went walking in the Lake District every summer. Anyway, it would soon stop being an issue because she had decided to drive to work in future now that Tom had offered to go halves on a new second-hand car, like the perfect ex-husband he was.

Caroline printed the letter off and took it across to Carstairs to sign. He was on the phone and mouthed 'Wait' to her.

Caroline waited, then put her coat on. She glanced at her watch. At this rate she would be late for Marcus and she couldn't remember if he had taken his front door key (never yet used) this morning. She gestured to Carstairs impatiently. He looked surprised, then angry, and Caroline suddenly realised that she had just acted like a mother rather than a secretary, a real person rather than an office person. At last Carstairs rose, smiled at her stiffly and said he would be with her in a minute. He closed the door behind him and Caroline heard Simone and Jackie walk past. Then Carstairs came back in, picked up an umbrella and ushered her out. He didn't have a briefcase. Caroline wished she had said something to the other secretaries.

The rain slackened as they got into the car, then came on again with new intensity. 'Don't worry, we'll get you there in time,' Carstairs said as the car stopped in a traffic jam. The windows were steamed up and it was unpleasantly humid. He loosened his tie with a crooked finger. Caroline flapped her blouse at the neck. Carstairs shot her a glance sideways and downwards. Caroline took an irritated breath and without looking at him was aware that he had glanced at the deep V between her breasts where the seat belt cut across her, and had blushed. According to the clock on the dashboard Marcus would be home by now. At this rate it would be quicker to walk. The car was so quiet she could hear Carstairs breathing and the tiny click of saliva as he opened his mouth.

'So, thought any more about the summer holidays then?' he asked. 'How do you cope on your own with a child?'

'You cope,' Caroline said.

'Where will the two of you go?'

'Oh, Marcus will probably go off with his father,' Caroline said. 'Somewhere.'

'What about you?'

'I'll just stick around.'

'You must have a bit of spare cash now you're working. Why don't you get away?'

'It all seems to go,' Caroline said. 'On this and that.'

'This, that and a bit of the other?' he said. Caroline inhaled sharply.

'Sorry,' he said. 'Out of order there. I forgot you don't like that sort of talk.'

'No one likes that sort of talk. It's hardly surprising that you've got a bad reputation.'

Without thinking Caroline had adopted a normal speaking voice. She might have been rebuking Marcus. It worked on Carstairs.

'I'm not so bad,' he said. 'Really. People talk – I expect I have got a reputation. It's just, I haven't found a way to get through.'

What is it about cars that makes men get confessional? Caroline thought. Tom had confessed to seeing Marina in the middle of a trip to visit friends in Northamptonshire. Marcus had wanted to confess and she had not let him. Because Carstairs's fringe had flopped down more or less square across his forehead, he looked like an unhappy boy again. Caroline said: 'You should relax. Try and be less of a boss and more of a person.'

Carstairs laughed knowingly. 'Oh, no. I've seen men go down that route. Try and be friends with everyone. I'm a boss and I – '

'People do what the boss says because he's the boss, whether they respect him or not,' she said. 'You think anyone can risk losing a job these days? If you're human, they will respect you as well.'

The traffic began to move again. 'Sorry for dragging you into the car,' he said.

'You want people to think we're having an affair,' she said. It had not occurred to her before. 'Oh my God, look at the time.'

'That's not – '

'Crap! I've just been too stupid to notice. Jesus Christ, even my son thinks that.'

As they drove into the Close Caroline saw a dark figure looking out of the sitting-room window.

She waved as she tried to find the catch, and as usual found the ash tray. When she finally located the door handle and pushed, the door stuck. Her coat had jammed in the lock. She twisted round but was impeded by the seat belt. Carstairs said: 'Here, I'll do that.' He leant across to the seat belt, and started fiddling with it because Caroline was putting pressure on it. She put her back to the door, fell backwards as it opened suddenly and grabbed the nearest thing, which happened to be his tie. For a second she hung half out of the car, as Carstairs fell towards her, and she was staring upside down at the sitting-room window, with Carstairs scrabbling at her. She saw Marcus's mouth open in shock. She waved to him, just to show him that she was all right, tried to smile and mouth 'Help!', then screamed as Carstairs dug his elbow into her belly. He backed off and then pulled her none too gently into the car. When she looked at the window again, Marcus had gone.

'Good heavens,' he said.

'God knows what Marcus must have thought. I'd better go and put him straight.'

'He'll know it was an accident.'

'You don't know Marcus at the moment.'

'Better tidy up a bit if you're worried.' He looked stolidly ahead while she pulled her blouse down and ran her fingers through her hair.

She opened the front door and called to Marcus. There was no answer. She ran through the house, upstairs first. It was not until she got to the kitchen that she saw the open door, and beyond it the gate to the woods, gaping.

The grass soaked her feet before she was even across the lawn. The forest smelled green. Rain smacked from leaf to leaf to earth. The place was hissing at her, all green and shadowy. She called Marcus's name but the shouts were deadened by the rain and the damp. She looked up and down the path, and called twice more.

What did he want? What was he trying to prove?

She yelped as Tom put a hand on her shoulder. 'I let myself in,' he said. 'You look a mess. What's up?'

'I think Marcus misread a situation and has gone belting off into the woods to make a point.'

'Why would he make his point there of all places? I know you've been worried ever since that murder but aren't you overreacting?'

'Oh – ' But to explain anything at all, she would have to explain everything. She shook her head. 'You wouldn't understand.'

'You're on his back, Caroline. All the time. Back off and he'll be all right.'

'You don't know anything.'

'Here we go again,' he said.

She bit back her anger. 'You wait in the house. I'm putting a coat on to look for him.'

Tom looked as if he might protest. Caroline left him and walked out into the rain.

She got lost in the woods. Paths she thought were familiar resisted her, twisting and turning. Thickets moved in the gloom. Brambles and nettles sprang up to hurt her. The third time she found herself on the path at the bottom of her garden she gave up.

There was a note from Tom on the kitchen table: 'Marcus came back. Very upset. Call!'

She called Tom to speak to Marcus and got Marina. Marcus and his father were out, she said, buying Häagen-Dazs. Marina sounded sniffy. She would ask Marcus if he wanted to call Caroline but couldn't promise anything.

She ran herself a deep bath, emptying half a bottle of herbal bubble bath into the water, and soaked luxuriously for half an hour. She stood up, reached for a towel and blacked out for a second, darkness spinning in from the edges of her eyes. Stayed in too long, she thought. Her skin was pink, and her fingers wrinkled. The room seemed slightly dimmer than it was before, as if the voltage in the grid had just dropped a fraction.

In the hall outside she paused. It was cold out there compared to the steamy fug of the bathroom – the temperature must have dropped. She walked to the bedroom dressed in a towel and put on comfort clothes: an old Island of Majorca T-shirt, huge baggy sweater and ancient jeans worn to soft strands over the knees. The touch of old clothes comforted her.

Then she went downstairs.

And frowned.

It was nothing specific, but the light seemed dirty as if something had got into it.

She shivered and hugged the sweater to her, switched lights on and the window suddenly sprang into blackness, a glittering dark mirror. She watched herself walk towards it. Cold air wavered around it. She cupped her hands against the glass, peering through. Outside in the garden mist was rising from the lawn. Beyond, the trees had solidified to a dripping wall. She hugged herself, bolted the back door, opened a tin of Heinz soup and set it on the ring.

If it didn't get warmer, she thought, she'd put the fire on. The air was clearer at the front of the house. She drew the curtains and flicked on the telly. *Blind Date*. She fell back on the sofa and watched a boy and a girl have a miserable time on a golf course somewhere green and wet.

'Ooh, pets,' Cilla said, 'we packed you all the way off to sunny Spain, and what did it do? It rained on the plain. Did you find plenty to get up to inside?'

'He played snooker,' the girl said.

'I must admit that I did,' the man said proudly.

Caroline remembered the soup. She walked back into the kitchen. The gas flame was a blue glow in the mist. Amazed, she closed the ventilation fan. The warmth immediately began to eat away at the mist. In seconds, it seemed, the kitchen was clear, and the soup was boiling. She laid a place at the table, broke off a length of elastic French bread, slopped some wine into a tumbler and sat down to eat.

The phone went suddenly. It made her jump. When she picked it up, all she could hear was a deep, dark electronic roaring. Why did they call it white noise? This was black noise. Space would sound like this between the high singing of the stars. She called the operator who said reassuringly that if it were someone trying to get through they would try again, but most likely it was a fault on the line and would right itself in no time. The phone rang to reveal eerie silence four times in the following ten minutes. In the end Caroline unplugged it at the wall. The TV chattered and flashed inanely and comfortingly.

She closed her eyes, just for a second, then for another second, then for another, and then blinked awake.

The sense that the forest had been resisting her had been real. The forest, or the things in it, had been deliberately preventing her from penetrating further. There was something she was not meant to see.

She stood up, feeling like a half-filled sack. Her shoulders were hunched, her head drooping. She folded her arms under her breasts and walked upstairs. On the desk in Marcus's room there was a gap where his Nintendo should have been, a clean space surrounded by the clutter of childhood.

She called Tom's house. The line was bad. His voice was faint, diluted and blurred.

'I want to speak to Marcus.'

'He's watching TV. He's very upset. Really, he's only just settled.'

Caroline closed her eyes. Grey thoughts, stiff shadows, moved relentlessly across her mind.

'Ask him where his Nintendo is.'

'That's the point. He says it's been stolen.'

'Stolen?'

'Yes. He came back. You weren't in. The house was cold and dark. The back door was open and the Nintendo was gone. He was in tears after he saw you wrestling with loverboy. He got upset and ran away. I mean, for fuck's sake, Caroline, if it's not enough –'

'He's lying'.

'He's what?'

'He's lying. Ask him where he took the Nintendo. Ask him –'

Tom's voice came back, fainter and fainter.

'The line's breaking up, Caroline. Caroline? Caroline?'

Then nothing. Only a faint hissing that could have been the sound of wind on leaves.

It was all wrong. Her hands were freezing. She was freezing. There was a cold, rotten smell in the room, like the smell of an old, broken fridge. Across from her the television was a coloured, flickering glow. While she had been talking the room had filled with mist. She reached for the throw on the back of the sofa and draped it over her shoulders. The lamps and overhead light glowed yellow in the pale hollows they had burned. She knelt and turned on the gas fire. Flames popped into life around the fake logs. Freakish weather. Freakish evening. She snapped the television off. The silence closed around her like a muffled shroud, heavy and thick. She turned it back on quickly.

Then she looked at the window. The fog was liquid and mobile. Tendrils formed, twisted, reformed against the glass. Soft rounded shapes bellied and billowed. She walked to the front window. It was there too, so thick it had almost blanked out the streetlight only fifteen feet away from her door. She could just see its vague, pinkish glow, a blob of dull candy floss.

157

The room was warming quickly, the air clearing. Where does fog go? she wondered. The answer was on the window. It was misted by moisture. Streaks were already running down it. The walls too – simple, white-emulsioned walls – were wet. They shone in patches with the condensation.

Never had condensation before, Caroline thought. You get condensation when the house has been too thoroughly sealed against draughts. She placed a hand near the angle of the window. The air was appreciably cooler there, but it was still. She went to the front door and knelt. The draught there sometimes lifted the letters off the door mat.

Nothing. Still, damp, freezing air.

The damp was getting into her. She went to the sitting room and huddled in front of the fire. She never saw the point in these fake gas fires. The heat didn't seem to travel from them, not like a real fire which could burn down to that warm, glowing mound of ember and ash.

Then in the silence she heard a sound. It was unmistakable and it didn't seem so much to travel to her as be delivered. It was the creak and the snick of the latch to the forest gate being tried.

She froze. She had to be wrong. No, there it was again. Of course, it was bolted. She exhaled, unaware that she had been holding her breath.

And then came the noises she had been dreading: the snick of the latch again followed by the odd, characteristic boom as the gate was pushed and burst free of the frame.

She thought of the door but could not move. She felt her skin tighten; her hair rise in a slow, stealthy rustle up the back of her neck and on to the crown of her head. The skin of her face dragged her mouth open. She saw her reflection, dim and distant in the grey glass.

A new sound. The creak of the swing. She imagined something walking across the grass, surely, confidently . . . in the mist.

And something compelled her to watch. She reached a hand out to wipe a streak of condensation from the glass; her grey arm reached back at her in the reflection. She brushed her hand across, withdrew it.

On the other side of the glass, the arm stayed where it was. A small grey hand stroked the glass. It moved across and where it moved, dew seemed to coat the outside of the window.

Caroline tried to run but her limbs simply would not move. She did not know if she wanted to move for fear of attracting whatever there was behind the hand, behind the arm.

A thin finger pointed.

It performed four strokes. A vertical. An oblique down. An oblique up. A vertical down.

M

Caroline felt her brain freeze. Another mark, and another.

A

R

C

U

S

The letters were reversed, so she could read them, and slightly shaky. Caroline stayed stock still. She felt a presence behind the hand, the presence of whatever was out there, hidden in the thick mist. She closed her eyes, desperately trying to stop her legs from trembling. If I stay still it can't see me. If I stay –

Something touched her mind. It was like a cold beam of grey light; light the colour of dirty old snow. It touched and seemed to lighten. Behind it she felt a quickening of interest. Excitement. Familiarity.

thank you, marcus

The voice was totally unexpected. It came from behind the window. A still voice. Patchy somehow – loud, then soft, then loud. There was a pause.

we'll find you

Again that sense of searching. Puzzlement now. A big, unexpected why.

and play

Caroline screamed and suddenly it felt her. Caroline could not understand how she knew the difference, only that there was one. The mist swirled. Threatened to break. She closed her eyes and screamed again. The presence retreated, then like a dog intent on a meal came back. It touched her, it felt her, and

159

then, overwhelmingly, it needed her. The feeling pierced like a shaft of heat and freed her.

She ran from the room. She heard a tapping on the glass, then a booming. The little grey fist was clenched.

She was in the hall. Found car keys on the stand. Pulled the door open. It resisted then came with a hiss, as if a vacuum had been released. The fog swirled to reveal the car. Without looking back she ran down the stairs, ran to her car and screamed away in first gear until the corner, sump grinding and sparking off the sleeping policemen.

Behind her the fog dispersed as silently as it had come. A few curtains in the Close twitched. An owl called and lulled the night to sleep again.

Chapter 24

It was the first set of traffic lights that brought her down from the cold height of terror. She drove towards them so fast that a car approaching sounded its horn. She looked up, saw the red light and instinctively slammed on the brakes. The car dug its nose down, fishtailed slightly and stopped ten feet over the stop line. Get a grip on yourself! Traction. That was what she needed. Control. A driver passing across her pointed a finger at his temple and revolved it, then said something smug to the woman beside him who looked at Caroline as if she hated her. Caroline swore at both of them.

Mad. Women drivers ... Mad women drivers. Mad woman. She kept her eyes fixed on the lights. 'Red light spells danger'. The line of a song tripped idiotically round her head. Who had had a hit with that? Billy Ocean. One of those songs that you only ever remembered the first line to, then it was all nana na naaaana. How could a red light spell danger? Spell Marcus.

Grey finger on the glass spelling Marcus.

The gate in the fence swinging open.

The swing creaking.

Marcus, won't you come out to play?

The lights changed. She floored the accelerator, feeling the back wheels slide, grip, push the nose to the middle of the road, slip again as she wrenched the wheel away, over-correct, then she was away, taking a pelican crossing on amber at forty, keeping an eye open for police cars since the station was down a side road somewhere near.

Out of the High Street. Scrubby common land, criss-crossed with paths and filthy with dog shit on either side. The forest a dark wall ahead. Cars flashed her. She flicked on the headlights as the road dived into the tunnel of trees. Tom's cottage was a mile down this long, straight Roman road that split the forest in half, then off to the right. There. Then half a mile. Left down a track. White fence posts nestling in a thick hedge. She swung the car into the narrow drive. He'd regravelled it; the wheels sank; stones spat like hail against the wheel arches; the car slithered and lurched as if it were on snow. A hundred yards between high hedges, and there it was, home sweet fucking home for them, lights warm on the new pebbles, a neat little dream cottage with a thatched roof, roses making red splashes round the old front door and black timbers patterning the pebble dashed walls.

She ran round the back. The kitchen was a modern extension. She could see Tom's head bobbing as he leant over the sink to scrub something. Caroline threw open the back door. He looked up, amazed, faintly absurd in his apron and pink Marigolds.

'Where is he? Where's Marcus?' Her voice was surprisingly quiet but shook as she spoke.

'Caroline. What is it? What do you mean?'

'I need to talk to him!'

'Talk to him? Caroline, it's gone ten.'

'Is he asleep?'

'Marina's reading to him. Caroline!'

He stepped in front of her, blocking her way through the door, and put a hand on her shoulder.

'Now what's all this about?'

'There's something in the forest! There's something that – I don't know – wants him! Let me see him!'

'You're talking nonsense.'

'He knows it. He knows more than he's letting on!'

'Caroline, I insist you calm down. You're over-excited.'

'Over-excited? I've just been sitting at home when this mist comes down all around the house and a grey hand comes out of it and writes his fucking name on the window!'

'Mist? Grey hand? Caroline, have you been drinking?'

'Stop thinking that I'm upset! Stop telling me that! Just let me see my son! There's something in the woods. It knows Marcus and Marcus knows it!'

'No.' He pushed her firmly back. She grabbed his wrist and bit. Tom yelled and struck out at her. She half-fell, pushed herself up off the floor and launched herself at him so fast that he had no time to react. He caught the small of his back against the edge of the sink, groaned, and sank to the ground. She threw open the door. Standing outside, eyes wide, were Marcus and Marina, curiosity and surprise in their expressions. They must have heard her shouting.

She took a step towards them. 'Marcus,' she said. 'Marcus.'

He took a step back. She saw that he was wearing pyjamas she did not recognise. Marina put a hand on his shoulder.

'Marcus,' Caroline said, 'it's me. It's Mummy.' She put a hand out, as if she were trying to lure a shy animal.

Marcus stepped back. He pressed into Marina, then looked backwards and up. At Marina.

'Marcus, where did you go in the woods this evening?'

His eyes strayed from her eyes to her mouth. He screamed: 'No! NO! Leave me alone! Don't let her hurt me!'

He turned and buried his face in Marina's belly. She clutched it automatically and protectively.

'Marcus, it's all right. It's all right.' She heard a muffled wail rise from him. Marina was looking horrified. She said to Caroline, 'What on earth's going on? Why are you frightening Marcus? What have you done to Tom?'

'He's got to tell me what he's been doing!' Caroline shouted.

'What are you talking about? Leave him alone. Leave him alone. Can't you see that he's terrified?'

Caroline grabbed Marcus by the shoulder and turned him round. His eyes stared out at her from a white mask of a face.

'Marcus, did you make a wish tonight? When you saw me fall out of the car?'

'Caroline, honestly. What were you doing falling out of cars?'

'I think it might have looked to Marcus as if a man was attacking me. I asked Marcus to help. I want to know what he did. The Nintendo's gone, darling.'

Marcus began to wail and snuffle. He threw his arms round Marina's waist.

'I didn't. I didn't. Mummy was with her boyfriend. I was scared!'

'You were scared by what? Darling, I know you were trying to help me. But what did you do?'

She was dimly aware of music in the background. The News

at Ten was just ending and the local news would be on next.

'Marcus! Tell me!'

'I wanted to prove to you – I wanted to show you – You said I was a liar! I'm not! Marina, I'm not.'

'What did you do?'

'You said I was a liar. I wanted to show you that – '

'Get out of this house,' Marina said. 'Get out. You're not fit to be a mother!'

Caroline tried to make Marcus look at her. 'Marcus. Sweetheart. Tell me what you've done. Tell me what you've met out there. Tell me, precious. Tell me how you wanted to prove that you weren't a liar. I'm not going to be angry. Mummy's not going to be angry. But I must know.'

She felt his back and tried to turn him again. In response he buried his face even deeper in Marina's belly and began to wail piteously. Tom emerged from the kitchen. He had wrapped a drying-up cloth around his hand and was walking with difficulty. He walked past Caroline and stood by Marina. He put a hand on her shoulder and another on Marcus's.

'What have you done to my family?' Marina asked. 'What are you trying to do?'

'It's time you went, Caroline. It's time you left us,' Tom said.

Their calmness, the solid front they were presenting almost finished her. She felt something give inside her and suddenly she was too weary to react. Too weary, too strung out, and oddly, too convinced that she was right.

She looked from Tom to Marina to Marcus. Only Marcus dropped his eyes.

'Last chance, darling,' she said.

'Take him up to bed, darling,' Tom said to Marina. 'There's something I need to say to Caroline.'

Chapter 25

Willis was on his second whisky and fourth chapter of the latest Spencer thriller. There was music coming from the next street, so loud that the bass was quite clearly audible, pumping solidly into the room and making the air shake like jelly. The newsagent had told him that squatters had moved into an empty house that was awaiting conversion to flats. This must be their housewarming. He pitied the poor policemen who would be sent, inevitably, by some irate neighbour (why were neighbours always irate in reports?) to do something about it.

The phone rang. He let it ring until the answering machine cut in but when he heard Caroline's voice he picked it up without thinking.

Twenty minutes later he was sitting in Tom and Marina's sitting room. Caroline was looking wild. Tom, whom he remembered from Kingsmeade Close as radiating smug composure, was grim and white-faced. He was nursing a hand that was bound in a rough bandage.

'Well, how can I help?' Willis asked.

'My wife is settling my son upstairs,' Tom said. 'Now might be a good time to talk. My ex-wife is under the impression that you can explain, or justify, her behaviour.' Willis looked polite and quizzical. Tom continued, 'She came charging in here, rambling the most obscene nonsense about Marcus being involved in the death of a man. Well, she's explained that a bit more clearly now. Apparently Marcus was watching when Caroline fell out of the car of a man who was giving her a lift. According to her, it might have looked as if he was attacking her. From what I can gather she thinks Marcus has made a wish that this man come to some harm.'

Willis hid his shock and resisted the temptation to look at

Caroline. Either she had come round to his way of thinking, or she knew more than she had been letting on. He thought very fast. He had told her that he had been suspended. The question was, had she told Tom?

'Sergeant Willis is actively involved in an investigation,' she began, then paused. 'He came to me because he thought that Marcus was in some danger. I'm afraid I rather shouted at him, didn't I, Sergeant? I was wrong. I think he can help us.'

'What do you mean, help us?' Tom said angrily. 'What investigation? How could Marcus possibly be involved? And why are you bringing the police in on this, Caroline? If there's any sort of legal question, I demand that we get a solicitor immediately.'

Willis waited until Tom had had his say, then tried to think of a way to shut him up. He just wanted Caroline on her own, so he could talk to her. 'Of course – that is your right,' he said. 'So far I've gone rather out on a limb to keep this from becoming too official, but if you want this matter put on a more formal basis, then I would suggest a solicitor, and of course a social worker, if you desire. I can easily furnish you with – '

'Now wait a minute,' Tom said. 'What's all this about Social Services? I didn't say – '

'I suggest you listen,' Willis said. 'At this stage, we do not know where the investigation is leading. All I want to make clear is that while your former wife may have overreacted, her behaviour does not seem quite as strange to me as it does to you. Are you with me so far?'

The man nodded. He looked exhausted.

'This is not the time or place to go into matters in any detail. All I can do is repeat that she is under quite understandable strain, and I would hope, given the situation, and the sensitivities of the matter in hand, that you would give us your full cooperation. At this stage, we are anxious to keep Marcus out of the frame as much as we can. I'm sure you agree that having managed to achieve this so far, interference from outside by any other party would be undesirable.'

'You're keeping me in the dark,' Tom said. 'That's what you're saying. Why?' He looked directly at Willis. 'What's in it for you?'

166

Suddenly he looked from Willis to Caroline, and back again. 'You two are – '

Before he could continue, Caroline broke in. 'It's helping Marcus,' she said.

'I don't understand,' Tom repeated. 'Oh God, get out. I don't pretend to know what's going on. I don't want to. Marcus stays here tonight. I won't involve anyone else and you can call me in the morning. I'll talk to him first thing and try to get to the bottom of it. Now leave!'

Outside Willis cut short Caroline's thanks. 'We're going to talk. Will you follow me home?'

She nodded.

They drove back without incident, Willis watching her lights in his rear-view mirror, half expecting her to swing off behind him and disappear. If she did, he had made up his mind, he would not follow her.

Back at his flat he waited until she had looked around the room, sniffed it as it were, before he said: 'Well, did I do whatever it was you wanted?'

He tried to read her face. During the drive she had obviously recovered her composure. She fiddled with a curtain, then pulled it firmly across the window. It seemed to him that she had reached some sort of decision.

'I was at my wits' end,' she said. 'Tom sent Marina and Marcus out of the room and said he was going to get a court order and go for full custody. I had to have someone there who didn't think I was completely mad.'

'Just a liar,' Willis said. 'The other day it was you telling me that I was mad.'

'I thought you could survive,' she said simply. 'I can't talk any more. I came here to thank you, but you can't get in any deeper. I can't let you.'

'You can't let me? What do you mean by that? You think you're the expert now?'

Caroline shrugged.

'You've known about this all along, haven't you?' Willis said. 'Why didn't you tell me?'

'I had my reasons. I can handle it.'

'Crap! You haven't handled a thing. For all I know, we could

167

have saved at least one life if you hadn't kept all this to yourself. I don't think you can handle this at all.'

'I have to,' she said simply.

'Look, you've been dealing with this for too long on your own – '

'What do you mean by that?' she snapped.

He was surprised by the sudden violence in her voice. Her face too suddenly sharpened. What was the significance of what he had just said?

'What do you think I mean?'

He watched her wrestle her feelings under control. As she closed her eyes, deepened her breaths, seemed to retreat into herself, he realised that he was watching a routine. The colour came back to her face. She nodded once, twice to herself, then looked at Willis.

'All right,' she said. 'All right. I'll talk. Don't interrupt. This evening Marcus made another wish. He left his Nintendo at the tree.' Then she lost her composure again. She buried her face in her hands: 'Oh God, oh God, oh God.'

She told him about the incident with Carstairs, and how she had gone straight out into the forest to look for Marcus. She was talking differently, relieving herself of a burden. He felt a rush of hope.

'And you think he might have made a wish – '

'He said he was trying to prove something to me.'

'Prove what?'

'It's what you guessed. I think Marcus wished for Carstairs to be punished, like he wished for me to get a job and for someone to take care of Tailor. Let me just talk, don't interrupt. The night before I went for my interview, Marcus asked me if I really wanted the job. Of course I said I did, but it was like he was checking, you know, to see if what he was about to do was worth it. The afternoon of the interview, the day I was late getting to him at school and he walked off into the forest, he was making a wish. When I asked why he had taken off like that, he said he was only trying to help. I took that to mean that he was walking some of the way home. He didn't deny it; he must have been feeling a bit odd about it himself. He meant that he had wished me to get the job. He got his wish. Dana Watkins was killed; her mother was supposed to have my job.'

'He admitted this?'

'He told me. I told him he was wrong. Things like that couldn't happen. Tonight he did something to prove it.'

'And you think he wished for this man Carstairs to be punished,' Willis said slowly. He was waiting for the full impact of her words to sink in but he felt like a stone in a river. The sense of what she was saying parted around him and flowed past. Evidence. There was no evidence, he thought, but then realised that there was just no evidence of the sort that could be tested and recognised by others. The sort of evidence he was used to dealing with, that brought you out of the world of doubt and supposition into the world of facts. This sort of evidence was the opposite: the more you knew, the further you moved from reality. He had memories of eyes in the woods, children that floated, a man raining to earth, in short a story so impossible that it defied light and reason. So far, it was this very sense of unreality that had protected him.

But now Caroline Waters had exposed the story's awful logic. Things were moving, things were happening. The story had its own, slow, cold momentum.

'Do you know where this man lives?'

'Ongar.'

Willis handed her a telephone directory. 'Call him. If he's all right, he should be in.'

Caroline dialled but handed the phone over to Willis. 'I can't talk to him.'

A nervous voice answered the phone with a sleepy 'Yes?'

'Hold the line please.'

He put a hand over the mouthpiece. 'What's the name of the company?' he asked Caroline. She told him.

He spoke into the telephone again. 'Is this Mr Carstairs of Smith's Car Parts.'

'Yes.'

Willis put the phone down. 'He's fine. So far.'

Caroline closed her eyes. 'He's away from the forest. I'm sure that makes him safe. Oh God, I'm so relieved.' She exhaled. 'What do we do now?'

'We have a drink.'

He poured two whiskies. She swallowed, paused for a while, then looked straight at him.

'And now?' she said.

'As I see it, there are two options. One is to accept it and try and fight it; the other is to go.'

'What?' Caroline said dully.

'Go. Just leave.'

'It's not that simple.'

'It's a lot simpler than staying. Clear out, both of you. Go far away and see what happens.'

'But –'

'Because apart from anything else, Marcus made another wish tonight. And if Carstairs is all right, and stays all right, it means he wished for something else.'

'This is never going to end, is it? This filthy bloody mess. How can we sit here and discuss it?'

'I don't know,' Willis said. 'But we do, and we'll find an answer.'

He saw her slump. She yawned hugely, and looked around the flat.

'It's like a nest at the top of a tree,' she said.

'Look – I've got a sofa bed,' Willis said. 'You look dead on your feet and I can't imagine that you really want to go back to Kingsmeade Close.'

'No. I could try for a hotel.'

'Don't be daft. It's no trouble for me. Anyway, as an ex-copper, I can safely say that those whiskies have put you well over the limit.'

She tried to read his face. He looked slightly awkward as he spoke. 'Haven't got a toothbrush,' she said.

'Got a spare,' Willis said. 'When you haven't got a job you do things like buy spare toothbrushes. I've even got a back-up tube of toothpaste.'

'I'm very grateful,' Caroline said. She stood up. 'For everything.'

'Look, I've just got to move some furniture around. Why don't you go and wash.'

'Let me help,' Caroline said.

She grabbed a small table stacked with books and moved towards a bookcase. The stack of paperbacks toppled to the floor. She bent to pick them up.

170

'Oh, don't worry. Just put them by the wall there.' Willis grunted as he moved the sofa further into a corner to give it more space in front.

'It's all right,' Caroline said. She knelt, and began to stack the books against the wall, then gave a little gasp. From the other side of the room Willis saw her face was white and shocked. She was staring at a book that she had just rearranged. Willis could not tell which one it was.

'All right?' he asked. Instinct made him disguise his interest in the book and look at her.

'Yes, yes. Just fine. Just a twinge in my back.'

'Need a hand?'

'No! No, I mean thanks. I'm fine.'

Willis bent and moved two cushions. He saw her slip the book from the top of the pile to the bottom, furtively. He caught a glimpse of a black spine. A reddish cover with the title in the middle. The problem was that he bought so many books, second-hand paperbacks especially. He collected some, like early Len Deightons, others he consumed and then recycled. That pile on the table had mostly come from a small junk shop a couple of miles away that specialised in house clearances and usually had a 10p paperback bin by the stack of old records.

The bed unfolded, he pulled a duvet, a couple of pillows and some linen from the airing cupboard in the hall and put them on the mattress. She had recovered although she looked a bit green around the gills.

'All yours,' he said. 'Anything you need?'

She gave a tense smile and shook her head.

'I'm fine. Thanks.'

'Well, there's plenty to read.' He made a gesture that took in the end wall that was one big bookcase, but could have included the pile of books she had stacked.

Pain danced into her eyes. Willis regretted what he'd said. None of his business, he was sure of that. Unless he made it his business.

Before he left the room he turned to her and said: 'You know, nothing you believe would hold up in a court of law. No one would ever find out either.' She nodded. 'But now I know I'm going to have to stop it.'

'I know.'

'You're very brave.'

She shook her head. 'If I were brave I'd do it on my own,' she said.

'Have you any idea what?'

She shook her head dumbly. 'Just so long as we save Marcus,' she said.

As he was undressing it came to him. The book he suspected of upsetting her had a red cover with a black and white snapshot laid on to it at an angle. The picture on the front had been of a young girl in a cheap, old-fashioned dress, socks and cardigan. The picture had been blurred and oddly cut, a group photo perhaps, where effect was more important than detail. Willis had picked the book up because the title had interested him, and he occasionally read true crime books, but it was a bit of a busman's holiday. He had bought this one because he thought the title was humorously camp: *Kids that Kill*.

Chapter 26

Sitting in his car, on Harris Drive once more, with his buttocks sweating against the plastic seat and the sun burning his left ear, he had a very clear picture of himself: naked, bruised, blind, trying to get out of a maze. But every time he felt, or thought he felt, freedom, a burning ram would piledrive into his soft body, knocking him back and so disorientating him that when he picked himself up again and staggered off, he was no clearer which direction to try. He simply knew he had to, and now, after everything Caroline had told him, more than ever. And that was why he was sitting in his car on Harris Drive, again, watching the Tailor house, again, trying to remember exactly what it was that Mrs Tailor had said to him when she had lured him away from the stake-out.

They don't understand? No one understands? Something like that. Typical words of a besotted mother – that was what he'd thought at first. 'Everyone's out of step but my Johnny. If people didn't pick on him so, he wouldn't have to go out raping teenage girls.'

Except Mrs Tailor had not been like that. He had done some research on the case. She had said nothing before the trial, had stared at her son with 'unflinching inscrutability' during it (according to the *Telegraph*'s courtroom drama critic), and afterwards had released a statement to the press which stated that, while she loved her son as a Christian and a mother, his sin was so abhorrent to her (her words) that she would have turned him in to the authorities without a thought had she known what he had done.

Hate the sin and love the sinner: a Sunday school phrase that stayed with him. How did that square with her shouting that no one understood? Had her love for the sinner begun to soften her hatred for the sin? Since his parole Tailor had lived with her. He

173

had become a Christian in prison and been re-baptised. He went to chapel every Sunday and Willis had confirmed this with the leader of the congregation who said it had been a test and a measure of their faith to allow him to worship, but they had emerged the other side with their faith untarnished and burning brighter.

So what had happened to convince Mrs Tailor that her son was innocent of Dana's death at least?

He glanced in his wing mirror. The quiet suburban street felt empty of everything but the sunlight; the sunlight and a slight haze. Cars drowsed like cows, drenched still with dew. A single sycamore seed dropped like a helicopter on to the car's bonnet and skidded off. A figure appeared right at the end of the street, miniaturised in the wing mirror. As it grew, Willis's heart gave a leap. It was her. He'd had a good hunch. There she was, walking back from the shops at nine o'clock in the morning, when there were fewest people around, and the few who were shopping would be too busy to notice who she was.

He watched her with an odd frisson. She was a figure he recognised but had half-forgotten, a figure from his childhood and a type that had all but disappeared: angular, hard-faced; hair chestnut-orange and tightly curled under her plain head-scarf; stockings the colour of artificial limbs; ugly, heavy shoes, and a string shopping bag which bulged with brown paper bags of veg and white paper rolls of meat.

She looked neither to left nor right, and passed so close to the car that Willis, by tilting the wing mirror with the knob on the inside, could see the face powder dusting the fine hairs on her upper lip.

He waited until she was up the steps to her front door and had taken the house keys from her shopping bag, then he got out of the car as quickly and quietly as he knew how, had a foot on the bottom step as she pushed the door open, was halfway up as she stooped to pick up the shopping bag, with half his body inside the house before she had turned to close it.

As she opened her mouth to shout, or scream, he said: 'It's all right, I believe you about your son,' and turned and closed the door behind him.

He stood back, his shoulders heaving from the dash to the house and from anticipation. Mrs Tailor closed her eyes and looked away. She said: 'You're the one who's been suspended,' and her face twisted into an expression of pure agony. 'You make me sick!'

Watching the hatred cross her face was like watching a cardboard box catch fire and burn. He said: 'I couldn't do a thing about it. I arrived too late.'

The silence was measured by the repeated ticking of a clock somewhere unseen in the house. Mrs Tailor came to a decision.

'Say your piece, and then I beg you in the name of God, go.' She bent her head and nodded him into the front room.

Brown-patterned wallpaper was sandwiched between high skirting-boards and a heavy picture rail. A sofa and two chairs were arranged around an empty tiled fireplace. From a heavy ceiling rose hung a bulb and a white plastic shade. The carpet was faintly patterned with pink and green, brushed to oblivion. They sat opposite each other on either side of the fireplace, Mrs Tailor bolt upright, Willis leaning uncomfortably back, feeling that the woman was bearing down on him.

Shopping in the bag shifted. Something fell.

'He went back for something, didn't he?' Willis said.

Mrs Tailor nodded, apparently aware and unsurprised that he knew. 'A newspaper. We have them delivered. They write our name on it.'

There was a pause while she considered him. It was funny, Willis thought, how some people had opaque eyes. Like a sheep's or a goat's. 'What are you saying?' she asked.

'I think he knew something but I don't think he killed the girl. If he had, he would have run when you lured me away. I'm saying that, regardless of similarities, this killing was different.' Something made him add: 'It was like a very clever copy.' Willis sensed a quickening of interest. 'Did he say something like that to you?' he followed up quickly.

He had been hoping for a reaction, and got one, but it was nothing like the one he'd expected.

'I vowed – I promised never – Have you any idea what it was like – the duty – the duty to love my son as a Christian – to forgive – not to excuse – never to excuse – but to love – and to sit here, after the news came on the television about the poor, brutalised child, and see him watch me, wait for – wait for me to break?' Her voice was rough and low and she barked the words out. 'But I did not break. He broke. It was he who sat at my knee and begged me to believe him.

'I said: "Why should you lie? If you did it, you'll know, and soon they'll know. Telling me will make no difference." That's when he cried. Big tears. I'd never seen him cry since he was tiny and I was shocked. They soaked my stockings.' Her eyes slid to the empty fireplace and narrowed, as if she were seeing flames. 'He said it was him who had been raped.'

Willis gave an involuntary start.

'That was my reaction,' Mrs Tailor said. 'We had this agreement – a bargain. No excuses; no evasions. Only the truth with each other.'

She straightened her shoulders and gave Willis the benefit of her ugly, strong face. He felt a mixture of admiration and visceral revulsion. She nodded, as if she knew what he was feeling. He felt guilty as he remembered what he must be to her: the policeman who'd stood by while her son was dismembered, but this only compounded his desire to shrink away from her.

'I'll be brief,' she said. 'He went out that day because – well, he wanted a walk and the forest gave him the shade he needed. His skin couldn't take the sun. He left looking good. He came back – I've never seen anyone in a state like that. Oh, he was clean. No blood if that's what you're wondering. But terror . . . he was stained with terror. He came in and collapsed. Crawled into a corner in the kitchen and curled up. I couldn't get him out. All he wanted was for me to get his shoes off and burn them.

'Anyway, he calmed down after a while. They taught him how to do that in prison. Take himself under control. And he told me what had happened.

'He had no suspicion at first. He was enjoying the walk. Said it was very quiet. Just him and the birds. What he liked about birds was that you didn't need to see them. You just heard them. You could take them for granted.' She paused. 'Anyway, at first he wasn't aware of anything wrong, but after a while he said it was like there were – fish hooks in his brain, so sharp you didn't realise they'd gone in at first. That was what he said. And that he was worried. Anything to do with his mind worried him, any pain. He never said, but I always knew that he thought something, a bad thought, might be growing in there and battling to get out. But in the forest it was like fish hooks. Slicing through first, then just sitting there while he walked and hoped the ache would go away. But then they started pulling.

'All those feelings . . . He'd been in therapy in prison and learnt techniques to control the feelings that came over him, and he'd thought that maybe the feelings had gone away. But suddenly he knew they hadn't. Suddenly he knew that someone or something was looking for them, rifling through his mind like an old drawer, pulling this out, that out, until it found the hidden thing. Fingers, he said. Squeezing and sorting. And as they got nearer to the desire to – hurt – young women, the feeling began to announce itself, fresher and clearer than he had ever felt it before. All that feeling, all that need, came into his mind like a revelation, he said, as if a surgeon had just pared away all the fat and blood and tissue to reveal a gleaming heart underneath.

'In the past the feeling had always been linked to a particular girl, a focus, but this time the feeling was pure, he said. Unalloyed. It was a wonder, he said. Exciting, but not dangerous. What he was feeling was so pure, so abstract, that he thought it could never linger. It would evaporate like – like pure alcohol. And just as that happened, she came into sight.'

'She?'

'Dana Watkins. She was walking towards him quite carelessly, not looking where she was going. He said he just stood there. He felt like the wall he knew she must crash into and die. I can't say what else he felt at that moment, what his conscience was telling him, and anyway it all became academic because he saw that she wasn't alone.'

'Who was she with?' Willis said sharply. 'A boy?' He immediately thought of Marcus.

'No. Children. A whole crowd of little children, following her silently through the forest.

'That was where the power was coming from, he told me. It was them. They had gone into him. They were grey, he said, with blank faces. No features. He got the impression that they were herding the girl towards him. She might take a step to the left or the right, but one of them would move up and she'd change tack, as if they'd influenced her without her realising. They were bringing her to him. She saw him. He said she smiled, as if she'd been really nicely brought up and thought that there was something wrong with him and she should be kind to people who had something wrong. He opened his mouth to warn her, but he couldn't. He said it was like fate. He said that there was this moment when things could have tipped either way. He saw it very clearly: the path ahead of him forking. This is what happens if I rape and kill her; this is what happens if I nod and walk away.

'He nodded, Officer. He nodded and turned. But it was too late. They lifted the top of his head open, he said, like a box. He was blinded by a curtain of blood, but he could see through it, and what he saw was the children – darting in and hitting her. He said it was like piranhas going for a horse. You couldn't see what they did; you just saw the creature jerk, this way, that way.

'She looked shocked; she looked to him for help. He couldn't move; it was all blood. His thoughts began to form. He couldn't stop them.

'And what he thought, they did. They took her, bit her, did her on her side and did her on her breasts. He couldn't move. Physically and mentally he was rooted to the spot. When it was over, one of the children came to him and – It stood in front of him and took its thing out and . . . ejaculated on his shoes. He had to wash them. I smelled them. I thought he must have accidentally stepped on a dead pigeon or something. Anyway, that seemed to break the spell. He turned and ran. They used him, Officer. A man who had thoughts like he had but managed to control them should have got a medal. For him, every waking hour – well, it was like a coward being forced to be a hero all his life. They took him, and they used him.

'And now he's dead and that's his story,' she concluded. 'What's yours?'

Willis found he could not talk. You heard a description of how a girl had been killed and you needed time to think; you needed to give the thought a space; to hedge it in; shrink wrap it.

Children.

He walked out of the sitting room without really thinking and found himself in the back of the house, standing in a formica and painted plywood kitchen, looking at a plain garden.

Children.

Children with no faces. Children waiting for a face. A shiver coiled in the small of his back and sprang up his spine, shaking him. Beyond the fence at the end of the garden the trees were huge green monsters.

Behind him he heard Mrs Tailor say: 'It scares me too, the forest. None of us know what goes on in there. Even now.'

Willis thought very clearly, I do. Tailor kept a memory of his original crime; a blueprint of the bite marks; an awareness of her slow death from asthma. This model had been lifted from his head and applied to the girl walking past him.

Tailor's brain was milked so that a girl could be killed so that Caroline Waters could get a job. And all because Marcus Waters made a wish. Who could you blame? Not Marcus; he didn't know what he was up against. Not Tailor; having your sick brain emptied could not be interpreted as an act of deliberate evil. Not Caroline; she didn't ask Marcus to make the wish. It was a paradigm of modern justice. Everyone was a victim. It was screamingly frustrating but it was the truth.

But why Marcus? Why not any one of the hundred or thousand other people who had gone to the tree and made a wish? The tree had been covered with notes, with gifts. But unless he was missing something big here, wishes weren't automatically granted to one and all. Just this time. Just Marcus. Why him? Why?

Chapter 27

Caroline looked at the clock. Maggie said: 'That's the tenth time you've done that since lunch. Got ants in your pants?'

She licked an envelope with a wide, rather grey tongue, then raised her eyebrows and looked at Caroline. Caroline ran her eyes down the figures on the screen and tried to remember how to sort them. She picked her handbag up from the floor and began to rummage through it for some chewing gum.

'I'm seeing Marcus's teacher.'

'That's why you're all done up like a Christmas present, I suppose. Problems?'

In return for a sort of heavy reliability, Maggie demanded a certain amount of information in return. She was never offensively intrusive, and once when Caroline had told her to mind her own business on some fairly innocuous question – where she had been brought up – Maggie had gone quiet on her for three hours, which is a long time in office politics.

She looked out of the window. There was a huge plane tree in the car park. Its leaves were already turning; there was the usual talk of water rationing. It seemed to happen every year. So how come it had never happened when she was a child? People never seemed to learn; things never got better.

'Problems at school?' Maggie insisted.

Yes, my son's in league with the devil, Caroline thought. And I'm worried that it might affect his prospects. She gripped the underside of the desk.

'He's – he's been acting strangely recently. Withdrawn. Short-tempered. I just want to see if anything's happened at school.'

'You know, I really hated it when mine went,' Maggie said. 'To school, I mean. They stopped being mine. They talked different. Smelled different. And they started having secrets.'

On the tree in the car park, leaves hung like big, flat hands. Caroline said suddenly: 'You're from here, aren't you? You said that once. The original Essex Girl. Did you ever hear of any legends about the forest? Stories, I mean?'

'Legends. Let's see now ... Robin Hood type stories? Headless horseman type stories?'

'That kind of thing.' Caroline saw Maggie's face sharpen and become curious. She felt her heart begin to race.

'Not really,' Maggie said cautiously. 'We never really had much to do with it, telling stories and that. My parents discouraged that sort of thing – chapel people, you see. Now the church people, maybe they told stories, I don't know. But I was a pleb and plebs went to chapel and kept things very buttoned up. There was one thing: my grandmother used to say that if you went in the woods at full moon you could see the shadows of everyone who'd ever died in the forest. You ever been in there at night?'

'Once,' said Caroline. She remembered the walk to the clearing the night Marcus had seen her with Carstairs; she had hardly heard a thing, she had been so focused on the goal, so taken up by worry of what she might find. The branch of a tree, blowing to and fro in the wind, had made her heart kick against her chest. But Maggie was talking.

'I did once. Full moon. Went in with my Roy – before we were married – thought it would be fun to scare ourselves. You know, not get really scared, but give ourselves a bit of a thrill as a prelude to having it off in the back of Terry's – that's his brother, by the way – Terry's Ford Popular. Well, to cut a long story short, we got really scared. Shit scared.

'We walked into the woods, I don't know – about two hundred yards from the road – and stood in a clearing. By God, if after we'd stood there five minutes we didn't start seeing the shadows move! Never in front of us, always out of the corners of our eyes. We'd turn and it would go still. Look away, and these shapes would begin to shift, just a little bit. Wriggle here, shift there. We legged it, and by the time we were out of the bloody wood, if every shadow wasn't moving of its own accord, we thought it was. Thanks, Gran!

'Anyway, we thought about it afterwards and realised that they *would* all seem to move, what with wind and the fact that

181

you're moving. And of course the great thing is, the more scared you get, and the faster you run, the more everything seems to move. We worked that out but we didn't feel like going back into the woods to prove it.'

'Why?'

'Suppose a shadow really did move of its own accord? Whoops! Talking on duty. Back to work.'

Barbara Neilson clacked down the room towards them on heels that would have defeated any lesser mortal. She looked at Maggie frostily. Maggie deliberately stroked the hairs that grew from her mole until the other woman shuddered and looked away.

'Caroline, you look very nice today,' she said. 'Going anywhere special?'

'Just back to school.'

'Good. Now have you got that breakdown Mr Fisher asked for?'

'Almost there.'

'Well, drop it in on him when you're done and then I believe you wanted to leave a few minutes early? Well, that's fine, but don't make a habit of it.'

She turned to walk away but as she turned knocked Caroline's handbag on to the floor. The contents sprayed from its mouth.

'Oh, sorry,' she said. And knelt to start picking them up.

'That's all right!' Caroline said. 'It's all right. Please!' She tried to stop Miss Neilson but the bag had fallen into a small gap between two desks and there was only room for one person.

Barbara Neilson handed her the bag and walked off, composure unaffected. Caroline looked into it then dived under the desk.

'Lost something?' Maggie said.

'Nothing important.'

'Let me help,' Maggie said, ducking down.

'Please, no. There's no need,' Caroline said desperately.

'It's all right,' she said. 'I've found it. A book? It had got under my desk. This the one?'

Caroline stood up. The book was on Maggie's desk.

'It must have skidded across. I picked it up. Sorry.'

'Oh, it's all right. Just something someone lent me.'

'Read it on the way to work?'

'Yes.'

'You drive to work now,' Maggie pointed out. Caroline flushed. Maggie held out the book.

'*Kids that Kill*. What is it? True crime or something?'

'I don't know. I don't know why anyone thought I might want to read it.'

'Well,' Maggie said, 'it looks interesting. If ever you want to tell me about it, do. I'm a good listener.'

Caroline said nothing. She reached out for the book. For a second Maggie did not release it. She looked at the picture on the cover, then at Caroline.

Caroline was early and was able to park near the school. A couple of other mothers were standing and talking, one leaning against her car, the other gesturing and laughing. The one who was talking was dark, lively-looking, wearing a singlet and jeans. The other was blonde and wore a white shirt with a mutton chop collar, and a long, loose skirt. They looked worlds apart, but were both mothers, both with children at the school. That brought them together. Caroline nodded to them stiffly as she drove past. In the rear-view mirror she saw them both follow her car with their eyes, then one said something to the other.

I don't fit in, Caroline thought. Anywhere. The book was burning a hole in her handbag. Maggie knew – Caroline had seen it in her eyes. Willis, after her display last night, would wonder why one of his books had disappeared, work out which one, and then he would know too. And then – then what?

She was aware of a sudden rise in the general noise level. School was out.

Marcus sat on a bench in the hall. He looked at the overhead lights gleaming in the polished lino – one, two, three, four, five in one row, and counting back from the main door – five, four, three, two, one. Where light came in through the frosted panels of the classroom doors there were big, blurred pools of light, splashing messily over the polish, running over everything.

His feet touched the ground from the bench, but only just.

He could swing them and scuff the soles lightly over the polished surface. A door opened down the corridor and Mr Summers came out of the staff room and walked briskly down the corridor, heels clicking in the way that grown-up heels did.

'Hello, Marcus. Killing time?'

Killed it dead, he thought.

'Yes.'

'Good. Good.'

Whoever said grown-ups were clever? Marcus thought. His mother wasn't, his father wasn't, Marina wasn't –

Mr Summers put his hand on the doorknob to his classroom.

'My mother's in there with Miss Dunlop.'

'Right.' He pulled the hand away.

Mr Summers fancied Miss Dunlop. Everyone knew *that* even if they did not know exactly what *that* involved. To most of the school it just meant that when he talked to her in the corridors he leant against the wall and tilted his head slightly to one side and laughed a lot, loudly.

'They going to be long?'

Another grown-up question. Who knew?

'I don't know.'

'You are all right, Marcus?'

If you even have to ask that, Marcus thought, you're as clever as Timothy (Timoffee) Fairburn (Fairbum), and he's not clever at all. Some people might know more than me, but that's grown-up stuff and they all know it together. No one else in the whole wide world knows what I know, he thought, so I win.

But then, he thought in the sudden sunburst of knowledge that occasionally lights up minds of nine years old, knowing what I know doesn't mean I'm clever. It means I'm –

But his mind did not have a word for what he had become. He could not imagine a word for it existing.

'But he is all right? I mean, in your opinion,' Caroline asked Miss Dunlop.

Miss Dunlop was twenty-two, going on nineteen. Would I have been able to tell at that age? Caroline wondered. A tissue had found its way into her hand. It was damp from her palm. She tore little bits off it with her finger and thumb.

Miss Dunlop kept records in buff concertina folders. She opened one and pulled out a sheaf of papers.

'This way you can plot how they're doing,' she said. 'It gives you an overview. No, you see, Marcus is keeping steady. School work falling off is a sure sign of things going wrong.'

'Unless he wants to hide the fact that something's wrong?' Caroline said.

'I've never heard of anything like that.' Miss Dunlop looked worried. 'Is something going on at home?'

'I wanted to know if something was going on here,' Caroline said pertly. 'Does he play? Does he fit in?'

'Ah. Yes. I had noticed that he was a bit withdrawn. I assumed – '

'What?'

Miss Dunlop thought, then said fluently: 'Just that something might have been upsetting him, but he'd work it through and get over it. Childhood only seems easy in retrospect, you know, when we look back on it.'

Caroline stared at her coldly. Miss Dunlop shifted uneasily. 'I mean, I know some childhoods are – '

'How about friends?' Caroline asked.

'Well, since you've asked, I'd say he was self-contained. I suppose I mean by that that he doesn't seem to have close friends, but he seems quite happy that way and is sociable and able to cope.'

'So this matter you called me about . . . ?'

'Oh, yes. He's been going about saying that he had the power – children do at that age. It's nothing to be worried about.'

'But you were worried about it? Enough to call me.'

'Yes.'

'Why?'

'Very well.' Miss Dunlop's face sharpened. 'I'll be absolutely straight with you. Without admitting any degree of responsibility, of course. But something he did – or something I neglected to do – may have triggered the situation. It was on a field trip into the woods. We came to a glade, an open glade with a tree in it, and Marcus said: "There's the wishing tree. You make a wish on it and your wish comes true." I asked him where he knew this from and he said he'd been told. Naturally I assumed it came from either you or your husband.'

185

'Not me,' Caroline said.

'I see. Well, as a joke I encouraged them all to wish. I mean, it's no different from, say, telling them about wishing wells, for example.'

'Did Marcus?' Caroline asked.

'Oh, he was very firm about it. He said that everyone was doing it wrong. He said you had to give away something you loved to make the wish come true.'

'And did he?'

'I don't know.'

Caroline looked around the room. It was big and square and high-ceilinged. There were posters on the wall: Flora and Fauna of Farthing Wood, Roman Soldiers, African Villages, Indian Deforestation. There were a few uplifting poems and paintings done by the children.

Caroline ran her eyes over them. Lopsided houses; vast, round heads with round eyes and triangle noses; huge fields with tiny black and white spotted cows; bright red flowers; a bare white tree; balloons and a sailing boat. Killer robots of the Nintendo variety were obviously censored.

A bare white tree . . .

She stood up. Her footsteps echoed against the walls.

'Marcus did this?'

'What?' Miss Dunlop screwed up her eyes and squinted at the wall. 'Why, yes, I believe he did. I never got round to putting his name on it. How clever of you to recognise it as Marcus's.'

She came up beside Caroline. 'It's good. Not much colour in it, but then – '

Caroline looked at the teacher, then at the tree, then at the teacher again. 'There was nothing else about the tree? Nothing he said about – fairies?'

Miss Dunlop gave an explosive laugh. 'Oh, goodness me, no. Fairies! I'd be laughed out of my job if we started having conversations about fairies.'

Marcus sat with his feet up on the dashboard, fiddling with a hand-held computer game that chirruped like a trapped bird. Caroline drove jerkily and too fast.

'Sit up straight and put your seat belt on, darling.'

186

'Am I in trouble?' he asked. She was at a T-junction. She looked at him. His face was still. His hands moved constantly. 'No, darling.'

'Then why did you come to the school?'

'I just wanted a chat with your teacher. That's all.'

'Miss Bumlop fancies Mr Bummers.'

'Mr Who?' It was so normal, so childish, she found she was laughing.

He looked at her anxiously, saw her eyes were warm and said, 'I don't know, the things you snigger about. Mr Bummers and Miss Bumlop.'

'Miss Bumlop?' Caroline repeated incredulously. She started to laugh again. She couldn't help it, it was just the way he said it. Laughter welled up in her, shivered through her. It felt as if joy was bubbling through every cell. She felt tears in her eyes, tears of relief and happiness.

'Oh, Marcus,' she said, between gasps. She had to get a hold of herself and watch her driving.

She looked down at him again.

'Bumlop,' he repeated.

She accelerated, as if the speed of the car might speed her thoughts. 'Marcus, if I was to tell you that we're going to move far away from here – '

She heard his sharp intake of breath.

'Mummy?'

'Yes, darling?'

'Not yet.'

'Why not, darling?'

'I made another – '

'No!'

'Yes, Mummy. My last – '

It seemed like the easiest thing in the world. You come round a blind corner and see children running across the road. You don't have time to think, and anyway you're not really looking and you've only got one hand on the wheel.

You don't see the old Morris 1000 van, parked with two wheels on the kerb, in an attempt to get it out of the way. You certainly don't think that this is a car built to last, not like some modern rubbish, which is what the proud owner of the van said only that morning. Morris 1000s are built on to a solid chassis of

187

steel. And cars built like that don't crumple like a modern car.

Not a huge noise, considering. Caroline yanked the steering wheel. All it did was slow down time, as if she were choking its flow.

The Nissan slewed, but too late. It caught the rear wing of the old Morris and pushed it straight into a lamp post. The Morris stopped dead, the rear of the van bucked, scraped down the side of the Nissan, buckling metal like it was tin foil, and came in at the door.

Marcus, half in the air and about to fly through the windscreen feet first, caught a wedge of malevolent steel, scraped to surgical brightness by the impact, in his side.

It twisted him and seemed to suck him round it. He folded, the hard corner almost splitting his small chest. His face bounced once, twice, three times. His arms slammed back. One hand caught Caroline on the bridge of her nose and gave her a three-month shiner. And that, apart from some seat belt grazing, was the sum total of her injuries. Marcus, on the other hand, was dead.

Chapter 28

The year was getting tired, Willis thought, and it was barely halfway through. He longed for an autumn gale to come pouring down the street, tear through the trees, rip up front gardens, lift roof slates, raise the dust of summer that seemed to lie thick on the ground, scour the forest clean. He felt he was sitting in tepid bathwater that the whole world had used first. He longed for a lick of clean wet air, for the bite of the cold. He pulled his sports shirt away from his back and flapped the material, feeling the tickle of cool air run up his spine. He took a swig of his drink, blinked sticky eyelids and listened to a sleepy pigeon croon.

A generic small car came buzzing down the street. He watched it without interest. It stopped outside the pub and Nancy waved to him from the front seat. He saw a young man with longish hair and granny glasses lean across the front seat to give her a kiss. Nancy got out and the man nodded amiably at Willis before slamming the door and driving off.

'The boyfriend?' Willis asked.

'The partner,' Nancy said.

'Should have asked him to join us.'

'I did,' she said. 'But shop bores him. Anyway he does that indoor speed climbing and he's in training. He hates sitting in pubs nursing orange juice. I think it makes him feel self-conscious. He says he thinks you sound like a nice bloke.'

'Oh, I am,' Willis said. 'A real poppet, but you know that. What are you drinking?'

'Lager top,' said Nancy. 'With ice.'

'Urgh,' Willis said.

'What news from the front?' he asked, putting down two pint glasses, spilling beer out of both.

'It's fine.' She trickled the slops into gaps in the slatted table top, then fanned her face with an envelope. It was a nice face, Willis thought. Broad cheeks, good bones. Nice finely drawn mouth. Very cool eyes. The sight of her with a boyfriend put her in a new context.

'Like what you see or are you just bored?' she asked.

Willis smiled. 'I like what I see,' he said. 'I was just thinking that I never really thought of you as a person before.'

Nancy opened her eyes wide and looked at him over the fan of photographs. 'Great. I don't think I can cope.'

'I'm sure you'll find a way. But that's just the effect I have on women. How are you, anyway?'

'Fine. A job's coming up in traffic that I'm thinking about.'

'Traffic? That's disastrous. I'd always assumed you'd stay with the detectives.'

'No,' she said simply. 'I mean, you're right. That's what I had been thinking. But a lot of things have happened recently and to be honest, I've changed. I mean, basically I don't think the game's worth the candle. But mostly I don't think I'd cope.'

'With what?'

'Oh, you know,' she said. Willis shrugged. 'The sheer bloodiness of it all.'

'You'll get plenty of that in traffic. Buckets of it. You'll be putting up with people in shock because they've seen their little boy or girl or whatever thrown through a windscreen. You'll have to caution the man who's babbling, because he's just taken his girlfriend out in his new wheels and killed her, that anything he says may be taken down and used in evidence. You'll have to move the ghouls along. You'll have to – '

Nancy threw up her hands and said: 'Stop! I didn't mean the blood. I meant, I don't want to meet people like Tailor in the first place and then I don't want to find out that they've been chopped up. I don't want my friends to be suspected of it. I don't want to be forced to confront every fucking minute of every day the worst of what people can do. And before you ask if I'm getting married, the answer is maybe but it's not why I want out. It's odd, but if I have to see people killed, I want it to be by accident.'

Willis bared his teeth and thought of saying something in a Humphrey Bogart voice, then thought he had better not. Did

Marcus stumble on the wishing tree by accident? He thought not. And if he didn't, was there a pattern that was larger than the simple reciprocity of gifts and wishes? For a moment the thought excited him.

Nancy was looking tense and bright-eyed. Very controlled and determined to make a point, or else get something done, something unpleasant. More bad news about his career?

'Well,' Willis said, 'I wish you love and luck among the contraflows, and may all your traffic cones stay upright.'

'Why are men so sarcastic?' she asked.

'Oh, because we're hurting inside.' He squinted at her over the rim of his glass. 'I think you're doing the right thing.'

'Oh, good,' said Nancy, overemphatically. 'I'm so glad.'

'And I'm glad you're glad.'

They sat in companionable silence for a second. A slight breeze stirred the air, bringing with it the tang of a giant lime tree that grew across the narrow suburban road.

'Anyway,' she said, 'I called because I thought you'd be interested in these.'

She handed over the envelope she had been using to fan her face.

Willis shook out colour scene-of-crime photographs and shuffled through them quickly.

'A skeleton.'

'Male; Caucasian; late-teens, early-twenties; height between five eleven and six foot.'

'How long's he been dead?'

'No one's sure. Some time, to be skeletonised. The dental work – I can't remember the details but something about it suggests it's any time between 1905 and 1920.'

Willis stopped shuffling through the pile.

'And found where?' he asked softly.

'In the forest. Just round the back of Blackthorn Way.'

Willis felt time and space contract. If he asked the wrong question the world would stop and everything would go shooting off into space. Nancy was watching him very carefully. Her eyes dropped to the pictures. Slowly Willis shuffled through them again.

Stopped. Looked at a couple of other images for comparison.

'They're calling it a dismembered corpse,' Nancy Freeman said.

'That's it?'

'That's it,' she said. 'Sorry.'

'Can I take these?'

'Yup. I had a friend in the lab run up duplicates. They won't be missed. To be honest I doubt very much if the originals would be either. He was found by a treasure hunter, or rather a man with a metal detector who happened to be walking around with it switched on. He was inside the Roman fort – where it's illegal – and insisted that we understood the distinction.'

'What happened?'

'A couple of big trees had fallen and he was sweeping the root hole. He got a signal and dug. Got the shock of his life, I guess.'

Willis thought for a while, then asked: 'And no one's linking this to Tailor.' It was more a statement than a question.

'Christ, no. That would take intelligence and imagination, and I'm afraid both those qualities are in short supply at the moment. The lab still can't make out the samples taken from Dana Watkins.'

'What do you think?'

'I don't know, Willis. And this is why I want out. I just don't know. They don't know. I don't *want* to know.'

She drank. He watched the ripple in her throat. He could see her teeth through the glass. 'There's one other thing. We just learned that Dana Watkins's mum was going to work for Smith's Car Parts. Do you know who works there as well?'

'No,' Willis lied.

'Caroline Waters. Now, who was the last person to see Dana Watkins? Caroline Waters. Who was lying about his where-abouts in the woods? Her son. There's something very fishy going on here. Me, I'd have her in for questioning if it weren't for one little thing.'

'What's that?'

'She's in hospital. She had an accident. Her son was killed. She ran into the back of a van. Crushed him. One of those freak things. I mean, it should never have happened. She's trouble, that woman.'

Willis felt as if he'd been given an electric shock. Jolted then numbed. Terribly cold. For a second he was too shocked to make any response.

The boy was dead. She was meant to take him away. She should have taken him away!

Dead.

It was such a flat word, dead. Rhymed with ted. The boy's dead. The boy's fed. The boy's ted. The boy's teddy. The boy's deady.

'Oh God,' he said. The back of his throat felt dry and hollow. When he breathed he felt something catching in his abdomen. Earlier he thought he had seen Nancy as a real person, out of context. He realised now that it was he who was out of context, that being a policeman gave you protection against things like this. Now he was feeling it as a real person did.

'The mother?'

'Fine, apparently. Hardly a scratch.'

Willis thought that it might have been better for her if she had suffered. It would be hard not to blame herself. 'Poor kid. He never looked happy.'

'No. Don't make too much of it though.'

'Mother in hospital?'

'North Forest General,' she answered promptly. 'Here, let me get you another drink.'

When she came back they chatted, as if by unspoken agreement, about anything else: the station, Nancy's family, how to break into a Mercedes – or was it a Lexus? – with half a tennis ball. They finished their drinks. Nancy was taking a bus back to her flat and the stop was a couple of streets away. Willis was walking back to his in the opposite direction.

'By the way,' he said as they both stood up, 'the accident. Where did it happen?'

'Ferny Road. She was driving him back from school. Just been to see the teacher apparently.'

'This end of Ferny Road or that end?'

'I don't know it too well,' she said. 'Oh, yes. They said there were a lot of accidents there in the autumn from fallen leaves under the wheels. It must be that place where the forest comes down to the road. Know it?'

He nodded.

'One other question.'

'Yes.'

'The treasure hunter. What did he pick up?'

'What do you mean?'

'He must have got a signal off something. What was it?'

She looked blank, then infuriated. Then she smiled.

'I hate you, Willis,' she said. 'Anything else you want?'

'Don't go in too hard on Caroline Waters.'

'Not my department,' she said. 'But I'd keep away if I were you.'

Then suddenly, like feeling a cobweb kiss your face in the dark, and stick, he felt fear, and knew it could be a condition of life, not a simple reaction to the great unknown or the simply misunderstood.

He opened all the doors and windows in his flat and made himself a jug of lime juice. He cleared the dining table – used for everything except dining – and laid out the prints that Nancy had given him side by side. He was living off scraps, he knew that, dealing with pictures of evidence rather than evidence itself, but it was better than nothing.

Dismembered corpse or just a stack of old bones, a skeleton? Now he thought about it, skeleton was a much nicer word than corpse. There was something jokey and rattly about skeleton. There was something clean and clever about skeleton, a sort of 'So that's how you do it' feeling. Skeletons were hard, skeletons were definite, skeletons could dance and grin with castanet bones and toothy smiles. Skeletons were fun. But a corpse . . .

If ever there was a word that was about to swell and burst it was corpse. That long vowel sound in the middle, that was punctured by an explosive 'p', and then allowed to hiss on with the last sound. Something swollen, something leaking, something awful. Corpses showed what would happen when that slender thread of life was broken. The worst thing he'd ever seen was the corpse of a baby in a house where the mother had died suddenly of God knows what – these things happen. He had made himself look; he thought it was an important part of the toughening-up process, but the sight had ended up tenderising him for weeks. The baby was in a cradle. It was a strange bacon-like colour. Its skin was slack, sunken and wrinkled around its face, blown out as taut as an aubergine around the belly. The baby was flyblown and bits of it, or him as it turned out to be, a little boy called Jason, stuck to the cradle when they lifted him out. That was a corpse. Corpses mocked the living. He'd never had these thoughts as a policeman.

He rubbed his face to erase the thoughts that played beneath it, then looked at the pictures. It had occurred to him that Nancy had given him them to have something to talk about other than Marcus Waters.

The first picture showed a hole in the forest floor with what looked like a white disc in the middle of it. A ruler placed in the hole showed the disc to be about four feet down. The white disc, other pictures showed, was in fact domed. Was in fact the top of a skull. The area around the skull was cleanly dug. In front of it was a deeper, rougher hole. He guessed that the treasure hunter must have dug past the skull to get to the source of the signal. But if that was the head, where was all the rest?

The answer lay in the other photographs. The limbs were stacked on the ground, as the treasure hunter had left them, Willis imagined. That meant they had been buried in front of the head. The trunk had been buried upright. The jaw of the skull, Willis noticed, was open. He hoped it wasn't in a scream.

Willis remembered Tailor geysering up from the forest floor in bits. When he was found, he had been arranged, the trunk in one place, the limbs stacked in front of it.

He looked at the pictures of the hip and the thigh. Ball and socket joints, they were called. The ball was there, so was the socket. That meant something.

He stood up and went to the window, glass of lime juice in one hand, the other somehow having come by a tumbler of whisky. No stars tonight, no sky really, if by sky you meant something far away and clean. This soupy sky was just deep air, as clear as the North Sea – and the North Sea wasn't clear at all.

The ball was there, so was the socket . . .

The limbs hadn't been cut off. They had been torn off. If they had been cut off there would have been marks of shearing or splintering. If they had been sawn there would have been tooth marks from the saw.

These limbs had been torn off, pulled apart, like Tailor's. Now, when Willis thought about the open jaw, he could hear the silent scream, muffled by earth.

Surely this was evidence enough to get Tailor's murder re-examined: I might even get my suspension quashed, Willis thought, then wondered if he ever wanted to go back to policing again.

Except . . . If the police weren't making much of a fuss about this, they must be thinking something else. Bones in the ground. Of course – it would be exactly what he would be thinking. A body, left to rot, re-interred somewhere else. That would be how it came to be in pieces.

He had an idea and looked at the photographs closely. No clothing – well, that could have rotted. Something else though . . .

He'd get the address of the treasure hunter off Nancy in the morning. To be honest, he couldn't care less what they had lifted off the corpse, but there were a couple of things that he would like to check.

Chapter 29

Waking up was the worst.

'There's really not that much wrong with us,' the nurses said, the doctors said, the mop man and the dinner lady said. 'We should be up and walking by now, shouldn't we?'

Or: 'Goodness me, haven't we got anything to say this fine and lovely morning?'

They all seemed to know that she should be up and walking now, talking now. She didn't.

'Goodness me, we shouldn't let a little thing like a black eye stop us from getting round the ward, making friends, should we?'

Almost certainly they were right. It was just there were other things as well.

For the first two days, when someone came up to her bed, Caroline hid her face in her hands and looked at them sideways. Not through her fingers – there was nothing peekaboo about it. She covered her face with her hands and only looked if they seemed to be doing something personal to her.

'Why are we hiding our face?' almost everyone asked her. 'We don't want to hide our face.'

But we did want to hide our face. We didn't want anyone to see it, or for it to see anyone. Why that was a preferable state of affairs than showing it to the world, she did not know. It didn't make her feel better or stop her from feeling worse. In truth there was no better nor worse in her, just as there are no dry deserts on the bottom of the sea or dew ponds in the depths of the sun. It was just a compulsion, the way a lobster raises its claws if you wave your hand in front of its face. Or a baby throws out its arms if you drop it.

There were eleven other patients in the mixed ward and Caroline could identify a recent amputee, a hernia, a colostomy,

197

a case of malnutrition and two broken hips, because they all talked around the table in the middle of the ward. She was by far the least ill.

'We'll have you up in no time,' the consultant said on his first flying visit, sitting on the end of the bed and exhaling a powdery sort of bonhomie, precisely metered as a drug.

Oh no you won't, Caroline thought. She could not imagine moving ever again.

'You've got some old scarring on your rear upper thighs,' the consultant said. 'Give you any trouble?'

But by that time Caroline was far away again.

On the second day a pair of medical students, owlish, self-important, soft-voiced, came and stood by her bed and said they would like to ask her questions, if they could, to try and diagnose what was wrong with her.

The man adjusted his clipboard and asked if he could try out his stethoscope while the girl did her blood pressure. This they did. From behind her hands, Caroline caught glimpses of them as they busied themselves about her person and noted the seat belt bruising on her left breast and right shoulder.

Then one of them noticed the tears that were falling now from her chin on to the cotton nightie – Caroline was crying so much these days that she was having to drink abnormal amounts to replace the lost fluids. The medical student pulled Caroline's hands away from her face. What they saw shocked them so much that the girl replaced the hands. Caroline wanted to tell them that she was broken and poisoned and would probably stay here for the rest of her life.

She thought that if she stopped eating she would die in three weeks. She thought that eating was sacrilegious. She could not understand how she could do anything so mundane after killing her son. She could not understand how they could not understand. She pushed her meals away, untouched, and spent mealtimes watching the mounds of carrot, potato and brown meat cool. The dinner lady got annoyed and said she should think of all those poor people on drips.

The ward was long and built on a north-south axis. The high windows, six feet from the floor, let in morning light and afternoon light. At the end of the ward was a little south-facing balcony that looked over the sloping hospital lawns to the dark line of the forest. Forty years ago even, the TB patients used to sun themselves there and hope the golden warmth would cure them, dry up the wetness that was rotting their lungs.

Grief felt like that to Caroline. She wondered whether the sun would bake the sadness out of her, whether the wound would dry, form a scab, and one day be ready for God's finger nail to pick. But when a bar of sunlight slid across her bed one afternoon, it just made her hot, so that was that.

Everything around her had a way of separating, so that nothing seemed whole. There was no ward, for example, just the irritating, nonsensical constituent parts: window pane, frame, stretch of wall between edge of window and edge of next window; floor tile next to floor tile; long bit of wood attached to a table top; foot; bit of ankle poking thinly out from loose leg of pyjama which itself was simply an odd arrangement of stripes and hems and buttons and things. Faces were a real problem. Eyebrows flexed; eyes rolled; noses twitched; lips stretched and filled; chins bobbed. It might have been at random for all Caroline knew.

The only whole thing about her was the compressed, swirling fury inside her that sent poison flooding through her body in shuddering waves. She had killed her son. It was enough.

She forgot all about it when she slept, and one of the reasons she did not want to sleep was that the pain of remembering was so intense when she woke up.

'No visitors today?' one of the nurses asked as she straightened the sheets, pulling Caroline's hands away from her face and laying them neatly on the bed.

Caroline looked at her. The other patients were friendly with the nurses, which suggested that they knew them. If they knew them it followed that they must be able to distinguish between them. For the life of her Caroline could not. It was just eyebrows, hair, lips, cheeks. It took too much effort to assemble all the parts together into a semblance of form, and then commit the form to memory.

No visitors. No. Tom might come, she thought, and even though she knew it was wrong, she had a mental picture of him walking down the ward, Marcus holding his hand, looking anxiously at all the beds, worried in case he might not recognise his mother ('She'll look a bit different, you know'), and then his sweet, pale face lighting up with shy relief when he did see her, and recognise her.

But he was dead. She had killed him.

Tom might come to see her, but he would not be bringing Marcus. She would never see Marcus again.

It was dark. The last time she had noticed it had been light. She must have slept without being aware of sleeping. Something strange was going on. When she looked out of the window at the end of the ward, she could see that the forest had advanced across the lawn and was surrounding the hospital. Trees were tapping the windows with their thin branches in a nervous rhythm, but she did not feel scared.

The balcony doors opened. A tree which was so huge that it had to lean down to touch the hospital reached a white branch into the ward. The branch was dead and polished to ivory smoothness by the elements, as pebbles are sometimes polished on the beach. The end of the branch touched her on the belly. She did not feel scared, and although the branches were dead and hard, their touch was like the laying on of hands. The tree seemed to be wishing her well. Marcus was perched high up in the branches, a tiny figure far away. He was looking away from her but he was looking alive.

It was light. A nurse was leaning over her when Caroline's eyes snapped open. The nurse jerked back with a start, then looked at Caroline again.

'My,' she said, in a lilting Scottish accent, 'we do look better today.'

Caroline reacted to the word like a baby reacts to a new food, sort of rolled it around, tasting and testing it, and said: 'I feel better.'

She ate breakfast and drank her cup of tea. The consultant breezed in and sat on the end of her bed and Caroline was so civil to him that he even suggested that they try a bit of make-up on her black eye to mask its full technicolour glory. Caroline smiled at the thought. Half an hour later the Scottish nurse walked down the ward, caught her eye and smiled at her.

'A letter,' she said. 'Who's having a lovely morning?'

Caroline took it. Typed address and illegible postmark. She tore it open.

No address, no signature.

Marina and I had a most disturbing visit from the traffic police yesterday. In the course of the officer asking routine questions it transpired that:

1) You were driving far in excess of the speed limit.

2) Marcus was not wearing a seat belt.

3) The car you struck was positioned off the road.

4) A witness claims that you were laughing, not looking at the road, driving with only one hand on the wheel while waving the other one around.

5) The same witness also states quite simply that there were no children on the road, which you used as an excuse to the police when they interviewed you after the accident.

In the light of these discoveries, and in the light of your recent behaviour, it is my opinion that Marcus did not die in an accident. He was slaughtered by an irresponsible, self-centred woman who had no right to be in charge of him, had no right to consider herself fit to be his mother.

You have destroyed my life – I know I hardly need say this but I doubt if you have ever taken anyone into consideration in your life. Apart from you, I mean. When I think that you tried to give my son's life a shape I feel physically sick.

This is not an easy letter to write, Caroline. Not an easy letter to write to one's ex-wife, mother of one's child.

God knows, I wish I had never met you, and that I had never known Marcus only to have him taken away from me. Marina and I have taken the arrangements for the funeral in hand and we would be grateful if you did not attend . . .

It was like a thump in the solar plexus from a giant fist. Then every muscle in her abdomen seemed to clamp and twist. She found that she was moaning, bent around a steel bar that was trying to cut her in half. The Scottish nurse, down the other end of the corridor, came towards her at a trot. Caroline, unable to talk, held out the letter. The nurse read it, pursed her lips. She gently unbent Caroline and forced her to drink some water. When she had managed to get some down, the nurse left her.

Caroline saw her talking with the Sister. After a while she came back with two pills.

Caroline took them meekly, and slid off into sleep. She never saw the letter again.

She woke up later that afternoon. The nurse was standing by her bed.

'Thought I'd let you sleep it off,' she said.

'What did you give me?' Caroline said.

'Two paracetamol.'

'What?'

'It's all in the timing,' the nurse said. 'Listen, I'm going off duty any minute, but look out for Fiona – she's on the next shift. I'll tell her about you at handover.'

'I won't be able to sleep tonight. I never can if I've dropped off in the afternoon.'

The Scottish nurse smiled at her: 'Then I'll make sure you get something to read.'

'Thank you,' said Caroline. 'My name's Caroline, by the way.'

'I know. Mine's Jessica.' She was about to go, then hesitated. 'You're in my team, and I'm on for the next four days – so if you ever want to talk – you know . . .'

She stopped as Caroline shook her head. 'Thank you, but I won't want to talk,' she said.

'It can help, you know.'

'It can't help what's happened.'

'No. I mean it can help you. It can help you get better, feel better.'

Caroline looked at her. 'What's the point in that?' she asked.

Jessica's friend did not look as if she was much of a one for talking either. She was small and had a definite, determined expression.

At eleven o'clock, while Caroline was staring at the ceiling, she came down the ward and stopped by her bed.

'Jessica said that you thought you might have a problem sleeping,' she said. 'Do you want anything for it?'

'Not really.'

'Would you like something to read? If you adjust your lamp I don't think it'll disturb the other patients.'

Caroline said that she'd like that very much indeed. The nurse came back a few minutes later with a stack of four well-thumbed books: three Mills and Boon romances and an old hardback.

'Good luck,' she said. And left her. Caroline found that she could read – that she could concentrate on something other than herself. It meant, she surmised, that she was on the mend.

Chapter 30

'Well, I really think it's a bit much.'

It must be one of Tom's relatives talking, Caroline thought. She turned. An elderly face, oyster pink with powder, dark, tight little eyes, and a ferocious hat. Caroline remembered her from somewhere – her and Tom's wedding? Marcus's christening? She began to cry. She was so used to the process by now that apart from a slight loss of co-ordination and an inability sometimes to focus clearly through the tears, she could live a life that was almost normal.

'I mean, being stared at like that. Letting them in. You'd think they'd put up a fence, wouldn't you? I'm surprised they don't have to. The mother here, d'you know?'

There was a hissing sound and Caroline could imagine the woman being nudged.

'Ooh,' the woman said. Caroline felt Tina tense, ready to turn. She grabbed her friend's arm and shook her head. She didn't want anyone to start swearing their face off at her son's funeral, even if it were Tina, even if it were fully justified. Things like that didn't matter any more. Tina muttered something like 'arse-faced bitch' under her breath and Caroline felt a giggle catch in her throat.

It was a beautiful day. A few high clouds drifting across the clear, pale sky looked as if they had been put there to remind you how big it was. A cooling breeze blew on her cheeks; she closed her eyes and let it play on her eyelids for a second or two.

Last night a sudden, stealthy downpour had come smacking down, soaking the ground. It smelled as fresh and mysterious as the grassy breath of a cow. The turf which had been baked to the colour of dried toast was already sending up tiny green shoots. Distantly, in the woods, she heard the monotonous throaty croon of a wood pigeon, the sudden rattle of a woodpecker, the disembodied call of a cuckoo.

She looked around. The service over, they were standing in concentric rings by the graveside. Caroline thought the proportions were all wrong: the hole looked too square. No, of course, that would be because the coffin was so short, so horribly short.

A sob rose in her throat like a bubble in a hosepipe. Then sank. It felt like someone else's throat. She wondered what she was doing standing here and not following the coffin out with Marcus's other parent, then she remembered the confrontation in the porch with her ex-mother-in-law, who had screamed at her, called her a wicked, wicked woman and then collapsed into bubbling, wailing, helpless grief – but not so helpless that she couldn't try to tear herself out of her husband's grip and launch herself at Caroline one last time, shouting: 'You've spoiled everything!'

Caroline, confused, had smiled at her and said that she was sorry, sorry, really sorry. When the vicar, anxious to spread oil on troubled waters, unction, balm and everything else, had smiled at her and moved across to comfort her, Caroline had fixed on him with lunatic desperation and said, twice, that it wasn't her fault that she looked fantastic in black. It would have been easier to pass the statement off as the deranged ramblings of a grief-stricken mother were it not for the unfortunate fact that it was true. And she had sneezed eight times when the flower-strewn coffin was walked down the aisle.

The cemetery was at the back of the church in a converted field. Caroline could see the pall bearers wobble down the church steps and begin to cross the grass towards them. They were followed by a cluster of black-clad figures: Tom, Marina, and Tom's parents. Everyone had their face in a handkerchief, apart from Tom whose face was tied up in a sort of fleshy knot so that it looked like a floor cloth being wrung. The procession was led by the chief undertaker while the vicar brought up the rear.

'What God hath given, God hath taken away.' Caroline hoped to God it *was* God.

She had gone through some process that she did not fully understand over the past few days. Grief and guilt were both still at home, but were locked inside their little rooms now, like bad children. She felt calm and at peace, almost miraculously so. She felt as if she were on drugs but she wasn't. Past and future had been snatched away by some cosmic cleaner; she was floating in the present tense and looking at the world with eyes that felt like cameras.

'What do you think that woman saw?' she whispered to Tina.
'What? Oh, kids, I expect.'

Caroline raised her eyes and looked for the kids. There were no head stones allowed in the council cemetery. No mounds. Graves were flat and plaques were set into the turf so that the council machines could mow the field in a clean sweep.

A short distance away the grave diggers sat on a mound of earth which had been draped with greengrocer's grass. They were tanned to the colour of hazel nuts, bare-chested, muscular, smoking roll-ups and talking in low voices. Their spades were dug into the mound and leaning against each other like rifles at rest.

Movement behind them against the line of trees. Four, no five, shapes had emerged from the shadows to stand in the sunlight, silhouetted against the shade. They shimmered across the hot earth. Kids. Was that woman really complaining about *them*?

Caroline blinked away tears. When she looked again the view was broken by the gently heaving coffin. She would never have put so much brass on it, she thought. She would have gone for something simpler. More elegant. It really wasn't her fault that she looked good in black . . .

The coffin had passed now. She saw the figures again. Four children. They looked as if they had always been there. The fifth was a little distance away, but looking at them. He took a step towards them. He looked nervous, she thought, tentative, but perhaps that was the heat haze. No. She could tell by the way he moved . . .

How – ?

Something shifted in her head.

No.

She gave a moan and felt her legs about to give.

'No,' she said. Tina gripped her arm tightly. Caroline tried to beat her off. She was vaguely aware that Tina was trying to hold

206

her, put her arms round her, pin her arms to her sides.

'Oh, oh. Oh my God!' Her voice rose to a shriek.

The coffin.

'I want to see him,' she said. She tried to free her arms. A soft breeze batted her cheek, cooled by tears.

'I know, dear,' Tina said.

'No,' Caroline said, 'I want to see him. I want to see his face again before they bury him! *I need to see him!*'

'Hush, darling, Caroline. Caroline dear, it's too late.'

'I do though, I do!'

She tried to break free. People were staring now.

'Please, everyone. I'M HIS MOTHER AND I MUST SEE HIM!'

The crowd in front of them parted suddenly. Tom's father stood there, his face working in rage.

'Stop it,' he said in a teacher's voice. 'Stop it this instant, please.'

'Please!' Caroline worked a hand free and grabbed him by the lapel.

'Stop this. Stop this now!'

She lunged, pulled him towards her. She felt his face crash against hers, her lips leave a wet smear across his cheek. He backed away, shouting: 'How dare you – how – dare you!'

Tom pushed him away, and stood in front of Caroline. He made as if to grab her. Tina turned her round and stood between them, taut as a bow string.

'Hey, get your hands off her!'

'I just want to see him,' Caroline insisted, her voice rising over the growing hubbub. The pall bearers stopped moving. The undertaker looked at the vicar, uncertain what to do next. Caroline was swamped suddenly by a vision of an earth precipice sliding past her face, earth smothering her, earth weighing on her chest, earth worming dully into her lungs. She flung herself through the crowd at the coffin, desperate suddenly to stop it. Tom grabbed her, spun her round, raised his hand and smashed it into the side of her face. Caroline felt a hollow flood of stars in her head, spun out of his hands and knocked one of the pall bearers who staggered against his companion. The coffin lurched, then fell. It hit the ground head first. Something slid inside it with a slight thud.

'Marcus?' Caroline cried. 'MARCUS!' She scrabbled towards it on her hands and knees, reached it, threw herself on to it and started pulling at the lid, trying to force her fingers under the rounded lip. All the time she was doing this, she was looking across the flat, flat field of the giant graveyard to the trees where the five figures stood, as still as guards, watching, watching.

Hands gripped her shoulders, pulled her up and twisted her around. Hands on her neck. Tom's face, mottled red now. She didn't want to struggle. She just kept on twisting round to try and get to the coffin.

There was a crowd round them. The sky thumped red above her. Tom's face was blending with the sky, the red of the grass. Blood and blackness filled her eyes, filled her head, she felt her lips pump up as if they might burst, there was black pressure behind her eyes –

Someone shouted, everyone shouted. She heard the words 'police, police', then a voice said – and it might have been in her ear – 'I am the police', and suddenly the pressure was off and Tom was being half-carried, half-dragged away, shouting that she was a killer, a murderer, a bastard and a bitch . . .

She struggled up from her hands and knees. People moved away from her, their faces closed or showing revulsion. She looked for the face she knew she would see. He would understand. Panting, breath whooping in and out, she saw him. He had managed to park Tom with his brother who was trying to calm him down, anyway keeping a firm grip on him. Caroline staggered towards Willis, hung on to his arms which he had opened for her and gasped in a cracked voice: 'The forest, the children . . . Don't you see?'

Through the course of the morning, Willis's anger at the behaviour of the mourners had given way to sickened contempt. He had seen the incident in the church porch, had seen the expression on Caroline's face change from shock and naked pain to something weird, a sort of opaque self-defence. He had not heard what she said to the vicar but wondered how a Christian could turn his back and walk away from a grief-stricken mother like that. He didn't see how anyone could behave the way the man had. The boy was dead. Nothing would ever change that.

He had stood at the back of the church. Its proximity to the council cemetery meant you could wheel the coffin right inside on a special ramp. The aisle was wide and newly carpeted, and the vicar disguised the fact that he did not know Marcus from Adam with a couple of good anecdotes which had set Marina howling and Caroline sneezing.

The church smelled of polish and heating oil. Willis stood at the back among the piles of hymn books and psalters, the unread newsletters, the parish announcements, and then followed the main body of mourners out of the south door.

Caroline had walked with her friend, a small compact woman with enough brass to wear bright red lipstick to a child's funeral. Wherever they went, whichever way they turned, the rest of the mourners kept a good five yards away. They went and stood by the graveside. The rest stayed back, at last settling round the grave in loose black rings.

Caroline had one black eye and one red. He imagined that the black eye would soon redden from weeping. Her hair was golden and white in the sunlight, red-gold and white-gold. The black brought the best out in it. She looked, he had to admit, inappropriately exotic, standing there by the graveside, peering in occasionally as if she were looking at a vaguely interesting exhibit at a museum. He wondered what drugs she had been prescribed.

The south door of the church opened and the coffin emerged, shouldered by four men, followed by the rest of the family. He recognised Caroline's ex-husband. Was that his wife? It was incredible that she was at the front, and Caroline, the boy's mother, was not.

By the grave the mourners moved restlessly, like guests at a garden party, waiting for the Queen.

And Willis felt that someone was looking at him. It started as a prickling in the back of his neck, then spread to his head and back – a feeling that his skin was actually contracting. As strong as the feeling was, he did not want to turn round and see. The feeling of danger was almost palpable – except danger was the secondary feeling. What he felt first of all was hatred, hatred pouring at him from a point behind him, concentrated like a torch beam at his back.

The coffin began its slow procession towards the grave. Willis felt as if the clothes on his back were being slowly burned and peeled away, and soon it would be his skin, then his bones. On that hot day he felt cold. He was torn between turning and looking at the presence behind him, and walking away, slowly at first, then a little bit faster, then faster still, then running –

He stopped himself, forced himself to think clearly. He was acting like a child in the dark, behaving like a cat with a tin can on its tail. He was a grown man; he was an adult. People didn't feel *presences*.

He turned.

Across the field that was really a graveyard, three, maybe four hundred yards away, a group of children were standing under the trees. The sunlight caught them and made them glow; they shimmered in the heat. That had to be why they seemed to float above the ground.

He turned back to the graveside procession to get his bearings, then looked again at the children. A light breeze was playing on the trees and the shadows were dappling the watchers, so that even though they stood as still as statues, they seemed to ripple with a sort of flickering grace.

Thin, weren't they? Willis thought, looking back at the mourners and thinking how plain and dumpy everyone looked. Perhaps not thin. Perhaps long.

He squinted through the haze which blurred the outline of the little group. There were four of them, and a fifth standing off to one side, moving now to join them.

He saw that he was wrong in thinking that they had been looking at him. The way their heads were turned they were looking at the grave.

He heard voices, shouting, then a woman saying words that he could not understand but plainly insisting on something.

It was her – Caroline. Her friend was restraining her. The coffin had stopped moving now. One of the men following it was going up to her, yelling at her; now another one was pushing his way through the crowd.

Jesus, he was hitting her!

Willis began to run. There was confused shouting now. He couldn't see much over the heads of the mourners, heard louder shouting, then a gasp as the coffin pitched and fell. He elbowed people out of the way. Caroline was half on her knees while that husband of hers bore down on her, having a good go at throttling her. Her face was swelling, her feet were flailing, but her hands were still outstretched towards the coffin. People were shouting for the police. Willis gave Tom a vicious little punch in the kidneys to warn him that someone was there, and then as both his hands were still around Caroline's neck, punched him scientifically on the part of the jaw just under the ear, driving the hinge up into a sensitive cluster of nerve endings. Tom went down, stunned, and Willis managed to bundle him into someone's arms.

The man looked shocked. 'Who are you?' he asked.

'I'm the police,' Willis panted. 'Hold him.'

He turned back to Caroline. She was holding her throat and making gargling sounds. She looked up as he approached. Willis saw relief wash over her face. She lunged for him, grabbed his arms and shook him. It wasn't her words, it was the look of sick longing on her face that sent a shiver down his spine: 'The forest, the children . . . Don't you see? One of them's Marcus! MARCUS IS THERE!'

Willis froze. He looked desperately around for her companion but could not make her out. The faces around them were hostile. He put his hands out to try and calm her. She knocked them down.

'Listen to me! Listen to me!' she shouted. 'Look at the woods. The little one is Marcus.'

She flung an arm out but looked at Willis. A gap opened in the crowd as people turned and stared nervously at the line of trees. Willis raised a hand and shaded his eyes.

The air had cleared suddenly and the children stood out in sharp relief. It was too far to make out their faces but he could see now that there was something terribly wrong with them, as if they were wearing those old-fashioned cardboard masks – strawberry pink ones. Again he felt that shiver grow inside and shake him in the heat. They looked at one another, and as if by a prearranged signal stepped backwards into the woods, melting into the shadows as if they had never been, the four of them.

One was left. He made a sad figure, standing all alone there. He made a gesture towards the crowd – held out his arms like a baby – then twisted and sank back into the forest. Willis pushed his way through the people and walked quickly and purposefully towards the line of trees.

The woods started suddenly, trees rearing up overhead like a frozen wave on the verge of breaking, the undergrowth thick and wet. A narrow headland of unmown grass soaked Willis's shoes; a triffid clump of wild rhubarb drenched his trousers.

The woods smelled of meat. Out in the open the night's rain brought out the freshness in the air. Here it only quickened awareness of the earth god's grinding two-step: grow and rot, grow and rot.

He blinked in the dark shadows, looked back at the light and saw the coffin lifted once more and pointed at the grave. The funeral was proceeding. Heat gathered under the canopy of leaves. Already he felt his face prickle, and a stream of sweat made its way down his back, joining shirt to spine in a long, wet zip.

He pushed in a few more feet, worried that although he had marked the spot where the children had disappeared and kept his eyes fixed on it from the graveside to the wood, there was no sign of any disturbance of the undergrowth. They had simply folded themselves into the woods.

Hey

He heard the voice, far away yet near, heavy but thin.

Heyheyhey

Then a long, long scream that made the short neck hairs crawl like a patch of lice.

It was impossible to get a fix on anything in the woods. He pushed on.

Hey
heyhehey

That awful cry again, broken this time, rising higher with each breath.

The undergrowth was thinner on his left and he veered instinctively towards it –

Hey
heyhehey

– aware that was what one always did in woods, and it was the best way to get lost. But this time the sound had cleared. It was in front of him somewhere.

'Hey,' he shouted. 'Hey, you. I want to talk.'

He pushed hopefully through the thin undergrowth, encased in his own noise. His body was a vast ungainly howdah, swaying and creaking on his bones. He glanced from side to side to peer through the trees, seeing movement all the time but knowing it was only the lines of perspective arranging and rearranging the pattern of the wood around him as he crashed through it.

Hey
heyhehey

Close. He stopped. He was in a small clearing, dry underfoot and strewn with beech nut husks. Above him the sky wheeled. He stilled his breathing. Swung around. Nothing. He traversed a full 360 degrees, eyes flicking ahead and back to try and catch a movement behind a tree or a bush.

The sense that he was being watched was palpable, and growing in intensity. He felt thoughts from outside come swarming round his brain, terrible thoughts, and all to do with what happened to little girls who met murderers and died under bushes; about what happened to bodies underground –

It wants to eat me!

The thought hit him, undeflected and unhindered. He whipped his head round, and round, and round, crouching and tense. The space around him was defined by the grey-green pillars of the tree trunks and the arching bows overhead. It was empty apart from the sound of leaves shaking.

Idiot!

You're just scared of dying. You've just realised that you're wearing away. You've heard about it before but now it's hit you. You are degrading. Crumbling. Dissolving.

It was so unfair, he thought, to pick on him. He was one of the good guys. He tried to save people, for Christ's sake.

The wood rustled at him with the whispery gluttony of rot.

You're part of the conspiracy that blinds us to the truth,

213

binds us to our frames. Authority – that's what you represent. You! A skeleton draped in lard, quivering like lights on a butcher's tray. But it's all rot! Flesh rots and drops from bones. Bones thin out to honeycombs. Skeletons of skeletons. It's waiting for us. All of us.

But not here.

The realisation was a cold light dawning: the early-morning winter light that tells you to leave your warm bed and go and do things, only not here. His mouth stretched into a grin of fear. Death was frightening, but where death did not happen –

Underneath his feet the forest floor twitched then rose. The dead leaves were massing, the ground beneath swelling into a huge, smooth, rounded hump, that was rearing up. He fell off; the dry ground split and a back, a great bare, earth-brown back, glistening and wet, shivered into view.

Willis screamed. If that was the back, where was the head, jerking, rising –

The shape crumbled and fell in on itself. Willis let his head drop on to the cold leaf mould. A few minutes later a leaf fell on his cheek.

His eyes flicked open.

From behind every tree trunk, in every space, a spider-grey face, eaten with twisted hope, stared at him. Young faces, or to be more accurate, one young face, dull as dust, hands that tapered to scratching twigs outstretched towards him. Willis opened his mouth but his spittle had turned to burning white string and his lips just chopped the air. Grey and thin, the wraiths advanced, twists of smoke in the sunlight, bright in the shadows. They moved slowly but it looked as if they were moving fast because pieces were trailing from them in a wavering slipstream. Bits of skin and shadow, woody bones in twin ridges shook and twitched, and when the things rose in the air, they looked like wings.

Sweet Jesus, Willis thought, it's the fairies. And they've all got Marcus's face. Steadily they moved towards him.

'Help me,' he said. 'Somebody, help me.'

His eye was pierced by a needle of light that expanded to make a tunnel. At the end of the tunnel he saw a girl walk towards him. Dana Watkins. Caroline as a child. His niece, Cordy. She was naked to just below her belly, her skin made whiter by the deep red of the long skirt that clung to her belly and her legs like a second skin. Willis saw that her lips and nipples were the same colour as the skirt. As she came closer he saw that the skirt was flowing behind her as she walked, unravelling almost, lying in a long twisting trail as far back as he could see. And then he saw that it wasn't a skirt: it was blood that was pouring from a hundred gashes that lay across her belly and thighs and fell in a thick curtain over her calves, over her feet, running in a river behind her.

'Help you?' she said. 'Save yourself.' Willis reached up. He touched her, felt the blood run down his hands. He put his hands round her waist but just then saw the children close in on her. They put their hands through her flesh and tore her as if she were dough.

'Now,' she said. 'Run, coward!' And Willis ran.

215

Chapter 31

It was dark when Willis walked from the forest and the cemetery was empty.

He drove to Caroline's, reluctantly but quickly, and although he felt like an eel advancing further into a trap, movement at least gave him an illusion of activity and choice.

Up and down Kingsmeade Close big front-room windows displayed framed vignettes of family life: TV, pyjamas, armchairs, supermarket meals on mail-order trays. Two doors down a man was weeding his borders. A boy was riding his mountain bike up and down the pavement. Two little girls were jumping on and off a battered Batman skateboard. Bonfire smells. The muffled rattle of a ghetto blaster.

Although it was hardly dark outside, the curtains in Caroline's house were drawn and yellow light seeped out from around the edges. It was funny what closed curtains could do to a house. A few summers ago while walking in the north-west Highlands Willis had come across a line of 'Keep Out' signs marching across a glen, a new landowner asserting his rights. He had walked past them and noticed that on the other side of the notices someone had written 'Keep In'.

A sense of apartness, of otherness, sweated from between the tightly mortared rough red bricks of Caroline's house. Perhaps this wasn't so much the modesty of grief as a response to some invisible outside pressure.

Keep In. We don't want death down our street.

Willis gave the bell a sharp ring and stood back. He thought he heard movement inside and waited expectantly. No one came to the door.

He pressed the bell again, for longer this time. He looked for the letter box but when he knelt to peer through it, found the view was blocked by a draught excluder. There was no sound from inside. Pretending to write a note, he pressed his upper arm against the bell and kept it ringing. He'd keep it ringing until the damn' thing burned out, he thought, but did not have that long to wait. He heard quick, heavy footsteps then the front door was flung open.

It was Caroline's friend. She had been on the point of saying something, but stopped herself when she saw Willis.

'Thought you might be Tom. I'm Tina.'

'I wondered how Caroline was,' Willis said lamely. 'How is she?'

'Right now, or in general?'

'Both.'

She stood back and let him walk into the sitting room. An ugly table lamp with an out-of-date hessian shade; the slightly worn carpet; a leather armchair; modern carriage clock on the stone ornamental fireplace. Now he thought about it, it was one of the most impersonal rooms he had ever been in, as if the character had been stripped away and all that was left were a few ill-assorted reminders of shopping trips. Was that because the husband had gone, and now the boy? He hadn't remembered the place looking so poor. Not financially poor, mind, spiritually poor. Life, or light, some binding agent had drained away. The room looked as sad as an empty lake.

Tina fetched whisky and two glasses from the other end of the room.

'How is she?' Willis asked again.

'I gave her some pills. She's sound asleep. All I could think of doing was immobilising her. Did you catch those kids?'

'No, but they nearly caught me.'

Tina looked at him, then turned away. 'I'm out of my depth,' she said.

'Me too. Truly. Who is Caroline?' he asked quickly.

'Who is she?' Tina looked both shocked and suspicious.

'I know I'm missing something about her. I know that there's something very important that is stopping me understanding her. There's been no opportunity to ask outright and every time I thought I was getting close, something happens.'

'That's the way it is,' said Tina.

'What? Every time someone tries to get close to her, there's a disaster?'

217

'Sometimes only metaphorically. Sometimes it doesn't end in the death of a child. Sorry. That was uncalled for. You were only doing your job.'

'Does Caroline think it was the investigation that killed Marcus?'

'Caroline thinks . . . ' Tina closed her eyes and inhaled. 'I don't know what Caroline thinks. This has brought a lot of bad things to the surface. Things she thought were locked away inside her head.'

'Things like what?'

Tina shook her head. 'I can't say.'

'What do you mean, you can't say? Don't you trust me?'

'It wouldn't make any difference.'

'It might to Caroline!'

'You like her, don't you?'

Willis shrugged. The question made him feel clumsy and therefore vulnerable.

'Tom calls me a lot,' Tina continued. 'He thinks you and Caroline are having an affair.'

'And you?'

'I know you're not. Caroline tells me . . . ' Her voice trailed away.

Willis pounced. 'You were about to say that Caroline tells you everything.'

'We share a lot. We're friends.'

'Tell me.'

'Tell you what?'

Willis thought: tell me why when I think of her my heart turns over and when I see her it turns over twice. He said: 'I'm attracted to things that move away from me. It's like I need to be tracking something to be involved. It's a useful quality in a policeman, but it makes relationships difficult.'

'You only get excited when they run?'

'And then I get too depressed to follow.'

Tina nodded. 'You're a sad case.'

'Thank you. So I know she's moving away from me, otherwise I wouldn't like her. But she seems to be moving away from everyone, everything. I just want to know why.' Willis saw there were tears in Tina's eyes. He must have hit a nerve. He continued: 'Is it because of Marcus? Look, she told me about the wishing tree; she told me about the job. I know about the creatures in the wood, and I know that she knows. But I just think that she's hiding more from me.' Now he noticed that Tina was looking at him sadly. 'She is, isn't she? There's more to this than just Marcus.'

Tina shook her head.

'I know there's more.'

Tina said: 'I'm not shaking my head because you're wrong. I'm shaking my head because you don't know how right you are. But I can't tell you anything.'

Willis spread his arms wide and groaned. 'There was a book at my place – *Kids that Kill*. That was it. She tried to hide it from me, then took it. Is that important?'

This time Tina shook her head. 'Of course it's important, you idiot.'

'You know the book.'

'Caroline's mentioned it. Please, believe me. I can't tell you more. I think Caroline might but I can't.'

Willis was thinking aloud. 'Marcus can't be in it; the book's too old for that. Someone's in it. Who?'

'I can't say.'

'Look, can't you see how important this is? You're playing games with me. This afternoon I saw things in the forest that either mean I'm mad, or the forest is alive. Actually fucking alive. What's wrong?'

Tina had opened her mouth. She shut it and frowned. 'I've heard that phrase before,' she said. 'Of course. It was Marcus.' She broke off, then looked at Willis. 'It was that bastard creep Temple that got him involved in this. Marcus said something like that when we found him down there.'

'Down where?' Willis asked.

'He lives at the end of the Close and I think he's got an unhealthy interest in children. Remember the day that Caroline called you in a panic because Marcus had gone missing? He'd been at Temple's house and he said almost exactly those words, like Temple had taught him or something. Caroline thought it was fine; said the poor man was just compensating. He lost a child apparently. Now it's you going funny. What's up?'

'The day Caroline called, when Marcus was missing, was the day that Tailor was killed.'

'Wait a minute – '

'I'm just thinking out loud.' Willis felt thoughts turn and tumble, seemingly out of his control but with a will and purpose of their own. 'Caroline's neighbour lost a child, you said. Girl or boy?'

'Teenage girl.'

'A girl called Stephanie Temple was raped by Tailor, and died later,' Willis said. 'What have they got themselves mixed up in? I'm going to see Mr Temple now.'

Chapter 32

Caroline stretched her toes. It was comforting to hear Tina downstairs making cutlery-on-crockery kitchen noises. There was the click of the kettle switching off; the scrape of a chair leg on tiles.

A stripe of sunlight lay across the duvet; the curtains were glowing and the bedroom seemed safe and neat. She felt odd after the sleeping pills, but no odder than she had been for the past two weeks. It was a different sort of feeling anyway; she was both wide awake and relaxed, a complete contrast to the angry, exhausted fog she had existed in since her release from hospital. She thought of getting up and preparing Marcus's breakfast, before she remembered that Tina would be looking after it. Then she remembered that Marcus was dead and cried. As she cried she realised that she had never really forgotten that he was dead; her mind was testing her in order to see how she would cope. This morning she was prepared to cope. She was prepared, full stop. After all, she was one of the few people who could say, after the death of their child: I've been through something like this before. Not as bad, not as awful, but generically similar.

She swung her legs over the side of the bed and immediately felt awful. The sun was too harsh; the room baked and swarmed with heat. She ran to the bathroom and splashed water on her face.

Tina called up from the kitchen: 'I'm up, sweetie. Got to go off in a minute. Tea's ready.' It all sounded quite normal. Caroline walked downstairs on shaky legs.

'Wow,' she said in the kitchen. 'Those pills knocked me out.' She took a sip of tea. It was a dark, smoky brown but she only tasted it faintly.

'You slept through a visit from your knight in plain clothes. Willis. The policeman.'

'Ah.'

'I think he's all right.'

Caroline shrugged.

'He wants to know everything about you. I think he'll be able to take it.'

'Fine.' It was fine. Everything she heard, all it signified, floated away from her like a helium balloon. 'Tell me what that means,' she said. 'I can't work it out.'

'I don't know what it means. I think he'd be relieved. I think he wants to know why you're under pressure.' She glanced at her watch. 'Shit, Caroline. I can't stay. There was one thing. He said to watch out for that Temple guy. He said that he thinks he might have . . . Well, he thinks he might be involved.'

'Ah. With Marcus?'

'Maybe. Listen, it might be better coming from him. He tried to get hold of Temple last night but there was no one in. He said he'd swing round this morning.'

Caroline smiled brightly. 'Right,' she said. 'I'd better have my bath in that case.'

The doorbell rang. She wasn't thinking or she would have seen that the silhouette in the glass belonged to someone smaller than Willis. So instead of finding herself a bit breathless, a bit confused, trying to find ways to thank him for defending her at the funeral, she opened the door to the concerned and serious face of Maurice Temple. His clean, rather large car was waiting behind him.

'Thank you for coming,' she said. She wasn't sure why, except seeing him crystallised something in her mind; something that had been swirling around in an inchoate form. Willis thought that Temple had been involved with Marcus in some way. She was going to find out exactly how.

'I thought we might talk in the car,' he said. 'There's something I feel I should show you.'

Caroline hesitated for a second, then thought that it would be easier to say what she had to while in motion, with someone else making the decisions about how and where to drive.

He kept away from the forest, cutting back through the town centre, unchanged to Caroline's dull surprise, and then out into farmland. He didn't gabble or talk nervously, which she

222

appreciated, just made a couple of comments about the weather and left it at that. Caroline felt like a child being taken for a drive by an adult. The radio chattered about the dangers of Chinese barbecue sets; the seat was so comfortable that she felt she was floating.

They passed fields of stubble and fields of grass; fields bordered by spinneys and bounded by small winding streams. The sky arched up above them. Temple pulled the car down a narrow lane which petered out at a ford. The stream widened and turned shallow at that point. There was an old wooden footbridge, and a willow that trailed long yellow leaves in the dark water.

'It's lovely, isn't it?' Temple said. 'Constable country, almost.' He gave a quick smile. 'Of course it was all forest once. Just forest.'

'It seems hard to believe,' Caroline said. 'It's so peaceful.'

'It is,' he said, 'now. Mankind has always hated the forest. Or feared it.'

'Why?'

'It's a threat.'

'To what?'

'Peace.'

'Why?' Caroline watched the willow branches sway and twitch as they were tugged to and fro by the current.

'The forest is a form of life – I might say, a rival life force. And by the forest, I mean the one forest that once covered Europe from the west coast of Britain to the shores of the Black Sea. We break it down to its constituent parts: trees, humus, undergrowth, birds, insects, flowers . . . ' He paused as a kingfisher flashed past them downstream. Caroline caught her breath. It was so beautiful, so quick, the moment so brief. 'Where was I?'

'Insects and flowers, you said. Why are you telling me this?'

He ignored the question. 'Ah, yes. And creatures.'

'What creatures?'

'Oh, you know. Woodland creatures. As I was saying, we prefer to look at them separately, but it's as futile as trying to pretend that a body is not a body but bones and corpuscles and teeth and hair. It's all those things and more, of course. So is a forest. Our forefathers knew about the forest – until they

223

became strong enough to beat it, that is. They had lots of strange gods scurrying about in it. Tended to keep to the high ground themselves. Left the forest to fend for itself. Stuffed it full of legends: wild men, woodwoses, Robin Hoods. The Germans have always had a feel for wooded places, a sort of violent, sentimental yearning; just think how many of the Grimms' fairy stories take place in a forest. The Romans once lost an entire army in the German forest, you know. Some say it was carelessness; others say it was Celts. The Romans thought they had been eaten by ghosts. The story of the forest is the story of struggle and defeat.'

'And you took Marcus there,' Caroline said dully. She remembered seeing Temple, peering into the forest, looking for something.

Temple opened his mouth then closed it again.

'Why did you choose Marcus?' she asked.

Temple shrugged. 'He was – willing to help.'

'You mean, because he didn't have a father you could influence him more easily.'

She had meant to keep calm but felt tears of rage prickle in her eyes.

'It wasn't as simple as that,' he said. 'Tailor murdered my daughter! You don't know what it's like – to have your child snatched from you.'

'I do now! Because of you, my son is dead!'

'The idea was – it got out of control. The idea was to do good things. Marcus wanted you to be happy.'

'So he made a wish to get me the job?'

'Yes. I arranged to meet him after school – he said it would be all right.'

'And afterwards, when you came to our house, it was to make sure that I hadn't seen you near the scene of a murder?'

'What with everything, I didn't want anyone to know I had been in the wood.'

'No,' Caroline said sarcastically. 'And Tailor just happened to be blundering past at the time, and he just happened to be the man who killed your daughter?'

'I didn't know, I swear it. I had no idea. But that's how it works. It traps you; you ask for something simple and it traps you.'

Caroline nodded. It had pulled her in. Why not Temple? Why not Tailor?

'What happened then?'

'I told Marcus that Tailor might have seen him. Marcus was very frightened. He didn't want anyone to know. I saw a way of – '

'Getting revenge.'

'And making Marcus feel better. So the next time, he asked for Tailor to be stopped from talking.'

'So Tailor was killed.'

'After that it was awful. Relentless. Marcus had woken something. They wanted more wishes, more gifts, more everything. They played with Marcus's rabbit; they came into his room, he told me. He said that you wouldn't listen to him when he was most frightened . . . '

'They?'

'The fairies. The children. Call them what you will. The story goes that if a child dies in the forest, it becomes one of them. The fairies are the ghosts of little children and they want to play. Granting wishes is part of their game.'

Temple swung the car off a main road and on to a narrow country lane. Ahead Caroline could see a small bare hill, crowned with a grey stone chapel. Now the car began to climb the little hill. The grass on its flanks was poor and uncultivated; the chapel looked exposed and temporary, as if it had been dropped there. Below them the irregular, familiar patchwork of fields dreamed beneath a dusty, golden light.

Close to, the chapel looked almost municipal. It had a green-painted door; the grass surrounding it was cut down to the earth. The windows were pale frosted glass covered in close metal grilles.

'What is this place?' Caroline asked.

'This? It was built by a wealthy local landowner just over a hundred years ago. I came across it when I was looking up local people who had a formative effect on the area.' He looked around. 'I imagine it was always a refuge: up here clouds and wind; down there the stifling, close, musty rotting mass of vegetation; the darkness, the constant whisper of leaves; the feeling of being watched.'

'I don't want to go in. I feel fine out here.'

'I think it will explain a great deal,' he said. 'It helped me, Caroline.' He came up beside her carefully, watching her out of the corner of his eye. He put a heavy key into the lock and turned, then pushed the door open and stood back. The air of the chapel, cold and slightly musty, was suddenly around her. She stepped inside, then exhaled, relieved by the sense of anti-climax.

The floor was of well-polished red tiles; the pews warm polished oak. The altar, hung with an embroidered cloth, was adorned only by a simple wooden cross. The walls were whitewashed to waist height, but above covered in purple velvet curtains. Temple pulled a long woven tassel and the curtains along one wall parted.

'They come in and out of fashion,' he said. 'Some people find them offensive.'

Caroline tried to shake away her sense of disorientation. Behind the curtains were two panels of a mural. Two on this wall, presumably two on the other. In the first a young man, thin, pale, and dressed in plus fours and a Norfolk jacket, was standing dejectedly on the edge of the forest. He carried a child in his arms. There was blood on his clothes. The style was modern without being contemporary – it reminded Caroline of early posters for the tube: clear, flat colours making bold, sunlit shapes. The effect was compounded by a background of neat surburban villas with whitewashed walls and red-tiled roofs, corn fields and a long dark line of trees. The picture was entitled: 'I was forlorn'.

In the second panel the young man was entering the forest. His face was already sharper and more alert. He stood poised as if he had just heard something and had frozen to hear and see better. The sun was slanting through the trees behind him; the artist had emphasised the clear columns of light that were slashing through the canopy of green. In one of the bars of light a little shape, a child perhaps, more suggested than painted, was dancing like a ballerina in a spotlight.

Then Caroline saw the eyes.

They were pale, almond-shaped, and looking at the young man through a bush. All their attention was focused on him. You could see nothing through the leaves and there was a clear gap between the bottom of the bush and the forest floor so you thought that the eyes had no body or the body had no feet or the whole thing was floating. This panel was called: 'I felt their presence'.

Caroline shivered and moved across the floor to the opposite wall. Temple opened the curtain. Here the man was standing in thick undergrowth, his hands thrown up across his face, though whether in wonder or terror it was hard to say.

In front of him on a bough sat three fairies. The first had no face, the second had blurry features, the third had the face of the dead girl in the first panel. The creatures were thin, nude, but seemed somehow oddly dressed in nakedness. Their pallid skin, greyed and yellowed with age like old towels, sagged on their tiny frames. Their feet were filthy and strange bony excrescences sprouted from their backs. They looked like ribs, streaked with dried meat, half-covered in a ragged membrane of dried skin. This panel was called: 'Salvation is promised'.

Hurriedly Caroline passed on to the last painting. It was the most dramatic, and at first sight seemed to show a crucifixion set in an English wood. Except, except . . . no painting Caroline had ever seen showed Christ's head thrown back, face stretched in such an ambiguous grimace: pain and ecstasy; defeat and triumph; sudden realisation and a sort of mindless revelling in the moment. The back too was arched and the hands and feet were straining to tear loose from the heavy nails that fixed them to an old dead tree. In front of the figure a swarm of creatures were crawling from the mud: naked, earth-caked, as plump as fruit as they emerged, but their skins drying to dusty tatters as they strove to reach the light. This panel was called: 'Salvation and pain'.

The face of the man on the tree was the face of the man in all the other panels.

'What is this place?' Caroline asked. 'Why haven't I heard of it?'

'It's mentioned in guide books but it's usually locked and the key's the very devil to get hold of. The painter was a man called Herbert King, a decent artist, I think. Studied at the Slade, moved to Epping just before the Great War. Died four years later after a spell of acute depression followed by a complete physical breakdown. He's usually referred to as a demented visionary, a sort of cross between William Blake and Stanley

227

Spencer. It never crosses most people's minds that he was painting what he saw.'

'He couldn't have seen the crucifixion.'

'Perhaps not. It depends what you mean by "see".'

Caroline looked at the murals. Then at Temple. 'You're going to do something. You're going to wish for something.'

'I don't think adults can wish,' he said. 'But I'm going to ask.'

'For what? Tailor's dead. What more do you want?'

Temple closed his eyes.

'Your daughter?'

'Just to see her. You can ask for Marcus. It's all we can do now!'

'You're mad.'

'She needs me; she needs love. So does he. That's why they are the way they are.'

'It won't work.'

'Look at the murals. It might. He lost his child – but he saw her again.'

'But *look* at the children,' Caroline shouted. 'I can't let you.'

'You can't stop me. My daughter; your son.'

'He's not my son! He's dead.'

'He's not. Children don't die when they're part of the forest. We'll go – '

'We will not.'

Caroline looked at Maurice Temple, then looked at the door. The key was still in it; the windows to the chapel were high, too high for him to reach.

She walked behind him, as if she was considering something, and lifted the edge of the heavy Bible. It fell with a satisfying 'whump' back on to the lectern.

'Let me think.'

Temple turned away. The important thing, Caroline thought, was not to hit him too hard. If she could just stun him, she was sure she could keep him pinned down. Temple half-turned, warned by the Bible's heavy hiss. It struck him on the side of the head and he fell on to his knees, then his face. She knelt and went through his pockets for his car keys, then checked his pulse and breathing. He began to stir and his eyelids fluttered.

228

'I'm doing this for your own good,' she said. 'Think about what you've just said.'

Temple protested feebly. Caroline walked to the door and locked it behind her.

Chapter 33

Things were bad when you woke up and felt more tired than you had the night before.

Willis stood under the shower, feeling punch drunk. He turned the water to cold – it was a perversion of the system that the only decent jet you got was when the water was cold – and hopped and flapped his arms involuntarily as the breath was sucked out of his body and his skin began to tingle.

Good. He felt better for that. He made double-strength Colombian coffee, deliberately didn't eat anything because he thought that anything else in his belly might delay the transfer of caffeine from gut to blood stream. He thought of taking a couple of amphetamine tabs that he had bought from a colleague who had found them surplus to the needs of a successful prosecution, but he knew the frightful fever-bright clarity they brought to his thinking and didn't want it.

He got to Smith's Car Parts by a quarter to nine. He wanted the reassurance of knowing that he had investigated as much as possible of Caroline's current life. The door was open and he walked into the empty reception area. Through a porthole in a glass door by the side of the desk he could see an empty office. A door behind opened and a tall, frosty woman said: 'I'm sorry, we're not open yet. Can I help?'

Willis summed her up as someone who would ask for identification if he was polite. He looked at her blankly, then around the room, and said: 'Not very clever, leaving the main door open and the room unattended. Police. Detective Sergeant Willis, North Forest CID. I'm here to ask a few questions about Caroline Waters.'

'Oh?' The head waggled slightly on the long neck.

'If possible I'd like to see her personnel record and talk to anyone in the office who might have any information regarding her employment here.'

A slight frown creased the smooth forehead. 'I would have assumed that – '

'Yes?'

'No, nothing.'

'Please. You were saying?'

'Well, it really isn't important but I assumed that you might be asking about the tragic accident.'

Willis gave her his nastiest smile and said: 'So you have information regarding the accident?'

The woman flushed and looked flustered. 'Certainly not. I . . .'

Willis raised an eyebrow and looked at the locked door. 'Perhaps we could talk in the main office, Ms – '

'Neilson.'

Willis stood back and smiled. He had just seen a personnel file open like magic in front of him.

Five to nine. He had no desire to be still reading the file while the office filled up. Someone might ask why. This must be the managing director's office, he thought. There were graphs on the wall of targets to hit and an onyx pen stand. By the window stood a fax machine with copy facility. Willis slid the top page of the file through, the one containing personal details, and called out of the door that he was finished.

'That was quick.'

'I knew what I was looking for,' he said. 'Now, if you'll just let me have a word with the people she works with – '

He was interrupted by a girl with backcombed hair.

'The copier's out of toner, Ms Neilson. Want me to call the supplier?' She stopped, looked at Willis as if she had not noticed him before and said: 'Oh.' Ms Neilson looked exasperated. Willis thought the whole exchange had been engineered so the girl could have a look at him.

'You know Caroline Waters?' he asked.

'Of course.'

'I'm interested in how she got the position here. Anything she might have told you – '

The girl looked taken aback. 'You don't want to ask me about that,' she said, looking pointedly at Ms Neilson. 'Wasn't anything to do with me how she got the job.'

She turned on her heel and stalked away.

'Bad feeling?' he asked.

'It was nothing,' Ms Neilson said. 'Let's just say that a friend of hers was up for it – '

She was interrupted by a loud snort. This came from an untidy middle-aged woman dressed in a worn velour track suit and battered trainers.

'Do you want me to phone about toner or not?' the first girl called from the other side of the room.

Ms Neilson threw her hands up in the air and walked off.

Willis squared up to the older woman.

'Can you tell me anything?'

'About how she got the job? I wondered how long it would be before one of the boys in blue put two and two together and made three. You weren't there when she found out. That cow – pardon my French but I believe in speaking honestly – didn't even tell her and caused a lot of bad feeling with the younger generation.' She nodded to the other end of the room where the girl who had asked about the toner was talking to two others of about the same age, gesturing at Willis while she did so to make her point. 'Simone was at school with Dana's sister, knew her mother, told her about the job . . . Lovely girl by all accounts. Anyway, not surprisingly Simone was upset. Something about funeral meats not even being cold springs to mind but then Miss Neilson has all the sensitivity of a pig in rut. Between her and Mike Carstairs – he's the boss – you had the combined sensitivity of . . . '

'Two pigs porking?' Willis said.

'Doing an injustice to pigs!'

'But I get the drift.' Drift. The fear he felt was the invisible, fatal mist of a driftnet; fear that too many people were involved now.

'Caroline's all right?'

He shook his head.

'No. I can't see how she could be. Parents shouldn't outlive their kids. But, like I said, you didn't see her when she found out. There was no way she could have faked that. Practically fell off the roof. Well, when she told me later that she'd actually seen poor little Dana just before she died, when I put that together with her past, I knew it wouldn't be long before you boys turned up. I knew you'd be asking so I thought about it a lot. And I repeat: no one could have faked her reaction. The idea that she could have killed Dana Watkins to get the job, well, it's absurd. Quite absurd.

'You're looking haggard. Not heard what you want, I expect? Well, that's the police for you and I'm very sorry if what I say doesn't fit in with your particular theories, but just because Caroline . . . well, just because that tragedy in her past occurred, it doesn't mean that she's dangerous in any way. Well, that's my opinion and I'm sticking to it,' she concluded with a harsh laugh.

Willis said: 'Very clever. How did you put two and two together?'

The woman looked rather pleased with herself. She leaned forward and said: 'Detective work – and a little bit of luck, I give you that. I don't have your resources. Caroline was looking for something one day. Seemed agitated to have lost it, so I looked too. Right under my desk, hidden from her by the pedestal, there's this book. I pick it up. Know what it's called?'

Willis shrugged, anticipating what she would say next but unwilling to interrupt her flow.

'*Kids that Kill*. Tacky, eh? *Kids that Kill: Victims of Innocence*. That was the full title. And blow me, I've got it in my hands, I'm looking at the picture on the cover and whose photo is it? Caroline's. Well, as a young girl but it was her all right. Then I remembered. Local story. Abusive father, mad mother. Found in the cellar of their home, dismembered. At first they thought it was Caroline. She was charged but they had to let her go. Mind you, if you heard what her parents did to her, you'd not blame her. Well, I wouldn't,' she added pugnaciously. 'I'm surprised you don't remember it.'

'I wasn't here then,' Willis said.

'Ah. I was a teenager at the time. It stayed with me. And to think it was Caroline; the woman who sat next to me at the office. Does this mean she's in trouble?'

'No,' Willis said shortly.

'Good. I like her. She's all right, is Caroline.'

233

'Will you keep this under your hat?' Willis asked.

She nodded. 'Of course. I think she's suffered enough,' she said.

Willis sat in his car with the windows open and smacked his hands gently against the wheel. Caroline Waters, or Emma Darby as she was then. What must she have thought when she came round to his flat that evening, what must she have thought when she came across that old paperback? What could it be like to be Caroline Waters, to walk through life with that burden?

Caroline Waters, Emma Darby. Caroline's colleague had given him the story with a directness and conciseness that impressed him. Her parents had been hacked to death with a hatchet one hot afternoon while they slept off a drinking bout. Emma Darby had been beaten so badly for so long that by the time her parents had died – she was twelve – they weren't cutting into skin, they were splitting scar tissue.

She didn't live in a trunk or anything, she hadn't been fucked to madness and back or sodomised by all her father's friends. The house was spotlessly clean, she was well nourished. But every night, if what she said was true, she was led into the basement, bent over a bar with her wrists tied to her ankles, and – left.

Some nights her parents came down later and beat her until she bled. Some nights they let her hang there on her own. 'It was,' she told the police, 'just what they liked to do.'

Emma Darby. What must it be like if, like her, you didn't want people to find out about your past? What must the past be like if at every turn it was there in front of you like a brick wall. She wasn't a celebrity, she wasn't even notorious. It was just every now and again, perhaps when you wanted help and felt you had nowhere else to turn – WHAM! There it would be. The past facing you whichever way you turned, just when you thought you might have beaten it.

He rubbed a hand over his face and squinted up at the sun until his eyes watered. He saw black for a good minute afterwards. What he needed, he thought, was something straightforward to get his teeth into.

He tried to clear his mind. Why had he gone to her workplace? To find out more about her, and now he had. He had to face it. Her parents had been torn to pieces; Tailor had been torn to pieces. The link went beyond Dana Watkins; went beyond Tailor. It went back to Caroline's childhood and then back beyond that. That let her off the hook but added a new element to his fear. It meant that Caroline was caught up in something bigger and older than he had thought possible: a great, dim, ragged driftnet of terror that stretched out of sight, and out of mind.

Chapter 34

Behind a bald privet hedge a dismembered Reliant Robin was spread over half the paved front garden. All the other houses had concreted-over front gardens, and a great many had bits of car spread out over them. A poor street, then, where people fixed their own cars and you did not have to be a detective to work that out. Two doors away someone was revving an old Marina. The exhaust smoke changed from white to black and the engine coughed and died.

The houses were two-storey pebble-dashed semis. For some reason they all seemed to be painted olive green, or perhaps that was just the impression they gave. Willis thought that if he lived there, he'd go treasure hunting too. He might even go train spotting.

The door was opened by a youngish woman with a goggle-eyed baby on her hip. Before Willis could open his mouth she shouted 'Dad' over her shoulder. She didn't close the door, she just stood in it, jiggling the baby on her hip and looking at Willis quite pleasantly. The baby looked at her and smiled. Willis smiled at the baby and it cried. Behind her he saw a narrow hall, narrow stairs, a narrow corridor leading into a narrow kitchen which gave on to a narrow garden.

The man who came down the stairs was narrow too. He looked at Willis and said: 'Oh my God,' and rolled his eyes. They were set close on either side of a high-bridged nose. Dark eyes. There was something assertively naive about them.

His daughter looked amused, the baby looked at the man and smiled, then looked at Willis and cried.

'Police?' the man said.

'Yes.'

'Blimey. It's about digging in the forest, I suppose?'

'Sort of.'

'Look, I'm beginning to regret I ever told you.'

'That's what I said, Dad,' the woman said. 'Isn't it?' she said to the baby who stuck its hand in her mouth.

'This is more in the line of general enquiries,' Willis said. 'For what it's worth, I'm not in the slightest bit bothered by what you did.'

'We're careful,' the man said. 'Responsible. I don't care what anyone says, people like us are the only ones out there looking. The archaeologists – they just hang around until some developer turns something up, and half the time they don't even do a decent job of it before it's all covered over again. At least with us we – well, we're always trying to turn something up.'

His hands were long and restless, thumbs constantly rubbing the pads of his index fingers.

'There's just a couple of things I want to check up on.' Willis pushed his way in.

The man rolled his eyes again and said: 'That's another fine mess I've got us into,' as he stepped aside and let Willis through. Without being asked he walked into the corridor and let himself straight into the front room. The man screwed his eyes shut and said: 'Oh, no.'

The woman followed Willis in. The baby smiled at him, looked at his mother and cried.

In pride of place, hanging on the wall above the gas fire surround, was what Willis guessed to be a very old sword. The grip had rotted away but the short, broad blade still carried an air of purpose and menace. On the alcove shelving either side of the chimney breast were other trophies: a twisted scrap of wood and leather which proved to be a leather shoe with a high, wooden heel; indeterminate bits of wood and metal and pottery; a ploughshare; numerous coins; an old pocket watch that looked fossilised.

On the mantelpiece, below the rusty sword, was a lump of metal that could once have been a service revolver. By it was the remains of a leather holster.

'World War One?' Willis asked.

'I can explain. I didn't know what it was, did I?'

'It might have helped, you know.'

'I told him,' the woman said. 'I said: This time, don't go helping yourself. Just give it all in. It's a police enquiry. This

237

might end up having serious repercussions. Didn't I say that, Dad?'

'Stow it, Raquel. All right?'

'I was right though, wasn't I?' she appealed to Willis with a perky, smug smile on her face.

'Perhaps I could talk to your father alone for a moment?'

'He'll only get himself into trouble,' she said.

'Exactly what I want.' He shooed her out of the door and confronted the man.

'And your name is?'

'Brian. Brian Borely.'

'And how long have you been a collector, Mr Borely?' Willis asked.

'Only a couple of years, really. Well, let's see now. I was laid off – the bakery, you know – laid off there three years ago come Christmas and I bought the detector with my redundancy package – so maybe two years, maybe more. It started as a hobby really, but it's grown. You might call it an all-consuming passion now.'

Willis looked up at the wall, at the alcoves, and said: 'I can see that.' He blessed the God of Archaeology. The man's hands, he noticed, stopped moving when he said something, and started when he was quiet.

'I want to know exactly what you found,' he said, 'and how you found it. I don't want to hear excuses or lies. The pistol. You found that where?'

The man followed his words so closely that Willis wondered if he were deaf. He replied, perfectly reasonably: 'I found the pistol on top of the arm. Nineteen-sixteen standard issue World War One service revolver – for officers, of course.'

Willis shook his head. 'You found the pistol first?'

'That's right. I was digging down, and found it.'

'And then you dug on some more?'

The man paused. 'Yes,' he said. 'Yes.'

Willis wondered what he had missed.

'And what did you find next?'

'Bones,' the man said enthusiastically. 'I've never found bones before.'

'Could you describe them?'

'Well, first I found big ones, then I found small ones.'

'Could you be more specific?'

'Well, first I found a very large bone, which I assumed was a thigh bone, then a smaller one that I thought might be a shin. I think all the other bones were there but everything was sort of clumped up with earth so it was hard to tell.'

'And how were the bones arranged?'

The man thought for a while, then gave a couple of bird-like pecks of the head. 'Neatly,' he said.

'And digging on?'

'Well, I seem to remember another leg, I suppose we must say, and then two arms.'

Willis could not restrain himself any longer. 'You came across four limbs and at no stage did it occur to you to stop digging and contact the authorities?'

The man looked unhappy. A hand twitched and flapped in the air.

Willis suddenly understood.

'You were still getting readings from your detector?'

'Yes. That's it. I was.'

'And you found . . . ?' he insisted.

The man shook his head. He got up, went to a drawer and took out a plastic bag. He shook it, then handed it to Willis who reached in and took out a polished brass button. He held the bag up. Six buttons and what looked like an old square-faced watch, the sort you could flip over for protection.

'Where were these?' he asked flatly.

'Oh, with the arm bones. It's the Greenbacks – that's the local regiment. They were amalgamated twenty years ago into the – '

'Exactly where did you find them?'

'Well, where you would expect.'

'Which is?'

'Well, the watch was on the wrist, and the buttons – they're from the cuff.'

'You're sure of this?'

'Quite sure.'

Willis closed his eyes. He summoned up the memory, never far away, of Tailor's body. How the bloody arms and legs, trailing muscles and blood vessels, had been cleanly torn from the sockets. But more than that. How they had still been wearing clothes. That was the key really to the scene's obscenity

239

– that little touch of detail he could not shift. A leg, an arm, one in trousers, the other in a sleeve, tumbling slowly through the air against a bright blue sky.

He dabbled through the plastic bag, was just about to hand it back when he had a thought. He fished out the watch and looked at it. The face was still pointing outwards. Whatever had attacked the man had not given him much warning. He got up.

'I'm only an amateur,' the man said. 'I don't really know the law.'

Willis held the watch up to the window. It had been thoroughly cleaned; the back even showed some signs of being polished. Under the intact crystal the face was black. 'The lettering on the back of this. Is it engraved?'

'I think so, yes. It's a bit hard to make out but with the magnifying glass I think it says "TW from CT". Then something like "My Love". I'm fairly sure about the initials. Have I been of help?'

Willis said: 'I don't know.'

'Am I still in trouble?'

'I don't know.'

He pocketed the watch without even asking, and saw himself out.

It was almost a relief to think that whatever had killed Tailor had killed this other person – this TW. If the revolver was standard military issue for 1916, it meant that this murder could not have occurred before that date. Equally it struck Willis as unlikely that officers would have gone around after peace was declared in full kit. What did he have then? An officer called TW goes for a walk in the forest and is killed some time between 1916 and 1918. He is dressed in military uniform – the local regiment – so he is likely at the very least to be from the county. He's been given an expensive watch by whom? A friend? A fiancée? Say fiancée, whose initials are CT. She's rich, because tank watches don't come cheap, so the chances are that he's well off too.

And it happened nearly eighty years ago, thought Willis.

He waited for the shudder to kick in, for the cold hand to grab him just above the coccyx and start hauling in the skin. It didn't. Must be getting used to it, he thought.

Chapter 35

Evening. Willis sat in his flat with the windows open, feeling the warmth leave the air, trying to relax. He had been given an indigestible mound of information and couldn't get through it. He kept on coming back to two points. The first was that neither Marcus nor Caroline was the instigator of this bloody mess. The second was that he was missing something, some last fact that would make the whole story gel. He knew it was there. He knew it was big and overwhelming but when he tried to think it through, he found himself diverted into the terrible history of Caroline's childhood. What would a child do in her circumstances? How would she have coped? How would he have coped?

Not having children himself, his own childhood had retreated into a blurred, consistent mass: hope, expectation, boredom, surprises – some nice, some not so nice. Sixteen childhood Christmas Days were now just a memory of one unchanging Christmas Day that he had suddenly grown out of. The sharp tang of each individual birthday had melded into a seemingly unbroken succession of steadily shortening years. Time accelerated as you grew older. He had a strange feeling that time was beginning to run out. The room grew dark around him. He heard a car draw up outside the house, and a door slam. When he looked out of the window he saw her looking up at him. Something inside him tightened excitingly. He walked down the stairs to let her in.

In the sitting room she turned and looked at him.

'What –'

There was an air of desperate excitement about her. She took two steps towards him, cupped his face in her hands and stopped his mouth with her lips. He was still at first, cold and still depressed, then something happened: a forgotten pilot light somewhere inside him lit into flame. He felt a warm glow spread outwards from his belly, catch in his groin, rise to his head and infuse his whole body with heady red heat. He grabbed her, more roughly than he meant to. She pushed him away and for a second they looked at each other, both panting, lips flushed, eyes glistening and dark. Then they grappled each other to the floor like wrestlers, face crushing against face and neck and breast. Willis slipped his hand under the back of her T-shirt, up her spine, round to the breast which seemed to strain against the fabric of her bra. He felt her hands tugging at his shirt, freeing it from his waistband, felt the sudden loosening of his trousers, then her hands were round his prick, pulling at it, running round and down it, cupping his balls. He dragged the T-shirt over her head, fascinated for a second by the muscle that ran down from her shoulder and sank into her breasts. She wriggled free of her bra, tugged open his shirt and pressed herself against his chest. Her breasts were full, heavy, low and he felt them crush against him. With a moan he lowered his face on to them, felt them envelop him, then started pulling her free of her jeans.

She stood. Kicked off her jeans and panties. Willis looked at her. There was an expression he could not read in her face: something brave and defiant. He stood and undressed. God, she is beautiful, he thought, and as if to confirm what he was thinking she straightened her back and lifted her chin. He stepped towards her. His prick seemed to rear up against her belly. He cupped a hand under her sex and let his fingers run over the warm furrow, touching the smooth skin of her thighs. She pushed her crotch at him, knelt, then lay back. When he entered her he wanted his whole body to follow.

He began fast then checked himself, but Caroline rolled her arms around his waist, pressed him into her. Her hips reared up then began moving. He started to say something but her eyes flashed open and something in them made him join the rhythm she was setting. Her teeth were clenched. He saw sweat start on to her upper lip, and darken the soft hairs of her fringe. Again he tried to slow, but her arms slipped down his back, held him just above his buttocks and began pushing him, harder, faster, harder, faster.

She was frowning, her lips were moving and he heard a

242

murmur come from her throat. Words started to form. Her frown deepened. He sensed she was coming, a pressure built up inside him and the first pre-orgasmic flush spread from his body, flowed into his prick. He was gasping, straining. White heat, black heat, red heat gathered like a small sun. His head dropped; her lips were in his ears, mouthing something. As the warmth exploded and he thrust deeper and deeper in her, breath jerking from him in short spasms, he heard something catch in her throat, and a wail joined the words so that they blended into a long, incoherent shriek.

She gasped as he thrust helplessly into her, then something in her gave. She loosened and collapsed. Her arms were clinging now and tears were running helplessly down her cheeks. Her breath came in sobs that racked her like a storm and all Willis could do was hold her, mutter 'shhh' in her ear and try to calm the shudders running up and down her body in waves.

The wind caught the curtain at the open window. It flapped loosely and Caroline brushed it away from her face. The tear tracks had dried the skin on her cheeks to a different, duller texture. She hugged the bathrobe he had given her and took a deep, long pull at a glass of wine.

'I'm sorry,' she said.

'Don't be.' Willis was still on the floor, wrapped in a throw that he had pulled off the back of a chair.

'I used you.'

'Any time,' he said. 'I mean it.'

She gave a quick smile and when she turned her head, the lights of a passing car seemed to catch in her eyes.

'Has it worked?'

'What?'

'Whatever you were using me for?'

She shook her head and seemed to be shaking the tears away.

'It's Marcus, isn't it?' he said.

'No.'

He stood and walked towards her.

'Please tell me.'

She backed away from him but there was nowhere to go.

'I said no!'

'For Christ's sake. Did you come here just to – '

243

She ran towards him, knelt and put her hand over his mouth. 'Again,' she said. 'Do it again.' Her hands fluttered down his chest to his prick.

'No,' Willis muttered thickly. 'I doubt I'm capable, and even if I was – '

Her head slid down his body. She took his sleeping sex in her mouth and began to suck with almost childlike insistency.

'No,' he said.

He pushed her away.

'Why?' she wailed.

'You've got to face it,' he said. 'Whatever it is.'

She looked at the floor and shook her head, hair swinging in a golden bell in front of her face. Willis felt drained. He tried one more time.

'Caroline, you've got to face the truth. I mean, in order to get to the truth you've got to get to the facts.'

'All anyone wants me to do is face the facts.'

'Anyone?'

'Everyone. Anyone. What's the difference?'

'Who else?' Willis persisted.

'No one.'

'Caroline, I know who you are.'

'What do you mean?'

'I know where you come from, who you are.'

She was silent. For a second Willis could not see what she was doing. Then he realised that she was rushing for him, scrabbling across the floor on all fours. She looked like something frightening and wild. Just before she reached him he sidestepped and dropped on to her back, pinning her down with his knees pressing into her waist and his hands holding her wrists. She struggled for a moment, then went still.

'How did you find out?' she hissed.

'I'm a detective,' he said. 'Finding out is what I do.'

'You weren't meant to know. Nobody was meant – '

'Neither was Tina, and neither was your friend at work,' Willis said. 'They both know. Tina wouldn't tell me out of respect for you; Maggie was sympathetic. As I would have been. As I am.'

'You people are never sympathetic. I'm just a freak. Did it give you a big thrill to fuck me? To touch my breasts, my hair, my back? Knowing?'

'People aren't like that,' Willis said. 'I've just told you of two people who know about you and care. Three people if you count me. Listen. All I'm interested in is the fact that this goes beyond Marcus and goes beyond you now.'

'What do you mean?'

She twisted round and looked up at him. He could see the skin stretch on her neck and two tiny tendons under her chin raise themselves as she struggled to keep her head up. He stood up and moved away.

'Your parents were dismembered, just like Tailor. I think you wished for it. We just found a dismembered skeleton in the forest. It's eighty years old. This has been going on for a long, long time.'

She sat hunched in an armchair, her hands wrapped around a mug of hot, sweet tea. The bathrobe swamped her. Her dark-ringed eyes were huge in her pale face. With her untidy hair and legs tucked under her, she looked like a sick child.

'What's your theory?' she asked.

'About what?'

'About me.'

Willis shrugged. He was in his flat's other armchair, half-facing Caroline. They were separated by a gas fire with a tile surround the colour of dirty snow.

'I think your parents beat you; I think it all got too much for you and like anyone else, you wished for it to stop. It stopped.'

'I told the police,' Caroline said. 'I told them everything. I told them that I made the wish and they dismissed it. They wanted to blame me at first but they couldn't. No human child could do what they do. Nothing could.'

'Who are they?'

'The children who live in the forest. The fairies.' She looked at Willis. 'That's what they are. Tinkerbells.' She gave a short, harsh laugh.

'You saw them?'

'They showed themselves to me. Once. I was standing on the edge of the wood and I saw them. They were very thin; they were badly made; they're dreadful and dreadfully unhappy.'

'But what are they?'

'Ghosts. Ghosts of dead children. They don't die here. It's

245

the forest. It's become too concentrated. Bits of it die, but bits of it grow. A forest goes on and on, and so do they.'

'And the wishes?'

'Oh, I expect that's how they make contact with people. Humans. They understand us, you see. And no one knows more about wanting things than children.'

'But they helped you. Why you? It's been bothering me all this time. The tree's a part of local legend. Hundreds of people make wishes there but only some people seem to get their wishes granted, thank God. I just don't understand it.'

Caroline shook her head. 'I don't either. I don't understand how they do it, why they do it. I don't understand what they did to me.'

'Did your husband know?' Willis asked suddenly. 'I mean, about your parents?'

'Tom? God, no. That was the whole point about Tom. Not only did he not know, he never would. He wasn't the type. He just recognised in me a craving for normality and that was it. When he saw my scars, I told him that I was orphaned young and sent to a home where I got beaten. I said I didn't want to talk about it and he certainly didn't. I wanted what he wanted; did what he did. I just couldn't manage the children.' She looked at Willis and shrugged. 'It was the one thing I couldn't fake. All the rest, things like living in the Close, being nice to neighbours, that I could handle. I just couldn't bring myself to have children. Even Marcus was an accident.' She grimaced as if the word was bitter-tasting.

'Who brought you up?'

'I was a council orphan. It wasn't great but it wasn't awful either. I wasn't one of the tearaways. I never wanted to burn things down or go shoplifting. I think I had a healthy terror of unforeseen circumstances so I kept to the straight and narrow. I got qualifications; I got a job; I met Tom; I got married. And it was all fine, even the divorce and being on my own. It was all fine until I found out that Marcus had made a wish and it'd come true.'

'But surely you knew that it could happen.'

'I knew, but I'd been persuaded otherwise. Early on after my parents were killed I'd had counselling. I was quite open, in fact I was desperate to confess. I told them that I had wished for my

246

parents to stop beating me and the fairies had killed them. They told me that it was a subconscious defence method. Don't you see? I was told that all the stuff about the tree, about the fairies, about the wishing was a fantasy, a result of abuse, guilt, anything they could drag in. They convinced me that I was making it up, in the nicest possible way, of course, and I got it into my head that the best way to overcome my fears was to live here. I tried to impose this grid of normality over my past and for a while it worked. Until my past came back. When Marcus told me what he had done, when he confessed to me, I told him it was nonsense.'

She was silent for a while. Willis tried to find the words to comfort her but nothing he could think of felt adequate. He was relieved when she stood up, yawned and allowed herself to be led into the bedroom. In bed she lay in the crook of his arm. Willis was surprised, and impressed, by her size. She felt substantial, the physical reality of her somehow belied the impression of nervy tension. Curious, he had watched as she got into bed. She had found an old shirt of his in the chest of drawers, had taken it without asking him, and slipped it on in the bathroom. Now she was lying so that there was no way he could see or feel her scars. He found the whole thing – her damage, her passion, her presence – disturbingly arousing and, if he was honest, the fact that she had been so abused, but had somehow chosen to use him, added to the thrilling warmth. Secrets, even dreadful secrets, were erotic.

He heard her breathing and felt her eyelashes move against his skin. She was awake. In the darkness he could see her face. She was thinking. She frowned; she closed her eyes; she opened them wide; now she looked lost and frightened. She made a movement as if she was about to turn her head. Something made Willis close his eyes. He gave a deep, sleepy sigh and turned on his back.

She had turned her head. She was watching him. He heard her eyelashes scratch against the pillow as she blinked. Still she watched him. He waited, hoping that she would turn, close her eyes and settle back down to sleep. But she didn't.

He opened his eyes. Immediately her face softened and she smiled. He smiled back and said: 'Want anything?'

She shook her head and rolled away from him, butting into

him with her buttocks. He lay awake, thinking. It was not the smile that concerned him, but the expression it replaced. It had been a mask, so expressionless that for a split second he was frightened.

But who was he to know what she was going through? he thought. She had survived more than he ever had and ever would. He knew, too, that survivors could drown the people who rescued them, but he had no desire to pull back. He would be careful for both of them, but he would not pull back.

Chapter 36

Over coffee the next morning, Willis asked Caroline what she knew of Maurice Temple.

'I've got a confession to make. I locked him up,' she said. 'I needed to think.'

'You locked him up? Where?'

'In a chapel he took me to. It's got these murals about the forest. You know Temple's daughter was raped by Tailor?' Willis nodded. 'I was confused. He wanted both of us to wish for our children to come back to life. I needed to get away, to clear my head. I was tempted. I needed to stop wanting it to happen. I came to you,' she said simply. 'I just wanted a bit of oblivion before – '

'Before what?'

'Before I had to make a decision.'

Willis nodded. 'Can I ask you something? Do you think that Temple asked Marcus to wish for Tailor's death?'

Caroline took a deep breath. 'Yes. No. He encouraged Marcus to make the first wish – for me to get my job. That resulted in Dana Watkins's death. That showed him that the whole thing worked. Marcus didn't need much persuading to ask for Tailor to be stopped, after that. He was frightened.'

'But Temple was behind it all?' Willis asked.

'If I thought that, I would have killed him,' Caroline said. 'No, he's just a pawn, like all of us. Can't you see the way events twist and turn to involve as many people as possible, to create as much hurt as possible? The way Tailor was brought in meant that even if Temple hadn't wanted him dead, someone else would have. It's been slowly poisoning Temple; he's convinced that he can bring his daughter back from the dead.'

'It creates its own momentum,' Willis said.

'Yes. And now I think it – this force – has stopped needing

us. Temple said the fairies just wanted to play with Marcus, and now they have him.'

'We don't know that.'

'We do. How can we get him free? How can I . . .'

She was crying now. Willis stood behind her. She leant against him, then gave a decisive sniff.

'Let's go and get Temple now. I can face him. Perhaps we can persuade him to let his daughter go.'

'What can you remember?' Willis said after they had left the shops behind. He drove quickly, trying to push away a cloud of apprehension.

'About what? My childhood?'

'No. About the day. The blank day.'

'Nothing.'

'What about after it?'

'I don't remember anything until a worried neighbour came round. She hadn't seen smoke from the chimney – it was a bitterly cold spring and in the country you notice that kind of thing. I was in the kitchen. The first thing I remember is sitting at the kitchen table and the neighbour screaming and shouting in the doorway, twisting this hideous floral apron in her hands. She thought I must have been hurt.'

'Why?'

'I was covered in blood, I mean caked in it, and had my father's guts draped round my neck like a garland. I'd made a garland of leaves for my hair – God knows how, I've never done anything like it since. They said later that I was crooning, evilly no doubt, and my expression was terrifyingly blank.'

Willis smiled.

'So the neighbour screams and what happens then?'

'She says: "Where's your mummy and your daddy?"'

'I said, in the basement. I knew, you see. I led her down and turned on the light. I remember what I saw. They used to beat me on a long wooden beam that they stood on two trestles. Their bodies were spitted on that. In the anus and out through the throat. Their heads and legs were off, stacked in a corner. They'd been largely emptied of their innards and stuffed with earth and leaves.'

'Your reaction?'

250

'Nothing. It was like I knew but didn't know.'

'And your neighbour?'

'Passed clean away. When she woke up she locked me in a cupboard and rang for the police. I was questioned. I never lied. There was one nice man, I remember, a sergeant. At first they invented a special syndrome for me: defensive rage-induced temporary insanity. Defensive rage was supposed to have given me the strength to shove an eight-foot pole through two adults' bodies; they came up with all sorts of stories of people gaining superhuman powers for a minute or two at moments of great stress. Most people focused on that. There was one man, a nice sergeant, local, I could tell by the accent, always asked me about what my parents did to me and what I felt. Grey he was called. Sergeant Grey. I liked him a lot. He seemed to understand.'

Willis's eyebrows shot up at the name.

'Slow down,' she said. 'The chapel's there.'

Willis's first thought was that the chapel had caught the last rays of the setting sun because the windows were glowing red. Caroline was fiddling the key out of her jeans pocket and hadn't looked up. Willis was about to say something when she pushed the door open, then swung round and spun down the pathway, retching. A faint smell of butchers' shops reached Willis on the breeze. He took a handkerchief out of his pocket, pressed it to his nose, then stepped inside.

A fine red mist, an aerosol spray really, hung in the still air. Willis's jaw dropped. He tasted something and closed his mouth quickly. The mist wafted past his eye in particles as fine as smoke. He blinked. His eyes blurred, felt greasy. His foot kicked something on the floor: a jacket, heavy with blood.

He stepped backwards, still not quite understanding. The mist stung his eyes; he felt it settle on his skin, in his ears, coalesce into little droplets. Even through the handkerchief the smell was pervasive: sweet and bitter, thick and thin, astringent and cloyingly nauseous. As he stepped back he bumped into Caroline. She was hunched, a hand held over her nose and mouth. He tried to push her out with him but could see her eyes swinging around the space until they fell on the altar. A broken skeleton was stacked on it, picked clean of flesh but coated in a

251

pale wash of blood. The bones looked oddly sculptural. The skull was facing into the chapel, pointing at the door. Then she turned and ran, slipping dangerously on the floor. Willis followed more slowly, kicking the sodden jacket ahead of him with the toes of his shoes.

Caroline was sitting on the grass, her shoulders heaving. Willis sucked in air, spat, sucked in air again. The wide, fatty smell of mince was inside his head. He touched his face. It was wet and the handkerchief he had held over his mouth was pink and damp. He went down on all fours and very carefully wiped his hands on the grass. When he had finished, he went to the hedgerow for a stick and prodded the jacket open. Very gingerly he reached into the breast pocket and pulled out a wallet. The credit cards belonged to one M. Temple.

'That was him,' Caroline said. 'That was Temple, wasn't it?'

Willis spat again. Caroline rubbed her face and left streaks of red across her forehead and down her cheeks. He nodded.

'You don't think I did it?'

Willis shook his head. 'How could you?' he said.

'Leave the door open,' Caroline said. 'When it clears I want to check something. Don't look so shocked. This is the second time I've been through this.'

Willis nodded weakly. 'Me too.'

He walked around the chapel. High in the west wall was a small circular window with no glass in it. Near to the wall a wellingtonia spread its dark branches. Below it was a beech, then a young chestnut, then a hawthorn. He saw a trail of green stretching between fields, inching its way back across the landscape in the direction of the forest. He wondered who had built the chapel and whether they thought it was far enough away from the trees.

Caroline was standing by the front door. 'Are you ready to go back in? I want to show you the murals.'

Temple had obviously closed the curtains on the murals. When they pulled back the curtains the paintings had been scored and scratched to oblivion. No feature was discernible.

Caroline walked to the altar. The cloth was densely embroidered in greens and browns, an interlocking pattern of leaves and branches. It was soaked with blood, and dripping where it fell in heavy folds at the front. She looked behind her. High in the west wall a small round window had been shattered.

'He wanted to see his daughter again,' she said. 'I think he prayed for it and his prayer came true.'

'Prayed to what?' Willis said.

Caroline pointed at the cross. It was simple, bare wood. 'I hope to God he didn't see his daughter.' Instinctively she looked up at the small window. She could see sky, then a shadow seemed to flit across it.

'We'd better go,' she said. By the door the blood was thinnest and on the floor were leaflets scattered from a rack set in the wall. They were headed: 'The Winterburn Chapel' in heavy print. She stooped and picked one up, and quietly closed the door behind her.

In the car Caroline skim-read the leaflet. 'It's about the murals. Painted in 1916 . . . believed to represent a unique interpretation of biblical myth through English pastoral tradition . . . Angels, crucifixion, fertility symbols, suffering and redemption all combine in work of mysterious, emotive power . . . Artist never spoke of his work . . . adds to their enigma. Work commissioned by local family, the Winterburns, during the First World War, after the death of one of the sons.'

'Are you up for doing some local research?' Willis asked. Caroline nodded.

'Come back to my flat. We'll make a plan.'

Chapter 37

The weather changed as they returned to the flat. Rain slanted down from a grey sky and cracked wetly against the glass. A wind shook the dormer window in its frame.

'I'll fill you in, shall I?' Willis said. Caroline saw him blush as he spoke and couldn't help smiling.

'By the way, before we start, do I have to keep on calling you Sergeant?'

'Donald,' he said. 'Don.'

Caroline nodded. He looked like a Don. Solid. He was solid. She had felt it last night. Not just the sex, but the feel of him. Sort of . . . like a newel post, she thought. Same all the way through, and strong. He had managed her well, caught that mad, burning, sensual desire to obliterate herself in flesh and allowed it to awaken an echo in himself. And then in the night she had woken to find herself curled up behind him, had reached round and found that he was sleeping with an erection, and coaxed him over and into her, not that he needed much coaxing, and that had been good too. She had held him inside her for a long time afterwards and drifted off to sleep. The memory of it still had good magic about it. She could think about the chapel, even think about what he knew about her, and not feel too bad.

'Don,' she said. He was, she thought, a bit embarrassed, her using his name, so she said it again and gave him her thousand-kilowatt smile, just to make him blush.

'I, er, I told you about the other body that was found in the forest,' he said.

She nodded. 'Yes, Don. You did, Don.' This was fun. Dear Don. Ducky Don.

He muttered something that could have been 'for fuck's sake', then continued, hands lying on the table in front of him.

'I suppose it's because I'm the only one who's actually convinced that there's something rotten in the forest that I looked at it more closely than the others. That and the fact that I've got a lot of time on my hands. They're busy. No one's going to waste their time on a death from eighty years ago.

'To cut a long story short, I found the man who found the body and think I've managed to build up a profile of the victim that should help us. He's male, aged between twenty and forty, I'd say, officer in the First World War with the local regiment. Rich, at a guess, possibly engaged to someone whose initials are CT. His initials, by the way, are TW. And that's it. What I'm saying is that some time about eighty years ago, he was walking in the forest and the same thing that happened to Tailor happened to him, except this one was buried. Tailor was left on top.'

'So you think that if we find out who this man is, maybe we'll discover something about – whatever killed him?'

'If the killing is for a reason,' Willis said, 'knowing about him might just help.'

Killing. It made her wince. She looked up but his face was impassive, and his eyes had deadened to flinty chips. He's testing me, Caroline thought. He wants to see if I can take it. He wants to see if I've got the bottle to find out what took my son.

She was quiet for a moment, then said deliberately: 'So what's the first step? Newspapers? Engagement announcements. *The Times*?'

'You want the newspaper library at Colindale. I'll see if there are any regimental records. After that we can look at the local press for people missing in 1916.'

There was a short pause. He seemed to be waiting. Caroline got to her feet and said: 'Well then, I'll be off.'

Willis found that the regimental records were now housed in Basingstoke and that the librarian, who was the only person able to give authority to do the research, was away. He consulted a local guidebook in a public library then spent the rest of the day driving around sites where he remembered travellers staying, even going down to the gutted wrecks of Wanstonia where the road protests had been held. All he found were half-demolished houses behind wiremesh fences, hard-faced men in yellow helmets, and a single stretch of wall where the graffiti read: 'Trees not cars'.

When Caroline came back he gave her the news.

'Why travellers?' she asked.

'Something I heard – travellers being chased out of the woods. Could mean anything. Anyway, did you have any luck?'

'Yup,' Caroline said. 'Thomas Winterburn, engaged to Constance Trent sometime in autumn 1915. Listed missing in action, late September 1916. And the Winterburns are the same family that commissioned the murals in the chapel.'

'Except –'

'Except if he's the right person, Sherlock, we know he wasn't missing in action. We know he died in an English wood not half a mile from his home.'

'How do you work that out?'

'The Winterburns lived in High Croft Hall.'

'Rings a bell.'

'It would do. It was rechristened Croftholme House. There was a plan to convert it into flats three years ago but it was abandoned halfway through. Remember that old pile behind all those trees, if you drive towards the forest then turn left just past the butcher's? Modern houses all around it. You only ever catch glimpses of it.'

'Of course.'

'Marcus and I used to joke that it was haunted. Marcus said he'd buy it for me when he was grown up.'

'You can't remember who the developer was, can you?'

'No. Anyway, that's where the Winterburns lived.'

'I was just thinking that there was an off chance that it was still owned by the same family, especially if it looked to you as if nothing had been done to it for years.' He frowned, thought for a moment. 'Killed that near to the house, then listed as missing in action? It's a cover-up, isn't it?'

'I suppose so.'

'There's an odd pattern to all this. It seems to work on two levels – there's the folk memory thing, and then there's the times something actually seems to happen. I mean, suppose it became widely known – general knowledge. What would happen then? It's almost as if there are people who know and who aren't telling, and people who half-know but don't quite believe.'

Caroline twisted suddenly towards the window and said: 'I want to get to the bottom of this. I need to. There's something – I'm so scared. There's something about all this that's almost attracting me. I'm thinking that all I want to do is go into the woods and never come out again, as if there's something there for me. And the awful thing is, when I look around me, I can't think of one reason not to.' She looked up at him. 'Sorry. That was cruel. I shouldn't have said it.'

Willis shrugged. 'That's all right. Just think of me as a way to make the present less horrible. I mean it. The other, the reason for carrying on, that might follow. I hope it does. Do you want to stay here tonight?'

Caroline looked around the flat. She nodded. 'I want to watch TV in bed and drink whisky and go to sleep.'

'And?'

'Maybe,' she said. 'We'll see.'

Chapter 38

The estate agents handling Croftholme House were only too pleased to pass on the property developer's address to Willis. Gavin Fairchild had gone bankrupt, leaving them with a half-built hulk that leaked. The bank had just pulled out of the development. He asked Willis if he knew any arsonists.

Fairchild lived a couple of miles to the north but if Willis wanted to get past the monogrammed security gates, he'd better not mention Croftholme House. They'd been trying to get in touch with him for the past six months.

It might have been just fancy but Gavin Fairchild's home looked as if it had been built from the bits left over from every project he had ever worked on. Behind the secure wrought-iron gates the house seemed to rise from a carpet of bricks. The wide, sweeping drive was brick; the terraced garden seemed to consist mostly of brick. A gnome sat by the side of a garden pond with a brick surround.

The house itself, once a straightforward cube of wall and window, sat on a small mound. It had been extended and added to until the original house was almost lost behind the portico, balconies, extensions, double garage, conservatory, and what looked like a riding stable but was, Willis guessed, a swimming pool.

It was funny, he thought, how some people went bankrupt and some people went bankrupt.

In front of the house a bulging Mercedes sports car squatted like a toad. It had just been washed and around it the wet bricks were dark red. The silence was broken only by the monotonous urgency of a sprinkler going zip, zip, zip at the back of the house. It was wetting a livid green lawn that looked as if it had come on a roll. Dwarf conifers stood like punctuation marks around the lawn. Behind rose the ragged wall of woodland, a broken silhouette of green. In front of it, at the back of the garden, stood a large wire cage, an aviary, half-smothered by a honeysuckle. The wild plant provided a dense, heavy shade.

Willis pressed the buzzer on the brick pillar and when a voice said, 'Yeah?' replied: 'Police.'

He half-expected to be told to fuck off. In fact he was told nothing. The crackling grille above the buzzer fell silent and the aperture in the TV spy camera shut. He waited.

A man walked round the side of the house. He was square, red-faced, dressed in jeans and designer sweatshirt. His face was puffy and creased as if he had just got up. He stood by his car and looked at Willis.

'What do you want?'

'Mr Fairchild?' No reply. 'I'm trying to trace someone.'

'Oh, yes. Who?'

The man was finding the sunlight difficult and kept on squeezing the bridge of his nose.

'Someone named Winterburn.'

The man paused, sniffed, and made a chunking noise somewhere between his nose and his throat. He cleared each nostril on the gravel, delicately holding his little finger outstretched while applying pressure with his index finger. He flicked his hand and approached Willis.

'What does that old coot want to see me about?'

'He doesn't. I want to see him.'

The man swallowed repeatedly. His eyes were watering.

'Fucking sun. Makes you feel all cheesy up the nose. Winterburn? Yeah, I know him.'

'I need to ask him some questions.'

'I'm not stopping you.'

'About his family.'

'Good.'

'I need to know where he's gone.'

'You been sent by the agents?'

'No.'

'Then how the fuck did you get my address?'

'Someone remembered the name of the development company. I checked our records and found you'd reported a theft from the site,' Willis lied. 'We kept a record of your address.'

'Fucking big brother. Why do you want that Winterburn?'

259

Willis looked through the gates. He knew a wind-up merchant when he saw one, and knew that nothing would be gained by hedging.

'We found a dead man in the forest. Murdered eighty years ago. We think he might be a relative of Winterburn's, that's all.'

'Strewth,' the man said. Willis could see him thinking, trying to work out if there was an angle he could use to come in on this. Willis waited for more, then said: 'Have you any idea where he is?'

'He's a silly old bastard. When I finally tracked him down – he was in Canada of all places – I put it to him that if he'd sold the house three years earlier he would have made another hundred thou on it easy. Silly money. He'd let it go as well. It was almost a ruin. Anyway, I caught him at the right time. His wife had died or something, and he was ready to move back to this country. He moved down to the south coast, when I . . . when we . . . bought that old house. He's in a nursing home in Hastings. High View it's called.'

'You remember that?'

'I should do. I own the fucking place and all. If he complains, don't believe him. Senile. We did a deal – reduced cost if I guaranteed him a place in one of my old folk's homes. He chose High View because the name reminded him of his old place. Hell of a negotiator, even at his age. Still, none of my business. 'Bye.'

They drove down in Willis's car, M25, A21, through a landscape that hadn't settled yet: sites blurred and stretched by speed; brightly coloured shopping sheds with cute clock towers surrounded by waxy half-grown trees; embankments with no flowers; bridges with no graffiti; service stations with nothing but space in their car parks. From the motorways the world seemed angled wrongly; fields and houses had happened at a different time, when there were different reference points. As they skirted the south downs Caroline saw bald, steep hills, shaved by man to a sort of prehistoric weirdness, white earth, no trees, wind that carried the freshness of the sea. She opened the car window and breathed in air that seemed to come from heaven. She looked at the grey, wrinkled strip of water, compressed to a flat sheen by a heavy blue sky, and thought of cliffs and rock pools.

Willis said: 'Doesn't look like the busiest waterway in the world, does it?'

'That's a pointless thing to say,' Caroline replied, thinking that Epping Forest didn't *look* evil.

And High View Old People's Home didn't look like a home for old people. It looked like a place where they were stored prior to dispatch: a large, grey-painted, pebble-dashed house whose original pitched roof had been replaced with a flat one.

They walked in through the main entrance, past an empty reception booth. They stood still on gleaming brown lino. The hall was filled with the amplified voices of Nick and Anne comforting a woman in tears. In the TV room, armchairs with plastic-covered seats were arranged in three concentric rings round a huge television. Faces looked at them, then looked away. Caroline opened her mouth to say something above the sound of the television but decided she could not compete.

They were still standing in the hall when a door at the back opened and a woman in a nurse's overall stepped out. She looked surprised, then said: 'Excuse me, have you – '

'The door was open,' Caroline said. 'We couldn't find anyone in reception.'

'And you walk through every front door you see open?'

'I'm a police officer and this is Mrs Caroline Waters. We're trying to trace a Mr William Winterburn. We were told he was living here.'

'And you've got identification?' the nurse said. 'I'm sorry to be fussy but we get all sorts in here. There was another old lady raped only last week in Brighton. Eighty-seven she was. Died of shock. What a way to go.'

Willis pulled out an identification card.

'From Essex, eh? Like Mr Winterburn.'

'That's right.'

'Why do you want to see him? He's very old. I don't want him disturbed.'

'We're trying to trace a relative of his.'

'A relative? He told me quite categorically that – '

'A deceased relative.'

'A tragedy? Like I said, he's frail.'

'It was a long time ago,' Willis said soothingly.

'Well, I – He's one of our favourite gentlemen – I only wish I had the time to talk to him more. Remarkable for his age. Really wonderful. Sharp . . . sharp as a knife.'

'How many of you work here?' Caroline asked.

'Well, looking after them,' the nurse said, 'not including the cooking and cleaning, there's me. I do my best. But anyway . . . why did you want to trace this relative?'

Caroline opened her mouth. Willis said quickly: 'I'm afraid that's something we should only discuss with him. Please. It is very important.'

The nurse looked from one to the other. Somewhere a bell rang; applause from the television echoed round the hall. She said: 'Upstairs and straight ahead. Best room in the house. Fairchild only gave it to him because he thought he'd pop off within the year. It's been three now and he's still going strong. All power to him, I say.'

'Me too,' said Willis, and hoped the old man's heart would hold out.

William Winterburn sat in a high-backed chair, looking out of a bay window. The window overlooked the street, and at the end of the street was a flash of bright colour where the council geraniums were doing their thing, and beyond that, wedged between a dwindling line of buildings, the sea.

William Winterburn turned and looked at them. His expression was resentful; his eyes, red round the rims and watery, were penetrating once he had taken their measure.

He said: 'Yes?' in a vague sort of voice. Willis stepped back to let Caroline walk ahead.

'Mr Winterburn?'

'Yes?'

'My name is Mrs Waters, and this is Mr Willis. We think you might be able to help us.'

The old man considered them for a moment, then waved a hand at a bedside chair. 'You had better come in and sit down and tell me what it is you want. Although I'm afraid I won't be much use.'

He gave a smile that might have been humble or else ironic. It was warm in the room but he had a blanket on his lap. He had large hands with blue knuckles that made Caroline visualise the bones beneath. His ears glowed red in the sunlight. It was a large room, and the furniture in it was heavy and old. The carpet on the floor was faded Persian. On the walls hung fine, precise watercolours of the Middle East – pyramids, palm trees, giant statues in red deserts.

'It's about a T. Winterburn,' she said. 'At least, that's what we think the initials are.'

'Eh? What's that? De Winter? What are you talking about? No De Winters I know of. Although, wait a minute, the Hertfordshire Winterburns once took a fancy to sticking "de" in front of their name. Stupid.'

Caroline had an odd impression that he had heard her perfectly well.

She said very clearly: 'No. I said T. Winterburn. Thomas Winterburn. We know he was engaged to a woman called Constance Trent.'

His eyes betrayed him, flicking towards a fine, bow-fronted chest of drawers. On it stood a mirror, a pair of ebony-handled hairbrushes and a group of photographs in dull silver frames. Caroline stood and pointed to one of them. It showed a handsome man in his early twenties dressed in a stiff officer's uniform. He was standing hand in hand with a striking dark-haired woman in front of a painted backdrop of misty vales and waterfalls.

She looked at Willis who raised his eyebrows.

'Thomas Winterburn?' she repeated. 'Constance Trent?'

The old man settled back in his chair. He waved a hand dismissively. 'Yes. My brother Thomas and his fiancée Constance. He died on his way to the front, you know. Shell hit the transport. Such a waste. Still, I dare say you knew that, but I can't think why you . . . why you . . . '

His hands sank to his lap and began to tug at the fringed edge of the rug.

'We found something belonging to him,' Willis said. He reached into his pocket and pulled out the clear plastic bag. He held it up. The watch could have been anything. 'It's not in very good condition. Been in the ground too long.'

William Winterburn frowned and leaned forward in his

chair. 'You'll have to bring it closer than that. My eyes.' He took the bag and lifted it. 'Goodness me. A watch.' His fingers darted, then picked the watch out. He looked at the face, head tilted back, then turned it over.

'I'm sorry,' he said. 'Who can tell?'

'On the back,' Willis insisted. 'The initials.'

The old man frowned, then picked up a large plastic magnifying glass from a cantilevered table and peered at the back.

'"TW from CT. My Love",' he read. He let the watch and glass fall into his lap and looked out of the window for a while. Then he closed his eyes. Still a striking man, Caroline thought, even into his nineties. She could see a vein working in his temple, blue-green against the papery, slightly yellowed skin.

And thinking hard, or remembering.

He opened his eyes suddenly, and looked at her. He didn't seem baffled or hurt any more. He looked defiant. 'So, how can I help you?'

Caroline shrugged helplessly, suddenly unwilling to continue.

'You do identify that watch as your brother's?' Willis asked.

He nodded, then said suddenly: 'I'm not going to pretend. By rights you should have found that buried somewhere in the mud of Flanders, some farflung foreign field.'

'We did not,' Willis said.

'He dropped it then?' Underneath the light sarcasm, Caroline thought she sensed a desperate hope.

'I'm afraid not,' Willis said. 'Not in Flanders.'

He struggled with the next question. 'Where?'

'In the forest. Half a mile away from your home. He –'

'*No!*' The old man covered his face with his hands, and rocked to and fro. Caroline was shocked by the strength of his voice, a young man's voice almost, slicing through the fug of the room. As he rocked, a bar of sunlight flashed across his head, making the white hair blaze. Caroline wondered how old he was now, how old he would have been in 1916. She looked at the picture of his brother and his fiancée. Wondered . . .

Willis hissed at her and jerked his head in the direction of Winterburn. Caroline perched on the arm of his chair and put a hand on his back. The spine felt like rocks.

'It's all right,' she said. 'It's all right.'

'Please, don't patronise me, young lady. You have no idea. No idea at all.'

'Would it help to talk?' she asked.

'Would it help? Would it help? You . . . For God's sake, woman, for seventy-five years or more I've wondered what became of my brother. Seventy-five years – that's more than twice as long as you've lived your bloody life. All that time I've wondered – '

'Why was it so important to know?' Willis asked suddenly.

'What?'

'Why was it so important that you knew?'

'If your brother had walked out of the house one fine morning and never been seen again, wouldn't you wonder what had become of him?'

Willis looked at him for a second. Their eyes locked. Willis looked down. He said: 'Yes.'

Winterburn's face twisted momentarily. Caroline thought that he was aging in front of their eyes. He sighed, then said: 'So he walked out, one fine summer's morning, and shot himself?'

Caroline missed the shrewd expression on his face as he spoke. She said: 'No. He – '

Willis signalled furiously at her, but it was too late. Winterburn had heard her.

'He didn't shoot himself? How did he die?'

Caroline felt a sudden surge of revulsion. The old man had almost pounced on her; now he was looking curiously avid. She sat down on the bed opposite him. From somewhere an image of Marcus, happy and carefree, settled behind her eyes. She felt cold determination steel her.

'He was killed.' Caroline's voice was level and she looked straight into the old man's eyes.

'Killed? How can you be so sure?'

'He was buried. His body was found.'

'Buried?' Winterburn licked his lips. 'You think he was murdered?'

'He'd been – ' Willis said 'Stop it!' just as Caroline said '– dismembered.'

Winterburn blinked, looked from one to the other. Caroline repeated: 'Dismembered.'

Willis grabbed her by the arm. 'For Christ's sake, woman, what are you trying to do?'

She tried to shake him off. She said: 'Something took away my little boy. My son. In the woods. What do you know? Why were you so sure your brother was killed? Why did you pretend he'd been killed in France? Why did you have those murals in the chapel painted? You've got to tell me! How did you know that he was dead!' Her anger built as she talked. She ended by tearing herself from Willis's grip and thrusting her face into Winterburn's.

'No.'

The old man looked terrified, his eyes flickering from Willis to Caroline. He lifted a hand weakly, then let it fall as if the weight was too much for him to support. His jaw slackened and his tongue protruded slightly, sliding limply over his lips.

'My son is dead! What do you know?'

There was a moment deeper than silence, a moment of significant stillness.

'Dismembered?' he said.

Caroline looked hopelessly at Willis. 'We think so.'

'Did he know anything? I mean, was it sudden?' His eyes peered first at one, then at the other. His cheeks seemed to have sunk, dragging his eyes down at the corners. He suddenly looked more ancient than old.

'As far as we can tell, yes, it was.'

'How can you tell?'

'I saw something like it happen to someone else.'

'No . . . ' This time there was wonder in the way he spoke the word. 'So it is true?'

'What?' Caroline asked.

'The stories,' the old man said. His face suddenly twisted. 'Oh, Thomas,' he groaned. 'My brother.'

And he lifted his head and made a sound that was something between a cry and roar.

Then the door to the room opened.

'What is the meaning of this? Go away! Get away! I should have guessed that you'd come from Fairchild, trying to frighten an old man. You, you – oh!'

Winterburn was gripped by a frightful bout of coughing, his

whole body twitching and heaving. His head suddenly slumped forward.

The nurse knelt in front of him. She kneaded his hands, then expertly took his pulse. Winterburn threw his head back. Sounds bubbled up from his throat, but his mouth seemed to lack the strength to form them into words.

'What is it, love? What is it?'

The nurse put her ear near his mouth. She listened hard. All Willis and Caroline could hear was the clicking of his tongue and the faint hoarseness of his breathing.

'Wait? You want them to go away?' the nurse said. She listened again. 'Yes, I'll get them to leave.'

Without looking over her shoulder, she said: 'You two – out! I'll see you downstairs when I've tried to make good what you've done.'

They waited in the lobby, heard the News come on. Institutional food smells filled the house. Willis's stomach rumbled. Caroline was remote, looking as if a key inside was tightening all her sinews.

Willis had to admit that all her instincts had been right. She had known when to push. He should have guessed that the old man was hiding something. The very fact that he suspected that his brother was dead at all – shot or whatever – was suspicious. Willis was not certain, but he suspected that a lot of young men must have gone walkabout before they were shipped off to be killed for their country. An awful lot of them must have succumbed to the temptation to change identity, just pack the whole thing in so that they could live. So why was William Winterburn so certain that his brother had died?

Whatever the reason, being forced to confront the truth had damn' near killed him.

Footsteps on the stairs. The nurse's face was drawn; she looked close to tears.

'Here,' she said. 'He wanted you to have this.' She thrust a leather wallet into Caroline's hands. 'I don't understand. He told you to go away, yet he gave you this. I don't understand it. But I do know that I want you to go. Get away and don't come back. Have you got me? Have you? Now go!'

'Tell him we're sorry,' Willis said.

The nurse's expression softened slightly as she looked at him.

'And her?' Her head jerked from Willis to Caroline. 'Is she sorry?'

'She's sorry,' he said.

'She's got a heart of stone,' the nurse said. 'Of stone. Shouting at a dear old man. Shouting! How could you? All he wanted was a place to live out his life in peace.'

The nurse pushed past them and into a small office.

'You *were* a bit rough on him,' Willis said.

Caroline opened the wallet. It contained two photographs. The first was of a beautiful dark-haired woman in a long dress and huge hat; an old studio picture.

The second picture showed the same woman and a man; she was now in her forties, her hair loose and blowing in the wind. The man was tanned and handsome. They were on horseback. Behind them stretched a vast field with a Canadian-style grain silo. They both looked radiantly happy.

'What is it?' Willis asked.

'The woman,' Caroline said. 'It's Constance. The man's Winterburn. There's no doubt about it. They're together. They're happy.'

'And they got away,' said Willis.

Chapter 39

Caroline asked him to drop her off at her house. He offered to take her in and stay but she said she would rather cope with it on her own this time.

Willis watched her from the car as she pushed her front door open, saw her fold suddenly as if someone had punched her in the stomach. He ran past her, following the outstretched finger that was pointing at something in the middle of the living-room floor.

At first he couldn't see what she was pointing at. The curtains were drawn and he had been driving a long time facing the sun. Gradually he was able to make out the shape of an old, balding teddy bear, lying face down on the carpet.

'What's the matter?' he asked, and walked towards it to pick it up. She had to swallow hard two or three times before she answered. 'His. It was his. Marcus's.'

Willis dropped it as if he had just been told it had last been hugged by a smallpox victim. He pulled the curtains open. The teddy bear lay on the floor near the door. At the other end of the room he could see a scrap of fabric. Willis frowned. Five long steps took him to the end of the room and showed him what he had feared. The kitchen door was open. When he looked out of the window, so was the garden gate into the forest.

He heard footsteps on the stairs. He ran after Caroline, and found her in one of the upstairs bedrooms, the boy's room by the look of it. She had collapsed and was rocking slowly from side to side.

The bed had been turned into a sort of nest. The quilt and bottom sheet were scattered with twigs and grass; mud was smeared over the fabric. Everywhere hung a sweet, cloying smell, that grew increasingly bitter the longer you were exposed to it. Toys and clothes had been pulled from drawers and dropped on the floor. The room looked as if a small bomb had hit it.

A burglar? He registered another noise in the background – a sort of gentle hissing. He opened doors. Her bedroom, spare bedroom, bathroom.

Same story here as the bedroom: chaos. Towels everywhere, taps dripping, shower running cold, soap dissolving in a dirty mess of – what? Twigs? Mud?

There was crud all the way up the sides of the bath. On the floor a grey towel lay like a wet animal.

'He was here.' Her voice was as bleak as a beach in winter. 'I was with you. He came back. He was trying to wash.'

Willis turned. 'Caroline, you can't – '

She brushed his hand away. 'He came. He tried to clean himself. He put himself to bed. And when I didn't come back, he took himself off.'

Her face collapsed and she seemed to bend as if she was about to be sick. Breath whooped into her lungs and came out, salty and black with pain and grief. She leant against the wall, then slowly sank down it.

Willis bent to pick up the towel. It carried the sweet bitterness of rot. Soft grey shreds fell from it and plopped on to the floor. The smell grew worse. The towel was dripping something thick and sticky that smelled of dead things.

He tightened the taps, regretting it when he felt his grip slip on more wet stuff. He imagined a small thin wrist, horribly weakened by decay, straining to force softening skin against the pressure of metal. Then he tried not to imagine it.

No. Just a burglar, or else kids. Just kids. What was that stuff they used? Goo? But grey goo? Goo that smelled of a broken meat store in a heatwave?

He walked down the stairs, noting this time that a battered Dinky car had been dropped on the landing; a T-shirt on the kitchen floor.

'No proof,' he said to himself. 'No proof.'

'What was that?' She had come up behind him.

'Just a mantra coppers use sometimes. No proof. No proof. It gives the job some limits.'

'It's no good. Those things – the fairies, the creatures. They're the ghosts of the children who died in the forest. Now

Marcus is one of them. And he came back!'

She bent and picked up the T-shirt, folding it loosely and absent-mindedly hanging it over her arm, a movement so natural and routine it made Willis wince.

'We've got to get you out of here,' he said.

'I want to see Marcus. I must. Don't you understand?'

'It won't be Marcus, any more than the creature I saw which lured Tailor to the glade was Dana Watkins. We have to stop them.'

'Stop them? How do you think you stop them? You might as well try and stop the world from turning! Temple – he said he'd do this. I told him not to . . . Marcus!' she howled. 'Marcus!'

Her voice bounced flatly off the walls of the room. She was being torn apart, and yet oddly she felt almost nothing except a sort of diseased energy coursing through her and, deep within, a yellow fire burning with a cold flame. She willed it to burn her in half so that part of her might stay and wait for Marcus and the other half might run.

But she didn't resist when Willis put a heavy arm across her shoulders and led her gently out to the car.

Chapter 40

It began with an argument. Nancy thought that her boyfriend was spending too much time on the walls, as he called them. Indoor speed climbing was all very well, but not as a full-blown obsession. So at seven o'clock on Saturday morning, for Christ's sake, as she saw him dip into the little basket on her dressing table where she kept her loose change and car keys, she sat up and said: 'Oh, I'll be needing the car today.'

'What?' He looked disbelievingly at her.

'I'll be needing the car today.'

'But you never said.'

'And you didn't say that you'd be away all weekend, crawling up gym walls in Solihull.'

'Bloody did!'

'You told me at half-past midnight last night.'

'And you didn't say you needed the car.'

'I'm telling you now.'

'But I always need it to get to – '

'And now I do. My turn.'

His face turned ugly. 'This is absurd. Listen, next time I'll make other arrangements, but this time I need it.'

'Take a train.'

'You're just pissed off because I forgot to tell you before. This is so childish.'

'Or a bus.'

He stormed out. From the half of the telephone conversation that she caught coming through the walls, she learned that she was pre-menstrual and that Rob, the club-mate he had promised a lift to, could borrow his father's Mondeo anyway.

It still left a large hole in her weekend, but at least it was a hole she could drive around now.

*

272

She went to the superstore for comfort as much as anything else and bought more than they could possibly eat before it went off – but that seemed to fit, relationship-wise – excess and rot to compensate for the little nibbles of affection and lust that had reduced their affair to anorexic torpor.

She also bought a lot of wine, a litre of Beefeater gin and another of Johnny Walker because Neil didn't drink these days. He said it did something to his muscles, or did something to something that did something to his muscles.

She had to admit that she was turned on by the way he looked, but, at the same time, when they made love these days he was distracted and self-contained. Once she had caught him stroking the ridges of his stomach during foreplay.

Sod him, she thought, and remembered she had bought the latest *Hello!* the day before and left it in her desk, so she dropped in on the station to pick it up.

'Anything up?' she asked.

Bob Gower, one of the older sergeants, gestured at a pile of papers on the left of his desk, and two sheets on his right.

'On our left we have what has to be done; on our right what has been done. What's up, you ask? A pile of shite. Listen to this: it's from Councillor Arse Fart Bagshot of Dildo Drive:

Dear Sir,
I am dismayed to have received neither reply nor notice of acknowledgement of my letter dated bahdedeblahblah. Once again I draw your attention to the continued and illegal presence of so-called hippy travellers on the Watkins Alarms site, and further draw your attention to their contravention of no fewer than five laws and four by-laws: to wit . . .

You know the rest. He wants us to go in and bust up the camp, and if possible send them to the next ward. And I'm just sitting here thinking: Why? Where's the harm? You been down there? It's organised. They've worked out toilet facilities. The kids are being taught stuff . . . They're not smashing up their neighbour's house or hanging around the shopping centre. And this little pillock wants us to move in with JCBs and 'dozers and level the place.'

'Plenty who'd do it for you.'

273

'I know. But we can't spare them. It'll take thirty-two officers three days if the travellers dig in. I've estimated ninety man days. Person days. Sorry.'

Nancy waved a hand. She was suddenly feeling guilty. She remembered Willis asking her to follow up on something he'd heard from or about some travellers. To rub it in, Gower said: 'And how is Willis?'

'Fine. Fine.'

'Right. Good. And, well, you know, I never asked . . . what do you think?'

Gower's face suddenly became a little less pleasant. What do *you* think? Everyone wanted to know whether Willis had actually seen Tailor being massacred, or even if he'd had a go at it himself. They thought he might have confided in Nancy.

'About what?'

Gower pursed his lips and looked shrewd. 'Still passing stuff on to him?'

'I –'

'Don't even pretend. Come on. What's he after?'

'Scene-of-crime stuff. That skeleton they dug up – remember?'

'That old thing?'

'Beats me too,' she said. But having answered his questions felt she could ask her own. 'Those travellers. Are they co-operative?'

'They know their rights, but they won't gob on your back or throw shit in your face. Why?'

'Oh, just want to follow something up.'

'For Willis?'

She scrunched up her face. 'I've got four days off. I'm not doing anything for anyone apart from me.'

'You're doing it for Willis. Be careful.'

'What do you mean?'

'You'll be on your own. There'll be no back-up arranged. No partner.'

'It's not going to be dangerous. You said so yourself.'

Gower shrugged. 'Who knows? When you're doing someone a favour, chances are you don't know the whole story. You don't know what *not* to do. I mean, suppose you turn up there the day after one of them's been busted and they turn nasty? It only takes one, you know, and there's an incident. Suppose . . . '

'I'll be careful. Anyway,' she said, 'I'll probably not do anything.'

'Take a radio,' he said. Nancy hesitated. 'For me?'

'Just for you then.'

It was idyllic, she thought, the camp on the edge of the forest. She could have lived there: a child's fantasy enlarged, elaborated, working with all the patched-up logic of a Heath Robinson cartoon.

Above the gates of the old factory a faded banner read 'Free Republic of Essexonia'. Honeysuckle crept up the poles that supported it. A rough track led through a patch of grassland sown with meadow flowers. Behind that, the caravans and buses, old grocery vans and army surplus tents, shacks and home-made wigwams, were dotted around the site, not following any grid, but allowing a wide path through the middle of the village that opened up into a sort of green. The area was surrounded by a high metal fence that had outlived the factory. There were a few cars parked on the concrete apron that must have been the factory floor – some of the travellers were earning money from restoring old bangers. In the middle of the area was a group of sculptures, all figures. A shower of white sparks gushed out from behind one of them and she heard the uneven whine of an angle grinder. Nancy noted with some surprise that they must have electricity.

'Can I help?'

It was a young woman, small, with a crumpled, tired face and a child hanging on to her knee. Behind her a man looked up from beneath the open bonnet of an old Saab; not aggressively, but a definite presence nonetheless. He laid the fan belt on the wing. Like the woman he was sunburned a dark brown. Like the woman, his hair was long and dull, matted into thick, tangled snakes and decorated with beads. Nancy reflected that she herself looked so clean she might have been peeled. It made her feel more vulnerable.

'I'm looking for someone. A woman.'

'Relative?' the young woman asked. The child sat down suddenly and began to knead a patch of gravel.

'No. It's – er – general.'

'Press? Private investigator?'

The man approached them. He was holding an adjustable spanner absent-mindedly. At least he was making it look absent-minded. She remembered what Gower had said about back-up.

'No.'

'What's up?' the man asked.

'She wants to know something,' the woman said. 'Checking up on someone. Snooping likely as not.'

'Snooping?' the man asked.

Nancy said: 'If you were worried about the noise coming from the fan, it'll be the bearing. It's nothing to worry about though. They wear but it's no big deal.' The man raised his eyebrows. 'Saab 96 V4. My dad used to rally,' she added.

'So I should leave well alone?'

'Probably. They'll do a ton with a hundred thou on the clock. So I've been told.'

'And you?' the young woman said sharply. She looked from Nancy to the man and back again. 'Are you police?' Two other men joined the group, looking interested.

'Off duty,' she said.

'I didn't think you lot ever went off duty,' the woman said.

'Oh, believe me, we do. Sometimes we're even mistaken for human beings.'

'Let her speak, Karen,' the man with the spanner said.

Nancy shot him a grateful glance, then spoke quickly. 'I heard a story. It was about a month ago, about how a family, or a group of travellers, was chased out of the forest. I think they were actually living in the forest when they got chased out. I want to find out more.' Her eyes travelled from face to face. A man with a shaved head and a spider's web tattooed on his neck smirked and looked away.

'And why do you want to find out?' asked the man with the spanner.

'I want to know what chased them away. What frightened them.'

The man with the tattoo looked as if he was about to say something, but the woman said: 'No, Spider!' in a voice like a

276

whiplash. The man looked sheepish, shrugged and shuffled to the back of the ring of people.

'No what?'

'None of your business!' The woman picked her baby up and gave it to one of the group members. She squared up to Nancy. 'Too late. Too fucking late!'

'For what?' Nancy began judging distances. So far only the woman seemed aggressive but she knew how quickly situations could turn, and knew it might not take very much. If the woman pushed her and she reacted, for example.

'You – ' The woman's face twisted. She turned away and looked at the man with the spanner. 'Well, Jake?' she said to him. 'Are you going to stand there? Or are you going to do something?'

'Perhaps *they* mean to do something,' he said.

'Do something? The filth?'

'I hate that word,' Nancy said. 'I'm sorry. It's just something I can't stand. I'm going.'

It was true, but she also thought it might be good to leave on a note of protest, rather than trying to conciliate someone who wouldn't be conciliated.

'Wait.' It was Jake. With a glance he dared Karen to say something.

'Why do you want to help?'

Nancy half-turned, then looked back. 'I'm helping a friend. Filth too, as a matter of fact. He thinks there's something bad going on in the forest but doesn't understand what it is. There's a woman he knows, thinks it's got something to do with her son's death. So it's personal, and I don't necessarily believe it, but I said I'd help him find out anything else I could and now I've tried and I'm going home.'

After she spoke there was silence. It was as if they were all waiting for something to happen; as if around them something had changed that encouraged them to think that it might. Nancy looked at the restless ridge of trees behind the fence, at the faces that ringed her. A car passed the gates of the camp; somewhere nearby a pigeon crooned then clapped its wings. The noise had changed. That was it. The angle grinder had stopped.

She looked towards the sculptures. A woman was standing

by them, staring straight at Nancy it seemed. A path opened in the people around her.

Nancy looked at Jake who nodded his head in the direction of the sculptures. Tentatively she stepped across the grass towards them.

'Good, aren't they?' Jake said. Nancy was no judge.

'Powerful,' she said.. She thought they were inept and Jake precious.

'She saw them,' he said.

'What?'

Nancy looked at the sculptures. Small thin figures clumsily made of wood and metal; for a face each one had a doll's face painted grey. Some had protuberances that looked like stiff wings poking out of their backs.

'She saw them in the forest.'

'Kids?' Nancy asked.

'She calls them fairies. They've got wings and everything.'

'Those aren't wings,' Nancy said. 'Those are ribs.'

Jake shrugged.

'Where is she?' Nancy asked.

'She's shy. A bit special, you understand. Joined us a month ago.'

'Oh.'

'You're special, aren't you, Shena?' Jake said in a loud, patronising voice.

'Special? I don't know,' a little girl's voice said.

She had materialised out of nowhere. Another woman, or girl more like. All of them seemed so young. Her face was round and blank and still plumped up with puppy fat, like a cushion. She held her head on one side, and carried a long bundle in her arms.

'This lady,' Jake said, nodding at Nancy Freeman, 'this lady wants to hear what happened to you in the woods, Shena.'

'I saw fairies.'

'Did they chase you out?' Nancy asked.

'Not me. They gave me a baby.'

Jake flinched.

'The fairies gave you a baby?'

'Look.'

She turned back the edge of the bundle. Nancy could not stop herself giving a little cry. Jake was looking at the ground with his face strangely twisted. Nancy felt as if a second tongue were trying to force its way up her throat. Her stomach hollowed, then contracted.

'He's beautiful.' Nancy had another glimpse of something grey and wrinkled with a face like a monkey. It writhed like a maggot and she thought it rolled wet black eyes at her and grinned. The girl looked down and crooned.

'What is it?' Nancy asked. Without thinking she had put a good fifteen feet between herself and Shena. She put her hands on her hips and took deep breaths.

'Something dead she picked up.'

'It's not dead.'

'Can't you smell it?'

Nancy sniffed. Yes, of course. The smell was strong and thin, sweet and old, bitter and stale.

'But it – it's got no hair.'

'It's been skinned, whatever it is. Some of us think it's a dog. Spider says it's a hare. She never lets us get a good look. Keeps it with her the whole time, even in bed. Pretends to suckle it. You know.'

'But suppose it – ' Nancy could not finish. She still felt jolted inside. 'Sorry. I thought I saw it smile at me. What was she saying about babies?' She took a deep breath and tried to expel the memory.

'Someone played a trick on her. A bad trick.'

'Carry on,' Nancy said. 'You don't have a cigarette on you?' She felt an overwhelming need to pull smoke deep into her lungs and burn her clean. Jake handed her tobacco and papers.

'We all knew her. She arrived here one day on her own about a year ago. She was a bit, you know. Then she got in with this guy, called himself Dog, sort of dominant male type. Macho, beads and muscles. Had two or three women. They were moving into the forest – right up in the north where there's that ruined house, you know? Anyway the plan was to set up a sort of home there – grow some vegetables, have children, all that frontier man stuff right in the middle of fucking England. Shena, she got crazy about wanting a baby. The other two fell pregnant just like that. Bang, bang. Shena didn't.

'She was like – it's hard to say and I hate to be judgemental, you know – but her head was always somewhere else. She got all secretive, that's what we heard, started going off on her own. Told people she'd found fairies and was talking to them. Told them that the fairies were going to give her a baby. All she had to do was find something that she could give them in return. Something really good, you know.'

He paused. Nancy picked tobacco off her tongue. She had pulled so hard on the roll-up that tar was marbling the paper. It was bitter on her lips. Jake looked back at the girl, his eyes narrowed.

'This is where the story gets confused, and we only heard second hand, you know? Or third hand or fourth hand.' He frowned and thought. 'Maybe fifth hand. Chinese whispers. You know?' Nancy nodded. 'Anyway, one of the other women said that Shena lured her into the forest, tied her to a tree there – I know it sounds crazy – then made off. This other woman managed to escape – wasn't tied tightly enough – and ran back to the camp. She was – a mess.'

'I'm not surprised,' Nancy said. What was it Willis had said about a tree? Or was it a clearing? Or was it shoes? She knew she should remember but to be honest she'd got into the habit of switching off when he started rambling.

'No,' Jake said. 'You don't understand. She said she was chased. I mean, she didn't just manage to undo the ropes that were tying her to the tree. She was being attacked or something.'

'What? Who by?' Nancy's attention was attracted by movement at the base of the tree line. Heat haze or smoke.

'Kids. I mean, that's really sick, isn't it? Kids chasing her. Don't know what they would have done. Better not to think. But kids – I mean, you hear about that kind of shit going down in towns, right? But out here . . . We think the kids must have given her that . . . thing. Knew she was a bit feeble up here, told her it was a baby when in fact . . . '

'Kids? How old?'

'Old enough to give her old man a bad scare that night. They came to the camp, see, started – '

The scream tore the sky in half. That was what Nancy thought, then it tailed off into a series of panting grunts. It was Shena.

She dropped her bundle and began to run towards the forest, arms outstretched. Her fingers were hooked ready to tear.

'Shit!' Jake said. 'What the fuck's all that about?'

'I think she just saw something,' Nancy said. 'Wait a minute. Are those – '

She shaded her eyes against the glare and looked again at the base of the line of trees. Children?

She hardly thought about it but was suddenly running across the grass, trying to find the angle to cut off Shena. The jolting stopped her thinking too clearly, but all the different things she had heard – trees, children, babies, the forest – suddenly sorted themselves into a jagged, menacing shape in her mind. At the very least, she shouldn't let that girl loose in the forest. Not in that state. She glanced over her shoulder. A couple of the men were following her but she was fitter and stronger and was outstripping them. She patted her shoulder bag. Her radio, switched off, was a hard shape banging against her hip.

Ahead Shena tripped, got up so fast that it looked as if she had bounced, and hobbled on, clearly injured. Her good leg sort of rowed ahead of her, while she held on to the bad one with both hands and forced it to take some weight. Nancy caught up with her twenty feet from the forest. Even the pressure of her hand on Shena's shoulder caused her to shriek and collapse. Her ankle looked badly swollen, darkening already, the flesh puffing around the thong of her Indian sandal.

She lay on her back and drummed her good leg into the earth, her hands clenched into fists. She was biting her lower lip and going: 'MMM MMMM MMMM.' Spit shone on her chin.

Nancy glanced behind her; the men were walking now, clearly blown. She gently opened the front of Shena's blouse.

Her small breast looked very white. The skin all around the nipple, and the nipple itself, was coated with grey slime. There were red patches on the skin as if something had been sucking there. Shena stopped her drumming. She grabbed Nancy's hand and pressed it to the breast. 'Can you feel it?' she asked. 'I felt it. I thought it loved me. My own. Look!'

She suddenly bent her knees and pulled up her skirt. Her legs from the knees upwards were coated in the grey liquid. It was as if the thing had nested there.

'What is it?' Nancy said.

'I don't know,' Shena said, and started to cry. Nancy rearranged her clothes as the men came up.

'She needs an ambulance for her ankle,' she said. She felt light-headed and very detached.

She looked at the group of sculptures. No one was there. The whole camp seemed to be moving across the grass towards them. Nancy stood up and walked back to them. 'She needs wet bandages and cold water round her ankle,' she said, trying to sound clear and commanding, even if wet bandages and cold water round her ankle was not quite what she meant. A couple of people broke off and went back to the tents. Nancy walked to the sculptures.

I was standing there, she thought, and Jake was standing there. Shena was there.

She looked at the ground where Shena had dropped the bundle. Nothing. But the cloth covering lay unwound on the ground a few feet away. A few feet from that the meadow grass grew taller, and Nancy thought she could see where the stems had been flattened, as if something had wormed its way through them. Through the stems, crawling towards the forest.

Shit. Shit. Shit.

She immediately thought of radioing in, to make a preliminary report, but then realised that she had nothing to say that would make sense. Suddenly she appreciated what Willis must have gone through. He had been put in a position where he could only report what he had seen, and that had not been good enough.

What to do next?

Sit at home and go mad wondering what she had seen, or follow up?

Neither. Call Willis. Tell him you understand. Or if that sounds inappropriate tell him you don't understand, but you understand that no one else understands what he doesn't understand.

She called from a new telephone booth by a bus stop in the middle of the forest. It was so new that the perspex box glinted in the sun, clean as a soap bubble. She swiped her Access card through the slot and for once the system worked first time. The phone in Willis's flat rang.

And rang.
And rang.

For all her great qualities, Nancy lacked imagination. Like many heroes and heroines, she embarked on her quest not so much with a sense of courage, as with a muted sense of fear. Fear did not usually come into her world; she had not been afraid of the dark as a child, had never seen the bogey man hiding behind a bush in the garden. Her mind just did not have a part in it prepared, softened up, for the image of a grinning maggot sucking on a teenage breast; the idea just would not embed.

And so Nancy decided to go to the old camp where Shena and her small tribe had lived, and from which they had fled.

Chapter 41

Her *Nigel Mansell Road Atlas of Great Britain* didn't show any ruins, and why should it? A friend had claimed that it marked only the short cuts to tax havens, ho ho. Why wasn't she doing something with friends? Why was she here? Because she was and because she was curious and because she *wasn't afraid*. It was like climbing to the top of one of those walls in the gym. Once you started, you just carried on.

Jake had said that the camp was somewhere up in the north of the forest by the ruins of a big house, and she remembered that as you emerged from the forest with the nose of your car pointing towards Cambridge, maybe half a mile away from the main road there were chimneys poking out of the trees to the left that had a stark sort of look. She turned the car round and headed north.

It was the sort of heat that made your nose prickle; Mediterranean heat that baked the scent out of long, coarse grass stems, pounded it out of the ungiving soil that was powdered to whiteness along the rough track. The house was somewhere ahead, hidden now by trees. In the shadows the air looked as cool as water. This, Nancy thought, would have been the back way in.

The front gates stood on the edge of a field of barley, which had gone beyond ripeness to a grim dusty brown. A single line of elms and chestnuts ran past them, marking the barrier of the next field. Nancy supposed it was one half of an avenue. It looked like a strange off-shoot of the forest, thrust stiffly out to touch, to sense, to sniff the hollowed shell of the big house that stood on its borders.

The traffic sounds receded with every step. Nancy heard a quick rustle that could have been a lizard and the buzz of heat and grass and insects. The road actually followed the line of a small ridge and the house was positioned slightly downhill from it, overlooking a hazy agricultural plain that faded to a pale, dusty mist in the distance.

Nancy blinked. She lifted the hair on the back of her neck where the heat was gathering and wiped sweat from her forehead. She was entering the realm, so to speak, of the house now. A ruined wall that might have sheltered a kitchen garden, the thin ribs and struts of a skeleton greenhouse, ugly outhouses, and the still uglier back of the house rearing up, lines broken by extensions and heavy piping, windows charred and blind, the walls still black where fire had broken through the wood and glass.

Nancy looked for signs of a camp, or cultivation, but there was nothing to see. Nettles four or five feet high began to encroach on the narrow path which was leading her to an empty doorway. She pulled her sleeves down over her hands and pushed through, but even so one of the nettles managed to whip her on the neck, just below her ear.

It was much cooler inside. The floors above had gone and she looked up through a lattice of burnt joists, past four storeys to the sky.

The plaster on the walls had been picked away or disintegrated back to the lathes. Where any plaster remained it had been scrawled on by graffiti artists. 'Kevin is a shit head'. 'Louise sucked my nob here'. 'Arsenal suck'.

Pictures of stick women with ballooning tits, stick men with dicks like baseball bats. The floorboards had gone. Underfoot a wet compacted layer of crushed slate, charred wood, moss. The place smelled of childhood, the ruined house that every child knows; the smell hits you the second you push past the jammed back door, something oddly animal and dangerous.

She stepped into a suggestion of a corridor, defined only by studs and smashed lathes. Peering through the gaps she could see a room tiled from floor to ceiling in white. It sent shivers down her spine, even though she knew it would only have been the kitchen or cold room.

Through the corridor and into the front of the house. She was in a wider corridor leading between great rooms. There were cellars below here; she jumped from joist to joist wherever she could, and tried not to look down. It was dark there. Ferns grew below the holes in the floorboards. The floor seemed to bend under her feet in places. She would be taking the long way back to the road, through the field; under no circumstances was she going back through the house.

And yet people had been busy here: ripping out panelling, fireplaces, shutters. The great staircase was gone: treads, risers, newel posts, banisters and all. Must have been marble. Above it the floor sagged forlornly round the hole it had left. To her left and right the vast reception rooms were just crude sketches of what they once had been. No walls, windows, ceilings, floors, fireplaces – just naked desolation – and as nasty, in some ways, as those pictures of funny people in the back of the house, impaling or engulfing each other with their swollen parts.

What a place to bring up kids.

She had to jump to get out – there was a huge hole in front of the empty front door, but if it had been a pit of cobras she would have jumped it, no problem. The sun was behind the house and it cast a short shadow on the grass.

She stretched and looked around her. The first thing she saw was a naked, one-legged doll, half in, half out of the shadow. Its thin hair was tied up in a ribbon.

About ten feet away, up against the wall, she found a fire pit, and a grate. Beyond that, a flattened mess of wood and green polythene that she thought might have been a tent.

She lifted the corner of the tent with a stick. The grass was already paling under the polythene. Small slugs like pellets of phlegm clung in the wet folds of an Indian print dress. There were pots and a pan; a mouldy paperback. They'd left in a hurry.

She ran over the story in her mind. Shena had wanted a child. She had lured one of the other women into the forest. Shena had tied her to a tree. The other woman had escaped, pursued by – what?

Nothing moved in the forest. For a second even the wind dropped and the constant mild sighing of the branches fell away. She was struck by the soft geometry of the shadows that the avenue cast on the grey carpet of the field; how black it was. It almost seemed as if a river of blackness were flowing from the forest and under the thin line of trees; no, a river was wrong. It was solid, many-coloured, like the shadow a painter might see, and while it was coming from the forest, it didn't so much flow as stain more deeply shadow that was already there.

She blinked and shook her head. What nonsense had she been thinking? The sun could do that to a person. Well, she'd been to see the travellers, she'd investigated them, she'd visited the site, and now she was ready to go and report back to Sergeant Willis.

She turned. The pit inside the front door reminded her that she had vowed not to go back through the house. Too dangerous. Nettles and a wall of brambles cut off all means of exit apart from the field, and as she could not walk across a field ready for harvesting, she'd have to walk under the trees.

She set off, then stopped.

There was a small scarecrow twenty feet away, standing on the edge of the field, a scarecrow with a raw, blank face that looked as if all the features had been shaved off. Its clothes were russet. Sacking maybe. Funny place for a scarecrow, on the edge of a field, and come to think of it, it was odd that she had not noticed it before.

She took another step, then stopped. The heat was building up again. The sky was a pale drumskin and something was tapping on it, causing ripples of heat haze. Heat prickled her face, her skin. Something had worked its way through her shoe and was scratching her instep. She blew upwards at her fringe, heavy with sweat. No breeze.

Then she thought she saw the scarecrow move. Nancy felt a prickle of unease and blinked sweat away. She sensed that she was experiencing fear but at the same time felt very strongly that this wasn't happening to her. She forced herself to think rationally, going over the sequence of events in her mind from the first time she and Willis stopped off at Kingsmeade Close and talked to Caroline Waters. Her mind flashed over the death of Dana Watkins; the death of Tailor, her killer; the death of Marcus Waters. And just yesterday there'd been a report of a man being spray painted on to the walls of a chapel fifteen miles away. Things happening in the forest and around the forest. Bad things. What were the links?

Dana Watkins's mother had been up for the same job as Caroline Waters; Tailor had killed Dana Watkins and was now dead. Marcus was Caroline Waters's son. The man who had been vaporised was one of Caroline Waters's neighbours. Everything centred on her. And now there were rumours that Willis was seeing her.

She was wasting her time here. She should be ringing his doorbell and warning him. She turned, and as she did the scarecrow moved again.

Nancy froze. Joints locked and muscles softened. There was a split second of relief when she managed to convince herself that it had been a trick of the light, wind, a wrinkle on her retina. But then it took a step towards her.

Terror built in her with the sudden explosive prickle and shiver of a sneeze. She didn't take her eyes off the figure; her fingers tugged at the catch of her bag where the radio sat, dense, heavy and comforting. As soon as her hand closed on it, she felt better. She found she could move, but instead of walking backwards, she took a step forwards.

She met this particular manifestation of the unexpected with a grunt. Odd things began to happen in her mind. She saw a picture of the flat; the new unmade bed; the clean litter in the clean bin; the fridge with eat-me-quick chilled meals; the freezer with its bottle of vodka, undrunk; ice cubes and frosted cardboard cartons of Chicken Tikka Masala and Chicken Kiev; the Ikea rug lying on clean cork tiles; the polished lustre of the antique walnut bric-à-brac box she had splashed out on in Islington – it all seemed curiously unfulfilled and empty, even though everything was the product of work, of planning, of maintenance and choice. A step backwards was a step towards it; a step forwards was into the unknown. She felt the loss of satisfaction in her ordered life keenly, almost like a be-reavement. She wondered if she were doing the right thing by moving to traffic. What had prompted it? Tailor. She had touched him and had felt polluted. She had washed her hand. Now her hand felt wet. She looked at it; it was covered in blood; it was sweating blood. She touched the blood with her tongue, then licked it. Her tongue left a wide, clean swathe on the red.

She shook herself. It was disgusting. A hallucination. Her hand, suddenly, was clean. She felt wheat tickle her legs and realised that she was standing in the middle of the field. The scarecrow was gone, or had she walked past it?

She turned.

A naked, child-sized figure with skin as soft and dull as a mushroom lifted its arms. It had no face and smelled of sweet decay; between its body and arms was a thin membrane. Nancy turned away and ran, shouting incoherently and making good ground through the field until the trees closed around her and she looked up and saw that the branches were crowded with small dead people.

She felt their thoughts swarming through her mind . . .

So wrong, Nancy, so wrong. Death is always an accident. Come to us, come to us, we just want –

Nancy shouted 'No!' She summoned up the last of her sanity and lifted her radio.

The fairies floated down from the branches and began to play with her.

Chapter 42

Willis spent an hour in a supermarket buying what he thought Caroline might want to eat. He had given her a sleeping pill so she would wake up feeling muzzy. Around three o'clock she'd need something savoury. Bloody Marys. That should do the trick. On the way back he drove past Kingsmeade Close and decided to check the house. The Close was quiet. As he swung out into the middle of the road before the turn into her sloping drive, he dimly registered an anonymous Vauxhall parked ten yards further up the street, and a similar car on the other side of Caroline's house pulling out of a driveway and stopping in the middle of the road.

Silly prat'll have to move, he thought, hearing a car door slam, turning to look at the first car and seeing Inspector Grey marching across the lawn towards him. He found reverse and pulled back into the road, rear bumper screaming as it hit the tarmac, but the car bounced so violently that his hands were thrown off the steering wheel and his feet from the pedals. The second Vauxhall shot up, sliding to a halt inches from his front bumper, meaning he'd have to knock them out of the way if he wanted to get out. Then he realised he had nowhere to go, nothing to do, and anyway, he hadn't done anything wrong.

The door was pulled open.

He had forgotten to lock it.

'A word, Willis.' He looked up into four faces that hated him. Behind them an elderly man with an officious face was trying to look between their backs and saying: 'Yes, that's him. That's him all right. He's been in and out of her house these past two weeks like a blooming yoyo!'

One of the constables turned round and said, 'That will be all,' heavily, and the man said: 'If I can be of any further assistance . . . ' before walking off with an exaggerated spring in his stride.

'What can I do for you all?' Willis asked, trying to give a breezy, insincere smile.

Inspector Grey said: 'We've got a tape that you want to listen to, Willis. Leave the car. We'll go in one of ours.'

A tape I want to listen to? A tape I want to listen to! God bless this country, Willis thought. I'm not frightened by the strong-arm tactics. I'm not frightened by six policemen bundling me into a car and taking me off to a police station. Perhaps I should be, but I'm not. I'm frightened by the way he said: 'We've got a tape that you want to listen to.' What tape? Why?

The High Street slipped past the window: window displays; fruit and veg; a butcher's. Meat is so many different colours, Willis thought.

He turned: 'What tape?'

Inspector Grey said: 'A funny tape.' He was leaning forwards from the back seat, peering out of the windscreen. They drove round the back of the station and parked.

'My office,' he said.

There was something chilling and brisk about the way it was being done and Willis was reminded of waiting outside the headmaster's study at grammar school, suspended in social limbo. Inspector Grey sat Willis down at his desk and checked the batteries in a cassette player which he left deliberately in the middle of the desk.

'Couple of minutes. All right?'

He came back a couple of minutes later, as he had promised, pushing Sergeant Gower into the room ahead of him.

'Hello, Bob,' Willis said, half getting up and holding out his hand. Gower flushed so red that his eyes actually watered. Willis shrugged and sat down. He'd always thought that Bob Gower was as interesting as a stale tea cake.

'Can you tell us again what you told me and the Super-intendent earlier, Sergeant Gower?' Inspector Grey said. 'Just like you said earlier,' he prompted. 'The conversation you had with WPC Freeman.'

Willis snapped to full alertness. 'Now wait a minute,' he said. 'You can't – '

'Shut up!' For the first time Inspector Grey showed feeling, showed it in his bared teeth and the spittle that hit the desk. 'Now, Gower.'

'I – yessir. You understand it was just in passing that she said . . .' Gower looked nervously at Grey. He settled his stance and put his hands behind his back, like a choir boy about to sing solo.

'It was this morning sir, I was – '

'Time?' Grey said.

'Ten-fifteen or thereabouts. I was undertaking routine administration duties when my attention – '

'For fuck's sake, talk English,' Grey snapped. Gower slumped a fraction, then pulled himself together and began again.

'I was sitting at my desk working when Nancy, that is, WPC Freeman, walks in. Says she's looking for a mag or something she left behind. Just to pass the time of day she asks what I'm doing, so I tell her I'm looking at a request to move on a posse of travellers who've put down roots in the old factory site off the Cambridge Road. She's interested, asks me a bit about them, and suddenly I start to wonder why. Then I remember all the rumours about her keeping up with Sergeant Willis, so I ask her if this has got anything to do with him. A hunch like, you could say. "No, this is for me," she says. But it's clear it's not really. At least that's what I thought.'

He paused and looked at Grey, who nodded. Willis felt tension gathering in the room. Grey dipped into his jacket pocket and pulled out an unmarked cassette which he tapped on the desk top.

'Anyway, that was more or less it. I did warn her, sir. I did tell her to be careful, that if you started messing with someone else's work – but she just said it wouldn't matter.'

'What was she going to do, Gower? Can you tell us that?'

'I got the impression that she wanted to talk to the travellers, sir.'

'About what?'

'That I don't know, sir. She wouldn't say. I tried to warn her. I told her to take a radio.'

At that moment the significance of the tape became clear to Willis. All calls into the station were automatically recorded, all calls and all radio messages.

'And she gave no indication of wanting to go anywhere else?'

'She didn't say, sir.'

'Thank you, Gower.'

'It wasn't my – '

'I said, thank you, Gower.'

He left.

'It wasn't his what?' Willis asked.

His hands were resting on his legs and he could feel the sweat on them.

'It wasn't his fault, I would imagine.'

It took two attempts for Willis to say: 'What wasn't his fault?' His throat had suddenly dried. Grey was almost shimmering in front of him. Black dots were blurring the edges of his vision. 'What wasn't his fault?' he repeated.

Grey flipped open the lid of the cassette player. Slid in the tape, clicked it into place, slammed down the lid.

'Ready?' he asked. And pressed the 'Play' button.

'I'm in trouble.' Nancy's voice was turned into a crackling squawk by the electronics.

'State name, state name. Over.'

'WPC Freeman, investigating disturbance of travellers next to ruined house on north edge of forest. Over.'

'State position. State position. Over.'

'In the fucking wood by the fucking ruin off the fucking road. Sorry. Sorry. Need back-up. Over.'

'State situation status. Range of danger. Over.'

'I'm surrounded by – things. I'm scared . . . oh God, I'm scared!'

'Maintain radio protocol and state danger.'

'Get me fucking back-up. The shadows are moving. It's gone cold. It's gone cold.'

Grey clicked down the 'Pause' button. 'It was a hot morning,' he said. 'Wasn't it? And where was Willis when the lights went out?'

Without waiting for a reply he set the tape moving again.

'Back-up alerted. ETA seven and a half minutes. Please describe subject. Over.'

'Can't. At the camp there was a girl, a traveller called Shena.

293

She'd picked up some kind of creature and was nursing it. The other travellers claimed that – shit! I don't know what to fucking DO. It looks like the Waters b—'

Her voice was cut off in a rising shriek. Control asked her to come in, once, twice, three times, then there was a shuddering grunt, and she said in a high, small voice: 'I think that was my tummy. I think I – ' Her voice thickened suddenly and was cut off in a wet, juddering coo.

Control continued to ask her to respond, then gave up.

'They got a car to her about five minutes later. It was a mess. Forensics are still trying to work the whole thing out. Got anything to say?'

Willis felt sick. Grey was looking at him with something like hatred.

'I warned you,' Willis said. 'I warned you.'

'You tried to sell us a load of shit. You used Nancy Freeman. And now she's dead. You – '

'What happened to her?' Willis asked.

'You what?'

'What happened?'

Grey reached into his desk and pulled out a folder. He slid it across the desk to Willis.

Inside were a sheaf of Polaroids, preliminary scene-of-crime stuff. They made skin curiously yellow and blood too pink. It was hard to decide at first what was what, but gradually Willis worked it out. After it had been pulled to bits, Nancy's body had been rolled in a thick coating of dead leaves. Her mouth had been filled with grass.

'You should have believed me,' Willis said hoarsely.

'What was she doing?' Grey asked. 'What was she doing? Who were these travellers? Is that what's going on? You and her, you worked out that travellers might be involved but you wanted to keep it from us? Is that it? Mr Fucking Liberal Pink Shit Willis thought that we might blame the hippies and the gippoes and start a fucking pogrom in fucking ESSEX? IS THAT IT?'

Willis closed his eyes and wiped spittle from his face.

'No. It isn't.'

'Then what is it?'

'It was just a rumour I heard. Not even a rumour. I was in a pub and the landlord said that some travellers sitting outside had been chased out of the forest by something. I mean by kids. I mentioned it to Nancy and she must have followed it up.'

Except that's not what happened and you know it, Willis thought. You asked Nancy to do it. You specifically asked her to do it. Not only that, you never told her the dangers.

You never told her that whatever is going on in there has been going on at least eighty years, and for all we know eight hundred, or eight thousand.

You never told her that and now she's dead.

'Nancy Freeman was transferring to traffic. I don't think she would have gone haring after some nonsense lead that you may or may not have passed to her, especially one that was going to get her dismembered. God! I don't know what makes me feel more sick. What happened to her or knowing that you're alive and she's dead. Now, tell us what you know.'

'I've told you.'

'You little bastard! All right. I'll play it your way.'

Grey led him from his office down corridors of thin partition board, into the back of the building. A short corridor opened off to one side. At one end was a store room; at the other the dead file stacks and evidence vault.

Grey unlocked the door but walked him past the vault. Halfway down one of the stacks under P he pulled out a box file labelled 'Petty Cash Receipts (Claimed)' and carried it to a small table. He said: 'Lock the door,' then opened the file.

There was a list of figures and numbers which Willis recognised as filing references.

'Unsolved crimes, Willis. Do you know what these represent?'

He shook his head.

'A betrayal. You think we're here to solve crimes. You're missing the point. We're here to make sense of it all, Willis. That's what police do. Crime is not considered normal behaviour – that's part of a tacit understanding that keeps society together. We explain to people, not why people commit crimes, but that it's wrong. We solve crimes, Willis. We solve mysteries. That's our role. It may be that most crimes don't get solved, but that's not the point. People believe that they do. If we start . . . opening things up, we've betrayed the public.

We've betrayed society. That's not for us to do.'

'You know?' Willis could not stop his voice from rising.

'No, Willis, I don't know. Neither do you. All I knew when I was interviewing a little girl called Emma Darby, all those years ago, was that I, she, we were up against something that no one understood. But that's not good enough!'

'You knew she was Caroline Waters?'

'Of course I fucking knew.'

'But you did nothing.'

'There's nothing to be done except keep quiet.'

'And all those other deaths – here in the forest?'

'What about them? And what about all the other deaths in the country? In the world? Unexplained, Willis. We give them our best shot, then we move on. You didn't move on. Because of that Nancy Freeman is dead.'

'But I can get to the bottom of it.'

'And then what? Keep it a secret? Let what you know slip, just once – have you any idea of the consequences if the press got hold of it?'

'But people do know. You saw the tree, you saw all the things that had been left on it.'

'Superstition, Willis. There's a world of difference between superstition and belief. Superstition can be comforting. Belief can be terrifying.'

'We've got to do something.'

'Yes,' Grey said. 'Forget it before someone else gets killed.'

'Jesus!' Willis said suddenly. 'I've been stupid. That's why Marcus – that's everything!'

'What are you talking about?'

'The children in the forest . . . I've got to get to Caroline. I'll tell you later.'

Caroline was not at his flat, so he drove to the close. He pulled up outside her house and ran across the pocket handkerchief square of front lawn. Terror came at him with shocking violence, a physical, sensate, enveloping force folding itself around him. His legs slowed and stopped. This was fear like pain, like extreme pain; his own body had put him into a state of shock. He could watch in horror in the same way that people could watch the ragged stump of their wrist pumping blood into

296

the place where the hand was meant to be, and not faint from the pain. He looked up at the blank front of the suburban house and saw with absolute clarity the terror that was stored inside; a terror that infected Caroline, her own son, him.

What had she done?

He remembered lying by her, entering her. The memory swelled in his mind and burst like a cyst.

What had she done?

The shape of the house, its flat façade, took on a cold significance which he could not properly understand. She was in there: he imagined her peering out from between the curtains, one dreadful eye pouring out its fear into the world, at him.

Where was she? Top floor? Ground floor? Above him, below him? Below him? He looked at the ground, at the grass stems, and saw them grey and wither. A high singing filled his head; held on a single, unwavering note. When the singing stopped the world would crash and all the evil in the wood would flood out like water from a cracked bowl, flood out and fill the world.

It all funnelled into this one truth. She had asked the fairies to kill her parents, *but what had they asked her to give in return?*

What had she done? What had she offered?

His mind spun; in his heart he knew.

Marcus. In exchange for killing her parents, she had been forced to sacrifice her unborn son.

The enormity of it almost crushed him. From somewhere far away he heard thunder. He looked up and saw clouds the colour of slate marching across the sky. Then the rain started to fall.

Chapter 43

The sky ruptured and rain poured down. The world below met it with a million hissing sighs as the wet smashed on to the hard earth, balling darkly in the dust, pooling, softening, cleaning.

Above the ruined house on the edge of the wood it fell on grass stems that were smeared with blackened, drying bits of Nancy Freeman. Softening, they reddened, ran down blades of grass, dripped from stems, fell gratefully at last to earth and mindless absorption.

The rain fell on the clearing where Tailor had died, mixing the last of him to mud; it fell on Sergeant Willis's upturned face as he scanned Caroline's house for signs of life; it fell on the lawn at the back of the house where a lifetime ago a mother had hosed down the remains of a dead rabbit to try and comfort her grieving son.

She still did not know for certain how it had happened, but she could guess. He had been playing with things that played rough.

She twitched a curtain. On the other side of the fence the forest drummed and roared as countless drops fell on countless leaves. Memories were emerging now as the fog in her mind was beginning to thin, and the blank space filled. Pain spread in sharp waves across her legs, up her back. She felt the flood of blood warm on her thighs, cold on her calves; the touch of bloody fabric, stiffening as she tried to move.

And now she remembered the figures in the wood. She remembered how they seemed to sing to her in high, grey voices, as fine as spun sugar, as light and friable as the crawling tendrils of a spreading mould.

It came back: the ugly square house, the wood; the grey and empty sky; the wind; the cold; the pain; the scars and scabs and the fairies from the woods who made her the awful promise.

The fairies? In the books she saw at school they were wispy hermaphrodites with gossamer wings, gorgeous legs and button noses. They smelt of sunlight and the soft thrum of their wings was the sound of dandelion seeds drifting through the air.

So where were they?

What were they?

They were as much like the slim wisps of air and sex that the story books showed as a mermaid is like a manatee. Through a hard membrane of wind-dried skin jagged the wicked outline of their ribs, splayed, racked, sharp, but fanning out behind so that it was easy to see why some might think they had wings. Flesh, caught between the memory of substance and the truth of decay, clung to their dry skeletons in a stinking, flowing jelly: frozen putrescence; an oily ice of rot.

And for one night Caroline had run with them. This she remembered as the raindrops knocked at the windows of her home, as the sky wept for her and her eyes bled tears.

Back in the field, night is falling and she hops from leg to leg in the ploughed field at the back of their home. She hears her mother call her.

'Little monster! Little monster!' Her voice rises and falls in a sort of coo.

'Come inside, you little monster.' A soft voice. Coaxing and kind.

Then from the woods another voice that cuts through her thoughts like a cheese wire.

no, come with us

She stands still before habit and fear twist into a noose to drag her to her home. Then:

no, come with us

This time she turns. She looks, she waits, her nerves tingling, fear spreading through her body, but a gorgeous, effervescent, heady fear that is all to do with anticipation and *not knowing*. So different from the fear her parents put her through.

The figures emerge from the woods. Two upright; two slithering. All somehow imbued with a lightness which she cannot understand until she sees that they are hanging six inches or so above the ground.

'Monster. Monster. Monster. Monster.' Her mother again. As if she's a cat to be called like that.

come with us run with us for a night be free tell us what you want

'To be free.' Her mouth forms the words and she thinks she can see one of the figures nod.

'You fucking shit! Get in here, you blood and shit! We'll fucking split you and skin you. Make your fucking arse grin.' Her mother's voice suddenly changes to a cracked scream.

She looks at the woods – at the house – fear jangles her – the figures are receding – floating – free – she looks at her feet caked in mud, smelling of mud, and thinks of the thick whips of pain and thin splash of blood and the red weals in her flesh splitting into smiles.

To be free. I want to be free! I want to be free! OF THEM!

That's it! Something real. Not just a vague idea but something real and achievable.

'Come here! Come HERE!'

It gets easier. This time she takes a step towards the spinney. The figures stop retreating and stand and wait. As her longing to escape becomes stronger, her weight begins to fall away until it is flowing off her in rivers.

One step. Two step.

Under the trees the figures are clearer. Dark and light, the mottled web of shadows makes sense of their ruin, fills in the gaps, as it were, and she sees them for what they really are. Her heart lifts, she feels joy blooming in her like a sun. One stretches a hand out, her tentative steps quicken and now she is running, then floating, her feet flicking above the ground as she runs towards the woods, her voice rising in a shriek of joy. Free of them. Free of them. To run in the woods forever, following the laughing children of the shadows.

follow us, follow us to the tree

Standing in her bedroom the adult Caroline shivers, tasting the joy all over again and the red salt of excitement.

She can't remember how she makes it, but it seems that an ancient path has opened at her feet. She is running with wonderful, exhilarating speed, branches flicking just past her eyes but never hitting them, the ground as smooth as a swiftly flowing river, effort and pain, limping and stumping along, way behind her, unable to keep up. She's watching the passage of the children in front of her, knowing that she will keep up, and knowing that they know. She is filled with awe.

★

There. She'd done with remembering for a bit. What came next?

She wanted a pee, she was hungry, she was cold, she needed a bath, she was tired. The feelings suggested an order of activity, real-time. Check the water's hot. If not, put on the heater. While it's heating up go downstairs and make yourself beans on toast. Eat it. Boil a kettle. Put a hot water bottle in the bed. Run the bath. Soak. Curl up in bed with a friend called Temazepan and wait for sleep. The thought made her feel delicious. At least that bloody man had stopped banging at her door. At least the phone had stopped ringing. She risked a peep out of the landing window. At least his car had gone.

She turned on the hot water and the central heating. She had just emptied a tin of beans into a saucepan when the phone rang. Without thinking she walked into the hall and answered it.

'Caroline – I've been trying to reach you for days now. How are you?'

'Tina? It was you?' Of course Tina would have been calling.

'Who did you think it was?'

'Oh, I don't know. Someone.'

'Listen, pet, I'm sitting here all alone watching the tennis court turn into a swimming pool and was thinking, well, maybe I could just look in – even for twenty minutes? I'd love to see you.'

That wasn't like Tina. She must be worried. There was a note in her voice.

'I – '

'I can be with you in half an hour.'

Caroline looked around the sitting room. At the plates half-covered with smears of food, at the general greyness and squalor of it all. Half an hour? She could wolf down her beans and maybe shove the plates in the dishwasher in that time. She could – She caught a glimpse of her face. Dark eyes in dark sockets seemed to hover above hollow cheeks. Even her lips looked thin. She felt ashamed of herself but at the same time knew that at last she *was* herself. She didn't need Tina any more. Tina had been her link to reality, to normality. Tina's friendship had been an anchor to keep her from drifting back to the shadows. Too late for that now. She put the telephone down

301

to break the connection, then lifted it. She didn't want anyone else to call.

She finished her beans, filled the dishwasher, lit the fire and opened a window to give the room a chance to air. Thunder grumbled across the sky somewhere over the forest and a couple of seconds later sheet lightning flared, giving her a perfect snapshot of her back garden, the summer-dried lawn awash with water.

Thunder again, this time more of a smash than a rumble. Was Tina coming? She couldn't remember. Perhaps she should go upstairs and do something about her face.

She sat at her small dressing table and looked for foundation to mask the black rings under her eyes, and blusher to put some colour into her cheeks. Another sudden crashing roar shook the house and made the windows rattle. Lightning flared across the sky as if it were a petrol flash fire; flared and kept on flaring. Shocked, Caroline stood by the window.

And froze.

In the last flicker of the lightning she saw the gate at the bottom of her garden open.

The lightning died. The doorbell rang. Caroline screamed and jumped, cat-like, away from the window, catching the back of her knee on the corner of the bed and crashing backwards. Her head slammed into the floor and sent stars shooting across her vision. The doorbell again. She got groggily on to her hands and knees and crawled towards the door, catching it with her head and slamming it shut. The pain boomed like a gong, reverberating in deep, dark waves. She sat back against the wall, trying to reach for the door handle, swallowing nausea. The ringing stopped.

They'll start to bang next, she thought. Then very clearly she saw the gate at the side of the house; very clearly she remembered how only that afternoon she had been trying to fix it, and how she had wedged it shut but thought that a good wind could well blow it open.

The wind dropped. She forced herself to sit still and listen. What would you do if you were Tina? You'd go to the back of the house to see if you could look in through a window. The back of the house where –

'Caroline!' The voice came through the window. Words were swept away by the wind.

She pulled herself to her feet, cupped her hands and peered through the glass for her friend.

A heavy growl of thunder – that should show up something when the next lightning flash came. Caroline looked down. Counted. One crocodile, two crocodile – flash!

Tina was walking backwards across the back lawn, looking up.

More thunder. One crocodile –

Caroline slammed her palms against the glass, tried to open the window, forgetting that it was locked, shouted, screamed.

Two crocodile.

Stopped.

Her hand froze on the handle as a fork of lightning split the sky.

Behind Tina's back a small figure detached itself from the shadows. She saw it for a second as the lightning flashed, then darkness swam back across her seared eyeballs.

Caroline screamed and beat on the glass. Another peal of thunder.

She waited for the flash then screamed again. Tina was backing into the middle of the lawn, peering up at the window, her hand levelled above her eyes to keep the rain off.

Thunder. Caroline drummed at the glass. At last Tina saw her. Maybe she waved.

Flash.

Maybe –

The next peal of thunder shook the house, the earth and the heavens. Almost immediately lightning tore across the sky, spear after spear, bolt after bolt. Caroline knelt on the floor and hugged herself.

Later she peered out of the window. The figure on the lawn was staring up at her. She flinched and tried to move back, out of sight, but something kept her at the window. Thunder grumbled. The storm was passing. The gate banged as the wind got up. Faintly she heard the creak as the swing moved restlessly in its frame.

The figure did not move.

Suddenly then the heavens were split by a bolt of white that sent the forest reeling. Caroline's eyes were blued by the magnesium intensity of the glare, but the image of a face like a shining white disc was stamped on her mind like a brand.

Marcus.

She screamed, wheeled round, but stopped, held by a single word cried out above the sound of the storm.

Mummy.

She could not tell if the sound was outside or inside. All she knew was that she heard it.

Mummy, I'm here.

His voice, recognisable but somehow slacker, as if the vocal cords were perishing, the palate rotting.

Mummy, please come to the window. Please let me see you. Please, Mummy, please.

And she turned.

Why did you do it, Mummy?

The voice came up through the rain, through the glass, into the room where it quietly surrounded her.

'Marcus, is that really you?' She mouthed the words, unwilling to acknowledge that she had said them, thought them.

Why did you do it, Mummy?

'Oh, darling, are you all right?'

She couldn't look. It was like communicating by remote control, but he could hear her, she thought, and she could certainly hear him.

Why, Mummy? It's not fair. I hurt and I'm bent funny.

'Oh, darling.'

Her heart was breaking. She could feel it. Inside her ribs it was suddenly the wrong shape. Her heart was going out to him. She could feel that too, feel the strain as it tried to fly from her breast to him –

It's hurting me. It hurts. It hurts.

His voice was coming and going as if he had turned and was now walking back towards the gate, looking over his shoulder to speak as he trudged forlornly away from her.

It hurts. Fainter now.

Caroline hurled herself at the window.

'Marcus, darling. Marcus, don't – !'

But he hadn't gone.

He was still standing there. A strong wind had torn the heavy clouds to shreds and broken moonlight played on the garden. Tina lay like a large, pale doll on the grass. Marcus stood over her, his face twisted in grief and anger. Rain washed down his face and bubbled across his lips.

I want to come in, he said. *Mummy, I'm cold.*

She could say nothing. She looked at Marcus and she looked at Tina's body.

I'm cold, Mummy. I feel terrible. Let me in, Mummy.

He started to float. His slack face became clearer. Closer. She closed her eyes. She could feel her heart pumping sickly but hugely inside her.

Mummy. Let me in, let me in. Let me get warm. I want you to hold me, Mummy.

It was Marcus but it wasn't Marcus. She opened her eyes. He was holding his arms up to her. His eyes were dark, brimming with pain. She could see through them and saw earth.

Please, Mummy.

Them. She could sense them now as she sensed them long ago, standing in the shadows, their shadows, making the wood their own.

They told me lies, Mummy. They told me things about you that weren't true.

Oh God, let the rain wash him away.

Mummy, I'm cold.

A sob tore from her throat. She put a hand to the window, felt it flatten against the glass, brought it down and rested her forehead against the pane. It was cool. She could feel the restless soothing rhythm of the raindrops through it.

It was coming now, she thought. It was coming.

Mummy, they said that they knew you.

'No.' It was more a groan than a word.

That's what they said. They said that they knew you, that they'd helped you. They said that you made a wish with them. They said that you'd gone to the tree and wished that your mummy and daddy weren't there any longer. They said that they'd done it for you, but Mummy, they said you didn't give them anything. A pause. *You were meant to give them something.*

No thunder, no lighting. In fact a hush, a stillness. Raindrops held themselves from falling, the long, trailing skirt of the wind stopped moving, the trees stopped rubbing their flat green fingers and creaking their hard, sappy bones. True, deep, silken silence.

Then Marcus said: *Me.*

It took a second to sink in, a burning, barbed arrow, burrowing into her breast and sinking into her heart.

'Oh no, no, no no no no.'

I tried to stop them but they took me. I tried to stop them by playing their games but they still took me.

'No. Please no.'

And look at me now!

She couldn't look.

Open your eyes, Mummy. Open them and see what happened to me because of you! Because of you!

But she could not. He carried too much with him. He was so swollen with what she feared that he would not fit through the door. There was no room for him in her heart.

Caroline retched.

She looked down hopelessly. Her mind was blurred with tears that would not come, her head was pounding with pain. She smeared her face against the glass.

'Please go,' she said. 'Please go.'

The little thing in the garden looked up at her.

I'll go, he said. *I'll go to someone who really loves me.*

She blinked and the garden was empty. Only the swing had gone crazy, jerking, swaying, ropes twisting.

The wind rose and the swing slowed.

She knew that what Marcus had said was significant but she didn't know quite why.

Chapter 44

Tom checked the windows of the house. A wind like this could get inside, prise one open and tear it off its hinges. That was the thing about a house like this, an old house. Things belonged to each other without necessarily quite fitting. Marina's parents, who lived in a semi in Amersham, said that old was quite nice, but they preferred the look of it to the real thing. 'What's the quarterly heating bill on a property such as this, Tom?' An I-thought-as-much nod resulted when he gave them the figure, while expounding on the insulating virtues of thatch. 'Ah, but what about your replacement costs? I'll wager you've not factored that in, squire.'

Jesus, that wind!

The forest sounded like the sea tonight, tossing and crashing. Somewhere, and it couldn't be that far away, he heard the creaking snap and sudden explosive cough of a bough breaking. He heard his father-in-law's comfy voice again: 'Hope you've stipulated falling tree cover in your policy, Tom. Haha.'

The wind was making the windows creak. Marina called him from the sitting room.

'Look, Tom, look.'

Another baby programme. The 'Record' light of the video was on. 'Within the next few weeks baby's horizons will widen to an extraordinary degree. Already their hearing can distinguish between bah and pah, their mother tongue and a foreign language. Next – '

'Tom, it's incredible.' Marina patted her stomach. 'To think it's growing inside me and it can already hear what we're saying.' He forced his mouth into a smile. 'And that thing about understanding. Did you know that, Tom? Did you?' He found he couldn't speak; could only mouth, 'No.' For once it was the truth. Everything else, all Marina was discovering – he'd been through it all before. He knew he should be with her but he couldn't bring himself to sit down with her.

Images of himself and Caroline, elbow deep in baby books . . . Every second sentence beginning: 'It's incredible; it says here . . . ' How could he tell Marina that all that love, all that interest, all that could be for nothing? How could he tell her without crying? How could he prepare her for the knowledge that all it took was a car badly parked on a corner and it was all for nothing?

'Better check the windows upstairs,' he said.

In the hall a sudden current of cold air on his face made him stop. He looked into the kitchen. The wind had blown the back door open, pinning it against the wall. Dead leaves and dry grass were dancing in a little whirlwind in the middle of the floor. He pushed the door shut, amazed by the ferocity of the wind. This time he bolted it. These old houses . . . Still, there was no way he was going to install a double-glazed storm porch with plastic window frames. The door banged and creaked on its hinge. The strip of felt he had stapled around the crack fluttered. Well, not this year anyway.

Marina called: 'Something's fallen down upstairs.'

'I'm on my way,' he said.

On the stairs he felt tired in the joints of his knees. That was something that had come on after Marcus's death. He was physically weaker, as if a bit of him had died too.

The stairs were steep with doors at top and bottom. It was on the little landing that he heard a thud.

A cat? He would not be surprised if an animal came in to find shelter given this weather. A cat, a dog, a fox even? No, not a fox. A fox would just make its way back to its den. Something domestic, perhaps, that had got lost.

He paused on the stairs, just a little bit nervous. Pushed open the door a few steps from the top because he didn't want to startle it.

The passageway, carpeted in pale grey, was empty, although there was something unfamiliar about it. He sniffed automatically: a strange, truffly, musty smell. His eyes fell to the top step where a dark stain lay in the middle.

Oh, no. The filthy little beast had pissed. Right! He felt decisive now. Ran downstairs, picked up a broom from the kitchen, closed all the doors except the one into the kitchen, and hooked the back door open so the cat or dog or whatever it was would have a clear run when he chased it out. It could shelter in the wood shed. More leaves gusted in. The outside light had switched on automatically as the door opened. The light just reached the first branches of the first trees of the forest. The noise was incredible, awesome, like a vast orchestra. He listened to it for a while then went back inside.

He paused again at the top of the stairs but all was quiet. He paced as quietly as he could down the corridor, then threw open the door to his and Marina's bedroom, his heart racing. Nothing. He checked the fitted cupboards, even though they were closed, prodded the broom under the bed before kneeling and peering there himself, painfully aware that teeth might suddenly sink into his nose. He straightened up. The room was clear, except – the duvet!

Was that a lump at the bottom of the bed? Had the creature crawled underneath it?

Holding the broom up, he twitched the duvet back. Breathed out with relief. His pyjama top. Good. So the bedroom was clear.

Feeling more confident he went into the bathroom, making kissy noises with his lips and crooning: 'Here, kittykitty. Here, you little pisser!'

Nowhere to hide there, not even behind the heated towel rail. Next room was the nursery. Marina would freak out if anything had been in there, and pray God it hadn't pissed or worse on the pastel all-wool carpet because if it had it would be another eleven hundred and seven pounds, twenty-seven pence to get it replaced because there was no way that Marina would allow it to stay if it had been sullied.

He flicked the light switch. The room filled with a warm, mellow light that picked up the Beatrix Potter frieze, the pretty flowered wallpaper, the fluffy sheep clockwork mobile, the already substantial collection of strange soft toys at the bottom of the canopied (canopied, for fuck's sake) cot.

No, the room just smelled faintly of wallpaper paste and the sherbert lemon scent that Marina somehow exuded everywhere she stayed more than a week.

Wait. Nonononono. Something in the cot. Something in the

cot. Can't make it out but it's dark and it's curled up. SHIT!

Broom raised, heart pounding, he took two steps to the cot, swung the broom down, and caught it just in time. Stared into the cot in disbelief.

Three days ago Marina had come back from the shops with a large toy rabbit, white with pink ears, poking out of the top of her shopping bag. It was lying on its side in the middle of the cot now, its stuffing spread around it, one ear torn off.

A cat did that? He'd never heard of it before but could imagine it lying on its side, raking the toy with its hind legs.

A dog? Dogs tore toys to shreds, but did they do it so neatly?

Marina? He knew all about post-natal depression: for three months after Marcus had been born Caroline had been convinced that he was going to be taken away from them in the middle of the night. Wouldn't it just be typical of Marina to get it slightly wrong and contract pre-natal depression?

He checked the room with painstaking thoroughness, even looking in the closed drawers. But it was empty. He looked at the rabbit's stuffing and the cot's mattress for hair but found nothing except for a single, dry leaf. He left the room, closing the door carefully behind him.

In a way it was a relief to have a real reason to go into Marcus's room. He had spent so long avoiding it, walking past it every time he went upstairs, never even looking at the door with the ceramic bi-plane trailing a 'Marcus' banner behind it.

The first time he went in it had been like walking into a vacuum. Everything had seemed empty, clean, and the sight of it had sucked the air from his lungs. He had walked round slowly, touching this, touching that, as if he had been in church. He had sat on the edge of the bed, not really understanding what he was feeling, but knowing it was nothing he'd expected. Somehow Marcus was still in the room, a presence, a feeling, something warm and comforting. He understood why parents might keep a room unchanged after a child had died – not in some vain hope that he might walk through the door and take up residence in their lives again as if nothing had happened, but in the calm and certain knowledge that something irrevocable had happened – the only irrevocable thing we come across in life – and the child was never, ever coming back.

Tom put his hand on the rustic latch that Marcus had just grown tall enough to reach – and froze. The hairs on the back of his neck rose and scratched his shirt collar. He felt goose pimples run in a cold wave down his arms. There was a noise coming from Marcus's room.

A low, irritating humming noise, rising and falling minutely. An electric noise.

It was. It couldn't be. This was bad. He was going crazy. It was the sound of the Scalextric – little plastic cars that chased each other round a track like mice. All this chasing after cats or dogs or whatever was sending him mad. He lifted the latch gently and flung open the door.

Chapter 45

Caroline was hiding from Willis. He had seen movement in her house, lights go on behind the curtains. He realised belatedly that if you wanted to see somebody and they didn't want to see you, the last thing you did was drive up to their house in your car, and park it outside for them to see. He drove down the Close, turned in the special area at the back, and pulled up about ten yards down from Caroline's front door, just as a natty Japanese convertible stopped and a slim, attractive woman – he was certain it was Tina, who he had seen at the funeral with Caroline – bolted for the front door with a newspaper over her head. He saw her ring and wait impatiently. Something about her made him think that she expected Caroline to be in. When the front door clearly did not open she ran round the side of the house where Willis remembered there was a gate. He should remember – he'd kicked it in.

He reckoned that she might hang around for two, maybe three minutes in this weather, but after that she would give up and come back, unless she had been let in, of course.

He waited five minutes, with rain exploding off the windscreen and bonnet of the car and the wind rocking it on its springs. Draughts pushed their way through tiny gaps in the door seal. He waited another five minutes for good measure, then another five because the storm seemed to be reaching some sort of climax and he thought it might begin to slacken. He stretched out his hand to open the door when something fat and black boomed against the windscreen before slapping off into the night.

He flinched and snatched his hand away from the door. At the far end of the Close a dustbin lid lifted off and went spinning against a metal garage door. He heard the clanging boom in the car, above the sound of the wind and rain. The dustbin toppled,

312

a black bag rolled out and was blown across the lawn.

A dustbin bag or something. That was what had hit his windscreen. He opened the car door gingerly, stood for a second. The wind was incredible. It tugged at the skin of his face, wrestled with his jacket, flapped his trousers while the rain drove in and soaked him. He thought he heard a scream but the wind was making the telegraph wire above his head bend like a bowstring and sing like a violin. The noise could have been anything, come from anywhere. Under the roar of the wind was a jagged timpani of things breaking.

He ran to the house. The wind was blowing rain straight into the vestigial porch. He doubted it was worth ringing and so ran round the side and into the narrow alley, feet threatening to slide out from under him as he turned the corner. The gate was rattling on its hinges but unlocked. He closed it behind him, hoping that she had left the back door open when she let Tina in.

It was pitch black in the back garden. Rain was still spearing the ground but the lightning had stopped and the thunder was low and distant. Light seeped from the edges of the curtains. He felt his way along the back of the house, brick giving way to the big french window, then brick again, the kitchen window. The door was to the side of it.

He grabbed the handle. Locked and solid. Back to the french windows. His palms squeaked across the plate glass as he tried to slide it. No good. The sudden crash of the back gate slamming made him jump like a cat.

He wheeled round, pressing his back into the wall. He'd forgotten about the forest gate. Suppose there was something in the garden. Having crept in. His eyes had adjusted enough now to see the fence as a pale line against the heaving, crashing wall of the forest. The gate was closed.

He peered through the darkness and rain, straining for movement, trying to block out whatever was directly in front of him and concentrate on the peripheries. Nothing moved. He took a step, then another, eyes flicking from side to side, shuffling forward until his feet met resistance. He jumped back and looked down.

He knew almost as soon as he saw it that it was a body. Tina was wearing black and that had hidden her. His foot had touched her leg. He knelt and felt his way up her body. He couldn't find her left arm – must be twisted under her – and he couldn't find the pulse in her right. He moved his hands up and tried to find the heart. He gave up, hooked his arms under her shoulders and began to drag her to the back door.

It opened suddenly and he fell across the sill on to the floor. Caroline. Together they pulled Tina across the threshold. In the light he could see a pulse twitching in her neck. He carried her to the sitting room and laid her on the sofa while Caroline fetched a blanket. Willis called an ambulance.

'Has he gone?' she asked.

Willis slumped against the wall, his chest heaving, rain running down his temples. He brushed the water away. His fingers smelled of sick. He supposed it came from Tina.

'Has he gone?' More urgently.

'Who?'

'Marcus. He talked to me. He wanted to come in. I wouldn't let him. He – '

'Let's get one thing straight,' Willis said. 'Whatever is out there isn't Marcus, any more than I am.'

'But you – '

'Marcus is dead. You saw the coffin, didn't you?'

'No,' Caroline said. 'He came back. He wants me and I can't give him love.'

'I understand,' Willis said.

'No,' Caroline continued. 'You don't. I did it. It's my fault.' She paused, swallowed and lowered her head as if she were butting her way through a wood. 'Years ago . . . They – those things in the wood – did something for me. Then they took me to a tree in the forest and asked me what I wanted. It was – I was just a child. My parents beat me. All I could think was that I wanted to be free of them. So I wished it. Then they asked me what I would give them. I said I'd give anything they wanted. They asked me for a baby. I didn't know. I thought babies just arrived. I didn't think it would be so bad for a baby, to live in the forest. All I could think was that it couldn't be worse than what my parents did to me. I never . . . I never thought that I would be me and my child would be Marcus. You see, what my parents did – '

'I know,' Willis said.

314

'But I didn't think that they'd kill them! I didn't want that. I just wanted them to stop – hitting me! Hurting me!'

'Yes.'

'Then they trapped Marcus – and they took him. And it's all my fault.'

'No.' Willis put a hand on her wrist. 'It's bigger than that. Remember Winterburn? It's years old, centuries old. I've just found that my inspector knows all about them. It's been going for ever. You. Me. We're just a little bit of it.'

'But he talked to me,' Caroline howled, her voice steadily rising. 'My own little boy. He blames me. He was right. He came here looking for love and I couldn't give it to him. He said that he was going to go somewhere he could get it.'

Willis, relieved at least that she was talking freely, gave a little shrug and said: 'I wonder what he meant by that.'

Caroline's eyes widened and darkened.

'Oh my God,' she said.

'What is it?' he asked, watching her closely.

'I've just realised what he meant.'

'What?'

'Tom. Don't you see? He's gone to his father.'

Tina groaned.

'Marcus didn't kill her. Perhaps that means Tom will be all right.'

Chapter 46

Tom stood in the doorway and screamed. The light in the room was bright and warm. He smelled sunshine, leaves and grass, earth and damp. He screamed again and wind came out. Dew spurted from his eyes and spattered against the thing on the floor with the faint crackle of rain on dry leaves. This could not be happening. He opened his mouth again, this time to call for help, and vomited lichen, wriggling fledglings, mud, leaf mould, puffballs. In front of him the racing cars careened crazily round the track. He tried to back out of the room but was drawn irresistibly to the thing sitting on the floor with its back to him. He felt its power as the direct opposite of his. His legs were snatched by the hips and jerked forwards, and as he toppled backwards a crushing force that threatened to snap his spine bent him forwards again in the middle. He proceeded across the room like a rag doll being manipulated by giant, invisible hands.

'Hello, Daddy.'

His mouth could only say 'Marcus', although he tried to scream again and say No, no, no.

'It's started,' Marcus said.

Tom tried to turn his head away. It was so unclear. There was a mass of liquid grey, and in it swum leaves and sticks and mud, the stuff of the forest. In place of the delicate pale triangle of Marcus's face was a soft wedge-shaped sculpture of leaves and mud that was always slipping and reforming. His arms were as thick as tree trunks, his waist as tapered and thin as a wasp's.

'Look.' He punched a hideous finger at the window. The glass and leading shattered, a gap appeared in the clouds and the stars began to flake and fall. All Tom could smell now was old meat. 'What do you want?' His mouth was so dry that the words seemed to stick to his palate.

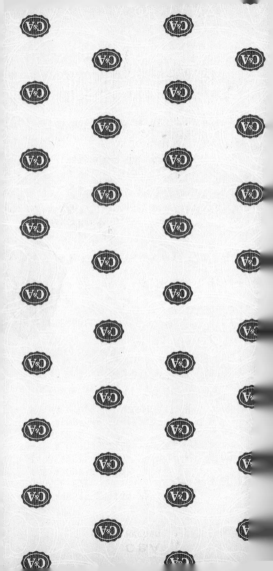

It could have been called a smile. Marcus rose like a thing on strings, and crossed the room. There was a dry rustle as he moved.

'A hug, Daddy.' He puckered his rough lips. Tom felt two columns like tubes of muscled clay wrap around him. Dead leaves whispered, wet with slime. Ripples of power ran around his neck; the stench was everything that had ever died in the forest.

'Who are you?' Tom managed to whisper.

'Marcus, of course.'

'You're not Marcus.'

'I am.'

'NO.'

Fingers slipped through his sweater as if it were tissue paper, then through his shirt. It was with dull surprise that he realised that his back was being gently flensed and blunt fingers were running up and down his bare ribs. Blood poured over his buttocks.

Marcus stood suddenly. Tom sat on the floor and rocked to and fro, bubbling incoherently. All he could think of was the spreading pool on the carpet. The thing looked down at him and said in a voice that was as bright as phosphorescence: 'Well, I'd better go and see Marina now.'

The room was empty by the time the words sank in to Tom's befuddled brain. The door was swinging on its hinges and a faint smell of forest floors hung in the air. Tom tried to move. His bones ached as they cooled. He tried to move but found he couldn't. The web of muscle that encased his ribs had ripped and with it had gone a lot of mobility. He felt like an unstrung guitar; he had never appreciated how gorgeously taut a body was before.

He fell. He could move his lower arms, and his feet. He was sure he would be able to move the rest of his limbs later but it was a question of finding how to without using the muscles of his lower back. He supposed it hurt. Right now he wasn't sure. He rolled, levering himself forward by the elbows, and wedged himself in the door. By wiggling his toes he moved his legs round and by pushing he managed to get his head and shoulders pointing through the door rather than across it. He pulled himself forwards, fingers digging into the thick pile of the carpet for purchase, until he reached the top of the stairs. He hooked his fingers over the edge of the first step, pulled himself over and allowed himself to slide.

At the landing he came across his first major problem. Momentum kept his legs moving after his body had stopped. Lacking any muscles across the small of his back, and angled upwards as they were, they flipped backwards, arching up over his shoulders like a scorpion's tail. The pain was sudden, lancing, cold and vicious, something like rusty knife blades being inserted between each vertebra and jiggled. He cried out in agony, wrenched his body round and forced his head down the next flight, praying that when he reached the bottom he would slide on the quarry tiles in the hall rather than stick.

He was more cautious on this flight, letting himself down one at a time. Moving more slowly he could hear what was going on around him. He was aware of strange and distant screaming coming from the front of the house. He thought he heard the dull crump and the high splintering sound of a car crash.

From the sitting room came a sort of muffled gasp. He let himself slide down the last few steps, then hauled himself round the corner. The sitting-room door, at the end of a short corridor, was ajar. He pushed it open with his fingers.

Marina was lying on the sofa, her eyes wide with terror. Marcus had stuffed her mouth with leaves and mud, and her mouth was working, spitting them out. The tendons on the side of her neck were standing out and her eyes looked as if they were starting from her head, as if her screaming was trying to squeeze round the edges of them.

Marcus patted her head clumsily with a blunt hand, leaving a trail of mud across her forehead. Marina writhed from side to side. Marcus put a gentle hand on her breast to keep her still, looked interested and tore her clothes until it was free.

From outside more sounds; two different sirens: ambulance and police.

Marina was trying to cover her belly with her hands; Marcus kept on taking them away, pressing his face to the newly rounded mound. Tom could see Marina's hands hovering above Marcus, not wanting to touch him to push him away.

Summoning all his strength, Tom hauled himself forwards. Marcus stooped and slid his arms under Marina.

Marina saw Tom. She managed to clear her mouth of earth and shout: 'Tom. Help me. They want the baby.'

Marcus turned. His foot landed on Tom's hand. It was like being pressed by cold mud and worms. He rolled feebly and tried to grab the other leg as it passed over him.

It was like trying to stop a tree from growing. But as he was pushed away he saw car lights brush across the ceiling. He tried to hang on to consciousness until help arrived.

Above the line of the shops and houses the sky was cracking, dark veins zigzagging up from the horizon. If it cracked . . .

The ambulance had taken forever to arrive. He had waited in the car; Caroline had let them into the house and then bolted. Now Willis was driving. Caroline sat hugging herself in the passenger seat, trying to imagine what she might do when she next saw Marcus, but her imagination was failing her.

'Oh my God,' she said. 'Look.' They were passing by a side street that led straight to the edge of the forest. She caught a glimpse of trees but instead of gathering darkness under their boughs they had gathered light, a dull, sickly light that was spilling out like liquid. 'We have to go through that to get to Tom's,' she said. 'Left here.'

Willis swung off the High Street.

Under the trees the light filled the road, lying on its surface like a motorway rain slick.

Heavy gobbets of rotting debris dropped from the trees and splashed on the windscreen. The washers couldn't shift it; soon they were peering through a smeared veil of grey and red. Even the ground was oozing.

Willis was muttering: 'What the fuck is going on? What the fuck is going on?'

'It's the forest,' Caroline said. 'Something's opened a channel to all the dead things in it. Dead things go into the ground. They rot. Trees feed on them. It's going on all the time. I think we're just seeing it magnified.'

A lump of ground, shaped like an arched back, reared up and in the tangle of roots and earth a dim shape seemed to be trying to assert itself over the vegetable matter it had become. Further away, she saw something like a huge black jellyfish hump across the forest floor before slitting itself on a tree and exploding with a sigh.

Willis beat the steering wheel with the flat of his hand. Caroline looked ahead through the filthy windscreen at nature turning in on itself, death coming to life.

By the time they arrived at Tom and Marina's the evergreen leaves on their hedge had turned into little spears of brown bone that rattled and hissed in the wind as they drove past. Out of the corner of her eye Caroline thought she saw the sky twitch like a blanket.

As Willis stopped the car Marcus appeared at the back door. He was walking backwards, dragging Marina by the heels. He saw them and started to drag her faster towards the forest. Willis left the car and began the chase. After he had gone a few paces he realised that Caroline had not followed him.

'What are you doing?' he shouted at her.

'I can't.'

'Can't? What do you mean?'

'Don't you see what it means to me? Don't you see what will happen to me? You're asking me to die. To volunteer. To choose to die. All because of something that happened nearly thirty years ago. My parents were monsters, now they've made my baby one. *I'm* a monster. It's just not fair!'

Willis looked at the forest. The light had stopped pulsing. It was held on a heartbeat. There was no more he could say.

Then he heard a low scraping behind him. Fear douched him. He turned, his back crawling, and saw a terrible wreck of a man pulling himself out of the back door of the cottage and along the gravel. His legs trailed behind him like a split tail. His face was blank, white, bathed in sweat. His back was all blood.

Willis went and knelt by him. Tom ignored him, simply kept on crawling with dogged persistence. Marcus half-turned, took a step towards the forest, stopped again and looked at Caroline.

Tom paused. He pushed himself up on his elbows and tried to call out. There were hard white pellets of spit in the corners of his mouth. Willis saw his lips form an 'M'. The word trailed off in a whispery exhalation.

Willis saw Caroline's mouth form into a hard, determined line, then suddenly relax. He knew then that she was going, and knew he did not want her to go, but were his wishes of any importance? The choice was simple: he could stop her, and let Marcus go back into the woods with his burden; or he could let Caroline go and perhaps this thing would stop, perhaps the circle would be broken.

She started to cry. He wished she wouldn't. He wished she wouldn't look at him so imploringly; he wished he had the strength to go to her and stop her. He did not even know if that would be strength or weakness. He lifted a hand towards her. It was meant to be a hand stretched out to rescue her but when he saw the expression on her face, it changed into something that could have been a gesture of farewell.

Everything was changing. Caroline's face was set. She was looking at the forest. He thought she would not look at him but at last she did and it was as if her eyes were on fire.

'I think I'm meant to go with them,' she said.

'You don't have to,' Willis said. He thought his insides were dissolving. He could hardly stand; he wanted to kneel.

'I know what Marcus's last wish was,' Caroline said. 'He wanted me to stop the children. This is the only way. We're all living in the wood. And all the paths come back to the same place in the end.'

'But we could have a life in between,' Willis said. 'Like Winterburn.'

'Winterburn didn't have Marcus,' Caroline said. 'He's mine. Still. I'm his. This might be a way to save him. Goodbye.'

The black trunks glared; the heavy canopy of leaves rustled and shimmered. As she approached the line of trees Willis felt, rather than saw, an eager stream of movement, rushing inwards to the forest. Shapes gathered on the margin of the woods, waiting in rows.

As Caroline reached the shape that had been her son, he saw it reach a blunt hand up to her, dropping the other woman's ankles. Then he saw Caroline stretch a hand down and clasp his, hesitate, then clasp again, as if she had found the shape of a little child's hand inside the glove of mud and rot.

He turned his back. He didn't see her disappear. He didn't see her running towards the trees.

Epilogue

In the weeks that followed Willis went down a very long way, dragged and drugged by guilt and a constant sense of fear. The waiting for something to happen was a state of mind now; he could not believe that things were over. When a tree moved, when a shadow lengthened, when a child looked at him, he flinched. He took to retracing his steps: Kingsmeade Close, the wishing tree glade, Tailor's house. Once he saw Mrs Tailor looking at him and guessed she understood something from the expression on his face. She nodded to him.

His interview with Grey had been short and sharp. Willis had resigned; Grey had given him a year's rest and recreation, the first three months on full pay, the rest on half. Willis had been too dispirited to argue, which proved Grey's point that he wasn't himself and could not be held fully responsible for his actions.

Willis developed a hacking cough that made people turn and stare at him; his cheeks sank, stubble seemed to sprout in new little crevices and fissures in his skin, like ferns in gullys. He drove past Kingsmeade Close but he never drove in.

One day, the first day of the year that breathed winter, he went back to the cemetery. It was how he remembered it, a flat field of stones. He found Marcus's grave and stood over it. There were fresh flowers; the grass that on other graves spilled over the stone had been trimmed here. Of all the people who had survived this, it was Marina who had come through the best. Marina, with a new baby and a crippled husband, found time to visit the grave of the child who in some other manifestation had come close to destroying her.

It was a mystery, but then there were so many in life.

He went over and over the events in his mind, never finding a way in, never able to think of anything that might shine a light on the mystery. He knew what had happened, he even knew why, but he didn't understand. On one level he thought he wanted to understand so maybe he could stop such things for good, even if it meant sacrificing himself. That would be fair: he had more or less asked Caroline to do the same. It would also provide an answer to all the questions.

Sleet hit his face and slid down it.

Winter, he thought. Winter . . .

Darkness gathered, then fell around him in wet folds. He had a journey to make, and a loose end to tie in.

This time it was raining. He drove along the front and looked at the waves rolling up the steep shingle. The municipal flowerbeds had been stripped for the winter; the seafront shops were boarded up apart from a single video game arcade with a bright yellow illuminated sign and Bryan Adams on the sound system.

The boyfriend, Nancy's boyfriend, had come up to him at the funeral. He had told him exactly why waves always broke on to a beach and not off it. Willis had not really understood why he had bothered to do this until later, and then it was obvious. He had been wasting his time on questions like that. The big question, the only question, was why people died.

He looked at the rain and looked at the sea and wondered how long it would have to rain for the sea to overflow and wash everything away.

At Winterburn's home the nurse was waiting for him. She showed him upstairs. The old man was in the same chair. He had been reading. When Willis entered he put the book down almost eagerly. There was tea in a Thermos and sugared biscuits on a tray. There was also, Willis noticed, an overcoat on the bed, and a hat. Winterburn motioned for him to sit down.

Willis had called the old man and told him all that had happened. He had said that the forest seemed quiet, that perhaps Caroline's sacrifice had worked, but to be on the safe side he needed to know whether Winterburn had ever paid for the death of his brother and the freedom of his bride. When Winterburn had told him that he had paid nothing, Willis

323

suggested that he might like to think of a suitable gift for a life spent with his heart's desire. After a moment's silence, Winterburn had laughed.

Now, on this wet afternoon with the rain lashing the grey sea at the end of the long street, it was time to set things straight.

'My father was an archaeologist,' Winterburn said once Willis was settled in a chair. 'Not a very good one, not good enough to be sent off to Babylon or Nineveh or the Valley of the Kings. There was fierce competition back then, you know. People clamouring to lead digs here, digs there. It seemed that every new discovery – Troy, Babylon, the Labyrinth of King Minos – brought to life a past that up until then one had only ever thought of as mythic.

'Anyway, the long and short of it was that my father never made it to the Middle East. Instead he busied himself with England. He was determined to find a past every bit as glorious as the one being dug up in those deserts: King Arthur's Tomb; the Holy Grail – anything would have done. He became a keen, not to say fanatical local historian and drawing on the stories he had been told as a child – we were always from these parts, you know – he started building up folktales into a sort of forest mythos. And one of those stories was that if you wished for your heart's desire on the dead tree by Ferny Dips, the fairies might grant your wish.'

He dabbed his lips with a very white handkerchief. Willis shifted in his chair, wondering when the pay-off would come. Winterburn glanced sideways at him and continued. 'Anyway,' the old man said, 'that's how we heard about it. There's no particular secret involved. Other people, well . . . it's just part of their local heritage. There are a lot of different, overlapping themes. Some of the stories contain dire warnings, others don't. But frankly, if you want something badly enough, you'll just ignore the warnings anyway, won't you?'

'And you did?'

'I didn't believe the stories,' Winterburn said. 'Not for a minute. Thought my father was a fool. I was driven to it out of desperation, the same way an atheist might pray on the eve of battle. Connie and I, we'd fallen deeply and profoundly in love while my brother Thomas was in France for his first spell. He was a staff officer, in no particular danger. His and Connie's engagement had pretty well been arranged. It was a farce, but he was a stickler for form. When he came back on leave, I told him. I thought he'd give her up, but not Thomas. Out of the question. Frankly he was surprised and disappointed in me – the army had made him frightfully pompous – and as for Connie, he would go and have a word with her.'

'And?'

'He told her that if she left him, he would say that she had been with the butcher, the baker, the candlestick maker, and every servant in the house. He would say that she was diseased, pregnant, debauched. He would ruin her so completely that she would never be able to show her face again in public. He said this to her, mind you. Not to me. Didn't have the guts.

'Connie came to me. Told me. She said she could bear it; said she'd sail with me to Canada to get away from him if needs be. All I wanted to do was kill him. In those days, a woman's reputation, you see . . . ' His voice trailed off, as if savouring his brother's iniquity, then gathered itself.

'Well, I don't mind telling you, I was presented with a dilemma: to take Connie at her word, rise to the challenge and take off without a bean, with the foul breath of scandal chasing after us, or to give her up and let her live a sort of death in life with a man she hated, who could do what he wanted with her. I'll be frank, the thought of him fucking her nearly drove me mad, Sergeant Willis. It put me on the rack.

'Anyway, the night after Connie told me of what Thomas said, I couldn't sleep. I contemplated killing him there and then, just to free her. He kept his service revolver in the hall stand; it would not have been difficult.

'Our house backed on to the forest and I staggered out into it. My nerves were stretched to breaking, so much so that I was hallucinating. I remember quite clearly how I thought I was followed by grey children with no faces. I got quite scared and started blundering through the woods until quite suddenly I burst out of the undergrowth and into a clearing, and there, in front of me, was the wishing tree.

'What can I say? I was desperate. I thought it was providence that had driven me there. I wished . . . in my frenzy I wished that my brother would die, and when I remembered that you needed to give them something in return, I said they could take whatever they wanted.

'I returned home. The next day my brother walked out and never came back. People suspected suicide – officers on leave did take their lives. My father was a colonel of the regiment and, to avoid a scandal, it was put about that Thomas was killed on his way to the front. I didn't know what to think.'

'And what did they take?' Willis asked. 'I mean, what did you have to give?'

'It came to me in a dream that night,' Winterburn said. 'The clearest, most vivid dream I have ever had. I was in the glade; it was bright, hot sunlight, I was looking at the tree, and there, crucified on it, naked, broken, was Connie. I'm ninety-four years old. The image is still here.' He cupped his forehead in a thin hand. 'To cut a long story short, we left the next day. Eloped. Connie took her jewels and we bought a farm in Canada. We were never hugely rich but we were happy, as they say. She died fifteen years ago. I stayed on, then sold the farm, came back, sold the big house, and settled in here.' He looked at Willis. 'Would you have done differently? Given the choice? Even knowing the price?'

Willis shook his head. 'I really don't know,' he said. 'I was never given the chance to find out. It seems to me, when I think about Marcus and Caroline, that choice hardly came into it. Fate would be a better word. Even what she did at the end was only granting Marcus's last wish.'

'Perhaps that was the only wish that won't be paid in blood,' Winterburn said. 'What was it you called me in your phone call? A loose end. Well, I'm prepared to let you tie me in now. Obviously, what I did before wasn't enough.'

Willis remembered the murals in the chapel.

'My solicitor was in touch yesterday. He said that a trust has been set up. The terms are clear: trustees are empowered to release what moneys they must for the purchase and unkeep of my old home, Croftholme House, and to maintain it for the purposes laid out in this document.' Winterburn patted a slim leather folder. 'Research into childhood development. That's rich. I never had you down as an ironist.'

'It's a skill I'm working on.'

'Loose end,' Winterburn chuckled. 'You think this will work?'

'I don't know,' Willis said. 'I'm going on the theory that they just want a place to call their own.'

'For how long?'

'For as long as we can manage.'

Winterburn rose and walked shakily across to the bed. Willis moved to help him into his coat. For a second it looked as if the old man would not let him, then he shrugged and his face took on a complex expression: amused, resigned, wistful. He led Willis downstairs and into the waiting car.

Imagine that you're driving through this pleasant corner of the country. You're passing through the forest, sweeping under the great boughs that summer and winter arch the road. Watch the way the trees shift as you pass them – it's only perspective – but notice how each inch you travel opens up another path, another vista, even as it closes the one that has just passed. It's a fast, straight road, a Roman road. But wait, the forest is falling away now. Houses are driving a wedge into it but it's still there: you can see it peeping over the roof tops, massing at the end of suburban streets.

Okay, slow down for the High Street. Right now, past the butcher and the greengrocer where Mrs Tailor still buys her provisions early on a Saturday morning, past the shops selling papier mâché finger bowls and Mexican tin work knocked up in Shotton. The turn's coming up but it's the sort of entrance that's easily missed. There. Missed it. You'll have to wait for a break in the traffic, then back the car, then turn. Perhaps this is a good time to hear about Winterburn.

Winterburn . . . They were gentle with him, actually. Willis drove him to the forest. The old man's head swivelled and twisted on his neck as he noted old landmarks gone, others preserved. They parked in a car park and as they stepped under the trees, Willis felt a sort of welcome shiver the air around them, and for a second experienced an odd sense of exclusion. This might have been how the prodigal son was welcomed, he thought. This is Winterburn's return.

By the time they reached the glade the rain had cleared to make a standard English grey day, the sun a tinfoil disc dipping around behind the clouds. Winterburn said: 'Well, I suppose this is it. It feels strange to be back,' and that was the last he said. Willis had not even seen them come up on him, and he had to admit that they were gentle.

Winterburn was stripped of his clothes like a banana being skinned. He stood there naked and very white for perhaps a second.

They opened him like a flower. He saw his mortality and the beauty of it; the white, white skin and the red, red blood; the gleaming coils of his gut and pulsing colours of lung and liver, two colours of blood, red and blue, heart and soul. He stood as if in wonder, then fell apart, although it might better be said that he fell away, a slow, silent firework, the parts meeting the forest floor with no more sound than the gentle patter of rain.

Space must be made for them, he had said to Willis. Space in time and place. Perhaps they'll find peace now.

Yes, it's a bitch of a turn and that's not entirely accidental, and yes, it is a horrid gate and that's not accidental either. It's high, metal, rusty and it sticks. It doesn't invite entry. You might think that there's a pumping station behind it, or something equally dull. On either side the trees grow high, the bushes thick. The drive curves so you can't see round it. Is that a house behind the trees? A big, deserted house? Must be worth a fortune – except there, on the fence, the only bright thing about this funny, cut-off road, is the sign: 'Keep Out. Condemned. Do Not Enter'.

And below it, peeking out of the long grass, another sign, rather rusty and mildewed: 'Croftholme House'.

Outside the world shoots past in smears of metal and hard colour: the road forms a barrier of a sort. Around the perimeter fence, where the grounds back on to the forest, nettles grow five feet high, brambles grow ten feet and weave in and out of the metal mesh. The ground underfoot is always soft and marshy. And if you got close enough to peer through the nettles, the brambles, the trailing curtains of cathedral bells, what would you see?

A big empty house that is frightening enough to deter vandals. Those that break in, break out again pretty quickly, too shamed to admit their fear. They don't go back.

Winterburn, bless him, left enough to secure the preservation of his old house. He left it to Willis.

If you hadn't seen the 'Keep Out' signs, you'd wonder what that house was doing on its own, and you might even think: What a waste. If I was a child I would kill to live in a place like that.

Yes. You might be right. Children did kill to live in a place like that; children, or fairies, killed and died and killed again – sorry. Wait, listen.

It's growing dark and the voices have started. No, no, it's voices, not traffic. That low murmur. Can't you hear? It's coming from the house. A sort of low, heavy buzz, that's all the poor things can manage, but you can hear another voice, can't you? It sounds almost human. Caroline likes to sing with them; she thinks they are sighing away their hatred because they have found someone to love. So it's nursery rhymes, half-remembered hymns, snatches of pop songs . . .

Yes, they've found someone to love. They do not even need it returned. They are nerveless, these ones. The dead take little in, but they sure can dish it out.

And they give Caroline a sort of peace. Gifts of rotting flowers clog the corridors of her home, piles of mud and sand, dead branches of dead trees. Marcus sometimes brings home a rag, some fragment of his rotting mind thinking: Pretty clothes, pretty clothes for Mummy. Mostly he just gives her moss and damp tree bark, puffballs and leaf mould.

The tree has gone. Willis cut it down with a chainsaw soon after Winterburn died. He stood back, thinking that he'd done a good job, but as he did so, he felt something brush his leg. He looked down and saw a sapling. That made him think, and then he looked up and saw he was standing in the middle of a forest and began to laugh. He lifted his head and laughed, and the sky boomed, and the earth trembled, and the trees shook, and for a moment he felt they were all sharing the same, great joke.

But he needn't have worried. The fierceness of feeling that focused on the old tree has gone; now they have Caroline they have been deprived of purpose. They're happy; they might even help you in a sort of misty, whimsical way. Ask them for guidance and they will take you by the hand and whisper the sweet poetry of rot. Ask them for money and they might shower you with golden leaves. They'll be around a while. They cannot die; the dead cannot.

All we can do is give them time to wear softly, gently away. With love.